At Left Linebacker, Chip Demory

A Winning Season for the Braves

Full Court Press

Nate Aaseng

Chariot Books™
A Division of Cook Communications Ministries

Chariot Books™ is an imprint of Chariot Family Publishing
Cook Communications Ministries, Elgin, Illinois 60120
Cook Communications Ministries, Paris, Ontario
Kingsway Communications, Eastbourne, England

Cover design by Chris Dall
Cover illustration by Dennis Jones

These stories were previously published in separate editions as White Horse Sports Stories for Boys by David C. Cook Publishing Co. in 1983, 1982 and 1990.
First compilation printing, 1995
Printed in the United States of America
99 98 97 96 95 5 4 3 2 1
CIP applied for

At Left Linebacker, Chip Demory

NATE AASENG

Contents

1 Doorway to the Unknown

There was no reason for the shove. The hallway that wound into the locker room was narrow, but two boys should still have been able to walk down it side by side without bumping shoulder pads.

It couldn't have been an accident, Chip Demory thought. Eric Youngquist had deliberately knocked him into the wall tiles.

The two had both arrived late for practice, so they found themselves alone in the dimly lit corridor. Searching Eric's face for some explanation, Chip held back for a moment. Had Eric turned and walked away, Chip would have ignored the whole thing. Instead, there stood Eric, leering and blocking Chip's path to the room. So Chip found himself shoving back, and he heard the clack of shoulder pads as Eric backed into the wall. Without hesitation, Eric took his turn again, with a harder push than before. The football gear cushioned the blows, and Chip recovered quickly and lashed out again at his opponent.

This is stupid; it could go on forever, he thought. What's more, it didn't make any sense. Eric Youngquist was nothing but a name and a face to him. What could he have against him? Chip couldn't remember even talking to him before. Dropping his blue helmet on the concrete floor, he braced himself for another round of attacks. Eric grabbed him by the shoulder.

Then, suddenly, it was as though a plug had been pulled. Eric's last shove faded into a harmless nudge. Without a word, Chip's mysterious attacker turned and disappeared, still smirking, into the locker room.

As Chip watched him go, he felt the warmth of the blood that had rushed to his cheeks and the tips of his ears. *That probably wasn't a smart thing to do,* he thought. Eric was bigger than he, and, Chip assumed, probably a lot stronger. But what else could you do when someone came at you like that?

Chip had seen the white block letters that spelled "locker room" above the door for as long as he had been attending Forest Grove School, but he had never been in the room before. He couldn't remember when he had made the final decision to step through the doors and join the football team. All he knew was that he was tired of being a nobody. The athletes seemed to be the ones who had it made, and Chip had finally decided he was going to join them. The way he had it figured, that uniform held the key to something. Respect, perhaps. Maybe even popularity.

When he thought of the evening he had broken the news to his dad, he felt he was already halfway toward his goals. The announcement had caught his dad by surprise at the supper table; the man had held that mouthful of food a long time before swallowing. Chip's dad had never tried to push him into sports, but he couldn't hide the fact that he was pleased.

"Sounds like fun," his dad had said. "What made you decide to try it?"

Chip had shrugged. "Like you said, it sounded like fun." There had been no reason to go into all of his motives.

"Is there a group of you boys in on this?" Dad had asked. No, he had done this on his own. Most of his current friends weren't the football type. Sometimes he was almost ashamed to know them. Take Tom, for instance. He was a nice enough guy, went to church, was good at music. But sometimes he was so innocent it was embarrassing.

"Can you imagine Tom in football pads?" he had said with a laugh. "Jason might be coordinated enough to play, but not Tom . . ."

"Well, I know *you'll* enjoy it, anyway," his dad had smiled. "I sure did!"

As he prepared to turn the last of three corners in the entranceway, Chip hoped that his dad was right.

The room turned out to be nothing but a long galley, packed with boys. Since the benches ran parallel with the lockers instead of facing the blackboard, everyone sat crowded on the floor on either side of the benches as Coach Ray Marsh stood before the blackboard. There were no showers, but that did not matter to the Forest Grove football team. Everyone was expected to change into football gear at home. In fact, the only way they used the room was as a meeting place.

The strange newness of the situation seemed frightening. Chip shifted his weight from one foot to the other, as if pulled by two magnets, as he tried to decide whether or not to stay. Finally he walked forward and knelt on the floor at the back of the group.

The coach had a wide face and short neck, which made him appear large when he was actually of average size. He certainly dressed the part of a coach, from his navy blue Windbreaker and white shorts to his high, white socks and heavy, black shoes. Chip wondered about the shoes. Why would a guy need special football shoes with cleats just to coach?

Had Chip been less self-conscious, he would have stood instead of knelt. He wasn't one of the larger boys, and he had trouble seeing over the group from his spot in the back. Coach Ray had been talking for some time now, but Chip hadn't heard much of what he said. He kept debating whether or not to sneak out and forget this crazy notion. But while he scanned the rows of white-jerseyed boys to see if anyone would notice his exit, he was suddenly jolted by a familiar face. Eric, in the back of the pack on the other side of the bench, was watching him with that same smirk.

Chip quickly turned away and started to concentrate on what the coach was saying. "Listen up now, boys. This is a big group and there's no way I can try and coach you all by myself. So I want you to meet Bronc Galloway. He'll be helping me out this year."

Bronc Galloway must have been stretched out on the floor in the front of the group, for Chip had not noticed him before. As the man stood up, Chip wondered how he could have missed him. It took no imagination to see this man in football gear in a starting lineup in high school or college. Under his sweater a huge chest puffed out, so large that his arms did not hang comfortably at his sides. Although Bronc appeared to be no older than his mid-thirties, he was almost bald, with only a few surviving hairs clinging to his temples. He wore gray, cuffed pants that had large loops for a belt, but no belt was there. The man snapped his gum so vigorously that he reminded Chip of a dog crunching his dinner.

"How're ya doin'!" grinned Bronc between chomps.

"OK, fellas," said Coach Ray, stepping in front of

Bronc. "I want all the backs to come with me, and the linemen to go with Bronc. Let's go and have ourselves a good practice!"

As Chip followed the stream of boys out of the locker room, he felt a wave of panic. *I thought the coaches told you where to play,* he thought. Everyone else seemed to know exactly where they were going as the team split into two sections and jogged out on the grass, but Chip stood still, trying to decide which of the departing groups to join. He had never thought of himself as a back; only the really good players got to carry the ball. But then he might be overpowered by the larger boys who played in the line. A last look at Bronc sent him scurrying to Coach Ray's side of the field. As long as he had a choice, Chip would shy away from that tough-looking brute.

Taking his usual spot at the end of a line, Chip wished for the hundredth time that one of his friends had come out for football. When he saw the players in line ahead of him fastening their helmets, he felt more foolish than ever. He hadn't been wrong about the better players taking to the backfield. There was Rennie Ruiz, the fastest runner in school. Bruce Wilkes was always the first person chosen for any sport in phys. ed. class. And nobody ever thought about trying to win the quarterback job away from Scot Schultz, who had a throwing arm like a missile launcher.

Coach Ray blew his whistle for silence even though no one was saying a word. He pulled out two rolls of tape from his pocket and tossed them to the boys. "Print your names, big enough so I can read 'em."

Most of the others paired off and used a friend's back to write on. But Chip bent down with one knee on the grass. His thigh pad was hard enough to make a good support, and he started to print on the piece he had torn off the roll.

While Scot's back was being used, he glanced in

Chip's direction. "Not your first name," he advised. "Coach likes last names."

Chip nodded, tore off another piece of tape and shakily printed "Demory." The exchange had reminded him that most of these players had been out for football before. There was more to joining a football team than just walking through the locker room door. *What am I doing here?* he wondered again.

After the group had run through tires and caught passes, Coach Ray grabbed a blocking dummy. "Some of you come and hold these," he said as he dragged one to the middle of the field. With swift cooperation, four dummies were soon lined up, five yards apart. Chip saw Bruce clutch the football and plow into the first dummy. There was a loud grunt as the boy hit the object and charged quickly toward the next.

"Well, here goes," gulped Chip, fumbling the football that Coach Ray had tossed to him. He picked it up and ran toward the first dummy, which was held by the coach. The collision stunned him. Those fluffy-looking bags were a lot more solid than they looked! Chip's helmet slipped over his nose. He took a step back and adjusted it before continuing to the other targets, which were held by other players.

"No, no, no!" shouted Coach Ray, rushing in front of the startled boy. The coach grabbed Chip's helmet and turned it slightly to see the name taped to it. "Demorg," he said in a softer voice, as if the patience he was showing took massive self-control.

"It's Demory, not Demorg," mumbled Chip.

The coach stared hard at the helmet and shrugged. "That's the darndest *y* I ever saw; looks like a *g* to me. OK, Demory, you were doing it all wrong. I didn't see any drive. For cryin' out loud, I don't want you to lie down on the bag, I want you to hit it. Here, watch me!" he said, shoving the bag at Chip.

From a standing start, he blew his whistle and

charged forward. The collision nearly blasted Chip off his feet. "Hit hard!" the coach puffed. "Legs pumping, always pumping. Spin away, charge, hit again. Now you try it. Hit! Legs going, legs going! Pump those legs, Demorg! Hit! Spin away! Charge! Legs!" Chip's turn probably lasted no longer than fifteen seconds, but he was relieved to take his turn holding up a dummy. Each player took two more runs through the drill. Chip felt his second and third tries must have been a little better; at least he wasn't yelled at as much.

No sooner had he popped into the last dummy than the whistle blew, summoning them for yet another drill. The group spread out into three widely spaced lines facing Coach Ray. At his command, they all ran in place, awaiting further commands. In rapid succession, the coach pointed left, then right, then to the ground, then left. The boys tried to keep up with his motions, running in the direction he was pointing, dropping to the ground when he pointed down. Within a few minutes, everyone had fallen hopelessly behind. It was obvious that no one cared for this drill.

"Coach, why are we doing this?" groaned Scot as he slumped to his knees. "What does it have to do with football?"

"We're doing it because I think it's a good idea," smiled the coach. "And because it's good for you. Let's go again! Left! Right!" A few minutes later he grinned and said, "Everyone around the goalpost, on the double, then report to where the linemen are."

Had Chip worn a watch to practice, his eyes would have been on it every thirty seconds. When he had been thinking about playing football this fall, he had expected some hard work. But this tedious, nerve-wracking routine was hardly worth it. Whatever excitement he had felt when he first put on the helmet and uniform had long since worn off. Although the slow trot around the posts seemed a waste of time, Chip enjoyed every second away from the coach and his drills.

When they returned to Coach Ray, he surveyed them with a sly smile. "One last drill for you, and then you can go home. Bronc, set up the bags for the one-on-one drill." The assistant swung around two bags, one in each hand, and set them on a worn stretch of grass, about six feet apart.

"I want the linemen over by the dummies, backs over here," said Coach Ray. "This is a simple exercise. You backs are to try to run between the bags. You linemen are to try to stop them. If the back gets through, he's done with practice, and the lineman goes to the end of his line. If the lineman makes the tackle, he's through for the day and the back gets in line. Any questions?"

There were none. It was all painfully clear to Chip. But for the first time, Chip found some competition for the last spot in the line. Two boys had quietly sneaked around and were now behind him. Chip glanced at the long string of linemen waiting to get their chance. He could be stuck running at them all afternoon while all the other backs went home.

Rennie looked as concerned about the drill as a cat settling down for a nap. Hands on his hips, he waited for Coach Ray to give him the ball. At the sound of the ever-present whistle, he flipped the ball from his left hand to his right, and started forward at an easy pace. A lineman crouched three yards in front of the dummies, his arms held out from his chest like a wrestler. Rennie put on a burst of speed to his right. When the lineman tried to cut him off, Rennie swerved sharply to the other side. Lurching off balance, the lineman tried to dive back, and made a desperate swipe at the speedster with his arm. But Rennie easily hopped over it and trotted between the dummies.

"Nice running," said the coach, clapping. "That

was a pretty piece of work, Ruiz. See you tomorrow. Next!"

I'm going to be the only one who doesn't make it, thought Chip. He saw Bronc whisper something to the boy who had missed the tackle. Then the assistant coach patted him on the pads and sent him to the end of the line. "That's going to be me," Chip muttered.

Another whistle blast brought Chip's attention back to the drill. Perry Clyde Brown, who liked to be called P.C., didn't exactly leap forward at the signal. Roosevelt Baxter was blocking his path, and he seemed to take up most of the room between the dummies. By far the largest kid in their grade, he had proven on many occasions that very little of his great bulk was fat.

P.C. rocked forward several times, then finally lowered his head and took off. Despite his determination, the huge arms of Roosevelt Baxter wrapped around him and slammed him to the ground. As P.C. hobbled to his feet, Coach Ray nodded his approval. "Good, clean tackle. That's the way to do it."

P.C. refused to let the hard hit silence him. Returning to the sympathetic group of backs, he muttered, "Welcome, to the 'Get Canned by Baxter Club.' It's always the same. Every time we do this drill, I get stuck with good old Roosevelt. Why doesn't anyone else get Roosevelt?" He tapped the helmet of the boy in front of him in line. "Isn't this fun? Boy, I can't think of anything I enjoy more on a nice day like this than being annihilated by somebody five times my size!"

For the first time that day, Chip joined in with the laughter as P.C. sputtered on about his misfortune. The smile had vanished, however, by the time he had worked his way to the front of the line. P.C. Brown wasn't the only one victimized by fate. Chip saw that the lineman he would have to beat was Eric! He still wore that same goofy sneer, although it was harder to detect underneath his helmet. With a deep breath,

Chip took off for the blocking dummies.

"Hey, wait a minute!" shouted Coach Ray. "You forgot the football. And I'd appreciate it if you'd wait for the whistle next time." Chip was too paralyzed with fear and embarrassment to come up with a plan for getting around Eric. After starting forward, he stopped and began to lean to the left to fake out the defender. But he had barely moved his head when Eric rushed forward and grabbed him just above the knees. Neatly picking him off the ground, he carried him toward the row of backs until the coach whistled for him to stop. Chip ducked back in line, too humiliated to even look up from the grass. "Next!" screamed the coach.

I might just as well put wimp *on my helmet instead of my name,* Chip thought bitterly. It had been a crushing lesson, but Chip had learned from that run. The next time he got the ball, he didn't waste time with timid fakes. He drove straight for the defender, and the two fell over each other. He didn't get through that time, either, but at least he hadn't been picked off the ground like a kindergartner.

P.C. finally got a break on his fourth try. He had been paired with the smallest lineman, and he could hardly wait to try his luck. As he burst through the defender and dove between the tackling dummies, he let out a whoop. "What power! What a runner! Sorry all you pro scouts, but I'm not signing anything until my agents look over your offers."

There were only two running backs left in line when Chip finally succeeded. He tore through an attempted tackle and sprinted past the dummies, feeling as though a huge load had slid off his shoulders. But he noted, bitterly, that none of the good players were around to see him break through. Besides, being the next-to-last to succeed was hardly an achievement.

Chip slammed his helmet on the sparse turf and

kicked it toward the school. Football was supposed to be his chance to prove he wasn't a dork. Instead it had proved, beyond a doubt, that he really was.

2
A Private War

Chip watched the last orange bus rumble off from in front of the school. Holding his breath until the exhaust fumes had drifted away, he sat on the steps in front of the glass doors of the entrance. He held a wadded Windbreaker in his hand; the day had turned out warmer than he had expected when he had left the house that morning.

Those guys are going to bake in practice today, he thought, *especially in those dark helmets.*

Chip had not quit the team. True, there were still about half a dozen times each practice when he wished he had never pushed open that locker room door. But it had been his decision to play football, and he felt it his duty to stick it out to the end. After all, he had told everyone that he was a football player. The best thing to do was just to get through the season, suffering in silence. At least none of his family or friends knew how badly he was botching things.

Then, too, there was still hope that things would change. He had overheard Bruce say that after the first few weeks, football started to get fun.

Despite this, it was a relief to be getting out of practice. Coach Ray had happened to schedule a practice for an afternoon when Chip was supposed to meet with the dentist. It was strange to feel almost glad to have a dentist appointment as an excuse.

A car engine rumbled noisily, and Chip stood up to see if it was his ride coming. No, it was a pickup truck, hardly what his sister would be driving. As he absently watched the dust kicked up by the truck, he thought of the practice field again. The lack of rain had hardened the ground so that his football gear didn't seem to be enough protection from hard falls. He was thinking back on one hard tackle when he heard a shout. "Hey, Chip!"

Leaning out the window of the truck, snapping his gum as always, Bronc waved at him. "You look like you need a ride somewhere. Want a lift? Practice won't start for another fifteen minutes."

"No, thanks," Chip said. "My sister should be here any minute. We have to go to the dentist."

"Going to get your fangs sharpened, huh? I knew you were a tiger on the field, but isn't that carrying it a bit too far?" Chip grinned at the attempted joke and shook his head. "Well, see you tomorrow," Bronc said. He waved and turned into the parking lot. Suddenly his truck lurched to a stop. The bald head poked out the window again. "Hey, Chip! What's the deal with you and Eric?"

Chip felt a shiver at the mention of that hated name. Before he could even think about it, he found himself denying it. "There's no problem," he shrugged. He had never imagined that anyone else knew about that trouble.

"Come on," frowned Bronc. "Hey, I've seen you two go at it whenever you get a chance. I mean, the fur is really flyin' in those one-on-one drills. There's got to be something causing that."

"You'd have to ask him," Chip said coldly. "I don't even know him that well, but that's the way he wants it, so—"

Bronc shook a finger at him. "I think we're goin' to have to get you two to talk it out sometime. It's not good when—What in the blue blazes is this?"

The squealing of tires as a Chevy swerved into the parking lot, barely clinging to the road, made Chip wince. "It's my sister," he said, bouncing down the steps.

Bronc had stopped chewing and stared, open-mouthed at the car. "Your sister! Sounds like one tough lady behind the wheel."

"That's the second time she's done that," said Chip. "At least this time it wasn't in front of a parking lot full of people heading into church."

"Oh, yeah?" Bronc smiled. "What church?"

"Trinity," answered Chip, feeling a little uncomfortable. Football and church were two areas of his life Chip had not wanted to mix. He was trying to think of a safe topic of conversation when Bronc changed the subject for him. "So, does she always drive like that?" the coach asked.

"I hope not," answered Chip with a grin. "See you later." He jogged around to the passenger side of the car and climbed in. "What are you trying to do anyway, Jill?" he asked the girl. "You're driving like the Indy 500!"

Jill swept back her long hair and looked at her watch. Chip knew she was embarrassed because of the way she refused to meet his eyes. "I'm in a hurry," she said. "We have only five minutes to get to the dentist's office, and it's a ten-minute drive." After a few seconds of silence, she finally peeked over at him and sighed. "Guess I did take the corner too fast. Well, live and learn. How long have I had a license—five months? Can't expect to be perfect yet. You know what, though," she added, almost in a whisper. "If Dad saw me do that, he wouldn't let me have the car again for about three eternities."

"I don't know why he lets you loose on the road at all," laughed Chip.

"Don't give me a hard time! Mom's got the flu, and Dad doesn't get home until 5:30. Besides, I need the practice."

"You sure picked a great time to practice. Right at the start of rush hour!"

Jill gave him a quick punch in the shoulder. "Quiet. You're making me nervous!"

"Who was the bald guy?" asked Jill, after announcing their arrival to the receptionist. "The one in the pickup. What an ape!"

Chip looked around at the sparse office furnishings. Except for a small coatrack, a window that looked out onto a row of car fenders, a table heaped with magazines, and half a dozen chairs, the room was empty. Pulling up one of the chairs, he said, "You mean the man in the truck that you almost hit?"

"I did not! It wasn't even close. Was he your football coach?"

"He still is, for all I know," said Chip. "At least, he's one of them. He's not a bad guy. I'm beginning to like him better than the other one we've got."

"I've had all kinds of coaches," shrugged Jill. "Somehow I've survived. So, how are you liking football?"

Chip felt important when his sister talked to him. Although they had their differences, and she talked too much for his liking, he'd seen other big sisters in action, and had to admit that he was lucky. At least Jill wasn't afraid to admit, once in a while, that he existed.

"Football's great!" he replied. He felt funny saying it, but he couldn't tell her what he really thought.

"You know, that's one sport I've never been able to figure out. I've gone to a few high school games, but if it weren't for the cheering, I wouldn't even know who's winning."

"That's because it's such a complicated game," explained Chip. "You see, you've got all kinds of games going on at once. Both sides are making secret plans, and there's passing, running, blocking, and tackling all going on at the same time." Chip was starting to feel more fired up about the game than he had in a long time.

"I figured there must be something to it, the way Dad loves to watch it," said Jill. "It sounds like fun. I'll bet you're glad you finally tried out for it this year."

Feeling uncomfortable with the false impression he was giving, Chip changed the subject. "So, do you like volleyball?"

"Love it," Jill grinned. "I think I like it even better than tennis, and you know how I've always loved tennis."

"It's easy to like something when you're great at it," sniffed Chip.

Jill turned on him, irritated. "That isn't true. I'd still like playing those sports even if I wasn't . . ." Seeing that she had been led into a conceited statement, she blushed. "Besides, I'm not all that great."

"Oh, sure!" scoffed Chip. "You're all-conference in tennis, and probably will be in volleyball, too."

"I do all right. You'll probably star at football."

"Don't make me laugh," grumbled Chip.

Jill squinted at the ceiling for a few seconds, as if mulling over something. "Wait a minute. If you really think you're no good at football, why do you say it's such a great game?"

Chip shifted uneasily in his chair. Jill was getting a lot closer to the truth than he could stand. "Oh, who says football is so great?"

"Well, it wasn't me! You're the one who went on and on about it. I don't know which is worse, getting my teeth drilled or trying to make sense out of you. Give me one of those magazines."

Chip scanned the pile and picked out the two with the least torn covers. "Do you want last year's *Reader's Digest* or the February *Boys' Life*?"

Just then the door creaked open. "Chip Demory?" called the receptionist.

Jill caught the magazines as Chip dumped them in her lap. "I think I've got it figured out," she said as he shuffled toward the door. "You went out for sports because you know how much Dad likes to come and watch me play."

Chip decided there was no need to tell her there was some truth in all her guesses. How could he help but want to trade places with her? Everyone in town knew who Jill Demory was. You could hardly flip through the sports section of the local paper during tennis season without seeing her picture. "Right," he grinned. "I figured if *you* could be a star, anyone could."

"Beat it! I hope the dentist broke his drill and has to use a jackhammer on you!"

"That's enough conditioning, boys. We'd better get going on learning the plays."

Coach Ray's words were like thick steaks thrown to a pack of starved dogs. Chip even joined the rest of the team in their whoops and howls. P.C. scurried through the ranks of players, shaking hands like a politician. "I want to personally congratulate each of the courageous survivors of this—"

"Knock off the clowning!" ordered Coach Ray. "We're going to organize you into units. Now, there's no such thing as a definite first team or second team at this point. Remember, the unit I put you on isn't necessarily the unit you'll stay on all year. It's just that we have to start somewhere. Now, when I call your name, I want you over here. Foster! Baxter! Torberg!"

Chip didn't know much about the linemen, other than Roosevelt and Eric, but he had seen the backs in action for some time. His suspicions of how the team was being divided were confirmed when the names of Ruiz, Wilkes, and Schultz were read off in order. The three pranced over to the coach, trying some awkward high-five handshakes. Then they started slapping hands with the linemen who had been selected.

"Knock it off!" shouted the coach. "I told you, it doesn't mean that you've made the starting team. In fact, the whole lot of you may wind up second-string by our first game!"

P.C. giggled and whispered what everyone else was thinking. "The coach is right. If Wilkes and Schultz break both their legs, they *may* get beaten out for a starting spot."

Coach Ray motioned with his clipboard to where Bronc was pacing in rhythm with his chewing. "I want the following to report to Bronc when I call your name." He stared at his clipboard for a second, as if trying to break the code of whatever was written on it. Finally he plunged into the list of names at a rapid pace. Eight of the eleven were mispronounced so badly that several boys were not sure whether they had been called or not. Chip, however, had heard the name "Demorg" so often that he automatically responded to the title. Trotting to where Bronc was lining up players, he glanced back at the boys who had not been chosen. He felt sorry for that glum group, whose hopes for playing time this year had just been crushed. At the same time, he felt glad, and a little proud, that he had been selected for the second group. At least it showed he wasn't a total loser.

Grabbing Chip by the shoulders, Bronc gave the boy a quick inspection. "You look like a linebacker to me, Chip," he said. "At least you will if you start eatin' three meals a day!" He rapped him lightly on the ribs with his knuckles. "Why don't you take the left linebacker spot?"

Chip was listening to Coach Ray explain to the unchosen players that their role would be to back up the offensive "starters" when he felt a tap on his shoulder. P.C. grabbed him by the pads and marched him to the defensive end on the left side. "Hey! Dave Atkinson! I can't tell if it's you or your twin!"

The tall lineman grinned down at the two of them. "This isn't me; it's him. I'm over there on the right side." He pointed to the gangly figure standing on the other end of the defensive line. "I'll bet it's hard to tell Dave and me apart when we've got our helmets on."

"Actually, Dan, the helmets make it easier," chuckled P.C. Nodding for Chip to come closer, he said, "As we all know, I'm a man of few words, so I'll make it short. We all know each other, at least, sort of. The way I see it, the best way to survive practice is to hang together. If I know this coach, we're stuck on defense for the rest of the year. What's more, we probably won't play much."

He must have caught the question in Chip's expression because he explained, "He likes to have the best players in for both offense and defense, and the best eleven are in that huddle over there. Practice can be a drag when you know you won't get into the games, so here's my idea. Dan, you're the left end, Chip's the left linebacker, and I'm the left cornerback. Let's set up our own game against the right side of the defense. We guard our turf better than they guard theirs, see? Only plays run outside the tackles count; if they run up the middle, we don't count it."

Chip hadn't followed all the details of the plan. He was still thinking about P.C.'s statement that they all knew each other. By name, maybe, but not beyond that. *But then,* he thought, *P.C. seems to think he's good friends with everyone.*

Dan shook his head wearily. Chip had always thought Dan would be a good person to know. He was a brain in class without being either obnoxious or self-conscious about it. Along with his twin Dave, Dan had a better build for basketball than football. But the lanky pair had never found a sport they didn't like. "Your game sounds like fun, I guess," he said in a doubtful voice. "But there's no way for this group to beat the right side."

For a second, Chip thought Dan must be thinking of him as a handicap in this contest. Instinctively he backed away. But then Dan pointed to the huge figure dwarfing his teammates in the offensive huddle. Roosevelt Baxter looked like a playground supervisor hovering over a circle of first graders.

P.C. unsnapped his chin guard and rubbed his chin. "I see the problem. We've got our good buddy Roosevelt blocking against you." Putting an arm around Dan, he said, "On behalf of all of us, I'd like to thank you for sacrificing your life for the good of the team. All right, so you have to play against him. We'll give ourselves a handicap of one yard per play." Before he slipped his mouthpiece back in place, he thumped Chip on the helmet. "Funny, I always thought your name was Demory."

"So did I, but I can't convince the coach," said Chip. "I got tired of arguing about it, so I just don't say anything anymore."

"Don't take it personally," laughed P.C. "He just

doesn't get along well with names. Well, I'd better shut up; here they come!"

As P.C. skipped back to his cornerback spot, Chip looked over the rest of the defense. It felt good to finally have a position to play—especially since he wasn't stuck at running back, where he felt out of place. But the best part was being in on P.C.'s little gang. If you couldn't get along with P.C., you couldn't get along with anyone, and Dan seemed nice enough. The problem was, would they put up with him if he made too many mistakes?

Even that worry, however, seemed minor when Chip discovered who was storming around a few feet to his right. Eric had been put at middle linebacker, and it was obvious he wasn't flattered to be there. Despite what the coach said, everyone knew this was the second-string group. Eric thought he belonged on the first team. Much as Chip hated to admit it, he agreed with Eric.

Muttering and spitting, Eric wandered in a wide circle around the defense. Chip tried to back out of his way, but Eric got close enough to recognize him. One look at the menacing glare and Chip turned away, pretending his shoes needed tying. If only he hadn't been placed right next to Eric! What was the kid's problem, anyway? Why was he always looking for a fight?

The offense ran through plays in a drill that seemed as silly as it was boring to Chip. Everyone simply walked through the play. The whole thing reminded Chip of a slow-motion square dance. At least there wasn't much for the defense to do, so Chip could concentrate on staying out of Eric's way. The middle linebacker was still steaming. Rather than let a blocker nudge him to one side, he would just turn his back and looked bored.

After what seemed like several afternoons strung

together, Coach Ray finally said, "Let's run through a couple of plays with some real blocking and tackling!"

The glare of the setting sun was getting under Chip's helmet as he watched the offense crowd around the coach in the huddle. Not until they broke their huddle and jogged toward the football to challenge him did he realize how little he actually knew about his position. He had watched football with his dad for years, and had thought he knew the game inside and out. But as the linemen bent toward the ground to get in position, he found that he had no idea what he should do. Eric stood close enough to touch the linemen, while the other linebacker stood several yards behind them. Where was he supposed to play?

Dan turned and called quietly over his shoulder. Unable to hear him, Chip darted up to the tall lineman. "They're coming to this side. Be ready for it," came the warning.

"How do you know?" asked Chip.

"No time now," answered Dan, digging his cleats into what little grass was left on the hardened ground.

Quarterback Scot called out a few numbers and then, in Chip's eyes, the entire field turned into a madhouse. He could make out that the general flow was in his direction. But all the movement distracted him so much that he barely moved from his original spot. There seemed to be nothing to do but wait until the ball carrier arrived and then try and tackle him.

As Chip inched forward, he was spotted by Rennie, who was leading the way for Bruce on the run. With a loud grunt, Rennie threw his body at Chip. Chip managed to keep his feet as Rennie stumbled. But as he was trying to find where Bruce had gone, he was suddenly jolted from behind. He fell forward over Rennie, who kicked at him to get him off. Neither saw P.C. end the play by bumping the ball carrier out-of-bounds after an eight-yard gain.

Chip finally untangled himself from Rennie, then cringed when he saw Eric standing over him, pointing a finger in his face. "If you're too wimpy to make a tackle," he sneered, "why don't you get out of the way so someone else can do it!"

Their private war had gone on in total silence up to this point. Whether it was Eric's mocking voice or just the fact that Chip had finally reached his limit, this time Chip was furious. His back hurt from where Eric had run into him, blood was trickling down his calf, and he was embarrassed in front of his new friends. It especially hurt because what Eric had said was true. Chip knew that he had been standing around like a clod. For all practical purposes, the defense did not have a left linebacker.

He spun away from Eric disdainfully. *I'm not afraid of that creep,* he said to himself. *Big shot thinks he's Mr. Tough. I'll show him!*

"That's a lousy way to start, guys," called P.C.

Chip found Dan still sprawled on the ground near the line of scrimmage, and helped him to his feet. "How did you know they would come this way?"

Dan scraped a clump of dirt off of his elbow. "Just a guess, but I'm right more often than not. See, the coach is right-handed, so I thought it would be natural for him to start off the year with a play to his right. Besides, how could he resist running a play behind Roosevelt?" He smiled weakly. "Of course, it doesn't help to know what's coming if you can't stop it."

"So what are they going to do this time?"

"I can't always tell. If I think I have it figured out, I'll let you know. Hey, P.C.," he called to the cornerback. "Why don't you come closer, and help out on those runs?"

"Come on, I can help some, but I have to watch the pass receivers."

"P.C., we watched that offense walk through three

million plays in the last hour, and none of them were passes. They haven't learned any pass plays yet!"

"Why didn't I think of that?" said P.C., joining Chip.

"My dad always says to pay attention to the little things," said Dan. "There's more to football than just banging heads."

When Eric shot one of his glares at Chip, this time Chip glared right back. He didn't shy away from the middle; in fact, he moved a few steps closer to Eric. The play was a basic, straight-ahead run. The blocking was so sloppy that no one even touched the middle linebacker. Eric met Bruce head-on, and stopped the fullback's forward progress. But Bruce kept his balance and squirmed ahead for a couple more yards. As defensive help raced in from all sides, Chip saw his chance to get even. Eric's back provided an inviting target, and Chip closed in. Quickly building up speed, he plowed into the growing pile of players, hitting Eric right around the shoulders. Eric lost his grip, and Bruce burst out of the mob for three more yards before being tackled.

"You moron!" shouted Eric, clenching his fists. "You don't even know whose team you're on! What are you doing out for football, anyway?"

Chip braced himself for a possible attack, but Eric made no move.

"Go on, smack him," said Scot, nudging Eric. That was all the encouragement Eric needed.

3
Forty-Two Red On Four

Chip met Eric's wild-eyed charge as best he could, stepping backwards and fending him off with his arm. When Eric finally got a grip on him and swung him around, Chip grabbed Eric's jersey, and the two toppled over. Eric must have been growing frustrated as they rolled around; he kept clenching his fist but couldn't find an unpadded place to swing at. Finally he aimed a punch at Chip's stomach, but Chip squirmed just enough so that he caught the blow on his hip pad.

Chip struggled to get out from under Eric. Surprised that he was finally able to wriggle free, he instinctively tried to wrestle Eric to the ground. But before he could try, he felt a steel grip under his armpits. Bronc swung him away from his enemy while Dan and Roosevelt grabbed Eric. Chip could hear Eric still cursing, and the calm voice of Dan saying, "Leave him alone!"

"Hey, save it for the other team!" barked Coach Ray, stepping into the middle of the scene. "There's no place for that kind of stuff on any football team of mine. I don't want any fights, or any cheap shots. If you guys want to stay on the team, you're going to have to learn to control your tempers!" Then, waving the rest of the group off, he said, "All of you, that's enough for today. Go on home! See you Monday."

Eric seemed to have settled down some, but Chip was growing angrier by the second. Who did Eric think he was, anyway? And what was the coach doing, chewing *him* out? Any idiot could tell it was all Eric's fault. *I don't care if I do get kicked off,* he thought. *In fact, there's nothing I'd like better!*

He felt a shadow as Dan walked by him. The tall left end was keeping an eye on both linebackers, and he seemed to be purposely adjusting his pace to keep between the two. "If you linebackers would quit pounding each other, we wouldn't be looking like such a bunch of idiots on defense," he offered.

"You're not the one who keeps looking like an idiot," said Eric.

Edging Chip away from Eric, Dan said quietly, "This fight probably isn't any of my business. But I think you two are a lot more alike than you realize."

"Thanks for the insult," spat Chip.

"No, I know Eric, and he's not always such a jerk. Not the friendliest guy in the world, but he's not terrible. Did you know that this is *his* first year out for football, too?"

"I hope it's his last."

"Tell me if I'm wrong," said Dan, tugging off his helmet and wiping back his sweaty hair. "Neither of you seemed to have gotten too comfortable with the practice routine yet."

"So we're both new," shrugged Chip. "Where's he get off trying to push me around?"

Dan started biting his lips and screwing up his face, making Chip think that he was debating whether to go on with this conversation. Finally he said, "Eric's fighting to get in with the guys. You have to admit it's not easy for him. He's probably as good as any lineman on the first team. Except for Roosevelt." He grinned, displaying a bruise on his forearm. "But Eric can't get the coaches to notice him, because they're busy watching the starters. So what does he do to get in with that group? He picks on someone to show how tough he is."

"We'll see how tough he is!"

"Maybe. But you can tell he wants to get in with the group. He never would have jumped you there if Scot hadn't opened his big mouth."

Trying to follow Dan's logic had taken some of the edge off Chip's anger. "All right, know-it-all, tell me why he doesn't pick on the scrubs who didn't even make the second team."

Dan stopped walking and gave him a sideways look. "Not a know-it-all, just a good guesser, remember? Now, listen: everyone knows the scrubs aren't good players. They may not like it, but they know what their role is. *You* don't know what *your* role is, and that gives Eric a good chance to try to teach you where you belong. Or where he thinks you belong. But don't worry," he said, leaning on the bike rack to change out of his football shoes. "The coaches are bound to find out how good he is, and then he won't have a chip on his shoulder. Your troubles are practically over."

Mine may be over, thought Chip, watching Eric disappear into the school. *But his aren't!*

As the rest of the class filed out into a noisy, jammed hallway, Chip stood by his desk in the back corner of the classroom. While waiting for Tom to collect his books and papers so they could go to band class, he examined his friend. He had done that often lately, trying to see him the way others must see him. As usual, the exercise made him frown. Those clumsy movements, hand-me-down clothes from what must have been a dozen years back, and the obviously home-made haircut marked him as someone who was really out of it. When Chip walked through the halls with Tom, he was beginning to feel awkward. He could just picture people saying, "Is that the best he can do for friends?"

This time, though, Chip couldn't help but notice something else. Tom's forehead was dotted with sweat, and his face seemed a pasty white. "Are you OK?" Chip asked.

"No, I feel sick," said Tom as he slowly gathered his books in his arms.

"Oh, no. Not you, too!" Chip said. The flu bug raging through the city didn't seem to miss anyone. At least half of Forest Grove school had been hit during the past week, he guessed. Chip had been one of the first to fall victim. Fortunately, the illness left him in as big a hurry as it had come. Chip had only been out of school one day, although he stayed out of football practice for two. But while the bug had lasted, it had been miserable.

"Did you feel weak, and have chills, and feel like you were going to throw up?" groaned Tom.

"Exactly. We'd better get you to the nurse fast. If you're like me, you're not just going to feel like throwing up, you're going to do it. Here, I'll carry your books for you."

It couldn't have been a pleasant trip for Tom, but Chip rushed him through the hall and up the steps to the nurse's office without an accident. Then he dropped off Tom's books on the nurse's desk and went off to the band room.

Poor guy, thought Chip. *At least he didn't throw up in the hall. Boy, neither of us would have lived that down.*

Later that afternoon, when Chip joined the football practice, he found even more evidence of the illness. The practice field seemed strange, almost ghostly, and not only because someone had marked the sidelines and the ten-yard intervals with chalk. It was as quiet as a funeral home.

Coach Ray marched onto the newly lined turf, staring at his watch. He looked over the sparse groups of white-uniformed boys and frowned. After a blast of his whistle that seemed to echo off the brick walls of the school, he said, "I know there's been a lot of sickness going around, and we're missing quite a few of our numbers. But we have our first game coming up next week, and we can't afford to go on vacation while we wait for everyone to get well. You boys badly need a full-scale scrimmage to give you a feel of this game before I can send you out to play for real."

He threw open a cardboard box and spilled out the blue bib tops. "I want the defense in blue today, so come on and grab a top. I want the offense and defense to go at it just as if this were a real game. Offense, you get four downs to make ten yards. Defense, you get three points every time you force the offense to punt."

As Chip bent down to pick out one of the blue tops, Scot called out, "Coach! We don't have enough backs!"

Seeing that only Bruce stood next to the quarterback, the coach waved irritably at the reserves. "Here's the chance you've been waiting for to step in and get some playing time. We've got two running back spots to fill today. Who wants 'em?"

The ranks of the substitutes had thinned out considerably since the first weeks of practice, and not all of it could be blamed on the flu. Many guys had quit altogether rather than stand around. Only one blue-helmeted player stepped out of the line to join Scot and

Bruce.

Coach Ray turned to Bronc, rubbing the stubble on his cheeks in amazement. "Bronc, don't we have any more backs? You mean the rest are all linemen?"

"If they're not, we've got the shyest backs in history," Bronc said. "But you know, some of the guys on defense used to work out with the backs."

Coach Ray scanned the defense, searching for the smaller, quicker players. Chip lowered his head, hoping to avoid the coach's search. But he had a feeling he was going to be chosen. Maybe it was because the coach liked saying his name, or what he believed to be his name.

"Demorg! How would you like to play right halfback?"

He felt as if he'd just been identified out of a police lineup of criminals. *Great,* he thought. *Another chance to make a fool out of myself.* Eric's shrill laugh didn't help matters.

"You can't do that, coach!" pleaded P.C. "You're breaking up this fine defensive machine on the left side."

"Do you mind?" sighed Coach Ray. "I need a back for this scrimmage."

P.C. hung an arm across Chip's shoulder. "Tough break, kid," he teased. "They finally get someone easy to tackle in the backfield, and you get switched out of the defense."

Dan winked at him and said, "You're still getting over the flu, right? Do me a favor and breathe on Roosevelt during the huddle."

"Sure thing," smiled Chip. "I guess our defensive contest is off for today."

"Are you kidding?" squawked P.C. "With you out of the way, we'll finally have a fighting chance. Do you realize we've given up forty-five more yards than the other side, even with our handicap?"

As Chip drew near the offensive huddle, he was awkwardly aware that the entire group was staring at him. Most seemed suspicious of the new runner.

"Sorry, you can't join the team," said Scot seriously. "Not when you're dressed like that."

Chip blushed as he looked down at his running shoes. He had always been self-conscious that he didn't have real football shoes like many of the players. But then Bruce snapped the elastic of his vest, and Chip realized he was still wearing the blue top of the defense. They were still snickering about that when Coach Ray poked his head into the huddle. From the way the coach rubbed his hands and grinned secretively, Chip could tell how much he enjoyed calling plays.

"This is the real thing now, boys. Any penalties will be called and marked off. Now listen up. Our first play will be 31 Red, on two. Let's go!"

Chip's clap came so late that it was only a small echo of the others. But the clapping didn't worry him; he was desperately fighting off a feeling of utter panic. What in the world did "31 Red" mean? He lined up an arm's length to the right of Bruce, searching the offensive formation for some clue as to what would happen. Although it was a cool, late-summer afternoon and he hadn't run a step yet, the foam padding of his helmet felt slippery with sweat. *How come they all know what the play is and I don't?* he thought.

P.C. was jumping and waving off to Chip's right, trying to draw his attention. Chip was dimly aware of the motion, but was so frazzled that he didn't even recognize him. Following the others in the three-point stance, he stared at Scot, who had started to shout out numbers.

Not me, not me! Chip pleaded silently. *Give it to someone else!*

But when Scot called out "Two," and the wall of blockers surged into action, Chip saw the quarterback directing the ball straight for his stomach. With a deep breath, Chip opened his arms to take the ball. What he would do once he got it, he had no idea.

At the last instant, Scot slapped the football into Bruce's stomach. Relieved, but still feeling out of place, Chip shuffled after the fullback as he ran into the line of blockers. Chip was still standing, untouched, when the runner was dragged down after a four-yard gain.

"How does it feel to be a star?" It was Dan grinning at him from flat on his back.

"Come on, can't you tell?" he whispered. "I don't know the first thing about what I'm doing."

"What do you mean?" said Dan, removing his protective mouthpiece. Suddenly he nodded. "That's right, you weren't here the day we went over the numbering for the plays. Let's see," he squinted at the other fallen bodies sorting themselves out. After retracing the path Bruce had run he said, "That must have been a 31 Red. Lucky for you! You were just a decoy."

Dan scrambled to his feet and caught Bruce by the elbow. After a whispered exchange, Bruce stared at Chip with wide eyes. "Are you kidding? He was fakin' it, and didn't know what the play was?" He laughed and poked Dan. "Hey, what if coach had called a forty play, huh?" Chip trailed the fullback to the huddle. "Tell you what," said Bruce over his shoulder. There's no time to go over the plays now, so I guess I'll have to tell you what to do on each play."

"Yeah, thanks," said Chip, his racing heart finally pulling back into his chest where it belonged.

"Fake 44, run 26 White, on three. Go!"

Bruce and Chip shuffled to the backfield positions together. "You're supposed to run over there. Oops! What am I doing, pointing?" Bruce dropped his hand in disgust and muttered, with his eyes fixed on the ground, "Scot comes to the right side and he's going to fake a handoff to you. You run between the right tackle and right end, just like you have the ball."

Chip nodded. "Then what about—"

"Don't worry about the rest; we don't have time," said Bruce. "Just worry about yourself and try not to mess up."

As Bruce had explained, Scot took the ball and veered to the right side. Chip ran forward, brushing past the quarterback, and looked for an opening to the right of Roosevelt. The area was clear and Chip found himself running free past the line of scrimmage. As an afterthought, he wondered if he shouldn't try to block someone. But by the time he located a blue jersey, the whistle had blown and the play had been stopped for no gain. Worse yet, the kid who had taken over his linebacker spot was the last to climb off the runner. It hurt to see P.C. give the boy an enthusiastic pounding on the back.

"Demorg!" shouted the coach. Chip cringed. Now what? "You have to hit that hole faster. Why bother to put a fake in the play if no one believes you have the ball?"

Chip stood awkwardly in the backfield as the offense tried one of their few pass plays on third down. But it fell incomplete. "Three points for the defense," growled Coach Ray. Chip saw P.C. and Dan slap each other's hands with glee. There seemed to be no doubt about it; with Chip switched over to the offense, the defense was playing better. Wiping his forehead, Chip called himself a few more names.

Bruce tugged off his helmet during the short break in the practice and signaled for Chip to join him. The fullback was breathing heavily, adding another load of guilt to the pile Chip already carried. The rest of the offense had been working hard, and Chip hadn't even touched anyone yet.

"Listen," said Bruce. "I can't concentrate on what I'm doing when I have to worry about you. So, quick, here's the system. It's easy. No matter what the play is, the system is the same. The first number is the ball carrier, see? Quarterback is 1, left halfback is 2, fullback is 3, right half is 4. The second number is the hole you run to. Anything to the right of the center is even, plays to the left are odd. So between the center and right guard is the 0 hole, between right guard and right tackle is the 2 hole, and so on. The 1 hole is between center and left guard, and so on. Got it? So a 25 play means what?"

Chip thought hard, trying to imagine the blockers at their positions.

"Um, the left halfback carries the ball, and he goes between the left tackle and the left end?"

"See, I told you it was easy," said Bruce. "Now the only other thing is the blocking code. The colors tell you how the backs block on the play. Red means the backs don't block; instead you fake it around end. White means the back nearest the hole leads the blocking through the hole. Blue means *both* blocking backs hit the hole before the runner. Got it?"

Before Chip could answer, Coach Ray ordered practice resumed. From the bark in his voice, the players could tell he was upset with the offense. No one said a word in the huddle. Chip gulped as the coach stared straight at him and snapped, "42 Red, on four!"

"You know the last number means the number the play starts on, don't you?" whispered Bruce.

"Yeah," Chip answered. He wished Bruce hadn't spoken and broken his concentration. Now that he knew he was actually going to run with the ball, he wanted to double-check in his mind where he was supposed to go. The system took some getting used to.

"Hut-one! Hut-two!" shouted Scot as he looked over the defense. Chip bit his lip and rocked forward on his toes. He was tired of being told that he didn't hit the hole fast enough. This time he was going to take off a fraction of a second before he was supposed to. "Hut-three! Hut-" Chip charged ahead just as the center hiked the ball. With one arm held high over his chest and the other low, he ran for the narrow opening between the center and right guard. Somehow, though, he smacked into Scot's shoulder. Dazed, he groped for the ball, but it slid out of his grip as he fell sideways. Luckily, Bruce saw what had happened and pounced on the ball just before two blue-shirted players arrived.

Scot coughed nervously and retreated to the huddle. This time Coach Ray said nothing, but the way he flung down his clipboard and glared with his hands on hips delivered his message perfectly. Before the coach stormed into the huddle, Scot gave Chip a puzzled look. "You came in a little close on that one, didn't you?"

Me! thought Chip. Scot's sloppy handoff had ruined his first run, and given him a scrape on the chin besides. And here Scot was trying to pin it on him! Suddenly, Chip's face flushed as he realized what had happened. The "2" hole was not between the center and guard—it was the guard-tackle slot. He had forgotten that the even numbers in the series started with zero and not two. No wonder he had bumped into Scot! And from the way Bruce was clearing his throat and shaking his head at him, Chip guessed that the fullback knew exactly what had gone on.

"I thought you said you were catching on to this!" said Bruce as they lined up for a 30 White play.

Chip nodded. He was supposed to be the lead blocker on this play. Still shaking with embarrassment from the last play, he didn't notice until he ran past the center that his blocking assignment was Eric! Seeing his enemy rush up to make the tackle, Chip lowered his head and braced himself for a jarring collision. But Eric was able to sidestep most of the block. "Get out of my way, you twerp!" he sneered as he pushed past Chip and lunged at Bruce. Chip's weak block must have helped some, though, because Bruce had gained seven yards by the time Eric wrestled him down. Still, he had to admit he should have done much better.

It wasn't until six plays later that Chip finally got his hands on the football. There was no path through the line, only a pile of bodies. But Chip plowed determinedly ahead for a yard or two before the massive weight of players pinned him to the ground. Wedged so tightly that he could not move until two or three layers of defenders got off, he could see Bruce looking down at him.

"You got a couple of tough yards," said Bruce.

Those few words changed the game of football for Chip from drudgery into an action-packed adventure. He wriggled to his feet and tossed the ball to Bronc, who was marking the forward progress. He knew that he hadn't done anything spectacular, but still he felt proud. He had carried the ball and won approval from one of the team's stars.

As he went out to block on the next play, he noticed for the first time how much he had learned in his weeks of practice. The plays no longer seemed like a confused scramble. As the patterns of play began to come into focus, he no longer had to rely on instinct and reactions. He could see where the tacklers were coming from, and where he had to be to block them out of the way. Of course, his blocking needed improvement. P.C. hopped over him, untouched, to make a tackle on one play. But rather than retreat silently to his huddle, Chip pointed accusingly at the cornerback and grinned. "I'd like to see you try that again!"

P.C. grinned back at him. "You liked that move, huh? Hey, do us a favor and warn us when the play's coming this way. We're still thirty-four yards behind the right side in our contest."

Two plays later, Coach Ray called for 41 Blue. By this time, Chip was able to decode the call in time to think about the path he would take. With a chill, he realized that he would be heading straight into Eric's territory. *I hope somebody blocks him,* he thought.

Chip waited for the other two backs to lead the way, then took the handoff from Scot. There was no mistaking the hole this time! No defensive player was within reach of him as he bolted through a large gap in the line. Bruce then knocked one of the safeties off his feet, leaving a clear field ahead.

Suddenly someone slammed into him from the side and put a bear hug on him. With one arm on the ground to steady himself, Chip somehow kept his balance and tried to twist out of the tackler's arms. As he turned, he found himself helmet to helmet with Eric. The sneer was gone as Eric stared straight into Chip's eyes. With a last bit of effort, Chip broke free from the grip and staggered backwards. A desperate swipe from Eric's arm caused Chip to stumble, but he lurched forward for eight more yards before being tackled from behind.

"Nice run!" shouted Bruce, sounding as much surprised as excited. Eric still stood where Chip had left him, holding out his arms and gaping at Chip as if the runner had passed right through his body.

As Chip filled his slot in the huddle, he could barely keep from shouting with joy as both Scot and Coach Ray offered their hands. The offense was on the move now! Chip could feel the energy in the huddle. Clapping twice as loudly as before, he dashed back to his position.

Fake 40 White, Run 27, Chip repeated to himself. He followed Bruce straight ahead and fell over one of his own blockers. Immediately, he craned his neck to see what was going on around the left end. The defense had fallen for the fake. Even the cornerbacks had rushed up to help plug the middle. The left halfback, running down the left sideline, was twenty yards past the line of scrimmage before many of the defenders even realized he had the ball.

"Ha! Faked you guys out of your pants!" laughed Bruce, elbowing Dan in the stomach.

When practice ended a half hour later, the offense claimed a 24-6 win. They walked off the field with just enough strength left to let loose a few howls and cheers. Chip decided he had never had so much fun in his life. He was walking off the field with the team's best player, or at least very close to him, and star players didn't walk off the field with nerds. Better yet, Eric Youngquist was limping off by himself.

Just before he reached his bike, he waved to Bruce, then turned to see what P.C. had to say this time. "Hey, thanks for running that sixty-yard touchdown to the other side," said the little cornerback. "That turned everything around. Now we have a twenty-yard lead in the great defensive race!"

"Don't thank me," said Chip. "I didn't call the play, and I didn't carry the ball on that one, either."

Dan trudged over very slowly after his day's battle with Roosevelt. "Now when you come back to linebacker we'll at least have a little cushion. It'll probably take you a good two practices to help us blow our lead."

"Forget the linebacker stuff," said Chip casually, spinning the combination lock on his bike. "It's fun being a back. You know, that Bruce is really a great guy."

4
The Punt that Got Away

"Chip Demory?" Rennie searched Bruce's face to see if his fellow running back was putting him on. When he saw that Bruce was serious, he burst into laughter. "Are you kidding? *He* took *my* place?" The peals of laughter cut deeply into Chip's pride, far deeper than Eric's remarks ever had. Eric laughed out of obvious spite, but Rennie had no such motive. He truly could not help himself, even though Chip was sitting well within listening range. Evidently the thought of Chip filling his shoes for a practice struck him as ridiculous.

Rennie had washed away all the confidence that Chip had so painfully earned in the scrimmage. But, just as suddenly, Bruce retrieved it. "Don't laugh," he said. "He did a good job."

As far as Chip was concerned, Bruce had just made a

friend for life. Rennie shrugged and trotted off to play catch with Scot. Chip tried hard to forgive Rennie's thoughtlessness. Who could blame Rennie for being surprised? Chip hadn't done much before to prove he could play.

Most of the team was lying against the brick wall of the school, where the shade had protected the last stand of lush grass from drying out like the rest of the field. Despite their lounging, very few actually seemed relaxed. In one hour the team from Monroe School would be there for the first game of the year. Coach Ray had done nothing to ease the tension in his players. He had been maddeningly secretive about what would happen, who would start, and how many reserves might play.

Those unsolved questions made it difficult for Chip to get comfortable. His legs refused to stay in one spot, and his stomach felt like it was turning upside down. He supposed that he probably should have had supper before the game. But even if his mom had been home in time to make him something, he wasn't sure he could have eaten it.

His new friend Bruce, however, seemed cool about it all. With his arms folded across his chest and his eyes shut, he almost seemed in danger of falling asleep. Chip tried to will himself to act that calmly, but then got twice as jumpy as before when he saw the school custodian plant red flags in the corners of the chalked end zones.

Stretching out his legs again, Chip noticed how clean his mom had gotten his practice uniform. "How come the coach waits until now to give the game jerseys?" he asked Bruce.

"Tradition, I guess," Bruce answered without lifting an eyelid. He yawned, then added, "He always waits till now. It's part of his pregame pep job. He likes everyone tense and psyched up."

Chip found himself yawning, too, though he was far

from tired. He ached to ask Bruce what he thought his chances were of getting in at running back. Everyone knew he had done well at practice, he thought. Maybe he and Rennie could alternate and carry instructions from the bench to the huddle.

Even Bruce sat up at the sound of the van as it arrived. Coach Ray hopped out one door, dressed in a sport jacket and tie, and pulled open the side door. Bronc, in a blue sweater with the sleeves rolled up, followed him and helped him carry in the boxes. Without a word or a whistle from the coaches, the team followed them into the school to the locker room.

What a change three weeks can make! thought Chip. Nothing in the room seemed remotely scary now. He was able to walk right into the middle of the group and find a spot on the concrete floor reserved for him by Dan and P.C.

"This doesn't mean it's permanent," said Coach Ray, waving his clipboard, "but this is the starting offensive lineup for the game. Come and get your game jersey when I call your name. The tackles are Baxter and Ellingsly."

Chip had to scrunch against the bench to help give the two a path to the front. They claimed their extra-large jerseys and held them up by a corner, as if afraid to wrinkle them. Midnight blue with white numerals, the jerseys looked professional.

"How do they assign numbers?" Chip asked.

"It's the usual pattern," Dan answered. "Quarterbacks are teens, runners twenties and thirties, defensive backs forties, linebackers and centers fifties, guards sixties, tackles seventies, ends eighties. Nineties are for subs."

Chip could not keep his eyes off the emptying box as the rest of the starting linemen came forward. This was his first game, he kept reminding himself. Now that he knew he was better than anyone had suspected, he pictured himself scoring a long touchdown in that sharp uniform.

"Wilkes, Schultz," called out the coach. When they returned, Chip saw Bronc pull out a number 20. *Wouldn't it be great if that were mine?* thought Chip. *Why not? Bruce says I was great.*

"Ruiz!"

Jolted back to reality, Chip felt foolish. *How dumb could I be to think I might beat out Rennie? Rennie can run twice as fast as I can.*

"All of these players will also start on defense," announced the coach, "with two exceptions."

Amid a chorus of excited whispers, Chip felt a nudge from behind.

"Hey, this could get interesting," winked P.C. When Bronc pulled out a large number 83, P.C. leaned over to Dan. "You might get lucky. That's a lineman's number."

"Atkinson," said Coach Ray, and P.C. pounded Dan on the back.

Dan made no move to get up, though. "Which Atkinson?" asked several voices.

"The one who plays right end."

"The lucky bum," sighed Dan as his brother hurried forward. No sooner had he grabbed his jersey and sat down than both Dan and P.C. poked Chip. Chip then saw a number 55 displayed in Bronc's hands. A linebacker's number!

Please, let me have that one! Chip pleaded silently.

"Youngquist." There was an extra swagger to his walk as Eric proudly strode forward to claim his starting position. Chip rolled his eyes in disgust. "What a joke!" he muttered. "He can't tackle. I ran right through his arms in that scrimmage."

"What did I tell you?" whispered Dan. "Now that he's in, he'll leave you alone."

As the rest of the names were called, Chip clung to

the hope of a reserve running back spot. He *must* have impressed them; Bruce had as much as said so. It was all right with him if he only got in for a few plays. He would show them what he could do.

"Demorg!" Nearly stepping on a few legs in his eagerness, Chip made his way to the front. The jersey Bronc held was rumpled, but Chip thought he could make out a number 37: a running back number! He grinned at Bruce and snatched the jersey, then held it out to get a better look. Fifty-seven! Chip hardly noticed the shoves from others trying to get past him to pick up their tops. The roller coaster of emotions he had been riding had just thrown him off at the bottom.

As he trudged back to his spot on the floor, the sounds of the bantering among the players seemed miles away.

"I hear football players wear their IQs on their jerseys," Dan was explaining, holding up his 99. "That makes me the smartest one here."

"Forty-six!" groaned P.C. "What a blah number! Name one great player who ever wore 46. Name just one."

Ignoring them, Chip glared down at his number 57. It was depressing how a number could ruin a perfectly good jersey.

"Hey, Chip!"

Chip swung his head around and, as if their heads were all connected by strings, half the players on the sidelines turned to look. Chip's surprise turned to anger when he saw that it was Tom grinning and waving at him. The disappointment of being demoted to reserve linebacker had put him in a grouchy mood to begin with. Throughout the first half of the game he had stared sullenly at the proceedings on the field. Some of the others had yelled encouragement to the starters, but Chip couldn't get into that. It especially grated on him to see Eric playing defense. Eric was playing the middle linebacker spot like a big shot, clapping and yelling warnings to his teammates, and jumping in the air after making a tackle. The coaches hadn't even looked at any of the reserves so far. And now there was Tom calling out to him, with that silly, homemade haircut and goofy grin.

What is he doing here? Chip wondered. *So what if he's a good friend; he doesn't belong here.* Tom couldn't have told if the Green Bay Packers were a football team or a labor union. A lot of boys thought of him as a wimp. It wasn't really fair: Tom just didn't happen to care about sports. He was a nice guy and a good friend, but Chip wished he would act a little more normal.

"What are you doing here?" Chip asked, so quietly that Tom barely heard.

"Come on, I came to watch the star in action," said Tom.

Eric, who was pacing the sidelines while the offense was on the field, overheard. "You told him you're the big star?" he laughed. "Then what are you doin' on the bench the whole game?" Several boys joined in on the chuckling.

"Shut up," said Chip, glaring at both Eric and Tom. Just then, a long pass from Scott to Andy regained the team's attention. Chip slipped away and led Tom far from the action, behind a row of parents watching from behind the bench. Chip judged from their lack of enthusiasm that many of them were parents of scrubs.

"What are you doing here?" Chip asked.

"I already told you—"

"I'm not the star," snapped Chip. "I never said I was."

"But you—"

"I said I did well in *one* practice. That's all. Now I'm on the bench. I haven't played all game."

"I'm sorry," said Tom, with his head down and

hands stuck in his pockets. "I just thought I'd come and root for you." Peeking through the row of parents, he asked, "Why was Eric Youngquist being so mean?"

"Because that's the way scum like him always act," Chip spat.

"I don't know him that well," shrugged Tom. "But I don't remember him being so bad when he was in my Sunday school class a few years back."

"Eric goes to our church?" asked Chip, suspiciously. "How come I never see him?" He couldn't imagine why God would want anything to do with someone like Eric. The thought of Eric in church made him uncomfortable, an intrusion on another part of his life.

"I don't know," answered Tom. "It's a big church. Maybe he goes in the middle of the week. Maybe he doesn't go at all now."

"That's more likely," nodded Chip. "If I acted the way he did, I wouldn't have the guts to step inside a church."

"We should get back to the game, shouldn't we?" asked Tom. "You might be called on to go in." Seeing Chip roll his eyes, he said, "Well, aren't you even interested in who's winning?"

Chip turned his back on the field. "Is that a good enough answer for you? This whole thing has been a big pain since the first day. It probably wouldn't be so bad if there weren't creeps like Eric around to spoil it for everyone." He paused as if coming to an important decision. "I'll probably stick it out for this year. But next year, I'm going out for soccer. Jason says it's fun most of the time. Hey, why don't you come out for it, too? The three of us could have a great time."

"Naw," said Tom, kicking a stone loose from the ground. "I'm no good at that." Then, brightening, he said, "I know one thing we can all do together next year. We'll be in the youth group at church. My brother goes to it all the time, and he says it's a blast."

"Yeah?" said Chip. "I'm not sure." The idea didn't sound the best to him. He was already working under a social handicap with Tom as a friend. If he was in a church group, too, well, everybody would think he was really out of it. He didn't think God would mind. What good would it do God if Chip lost friends over something like that? "Trouble is, they probably pick on the little guys. It might be better to wait until we aren't the youngest in the group."

"Come on," laughed Tom. "This is a church. What are they going to do, mug you and dump you off in a dark alley?"

"Very funny," said Chip. He heard Coach Ray's booming voice ordering the defense back on the field. The offense must have been stopped again. There was Eric strapping on his helmet and sprinting back on the field like a madman. "Hey, Tom. Do they let anyone join? The youth group, I mean."

"Well, I think you would have to belong to the church."

Frowning, Chip went on. "You don't suppose Eric would join."

"Eric who?" Then, following Chip's gaze, he said, "I don't know."

"I'll tell you one thing, if Eric joins that group, I wouldn't come near it if you paid me!"

Tom whistled. "Boy, the guy must be pretty bad!"

"You wouldn't believe him. I'd stay away from him if I were you."

"Relax," said Tom. "If he doesn't do much in church now, he's not likely to join then."

"Demorg!"

Although the voice barely filtered through the noise of the sideline chatter to his ears, Chip jumped. When he heard it again, louder and more urgent, he wheeled and dashed back to the bench.

"What are you doing? That's not your name," said

Tom, but Chip was in too big a hurry to explain.

"Demorg, for cryin' out loud, where are you?" Coach Ray was saying when Chip reached the sidelines. Forcing his way through a cluster of players, he reported to the coach.

"Where have you been?" demanded the coach. Without waiting for an answer, he shoved him toward the field. "Ruiz has the wind knocked out of him. Take over at left linebacker!"

"Go get 'em, Chip!" yelled P.C.

Chip didn't know how many more shocks his system could take in one day. The switch from total boredom and hopelessness to a supercharged high in just twenty seconds had him dizzy. He raced onto the field about two steps faster than he had ever run in his life. The Forest Grove defense didn't bother with huddles, so he headed straight for his position. Eric happened to step backward into his path, and he brushed lightly against him. *Oh, no,* thought Chip, poised for another confrontation. But the middle linebacker seemed lost in his own thoughts, and barely recognized that a new player was in the game.

In fact, none of his teammates seemed to have noticed his arrival. Chip was used to P.C.'s constant chatter between plays, and Dan always had some comment, even if he just groaned. Chip felt as though he were an intruder in the silent wave of blue shirts.

It didn't help matters that he had been ignoring the game. Chip had no idea what down it was, or how many yards there were to go. He wasn't even sure of the score, although his team had been ahead, 13-6, the last time he checked. But as the green and white Monroe team lined up, he began to feel more sure of himself. For one thing, it gave him a huge shot of confidence to see Roosevelt Baxter crouching a few feet away on the left side of the line. Better yet, the Monroe players, even the linemen, weren't very big.

This is a real game, Chip kept reminding himself as the Monroe quarterback gave out signals. They tried a running play up the middle, but the smallish blockers could not make a dent in the Forest Grove line. Five Forest Grove players had already wrapped up the little back and were driving him back when Chip arrived. Just to be in on the action, he pushed along with the rest of the tacklers until the whistle blew.

This is lots easier than stopping our own offense, thought Chip. For the first time in his life, he felt like a real athlete. It was such a feeling of power that he could almost forgive Eric for strutting around all game. Having easily brushed aside his blocker the play before, Chip hoped they would run a play to his side. He could see himself storming into the backfield to wreck the play before it started.

Roosevelt seemed to be waving him forward. Chip ran up, wondering what the star lineman had to say. But Roosevelt said nothing as he dug his cleats into the ground. Confused, Chip looked around and saw Bruce backpedaling all by himself. A quick look at the Monroe formation confirmed that this was going to be a punt. No wonder Roosevelt motioned him forward; they were all supposed to be on the line to try to block the kick!

Chip relaxed as he imitated the lineman's stance. He had never practiced rushing a punter, but he knew what would happen. No one ever blocked a punt; you just went through the motions, pushing and shoving a little until the punter kicked it away.

What he couldn't figure out was why there wasn't a Monroe blocker in front of him. There didn't seem to be anyone between him and the punter. When something didn't make sense, Chip usually suspected that he was doing something wrong.

Am I in the wrong spot? he wondered. *But where else can I go?* Chip finally shrugged, figuring some Monroe player would show up to block him. They must know what they were doing.

When the ball was hiked, Chip ran forward. To his amazement, no Monroe player showed the slightest interest in him. Chip was so startled that he slowed up. What was going on? It couldn't be a fake punt, because he saw the punter right in front of him step forward to gain momentum for his punt. Chip was close enough so that, with a quick spurt, he could easily smother the kick. But he had never seen it done or prepared himself for just *how* to do it. Were you suppose to hold out your hands, or run into the kicker? And how did you keep from getting kicked in the stomach?

The questions paralyzed him so that he had stopped moving altogether by the time the punt sailed away. Chip watched it bounce out-of-bounds, which saved him the trouble of blocking for the kick return.

As he stood there watching the punter walk off, it suddenly hit him how stupid he had been. A Monroe player had blown his blocking assignment. If Chip had been at all alert, he would have taken advantage of it. As it was, he had had to work hard to *stop* himself from tackling the kicker before the ball had even dropped! On the second play of his career, he had been given a great chance to be a star, and he had been too timid to accept it.

His eyes shot quickly to the bench. Had anyone noticed? The players milling around the field didn't even look his way; they must have been too busy with their own assignments. But a dreaded tap on the shoulder convinced Chip that Coach Ray had detected the error. A substitute had come in to take his place.

Chip was certain the coach had seen it all. The man didn't look at Chip for the rest of the game. Chip's substitute stayed in the game even when Forest Grove went back on defense. *Too chicken to block a kick,* thought Chip. *I won't get another chance to play for the rest of the year!*

Forest Grove wore down the smaller Monroe team for another touchdown in the final period. The referee shot off a gun to signal the end of the game, and Forest Grove danced off the field celebrating a 19-7 win.

"Way to go, Chip!" shouted Tom, above the uproar. That crazy Tom seemed more excited about the win than most of the players.

"Yeah, way to go, star! " said Eric. Chip saw Eric's uniform, coated with smudges of dirt, and looked down at his own spotless pants. Although he had done almost nothing for the past four hours, he felt as though he barely had the strength to walk the three blocks to his home. His anger had faded. He couldn't blame Tom, or Eric, either. He felt totally defeated. And he didn't care if he ever got another chance to play. *A loser like me would probably just blow it again, anyway,* he concluded.

5
Trumpet Call

The long line of cars waiting to pull into the senior high school parking lot were starting to tie up traffic on Princeton Avenue. From their spot at the end of the line, the Demorys could see their prospects of finding a parking place in the school's cramped lot were poor.

"You can tell this is a game of unbeaten teams," said Mr. Demory, his eyes darting, looking for a spot on the street. "Last time I came to one of Jill's games, you could have camped out in that lot and never been disturbed."

Chip scanned his side of the street. Just behind them, a turn signal blinked as a driver prepared to pull away from the curb. "There's one opening up behind you, Dad."

"Come on, fella, move it," said Mr. Demory. The car edged out of the spot and went around them. Seeing that no one had come up behind them yet, Mr. Demory backed up and moved into the spot. "I was wondering when he was going to wake up. I paid him a fortune to sit there and reserve that place for me."

"Really? How much did you have to pay?" asked Tom.

Chip groaned. "Come on, Tom, can't you tell he's teasing?"

"Lock up, men," said Mr. Demory. "Glad you could come along tonight, Tom. I didn't know you were a sports buff."

"Well, I'm not really," grinned Tom. "But Chip's football game was kind of interesting, so I figured this might be, too. Besides," he said, patting his black instrument case, "I think this'll be a riot with my trumpet along. Maybe I can add some excitement to the game."

"You're crazy!" said Chip, hurrying to keep up with his dad's pace. "Why did you bring that thing, anyway?"

"Chip's right," said Mr. Demory over his shoulder. "I'm not sure they'll let you bring that into the gym. You'd better talk to the coach about it."

While Tom sought out the volleyball coach, Chip and his dad headed into the stands. The movable bleachers seemed to wobble with each step, no matter how lightly they walked. Finding a spot halfway up, they sat back and watched Jill warm up. The team didn't have any official warm-up suits, and Jill stood out in the sky blue one Dad had bought her for her birthday. During the spiking drill, she crouched and then floated high in the air. Chip wished he could jump that high. At the top of her leap, she drilled the ball across the net—but it landed beyond the end line of the other court. Frowning, she swung both arms like windmills to get them loose.

The Demorys had room enough to put their feet on the seats below and to lean back on the ones behind.

Still, the gymnasium was almost half full on the home side, far different from the last time they had come. "A little success really brings people out," commented Dad. "We're ranked third, and East is fourth in the state coaches' poll." Chip hadn't ever heard of a state ranking for high school girls' volleyball. But, knowing how his dad combed the sports pages, he didn't doubt the statement.

Even if they hadn't seen Tom run up the steps toward them, they would have heard him coming. *Clomp! Clomp!* Chip thought the bleachers were going to collapse. "Hey! The coach, Mrs. Campbell, thought it would be a great idea!" Tom spouted. "The more noise, the better. Know what else? She asked me if I wanted to play the national anthem before the game. Usually they use a record."

Watching Jill muff an attempted setup, Dad said, "Well, bugler, do you happen to know reveille? I don't think Jill is awake yet."

"Sure, that's easy," answered Tom, putting the mouthpiece to his lips.

Chip pulled the instrument away from him. "When are you going to stop being so gullible?" he asked, shaking his head. "Dad's only kidding." A group of girls were standing in the aisle, shielding the clock from his sight, so Chip leaned across his dad's lap to check his watch. Three minutes until playing time.

Chip was watching the trickle of latecomers on the home side when he spotted two familiar faces. Bruce and Scot made their way into the gym and stood in the entrance for a moment. With their curly hair, jeans, and matching baseball league Windbreakers, they looked almost like twins from a distance. Scot shrugged and followed Bruce to a first-row seat near the door.

Those two were like a harsh light that exposed the blemish sitting on Chip's left. Until that moment, he had been happy to have Tom along. But he had never dreamed that some of the best players on the football team would be at the game. It was bad enough if they saw him sitting with his dad, but what would they think if they saw Tom with him again? Chip was especially worried about Bruce. The guy had been nice to him since that day he filled in for Rennie. If Chip had any chance left of getting important people to notice him, Bruce was his best bet. But Bruce was probably already going out on a limb just by talking to him. *He wouldn't come near anyone like Tom,* thought Chip. *If Bruce sees us sitting together, he'll really wonder about me.*

Well, at least there are a lot of people tonight, he thought, looking at the crowd. *They aren't going to notice me.* Just to be safe, though, he leaned back in his seat so that his dad's shoulder would block his face from their view.

Then he saw Tom with his horn up, waiting for a signal. East had already assembled on the sidelines, and Mrs. Campbell had just ended the drills for her squad. *If he blows that thing, everyone in the place will be looking at us,* he thought.

"You're not going to play the national anthem up here, are you?" Chip asked quickly.

"Why not? They'll all be able to hear just fine."

"But wouldn't it be more, uh, proper to have you standing out on the floor?"

"Not a bad idea," said his dad.

"OK. Wish me luck." Tom grinned as he pounded back down the steps. Chip had to admit he played well. He didn't waver on a single note. While some of the crowd near them joined in singing, Chip's mind was working feverishly. He had just barely dodged this catastrophe. But Tom was planning to use that crazy horn the whole game. Bruce and Scot couldn't help but notice Tom; Chip had to make sure that when they did, he was out of the picture.

"Well played, bugler," said Dad when Tom returned. "What do you plan to do for an encore?"

Grinning and brushing back his jaggedly cut hair, Tom blasted a brief familiar sports tune. "Charge!" yelled most of the home team spectators in response. Seeing that practically everyone in the place was turning to look at them, Chip quickly let his jacket slip down through an opening in the bleachers. Dropping down after it, he said, "Oops. Dropped my jacket. Be right back." It was an easy climb down the ironworks supporting the collapsible bleachers. There were already a few candy wrappers and popcorn containers littering the floor next to his jacket. It was a fine excuse to kill a little more time, and Chip collected as many as he could in one armful. Dumping them into the trash can by the wall, he returned and tried to locate the section in which he had been sitting. At the same time, he wished for a plan that could get him through the rest of the game.

"Hey! What's taking you?" Tom's head was poking through directly above him.

"There was a bunch of garbage down here, so I picked some of it up." Climbing back up through the supporting works, he had to admit he was beaten. With Tom carrying on, Bruce would notice him for sure—unless the games were so exciting that no one paid attention to that stupid trumpet.

Unfortunately, the first game dragged on with neither side scoring well on their serves. Chip spent most of it watching the two heads in the first row, and leaning back whenever it seemed one of them was turning around. *If Tom plays that 'Charge' thing again, I'll scream,* he thought. But of course, Tom kept at it. All Chip could do was try to make himself as small as possible. From what he saw of the game, Jill was playing well. That got his normally quiet dad talking nonstop. He always did when he got excited at one of Jill's games.

After Jill's team finally won the first game, Tom sprang another surprise. "How about a little intermission entertainment?"

Resisting the urge to slug his friend, Chip got up and walked down three rows before turning to his dad. "Want something to drink from the concessions?"

"Not for me, thanks," Dad said, prying a dollar out of his wallet. "I get so wrapped up in these games, I'd probably just spill the whole thing. But the bugler's probably running pretty dry. Get something for the two of you."

Tom was into his first number before Chip snatched away the dollar. Chip sighed heavily after yet another narrow escape. He started cutting straight across the bleachers to avoid running into Bruce and Scot. But when he checked on them again, he found their seats empty. *Maybe they left,* Chip hoped as he bounced down to the floor. Somehow, though, he still didn't feel that terrific. Even in his narrow escapes, something was gnawing at him. His feelings of guilt were harder to escape.

He stepped straight from the sounds of Tom's trumpet into the smoke of the lobby. It was always the same at these events. No matter how small the crowd, the smoke was still penetrating. Chip glided through the clusters of people, pretending he was a running back dodging open-field tacklers. No one so much as touched him by the time he reached the concession stand.

There was nothing there resembling a line. People jockeyed for position and tried to catch the attendant's eye before someone else did. Moving quickly into a vacated slot, Chip discovered Bruce just ahead and to the left. The fullback had made it to the counter and was tapping his quarters on it, waiting for his drink to come. At first Chip thought of backing out of line, but the space behind him had already been filled in. He found himself being funneled closer to Bruce, with only one man screening him from view. Chip saw the attendant bring two plastic cups of orange soda pop, then felt a nudge. It was his neighbor, Mr. O'Neill.

"Hi, there, Chip. Your sister's doing a fine job," he said, scratching his beard.

His cover was blown. But Chip saw a way to turn it to his advantage. Pretending he hadn't seen Bruce, he announced loudly, "Oh, Jill's doing all right, I guess. But I think she'll really get going in the second game. It always takes her awhile to warm up, you know."

Bruce took a long sip and turned to Chip on his way out. Without any greeting he said, "So that's your sister out there, huh? Number 15?"

"Yep," said Chip, acting as matter-of-factly as he knew how.

Bruce nodded. "We're taking off. Their games take too long. Scot and I are going over to the arcade before it closes."

It all worked out after all, thought Chip as Bruce pushed past. *They have to be impressed that I'm Jill's brother, especially after the way she played.*

Suddenly Bruce stopped and grabbed Chip's shoulder. Chip waited for him to finish swallowing. "You know, you should get your buddy to bring his horn to our games," said Bruce. "The last one we had was so quiet it didn't even seem like a real game."

"He's not really my buddy," Chip found himself explaining. But Bruce and Scot had already moved away and were pushing through the outside doors. *So they saw me with Tom,* Chip thought. *Why does he have to be so weird?* Chip couldn't see any way around it. He was going to have to avoid Tom for a while. At least for the rest of the football season.

When Chip returned to his seat, Tom was making a

bigger spectacle of himself than ever, bowing to the applause. The adults seemed to think he was funny, anyway. Chip slumped in his seat, muscles aching from the prolonged tension, and handed Tom his drink. A man several rows ahead of them waved at his dad.

"Hey, Chuck! Your Jill looks good out there!"

"Not only that, but she's playing well, too," laughed Dad. He was beaming, and his chest was swelling as if he were savoring the most delicious moment in his life. Chip had seen that look a few times before, and always when Jill was playing exceptionally well at something. Before this, Chip had always joined in the applause for Jill. But he wasn't feeling at all gracious anymore.

I've never seen him act that way when I *do anything,* he thought, watching his dad's eyes as they followed Jill. *Not likely to, either. Don't you think I try as hard as she does? All Miss Perfect out there has to do is show up and everyone* oohs *and* ahs *over her. I'm just her klutzy brother.* He ignored Tom throughout the second game, and took a morbid delight in how it was turning out. Jill's team fell behind early and lost the game badly.

Chip listened to his dad nervously mumbling unheard advice to Jill's team, and finally turned to Tom. "You mean you aren't going to treat us to another concert?"

Tom's eyes lit up. "Oh, I almost forgot. Any requests?"

But before he could play, Chip pulled him back down to his seat. "That was such a short game they're not even taking a break. See, they're already serving." Bitterness had ruined the evening for him. When the East team scored he grumbled, and when Jill made a good play for her team he sulked about why God had given her all the talent when he needed it worse than she did. When Jill won a round of applause with a diving save of a hard spike, Chip didn't join in.

But as the game went on, even Chip was drawn into its intensity. The teams were so evenly matched and were playing so hard that the spectators began to look as drained as the players. Tom's latest "Charge" number had attracted only a few hoarse cheers.

Tom shrugged and packed away the instrument. "My hands are getting too sweaty to play anyway," he said.

The gymnasium grew quiet when the ball was served. Spectators on each side seemed to be trying to will the ball to hit the ground on the other team's court. Chip's dad was still muttering instructions under his breath, and his clenched fists jerked in spasms, as if he were trying to play the game for Jill.

The tension pulled Chip back to Jill's side. When an East player stood back and let a ball drop near the line, he and a large share of the home crowd started yelling, "That was in!" But the referee refused to be swayed, and awarded the point to East. That put them ahead, 19-18. Two more points and they would win.

East served again, a deep, spinning shot to the corner. A good save by Jill's teammate sent the ball to her spot on the corner of the front row. As Jill wound up her fist and jumped, two East players crowded the net to attempt a block. "Spike it!" gasped Chip. But Jill eased up and tapped the ball down the row, almost directly over the net. Somehow, though, her teammate pounded it straight down into the netting. The muffed spike gave East a 20-18 lead.

"Why didn't she take the spike herself?" complained Chip. "She's the best player out there."

"Now, don't get on your sister for that," his dad whispered back, wiping his palms on his pants. "You see, that's another example of what makes her a good player. Sure, she could have hit it over the net. But it wasn't a good set. Why, she was at least three feet from the net! So she gave it to another girl. Jill doesn't hog the ball even if she could do better herself. That keeps the team playing as a team. See that? She just told the girl who missed not to worry about it. The game's on the line, and she's still a good sport."

All right, already, thought Chip. *You'd think she was a saint.*

A burst of relieved applause and cheering followed a wide serve by the East team. Now it was Jill's turn to serve. The room was so quiet, that Chip could hear the echoing thud as Jill pounded her serves across the net. Three straight points brought the home fans to the edge of their seats as their team took the lead, 21-20. Then Jill hit one final overhand serve that spun crazily away from an East player, beyond reach of her teammates.

The gym exploded in noise, and soon all the girls were hugging each other, even the ones who hadn't played. Chip saw his dad rush down toward the floor, and he and Tom followed at a more cautious pace. By the time they reached the court, a reporter had pushed his way next to Jill. "Everyone on the team works hard," she was saying. "We're all part of this win, 'cause we push each other in practice."

Chip bristled when he heard it. It was almost as if she were aiming her comments at him, insisting that everyone was the same. For a second, guilt washed over him as he thought of how he was considering abandoning Tom to avoid being tagged as a loser. *It's not the same,* he thought, fighting the feeling. *It's easy for her. She's got it all. What's she got to lose by being that way?*

Jill finally made her way over to them. "Hi!" she said, with a bright smile at each of them. "Thanks for coming!"

She's so perfect I could throw up, thought Chip as his dad swung her around in a hug.

6
The Penalty

Chip had not been wrong about that punt play coming back to haunt him. At the next practice, Bronc took him aside and asked, "What's wrong with you, Chip? You were a tiger during that one practice, but you haven't done a thing since." Chip could only shrug, paw the ground with his foot, and promise to try harder.

Worse yet, Coach Ray didn't call his name once during practice, not even to yell at him. He remembered a remark Jill had made once when Dad had complained that a coach was always picking on her. "It's when they don't think you're worth yelling at that you have to worry," she'd said.

When Forest Grove went to the municipal park to play Willow Creek, Chip found himself, as usual, on the wrong side of the white lines. He had been standing and watching so long that his legs were starting to throb. The lights over the field made even the scuffed helmets shine against the black of a moonless night.

The uniforms seemed brighter, the grass greener, the game more real.

But as had happened so often, Chip's thoughts drifted away from the game in front of him. His dad had dropped him off at the field on the way to a meeting. Before he had left, he had completely caught Chip off guard.

"You've got a game next week, too, don't you?" Dad had asked.

"Yeah, cross town over at Brycelin Heights. Tuesday night."

Dad had pulled out that black book that he kept tucked in the inside pocket of his suits. "I'll work on getting it cleared so I can come watch."

"Uh, well, if you've got something better to do . . ." Chip had stammered.

"Think you can get me a good seat?" Dad had said, knowing full well that there weren't any stands at Brycelin Heights.

Chip's first thought had been that his dad would find out for sure next week that he was not good enough to get into a game. For the first two quarters of the game, he moped about his klutziness and his bad luck. But by the third period, a stubborn streak had surfaced in him that refused to accept humiliation in front of his dad. *Somehow I've got to get into the starting lineup,* he thought. Then he laughed at himself for even imagining such a thing. But gradually, the scene before him captured his interest. Each missed tackle or block, each dropped pass, and each penalty gave more proof that the starters weren't perfect.

"Hey, all-star!" Eric jarred his thoughts loose with his shout. The middle linebacker threw back his head to gulp water out of a paper cup, crumpled the cup, and tossed it on the ground. Eric had been getting laughs calling him all-star ever since the last game. Although Chip had vowed many times to get even, he began to see that it was no use. Eric had won the starting role, and at the same time had won their private war. "Wake up, all-star, you gotta be ready to save the game for us."

"Shut your mouth, Youngquist!" said Chip.

"Oh, sure thing! I don't want to get an all-star mad at me."

Dan moved over to Chip, pounding his helmet on his thigh pad. "I guess I blew that call. I really thought Eric would settle down once he made the starting lineup. He must be more insecure than I thought. You know, that's the trouble with making predictions. There's always a chance that you may be wrong."

"Just a chance?" hooted P.C., sitting on his helmet in front of them. "Atkinson, if you predicted the sun would rise tomorrow, I wouldn't bet on it."

Chip was pretty sure of the answer to his own question, but he had to voice it anyway. "Dan, is there any chance of us getting in the game?"

"You're asking me?" said Dan. "I don't want to go out on a limb one way or another. But I haven't seen a substitution all night."

Chip was aware of that, and he knew the reason why. Willow Creek posed a far greater challenge than Monroe had. They were well-coached, fast, strong, and even had one boy who could make Roosevelt work awfully hard. Chip could see the strain on the starters' faces on the rare occasions when they came close to him. Even Bruce hadn't said anything to him at halftime. He had just squinted through the harsh lights at the Willow Creek squad, doubled over with his hands on his hips. Although Forest Grove held an 8-6 lead into the third period, this was serious business.

Rennie found out just how serious it was late in the third period. While trying to fake out one defender, he was hit hard from behind, bounced through the air, and landed on his back. Dazed, he limped off the field.

Seeing his chance, Chip sought out Coach Ray. He stood close enough to the coach to rub shoulders, and even ventured a foot out onto the field, trying to attract the coach's attention. But if Coach Ray did happen to turn his way, he looked right through him. After a time out, Rennie ran back on the field. All the starters were still in.

With nervous energy building up inside of him, Chip pushed his way behind the line of reserves. *Maybe if I do some really hard sprints, I can show them that I'm ready*, he thought. Somehow, the strange lighting and the darkness made him feel as though he were flying as he raced down the sidelines. He pictured himself running into the middle of a packed stadium with an announcer shouting, "At left linebacker, 6 feet, 4 inches, 230 pounds, number 57, Chip Demory!"

As he puffed back toward the bench, Dan reached out and slowed him down with his arm. "What's the matter? Your pants on fire?"

"No," gasped Chip, "just trying to stay ready in case I get in the game."

"Now there's an optimist for you," said Dan.

"I suppose you always keep your wallet open just in case some dollar bills happen to be falling from the sky," added P.C. But Chip thought he saw Bronc give him a quick glance. Just for good measure, he sprinted down the sidelines one more time.

Late in the fourth quarter, however, Chip had conceded that he would not play this game. He hadn't really expected it would be that easy to work himself back into favor with the coaches. In fact, as he watched the furious action on the field, he had a twinge of doubt about even wanting to be out there. Still trailing by two points, Willow Creek had driven deep into Forest Grove territory. Most of their yards came on power plays off tackle. Eric was no longer prancing around and hollering; he had all he could handle battling the opposing center. The Willow Creek center, a stocky guy with his red shirttail always hanging out, seemed to be a tough character. He and Eric were often still wrestling around after the whistle had stopped play, and Chip could see that they had a running argument going. The referee had tried to put a stop to it by calling a roughness penalty on the center, but neither had backed down much.

With two minutes left, Willow Creek drove their way to the 16-yard line. There they faced a third down with three yards to go for a first. Both teams' reserves were on their feet, crowding around their coaches at the end of the field where the action had moved. *This is just like the volleyball game,* Chip thought, watching Coach Ray pace a tight circle. When the coach suddenly wheeled and searched through the ranks of his substitutes, Chip was the only one with half an eye on him. Coach had that look that said he was sending someone into the game. He looked straight into Chip's eyes. Chip started forward, pointing to himself with a questioning look. But the coach's eyes darted away and he grabbed another boy near him. "Go in for Rogers. Tell Baxter to switch over to the right side. That's where they've been makin' all their yards. We've got to stop that play!"

Well, he's just going in for one play, shrugged Chip. *It's no big deal to be a messenger boy.* The coach's move had been a good one though, he thought. By the time Willow Creek noticed the change, it would be too late for them to change the play.

Chip saw the red and blue units grimly take their positions. Even with the dirt and grass stains, their colors still sparkled under the lights. The red backfield charged to their left, as Chip had seen them do countless times that game, with the runner following two blocking backs behind his left tackle. They hadn't expected Baxter to shift! The huge Forest Grove lineman plowed into the blockers like a tractor pulling a heavy load. Slowly, he forced his man right into the path of the runner. Then his long arms grabbed the runner around the waist.

"We got 'em! We got 'em!" shouted Coach Ray, jabbing a fist in the air. All the Forest Grove players began to whoop but were brought short by Bronc's booming voice. "Reverse!" he yelled. Confused, Chip squinted through the scattered piles of players, and then he saw it. Somehow, the running back had sneaked the ball to a wide receiver going in the opposite direction. The player Roosevelt had just stopped did *not* have the ball. All the Forest Grove players had been drawn in to stop Willow Creek's favorite play. Only Rennie and Bruce recovered quickly enough to have a chance to stop the runner racing around right end. Bruce was ambushed by a block from the quarterback, which slowed him up long enough to keep him a step behind the runner.

"Rennie, get him!" shrieked Coach Ray. Chip was thankful that the earlier hard tackle hadn't slowed Rennie. With long, quick strides, Rennie closed in on the runner near the far sideline. But Willow Creek apparently had their fastest runner carrying the ball. He sped toward the goal line, inches from his cheering teammates bunched along the sideline.

Since the action was clear across the field, it was hard for Chip to see exactly what was happening. At first, Rennie seemed to have a chance at him, then the runner seemed to be sprinting into the clear. Too late to get a good shot at him, Rennie stretched out one arm to grab the Willow Creek runner's elbow as he went by near the 5-yard line. The runner pulled away, but suddenly whirled and dove toward Rennie, who was sprawled near the sideline. The ball had popped out and was tumbling just out of Rennie's reach near the chalk line.

Hundreds of voices seemed to be shouting, "Fumble!" Bronc still managed to be heard, bellowing, "Get it before it rolls out-of-bounds!" As the Willow Creek boy scrambled over Rennie to reach the ball, Bruce dove in and knocked him away. Chip couldn't tell if Bruce was out-of-bounds or not when he covered the ball. The Willow Creek coach signaled vigorously that he was. If true, the ball would go back to Willow Creek. But an official peered down briefly, then swung his arm in a wide arc toward the Willow Creek goal.

"Our ball! Our ball!" yelled Coach Ray.

Chip found himself joining Dan and P.C. as they gave each other a joyful victory pounding. "Did you see him run? That Rennie can sure scoot!" marveled P.C. as he jumped on Dan's back.

"He saved the game!" said Dan, flipping him into Chip's waiting arms. "We won it. They can't get the ball back! With only a minute to go, Scot can just fall on the ball until time runs out."

The Forest Grove players on the field ran over to congratulate Rennie and Bruce. Their departure left two boys in the middle of the field, one of them being held back by the referee. The other, the Willow Creek center, hovered menacingly nearby.

"Uh-oh," said Dan. "If that's who I think it is, we could be in trouble."

The referee pushed the boy back with a stern warning. It was blue uniform 55. "So Eric's fighting with that center," laughed Chip. "Big deal! I hope they knock each other silly!"

Dan grabbed Chip's elbow and pointed to a bright yellow object wadded on the ground near the line of scrimmage. "Maybe it's a bigger deal than you think. There's a penalty on the play. If it's on Eric, it could give them the ball back. And I have a sneaking suspicion from the way that center is clapping his hands that it *is* on Eric!"

The Forest Grove players who had mobbed Rennie and Bruce now crowded around the two officials. The group shrank back only after the referee ordered them away. He held out his hands and his partner flipped the ball to him. The stunned Forest Grove players parted grudgingly as he marched through them toward the Forest Grove goal. Setting the ball gently on the 8-yard line, he signaled a first down for Willow Creek. Then he stepped back and made a motion to both benches.

"Personal foul, face mask!" groaned Coach Ray. Chip had never seen the coach's face so red. In fact, he hadn't ever seen a human being that color. Chip expected the man to blow up at any time. But he just stomped his foot and turned his back on the field, covering his eyes with one hand.

"Craig! What have you got out there?" Bronc shouted to the referee.

The man jogged slowly over, leaving behind him a trail of dejected Forest Grove starters. "I've got number 55 on the blue team with a personal foul," he sighed. "He grabbed the boy by the face mask and pulled pretty hard. I know it's a tough break, but that's one I've got to call!"

Bronc rubbed a hand over his bald spot while he ground his gum. "How about the other kid? Didn't he do anything to start it?"

"Oh, they've both been looking for trouble. To tell you the truth, I probably should have thrown them both out of the game long ago. But no, I didn't see the center do anything illegal on *this* play. It's a first down for the red."

The lineup for the Forest Grove defense hadn't changed. But it was hard to believe that they were the same group that had fought off Willow Creek just a minute ago. The pent-up energy that had been building all evening had finally been let loose in a premature celebration. Now the blue-shirted team looked tired, confused, and beaten as they lined up. It took only two plays for Willow Creek to run the ball in for the winning score.

It was like watching a movie that ended tragically in the middle of a funny scene. Chip couldn't believe it was over. Like most of his teammates, he stared at the leaps, hugs, and whoops being performed on the far side of the field. He kept waiting for someone to change the referee's decision, or to give them another chance, or something. But nothing could be done.

Coach Ray sent them on their way, muttering only about "bad breaks" and "nice tries." Chip had begged a ride home with Dan and his parents, but he risked lingering a few seconds near the coach. He suspected that Eric might not have heard the last of what had gone on. Sure enough, Coach Ray caught Eric by the arm and pulled him back, quietly but firmly. Chip shuffled away slowly with his head on his chest, as if depressed about the game. Listening carefully, he heard, "I told you back in practice that we don't play that way on this team. No, I don't want to hear any excuses. I know what kind of kid you were up against, and I know it wasn't easy. But you have to keep your head in this game. Your temper cost us the game. A lot of fine effort just went down the drain. It's fine with me if we get beat by a better team, but I am not going to stand around and watch us beat ourselves. You're back on the bench until . . ."

Chip had heard enough. As he broke into a run, the close loss was the last thing on his mind. There was a linebacker position open. And now he had a fighting chance to earn it before his dad came to watch him.

In practice that week, Chip learned a lesson about the power of fear: one big fear can wipe out a lot of little ones. Chip was so desperate to have his dad see him start that he pushed all caution aside. Whenever there was a runner or blocker in sight, Chip ran in to challenge him, without any debate. He struggled away from blockers as if fighting for his very life. On one play, he ran right over Rennie's block, ignored Bruce's fake, and latched onto the fullback's leg. There he hung like a leech until more teammates arrived.

"If he's such a bad player, why can't you block him?" Bruce scolded Rennie.

The play drew no comment from the coaches, but Chip knew that they were watching him. He was going to make them notice him if he had to make every tackle this afternoon. On the next play, though, he found out that it wasn't going to be so easy. He had caught Rennie off his guard. The starters had been going at three-quarters speed, as they often did in practice. But Chip had woken them up. Embarrassed they started to put out a better effort.

Chip fought harder than ever, though, as the afternoon wore on. He even embarrassed himself with his loud grunt as he fought in vain to force his way through a wall of blockers on a pass rush. But nobody else seemed to notice. As Chip looked around, he saw Eric quietly return to his position. *He hasn't said a word all afternoon,* Chip noted with a smile. Eric hadn't been in on many tackles, either. He spent most of the time looking at the ground, avoiding eye contact with anyone. Like an athlete who discovers his opponent is weakening, Chip felt even stronger as he watched Eric struggle.

It was at the following practice that Dan called together the "Left Side Three," as P.C. had named them. "How are we doing in our contest?" he asked.

"Still sixty-four yards behind going into today," answered P.C. Chip could not imagine how P.C. kept the running count in his head. After all, the guy wasn't that good a student.

Dan leaned in closer to the two and whispered, "I've

been keeping my eyes open and I've finally found the offense's fatal weakness. Believe me this is going to help us beat the right side. You'll never guess what the weak spot is!"

After a short pause, P.C. said, "Well, if we can't guess what it is, what's the point of making us guess? What's their weak spot?"

Dan looked each boy straight in the eye. "Roosevelt."

P.C. hung his arm around Dan's neck. "Medic!" he called. "I think this boy's been knocked dingy. We'll find a nice, padded cell for you."

"Shhh!" whispered Dan. "You'll give away the secret. I'm serious. I've been studying him for a long time, and I found a tip-off. When Roosevelt gets set to block for a run, he puts all his weight forward. That makes his knuckles turn white. When he's blocking for a pass, he sits back on his heels because he doesn't have to charge forward. I can tell you every time if it's a pass or run just by the color of his knuckles."

"Sure," said P.C. "What's your signal going to be?"

"Let's keep it simple. I'll just brush my leg if it's a pass; otherwise, it's a run."

"This I've got to see," said Chip, backpedaling to his position. No sooner had the offense lined up than Dan started rubbing his leg. Chip looked at P.C., who shrugged and backed up a few steps. Both players were so amazed that the tip turned out to be true that they merely gawked as Gary Rogers caught a pass between them.

"Didn't you see my signal?" asked Dan.

"Sorry. I'll believe you now," said P.C.

This is perfect! thought Chip, watching Dan move back into his lineman's stance. *Dan's tip-off can't help but make me look good.*

Dan left his leg alone on the next play, and quickly both P.C. and Chip crept closer to the line of scrimmage. Both bolted into the backfield the instant the ball was snapped, and they tackled Rennie before he had taken two steps.

"They were offside," complained Scot. "They had to be!" But neither of the coaches backed up his argument; instead they chewed out the blockers on the right side. By the time Coach Ray whistled the starters off and let the offensive reserves run some plays, the Left Side Three had narrowed the gap in their contest to seventeen yards.

Chip, P.C., and Dan manhandled the reserves with greater ease than they had the starters, even without Roosevelt in the lineup to accidentally tip off the plays. After each tackle, Chip looked up at the coaches for some word of approval. Coach Ray ignored him, concentrating on what the blockers were doing wrong. Chip hadn't expected the older coach to say much, but he couldn't figure out why Bronc was so silent. *He must still be thinking of that punt,* he thought. *He knows I had a good practice before that game, and then bombed in the game. But what more can a guy do in one practice?*

Again, it was Dan who came to the rescue. "Say, this is my lucky day! I wonder if the CIA has any openings," he grinned. "Chip, take a good look at Gary before he goes out for a pass."

"Forget it," said Chip. "He's P.C.'s man on passes. I'm supposed to watch the backs."

"That kind of thinking never got anyone into the Hall of Fame," said Dan. "Whenever he's the main pass target, he suddenly starts acting really cool and relaxed. It's a poor acting job covering up the fact that the play is going to him."

"So Gary won't win any Oscars," said Chip. "What's that have to do with me?"

"Oh, I was just thinking that you could trail him and cut in front to intercept. But if that's too much bother . . ."

For a while, Chip wished Dan had kept this advice to himself. Every time he thought he saw Gary make a suspicious move, he followed him. As a result, he was caught out of position on a couple of plays. *That isn't going to impress the coach,* Chip thought angrily. After that, he ignored Dan's latest hint and was in on several more tackles.

Just when Chip expected the long practice to be called off, Coach Ray ordered the first team back in. Chip's legs ached and his muscles were starting to feel slow and numb. Only the sight of Eric tripping on his own cleats from tiredness spurred him back to his high level of effort.

Then he saw it! Dan hadn't exaggerated when he said Gary was a poor actor. Chip had been looking for subtle changes in Gary's stance and walk. But there was no mistaking the difference this time. Gary looked sleepily at Chip and P.C., and even yawned while the quarterback barked out signals. He was the last to bend down and take his stance, as if he didn't care whether the play worked or not. Out of the corner of his eye, Chip saw Dan brush his leg. It was a pass play all right!

I hope Dan knows what he's doing, thought Chip. He inched to the outside, as warily as an inmate sneaking out of a jail. Scot shouted "Hut-three," and Gary lazily jogged toward the middle of the field. Keeping his eyes on the quarterback, Chip shadowed the receiver, staying a good five yards away from him. For a split second, he checked to see where Rennie was. The speedy back had stopped blocking for Scot and started downfield.

That's my man! Chip thought. A wave of fear swept over him. If Dan was wrong and the pass was to Rennie, Chip would look like a total fool. Suddenly, Gary burst into a sprint, and cut sharply to his right. Chip and P.C. both scrambled after him, P.C. in the rear, Chip moving between Gary and the quarterback.

Chip saw Scot release the ball. He had only to move two more steps before the ball hit him near the throat. Without even juggling it, Chip snatched the ball and raced downfield.

After crossing the practice field goal line, Chip flipped the ball high in the air, caught it, and trotted back toward the coaches. Coach Ray had seen enough from his offense. He ordered the team off the field, and unleashed a parting shot at Scot. "What kind of pass was that?"

Bronc took the ball from Chip and winked at him. "That was a professional move you made there," he said, rubbing his sleeve over his bald spot. "You took a big gamble, you know. But that's what great plays are made of."

"I just guessed right on the play," Chip beamed. He was enjoying Bronc's puzzled look. It looked as if the assistant coach were trying to figure out which Chip was the real one, the timid bumbler or the bold gambler.

Bruce whistled. "Don't suppose you could pull off one of those interceptions in a real game, do you?"

"Yeah, I couldn't believe it," marveled Rennie. "The pass was right in his hand, and he didn't drop it."

Flushed with success, Chip could afford to toss off Rennie's comment with a laugh. Nearly everyone on the team came up to him to offer some comment on the interception. And even Rennie said, right out loud, that he thought Coach Ray would have to start him on Tuesday.

"You put us fifty-three yards in the lead," called P.C. as he turned to ride his bike down the hill.

Waving proudly to P.C., Chip finally noticed Dan fumbling at the combination to his bike lock. "You were right about Gary," Chip laughed. "He really is a bad actor."

"Right," said Dan quietly.

7
The Mud Bowl

When the rains finally arrived, they tried to make up for their month's tardiness in a single, week-long cloudburst. The torrent fell so hard all weekend that even a quick dash from a car door to a house couldn't be done without a drenching. Football practice had to be canceled on Monday, and even by game time on Tuesday a light drizzle was still falling.

Mr. Demory leaned out of the front seat of his car and snapped open his umbrella. Picking his way through the puddles in the parking lot, he arrived at the other door just as his wife got out. Jill, standing safely on a high spot on the asphalt, looked over the field from under her rain parka. "Look at that mess!" she laughed. "Is that where you're going to play?"

The Brycelin Heights field had suffered the same fate as the Forest Grove practice field. The dryness had withered the grass, most of which had been worn away.

Now the rain had softened the hard dirt, leaving a muddy swamp with sparse patches of green poking through it. The midfield was dotted with small ponds of standing water. Although the field's boundaries were chalked, the lines were spotty, since there was little solid material for the chalk to hold on to.

"Oh, Chuck, they're not going to play in that!" said Mrs. Demory.

"Football is a game played under any and all weather conditions," started Mr. Demory. But as he noticed the ripples in the standing water, he, too, frowned.

Chip was the last out of the car. After lacing his shoes, he took a deep breath and stretched his arms, as he had seen Jill do before her game. "A little water never hurt anyone," he said. His only worry was that the coaches might be tempted to call off the contest.

"Where is Tom tonight?" said Mom. "I thought he mentioned something about coming along."

"You know, I haven't had time to get back to him," said Chip. "I've just been so busy this week." He really hadn't been that busy, but he didn't see why Tom should have to come with. He waved and went off to look for the coaches. It was close to game time, and no one had yet announced who was starting in place of Eric.

Apparently, Coach Ray had doubts about the field, too. Chip found him by the end zone with the Brycelin Heights coach, pointing at the field. After a lot of headshaking and shrugging, the two parted.

Chip heard the snap of gum just before the hand touched his shoulder. "You're starting at left linebacker," said Bronc. Chip turned and broke into a grin. He wished he had a tape recorder so he could play those words over again and again. "You're starting at left linebacker," he repeated to himself.

Bronc seemed unaware of the emotions bubbling in the boy. "We felt you earned the shot in practice," he went on in his grave, pregame voice. "You've been with us long enough to know what you're doing out there. Let's see a good effort. Be a tiger out there, remember!"

Chip nodded. Bronc could have asked him to stand on his head in the mud and he would have done it. "I'm a starter!" he said out loud to himself. He searched for his family and found them in the middle of a group of parents, most of whom huddled miserably in the drizzle. Chip wanted to rush over and tell them the news, but then he remembered it would not be news to them. For all they knew, he had always been a starter. *Well, just wait until they see me run out on the field,* he thought.

Brycelin Heights started the game dressed completely in white with purple numbers and helmets. But already their legs were plastered with muddy spots. They seemed to have only half the number of players as Forest Grove, and Chip had the feeling that meant they weren't that good a team. His hunch seemed to be right as Forest Grove drove down the field the first time they got the ball. Rennie was slipping all over like a deer on ice, and so the team went to their strongest ball carrier, Bruce. There was nothing fancy about the attack. Just Bruce running between the tackles, and ramming forward for about five yards a try.

Chip, meanwhile, hopped up and down on the sidelines. He was trying to stay loose, and at the same time get rid of extra energy. While the offense drove down the field, he pictured himself making tackles and interceptions. Already covered from the top of his helmet to his toes in mud, Bruce ended the long march by sliding into the end zone.

Here we go! thought Chip. But to his disgust, Brycelin Heights fumbled the kickoff. The ball kept squirting out of piles of players like a greased eel until Roosevelt finally surrounded it at the 23-yard line. That meant more minutes of waiting while the offense went at it again. The Brycelin Heights defense stiffened, but Forest Grove was finally able to score on a fourth-down run by Scot. The first quarter had almost ended, and Chip hadn't gotten into the game yet.

"Come on, hang on to it this time," he muttered as Scot prepared to kick off.

"Whose side are you on, anyway?" asked Dan.

"All right, defense! Let's go!" shouted Coach Ray, as Brycelin Heights took over the ball. Chip turned to make sure his folks were watching. No, they weren't! They seemed to be having a good chat with the people next to them. Chip lingered as long as he dared with his helmet off so they could still spot him if they liked. Finally Jill waved and nudged her dad, and Chip raced onto the field. This time was worlds different from the last time he had entered a game. He *belonged* on the field; he had earned his spot. He wasn't just filling in for a few plays as someone's sub. Instinctively, he stepped away from the middle linebacker. But then he remember it wasn't Eric. Bruce had moved over from the outside to fill his spot, while Chip had taken over for Bruce. Where was Eric, anyway? Chip glanced at the sidelines but did not see him.

"Let's see you play like you did in practice," said Bruce.

Chip grinned. He certainly planned to. This taste of success made him feel stronger and faster than he had ever felt. As the Brycelin Heights players came to the line, Chip crouched low, coiled for action. He was probably the only player on the field who wasn't thinking about the horrid playing conditions. That proved costly on the first play. The running back darted to his side of the line, and Chip slid off the block of the right end. When the back cut to the inside, Chip planted his foot sharply to cut with him. His foot slid out from under him. Before he could even get his hands out to break the fall, he landed heavily on his seat, splashing mud around him. With Chip out of the way, the runner gained nearly fifteen yards.

Shocked by the coldness as the water penetrated his uniform, and trying to ignore his bruised tailbone, Chip returned to his position. He shook the mud off his fingers and looked for a clean spot on his pants to wipe them off. Chip braced himself for some smart comments by his teammates, but no one said a word. As he had already found out, it wasn't a chatty group on defense. They took their jobs seriously. Judging by the way many of them grimaced as they walked around in the slop, they weren't enjoying the conditions.

It's a wet field, you dummy, Chip scolded himself. *You can't make sharp cuts on a field like this. Pay attention now.* He didn't need to worry for a while. On the next play, the ball carrier suffered a similar embarrassment as he slipped, skated a few steps, and finally fell without a player near him. The next two plays went to the other side of the field, where they were stopped short of the first down. Chip jogged off the field as Brycelin Heights prepared to punt.

Before he reached the sidelines, he again searched out his parents. He longed to run over to them to hear their reactions. Was his dad growling advice that no one would ever hear, as he did when Jill played? But he also felt, as never before, that he was part of the team. He would have to try and forget about Mom and Dad until the game was over.

With Forest Grove safely ahead by two touchdowns, Chip secretly cheered for the Brycelin Heights defense. He had enjoyed being in the game so much he could hardly stand pacing the sidelines. The sooner he could get back on the field, the better. Seconds later, Scot bobbled the snap from center and accidently kicked it forward. When the teams unpiled, the referee had to ask the boy on the bottom which team he was on. The mud-caked lad turned out to be from the home team.

"Defense!" shouted Coach Ray.

The deep breath Chip took as he sprinted out felt so fresh! "This is great!" Chip said to himself. This time the quiet of the field felt strange. No one else seemed to be having such fun. What was the matter with them? Instead, he heard murmurings, some of them pretty foul, about the weather and the field. All the grumbling took some of the excitement away, but Chip played well for the rest of the half. Neither team had chosen to pass with the wet football, and the offenses were bogging down. With the lead still 14-0 at the halftime break, Coach Ray announced that it would be a good chance for the reserves to see some action. Everyone seemed thrilled with that news. In fact, Chip thought the grimy starters cheered more loudly than the reserves.

Chip bit his lip, thinking the fun was over. But then Bronc called him over. "We're leaving you in. You can use the experience."

As Chip looked over the group that charged on the field with him to start the second half, he felt almost cocky. With the other starters all on the bench, that made Chip the best player on the field. He caught himself starting to give out advice to the others until he saw that Eric was now in the game.

"Hey, help me pin this on!" said P.C., who had come in at defensive back. He pulled a stiff sheet of paper from under his jersey and a safety pin from his hip pad. The large letters on the tag spelled "Killer."

Chip gawked at him. "You're crazy!"

"So? Come on!" begged P.C., eyeing the Brycelin Heights huddle. "I've wanted to do this all my life." As Chip made no move to help, P.C. chuckled, "All right, I'll do it myself." As he pinned on his name tag, several teammates broke out in laughter and jostled those next to them to look. Even the Brycelin Heights tackle noticed and started snickering.

What a nut! smiled Chip as P.C. strode around, soaking up the attention. *I'll bet Coach Ray is having a fit.*

If P.C.'s fun was upsetting the coach, at least it didn't last long. On the first play, P.C. helped out on the tackle and found half his tag ripped away when he stood up.

"Hey, what happened, Killer?" teased his teammates.

"Just call me P.C. now," he said sadly. "Killer lies buried somewhere around the 35-yard line."

The wind had shifted direction and was now gusting from the north. It cut through their uniforms, chilling their bones as the temperature seemed to drop by the minute. By this time, the field had been almost totally chewed up. From one 30-yard line to the other, not a blade of grass was left standing in the center of the field.

"Isn't this great?" howled P.C.

Chip felt a little warmer just hearing his cheerful chatter. "You like the mud, huh?" he asked.

"Like it? I love it. This is how football was meant to be played—in the middle of a rice paddy."

P.C.'s enthusiasm was contagious. Although the lineup was full of reserves, the defense swarmed all over the Brycelin Heights team, charging and leaping through the muck like kittens with a new toy. After stopping their opponents on three plays, they ran off the field, dripping wet but laughing, while a new unit took over on offense. Coach Ray, his clipboard tucked under his elbow, looked on curiously. Chip noticed the man was standing straight up, instead of hunched over like a coiled spring, his usual stance during a game. Somehow this contest had lost much of its meaning for the coach. He apparently had no doubt that Forest Grove would win.

Sure enough, the offense scored again to make it

21-0. The defense galloped onto the field, purposely sending a shower of mud on each other. This time Chip led the way. It felt as refreshing as the first time he got permission to run outside in the rain with a swimsuit on.

"Yoweee!" howled P.C. as he charged in to help finish off a tackle. "Way to go, you mud puppies!"

The time between plays got to be as much fun as the actual plays as P.C. triggered an unending stream of jokes and teasing. "I give up!" he announced. "I can't tell who's on what team anymore. From now on, I'm tackling anything that moves in my area."

"Better be careful," Chip warned. "We found a few alligators living in this during the first half."

"Speaking of safety," P.C. grinned. "Maybe we should form a buddy system out here in case someone goes in over his head."

"It's too late," said another boy. "I think we lost Peterson on the last play."

"Call a time-out!" said P.C. "Ask the ref if we can form a human chain and find him."

Brycelin Heights was unable to cross midfield the rest of the day. Meanwhile, the Forest Grove offense was content to run time off the clock. The fourth quarter flew by, and Forest Grove finished with an easy 21-0 win. As the defense ran off the field, Chip saw P.C. go into a baseball slide which carried him nearly to the sidelines.

"Look at you!" said Chip's mom as Chip came over to accept their congratulations. "You're filthy!" She shook her head and then added, "It was fun to see you play. But you were all so dirty it was hard for me to see which one was you."

"Nice game, Chip," said Dad. "But you'd better keep your distance until we get you hosed off. Don't ask me how we're going to get you home without ruining the interior of our car."

"You did great!" Jill added, wiping a blotch of mud off his nose. "Say, who's the little guy who played with you in the second half? He's a riot!"

Basking in their compliments, Chip didn't recognize that he was being asked a question. "Well, the coach is calling," he beamed. "I'd better get over and see what he has to say. Be with you in a minute."

Sensing that his players were getting chilled, Coach Ray limited his postgame summary to a brief notice of when the next practice was. As Chip listened, he saw one pair of white pants standing out like a spotlight from the rest of the team. It was Dan. Obviously, everyone had gotten into the game except him. The thought of Dan being left out took some of the silliness out of Chip, and he started to edge through the players towards him. Just then the meeting broke up, and everyone scattered to their cars. Before Chip could get to Dan, he bumped into Bruce.

"Hey, you really played a good game," Chip said.

"Oh, it was pretty easy," Bruce said. The next sentence clued Chip in as to why Bruce was talking so softly. "Hey, there's going to be a party at Scot's house on Friday. It's for starters only, and I guess you qualify now."

"Just got in under the wire," said Chip.

"Yeah, well, it's a good break all around. None of us were too thrilled about having to let Eric in. He's really bad news. But now he's out and you're in, so no sweat. Don't go telling anyone about it, though. It's only for starters."

Chip saw the white pants as they moved slowly across the parking lot. "But what about the Atkinsons? Dave's a starter, but Dan isn't. Being they're twins, he's going to know, isn't he?"

"Naw, Dave can keep quiet about it. By the way, there'll be some girls there."

"Really?" said Chip. "Like who?"

Bruce grinned secretively. "Nothin' but the best. Tammy, Gail, Laura, and a few of their friends. Now don't go telling anyone," he repeated as he walked off.

Dan had already disappeared by then, and Chip trudged off to his family. His muscles were starting to ache from fatigue. But it was a pleasant ache that kept reminding him of all he had done that night. Shivering slightly, he found his way back to the parking lot, where his dad had already warmed up the car. He didn't even mind when his dad asked him to take off his jersey and put it in the trunk. Scrunching in the warm backseat, sitting on sections of shopping bags that Jill had ripped up, he enjoyed answering Jill's questions about football. Occasionally, she had to repeat herself because Chip's thoughts kept wandering to the game and to the party on Friday. *I can't believe it! I've actually done it!* he thought.

8
Injury

There was no reason why Bruce should have made such a big deal out of hushing up the party. By the time Chip reached school on Monday, everyone on the team knew about it. Scot, Rennie, and some of the others were even talking about it right in front of the rest.

Chip and P.C. paired up for the prepractice calisthenics. One would hold the other's leg or legs while he did sit-ups or stretches, and then they would switch off. Chip was reaching out to touch his toes when P.C. first brought it up. "Pretty wild party from what I hear. Were you there?"

"Yeah, I was there, but you heard wrong," Chip said. He finished his last two sit-ups and looked at his partner. "Scot's parents were there the whole time, so how wild could it have been?" He had heard some gripes from other reserves about the starters' "private" party, but apparently P.C. held no grudges.

"I should ask my folks if we can have a scrub party at my house," he said as he let go of Chip's ankles. "Of course, we'd have to call it something else," he frowned. "I mean, if you call it a scrub party, everyone would think all we're going to do is wash floors or something. Nah, it probably wouldn't be much. What kind of girls could you get to come to a scrub party?"

Your party would probably be a lot more fun, Chip thought, grabbing P.C.'s ankles. With his partner silenced for a moment by the strain of the exercise, Chip thought back on the evening. He had been so tickled to go he could hardly believe it was true. Some of the most popular girls were there, ones he'd never even talked to. Just by being at the party he had shown that he was important, a starter on the football team. He had been so flushed with the honor that, for a while, he had convinced himself that he was having a good time. But he had begun to feel more and more awkward. *Just what's going on?* he had finally asked himself. He was sitting in a stuffed chair in the corner, trying to act like an adult like everyone else. Sure, the girls were cute, but they didn't seem anything like Jill. They were just trying to seem important, like he was. After a while he had gotten tired of running down the reserves and laughing at some of the dumb plays they had made. *They could really have a great time talking about all the dumb things I've done since I came out,* he realized. Then Bruce had finally gotten a card game going, and Chip had spent the rest of the evening at the table either watching or playing.

Now P.C. could really give a party! Chip thought to himself as Coach Ray whistled a stop to the exercises. The coach continued to use the starters on offense in practice scrimmages, leaving Chip with his old "Left Side Three" gang. Unfortunately, the third member of the group didn't have much to say. Dan was still upset about being the only one on the team who didn't get in the last game. Chip tried to ask him about it once, and Dan mumbled, "It was a mistake. The coaches told me they were sorry and said they had too much to think about to keep track of everything. Coach Ray said they ought to have a student manager or something to handle the little things so they wouldn't get distracted."

Chip couldn't think of anything helpful to say, and Dan wearily took up his position in front of Roosevelt. He wasn't giving out any tip-offs from Roosevelt, and he gave more ground than usual to the blocker in front of him. Chip shook his head. *Must be rough having to face Roosevelt every single practice.* P.C. continued to banter, even though Dan wasn't responding. But then P.C. could keep up a running conversation with the grass.

It was the first cold day of the fall. Chip tucked his hands inside his sleeves while waiting for the first play. Quickly, though, he poked them back out when he saw Eric purposely roll his sleeves up to the elbow. Chip had a feeling that the middle linebacker was starting to resurface after a peaceful week and a half. Ever since his crucial penalty against Willow Creek, Eric had tried to melt into the background. He had said almost nothing. When he played, it was listlessly, as if he could best avoid attention if he stayed away from tackling the ballcarrier.

No one had been too hard on him about blowing that game, at least not to his face. But there had been enough comments behind his back, especially among the starters, who hated to think of their unbeaten record being ruined by that call. Eric must have overheard a few of those, and he probably imagined the rest. It was obvious after the first play of practice that he was starting to fight back. On a simple running play, Eric threw one blocker to the ground and blasted Bruce with all his might. Bruce gasped and brought his feet up to his chest, the wind knocked out of him.

"What do you think you're doing?" spat Scot. "That was a cheap shot!"

Chip saw the starters gather around Bruce and glare at Eric. Bruce had already recovered and was slowly getting up. Chip thought he heard him muttering swear words at Eric. Lashing out at the whole lot, Eric sneered, "What's the matter? Can't take a little hit?" With that, Eric's mouth got going. He shot a cutting remark at someone after nearly every play. Chip realized that the peaceful era of playing next to Eric was over. Sooner or later, he knew, Eric would start in on him again.

Chip's turn did not come until midway through practice. Several plays had driven home the fact to Chip that he wasn't a star because of natural talent. He had won his starting job with a determined, almost desperate energy, far beyond the practice level of most boys. But when he routinely chased Rennie on a quick pass to the right halfback, Rennie faked him completely off his feet. As he sprawled on the ground, he heard that familiar voice. "Nice tackle, all-star!"

Their truce dissolved. Chip found himself more angry than ever at his enemy. This time he could fight back, because *he* was the starter. "Like to see you do better, scrub!" A flash of hatred in Eric's eyes showed that Chip had found the perfect weapon against Eric's mocking title. Eric stopped calling him "all-star," although Chip continued to throw in a few more "scrub" remarks at him, just for good measure.

The victory didn't last long. Chip realized that it was Eric who was now playing with a desperate, almost enraged force. When Eric—who was stronger and a little more coordinated than Chip—played that way, Chip began to worry about his starting job.

"Hey, Dan! What about those tip-offs about whether it's a run or a pass?" Chip pleaded. Dan squinted at him as if he didn't know what he was talking about, then nodded slowly.

"Yeah, we've fallen behind the right side again. They've got two yards on us," added P.C.

Seeing no signal from Dan on the next play, Chip wondered if his tall friend was back at his detective work or not. He decided to gamble that no signal meant a run was coming, and moved up next to Dan. Sure enough, it was a quick burst off tackle. Although Roosevelt pushed Dan out of the way, Chip filled the gap with only one blocker between him and the ball-carrier. Rennie ordinarily considered blocking a necessary evil, and Chip had found it easy to fend him off. But on this occasion, Rennie flung himself at just the right spot to knock Chip to his knees. Bruce ran past him before being brought down by the pursuing Eric. As the middle linebacker stomped back to his position, he said, "We'll see who's the scrub!"

Chip glanced nervously at the coaches. They were huddled together, looking at Eric. It hadn't been his play that had benched him before; it was his temper. Chip noted, sadly, that Eric had walked away from several players who had wanted to goad him into a fight after his hard tackle of Bruce. *How am I going to keep my job?* he thought. *I did pretty well against Brycelin Heights, but is that going to be enough?* Spurred on again by Dan's signals, Chip fought hard to outshine his rival.

On one play to the other side of the field, Chip sprinted all the way to his right, hoping to cut off the run. "Reverse!" came P.C.'s voice from back across the field. Chip froze and saw that the offense was trying a trick reverse just like the one Willow Creek had used. But he knew before he even turned that he was trapped way out of position. Eric had spotted the deception before Chip, but even he wasn't going to reach the ballcarrier. Scot blocked out P.C., and the play went for a touchdown.

"Duh, I'm Chip Demory!" Eric started hollering in

a dopey voice. "I don't have more'n a little bitty part of a brain. You can fake me out of my shoes, my socks, my underwear, you name it. Yessir, try anything on me, I'll fall for it."

"Shut up, scrub!" Chip shot back, but the name had lost its force. They both knew that if Chip kept making mistakes and Eric kept up his good play, there would be a new starter come Wednesday night against Van Buren. Chip looked around at his defensive mates and found some laughing. *So I make mistakes,* Chip thought. *I'm still new at this, you creeps.*

"Keep it up, all-star," laughed Eric.

As he had many times before, Chip searched his mind for some chance to get even. But this time he found something to work with. Chip picked up the clue when it dawned on him that the offense wasn't gloating over the play. On the very next play, Chip charged past a weak block by Gary, the end, and stopped Rennie in the backfield.

"Nice play," said Bruce loudly.

It seemed almost too easy. On the next play, Gary completely missed his block on Chip. Rennie, blocking for Bruce, ignored Chip and headed out to block P.C. That left Chip with a clear shot at Bruce and he stopped him for a loss.

"Can't anyone block this guy?" Bruce said as he slammed the ball down. But he winked at Chip as he turned. Then Chip saw another wink from Gary. As Coach Ray stormed over to Gary to show him how to get his body into a block, Chip figured it out. The starters couldn't stand Eric. Bruce had told him that after the last game. That meant they were on his side! They wanted him to keep his job. Those poor blocks had been little gifts to keep him in the running. But with Coach Ray on Gary's back, Chip could expect no more such plays.

That was fine with Chip. Just remembering that he

had allies put some of the fight back in him. And while he improved his play, the idea of revenge kept coming back. It was he, Chip, who had the advantage. The one thing Eric wanted, according to Dan, was acceptance from the starters. Thanks to Eric's mouth, that wouldn't happen.

When Coach Ray gave them a five-minute break, Chip decided to put his plan into action. He didn't want to make it obvious, so he stared at Bruce, hoping to attract his attention. When the running back finally did look his way, Chip called him over with a nod of his head. Bruce walked over, spitting his mouthpiece into his hand.

"Are you getting as tired of that blabbermouth as I am?" Chip asked.

Bruce's eyes narrowed as he focused on Eric. "Probably."

"Do you think Roosevelt feels the same way?"

"Why, what have you got in mind?"

Chip grinned. "How about a triple-team block? Next time you're blocking up the middle. Dan is kind of out of it today. Roosevelt could let him go for a play and cream Eric."

"While I get him from the other side," nodded Bruce. "A sandwich."

Chip's eyes lit up. "Now you're talking!"

"My pleasure," said Bruce, and he jogged back to his huddle.

He's been asking for this for a long, long time, Chip smiled to himself as he moved back to the defense. He had sworn he would get revenge. If Eric had kept quiet, he would have forgiven all he had done. But there was no turning back this time. *He won't know what hit him!*

Meanwhile, P.C. had finally gotten Eric to settle down. "Hey, you're ruining my reputation as a motormouth," he said to Eric. "Give me a break and leave the jabbering to me. It's the only thing I do well on this field."

Eric had flashed a smile, almost a genuine one. Chip marveled again at the way P.C. could say anything to anyone without getting them mad. On the next two plays, there wasn't one sarcastic remark from the middle linebacker.

Chip knew when he saw the offensive formation that this next one was the play. Dan was indicating a run. Chip saw Bruce fix Eric with a cold glare. It was all Chip could do to keep from standing back and watching. Just before the hike, he backed up so that at least the whole thing would be going on in front of him.

"Hut-one!" Roosevelt brushed past Dan, who stood straight up in surprise. Bruce led the way through the "1" hole and veered toward the right linebacker. Suddenly, he cut back toward the middle. Eric, busy fighting off the center's block, never saw him. Roosevelt blasted Eric from one side just as Bruce hit him from the other. Chip had to admit Bruce was a good actor. He immediately turned upfield and threw a block at the safety. Satisfied that justice had been done, Chip moved over to help on the tackle.

Eric raised himself to one knee but kept both palms on the grass to keep himself from tipping over. When he didn't move, Bronc came over and stared into his eyes. "Why don't you go on the sidelines and walk around for a little bit."

After one wobbly step, Eric steadied himself. By the time he reached the sidelines he was already shaking off that glassy look. He wasn't really hurt, just stunned. Chip smiled to himself as a replacement came in for Eric. *That'll slow him down for a while,* he thought.

It was amazing how much freer Chip felt when Eric wasn't around. For the next ten minutes he felt lighter and faster, as if he had shed a weight from his ankles. His mind seemed to work more clearly, too. On another end sweep to the other side, Chip trailed the play and then checked to make sure the left end wasn't coming around to take a reverse handoff. Without breaking stride, he kept going, and joined a group of defenders who were closing in on Rennie. The running back had waited far too long for his blockers to do their jobs. He was trying to dance away from the tacklers, but too many had arrived. Rennie finally just lowered his head and leaned into the blue-shirted mob. Chip fell beneath him and smelled the musty odor of grass as his head was pushed right down to the grass.

It was then that he heard the cry.

"No! Ow! Ow!"

"Get off him, quick!" ordered Scot.

By the time Chip got to his feet, Coach Ray had pushed back the players. They stood in a tight ring around one boy, who was slamming his fist against the ground. At first Chip thought it was Dan. But then he saw him standing, leaning as close as he could to the injured player. *It must be Dave, then,* Chip thought.

"Ow! Help, please!" Chip saw Dave's leg twisted at a bad angle near the ankle. Coach Ray stared at the leg for a minute, licking his lips. There seemed to be fear in his face as he yelled hoarsely for Bronc. The big assistant forced his way through the pack, and snapped at everyone to move back.

"Don't try to move. Just lie down," he said, easing Dave's helmet off and gently laying his head on the grass. Dave's jaw clenched, but he didn't say another word. Bronc fumbled for keys in his back pocket. Without taking his eyes off Dave, he tossed the keys to Chip and said, "In the gym there's a door by the stairs next to the stage. Get the stretcher and some blankets."

He didn't say to hurry, but Chip dashed off in a panic. Racing through the dark, narrow halls, he came to the gym and found it locked. There were eight keys on Bronc's chain. Chip jammed each of them into the lock and broke out in a sweat as none of them worked. On the second try, one finally slid in. He twisted and pulled until the door finally came open.

By the time he got back, many of the boys had started to leave. Practice had been called off. Bronc flung the blankets on Dave. Working so carefully he seemed to be in slow motion, he maneuvered him onto the stretcher. Coach Ray had backed his van onto the field, and Bronc and Dan lifted Dave into the back. Then Dan climbed in with his brother, and Coach Ray drove off.

Chip started to walk home by himself, feeling a little sick to his stomach. He had heard of football injuries, and even knew a boy whose parents wouldn't let him come out for the sport because they thought it too dangerous. But this was the first time he had actually seen a bad injury. It wasn't anyone's fault. Dave's leg happened to be in the wrong spot when a pile of players fell down. That didn't help to erase the memory of Dave's face, though.

Buttoning his jacket against the cold breeze, he heard a jingling in his pocket. Expecting to find some change, his fingers instead found an unfamiliar, cold object. Chip pulled it out and groaned. Bronc's keys. He had forgotten to return them. From where he stood he could see the truck still in the parking lot. *Of course,* thought Chip. *I've got the keys to his truck, too. Typical dumb move, Demory.*

Bronc was standing next to the truck when Chip arrived, out of breath. He didn't seem surprised or angry. Tucking away his handkerchief and accepting the keys, he said, "There's a mean snap to that wind. Want a ride?"

Chip accepted and climbed into the front seat. Bronc saw him step carefully over a gym bag. "Aw, don't worry about that. Just sweaty clothes that need washing," he said as he started up the truck.

"Sorry about the keys," Chip repeated. "It just slipped my mind. I guess I was kind of shook up."

"I think we all are," said Bronc, popping two sticks of gum into his mouth. Shaking his head, he said, "You know, when I was in college we used to all sit around and say a prayer before the game, asking that no one would get hurt."

"Not a bad idea," Chip said. Something about the way Bronc angrily cranked the wheel made him uncomfortable. He was glad it was only a short drive home.

"You know what the crazy thing was?" Bronc went on. "Some of the same people in on the prayer would lose their heads in the game and start gettin' mad. You can't play that way," he sighed. "You have to take it more seriously. Once you get out of control, it's not a game anymore." He looked at Chip, who wished he could scrunch down and hide from those eyes. "You know, we could have had two bad injuries today."

"What?" said Chip, his voice cracking.

"I've got good eyes and better hearing," said Bronc. "When you don't have any hair, the sound waves get a clear shot to the ears. It looked to me like someone planned to *get* someone."

"What do you mean?" started Chip. But Bronc didn't answer. He pulled up to Chip's house and put the car in park. All Chip heard was the whir of the engine. He knew it was time to drop the charade.

"He had it coming," he said, avoiding Bronc's eyes.

"Revenge and football are a bad mix. He could have been seriously hurt."

Chip felt like pulling open the door, but he knew he couldn't leave yet. Searching for some answer that would satisfy Bronc, he said, "You don't know how much I've taken from that guy. I had to stop it somehow."

"I know what you've put up with," smiled Bronc, pointing to his ears. "Remember how well these work? I wish you could find a better way to solve the problem, though. I've never seen a kid fight so hard to get accepted as Eric. But he does it all wrong. I don't think he has a friend on the team, does he? So you go and get the best players to gang up on him today. You think that'll help?"

"So what do you want me to do?" protested Chip.

"Hey! I don't mean to keep workin' you over, and I'm not here to tell you how to run your life. It's just my job as a coach to tell you there's no place for that nonsense on the field. As far as Eric goes, I wish you would have talked it out earlier, but it's too late for that. I know you're a good guy, Chip. I thought maybe the team could somehow help a kid who's got problems. Looks like we're blowing it, though."

Chip hopped onto the driveway. "Some people are just too far gone to help," he said. He felt a desperate need to slam the door.

Just before it shut, he heard, "Hey, we're all God's children."

Revenge. He had been waiting for the chance all year, and now that he'd finally gotten it, the taste was all bad. Chip plopped down on his bed and ran his feet up the wall. Mom hated it when he did that with his shoes on, but he didn't care at this moment. *Bronc's the one who's wrong about all this,* he decided. *It's always us good guys who get caught. I take all kinds of garbage from Eric all year. The first time I try to fight back, I get jumped on by that big ape. He never cared a bit when Eric was doing all that stuff to me!* Or did he? The more Chip thought about it, the more he admitted that it wasn't like Bronc not to care. He was the coach who knew all the first names, watched out for the subs, and had a private word now and then for everyone.

So what did Bronc want him to do? He wouldn't say. Was he talking about turning the other cheek? Chip had heard that phrase often enough in church.

Come on, this is football, thought Chip. *They'd think you were a coward and walk all over you.* His thoughts drifted back to that crunching triple-team block on Eric. For a second he savored it against all the mean things Eric had done.

But the word *coward* stuck in his mind. How much courage did it take to watch the strongest guys on offense wipe out someone who didn't even know it was coming? Chip's feet dropped back on the bed as he thought about it. That was his problem with Eric: he was afraid of him. Dad had read something at family devotions about trust in God and about courage. "Whom should I fear?" was what Chip remembered of it.

I don't know why I'm afraid of him, but I am, he thought glumly. *Face it, I'm afraid of everyone. A starter on the football team, and I'm still afraid. Football hasn't done a thing for me.*

The door burst open after a knock. "Didn't you hear the phone?" asked his mom. "I was in the basement and thought for sure you'd get it. I finally got there on the sixth ring. Anyway, it's Tom."

"Great," muttered Chip, rolling out of bed. "More problems."

9
Life at the Top

Chip had been successful at avoiding Tom for the past two weeks, at least in public. Much of it was due to luck. Tom happened to be busy completing a computer project for the science fair, and that had kept him from popping in on football practices. Besides that, Chip had managed to be gone whenever Tom had called, and made excuses for not getting back to him. Just to keep Tom from getting too upset, Chip had gone over to his house one Saturday night to watch tv and play chess, Tom's favorite game.

But this time Tom had caught him. Chip hated having the phone in the kitchen, because Mom was close by. She had been wondering aloud what Tom was up to, and was sure to keep an ear on the conversation. "Hello?"

"Hi, Chip. Hey, I got a great surprise for you. Just found out for sure this afternoon. You know how you were feeling bad about no one you knew being out for football, and how you were kind of lonely? Well, better late than never. Good ol' Tom to the rescue!"

Chip stared dumbly at the wall. "You're *not* going out for football," he said, more a prayer than a question.

"Oh, no!" Tom laughed. "You know I wouldn't be much good. I don't even know what's going on half the time, yet. They'd laugh me off the field. What I was going to say is that I was talking with one of the players. You know Dan, right? He's a nice guy and he's into computers, too. Did you know his brother broke his leg?"

"Of course I know, you dope."

"Chip!" scolded his mom.

Chip turned away from her and stretched the phone cord as far toward the stairway as it would go. "I was there when it happened."

"Oh, that's right. Well, we started talking about football, and I said that I liked to watch the games. Then he asked me if I was interested in being a student manager. He said they could use someone who wasn't playing to help out with some details, equipment, keeping charts, and stuff."

"Yeah, and what did you say?" asked Chip. He was sure of the answer, but hoped for a miracle anyway. He felt a headache coming on.

"Sounded great to me!" Tom said. "I told him I thought I could do a good job at it, so he set me up to talk with Coach Marsh."

"And he gave you the job," said Chip.

"I start tomorrow. How's that for wild?"

That pest! thought Chip, then tried to sound excited for Tom's sake. "That's great—but I hope you didn't do it for me. You know, I *have* made quite a few friends lately."

"Aw, I know that. I just thought it would be fun."

Chip grabbed the top tray and slid it along the ledge. As the cafeteria line slowed down, he grabbed the tray with both hands and breathed heavily. This was bad news, and it was Bruce, of all people, who had put him in this spot. Bruce had gotten carried away with Scot's idea of a starters' party and had decided to form a starters' club. He called it the "Blue and White Club." Some of the starters were making a big deal out of it. They met before nearly every practice, and shooed away any nonstarter who wandered too close. After the first two meetings, there were no more intruders, as word must have spread. Chip felt bad sitting there while guys like P.C. and Dan looked on from a distance. Once Bronc drove up while they were still meeting, and Chip broke out in a bad case of the guilts.

Bruce had been elected president of the club at the last meeting. He had wasted no time in pushing through his plans of sitting together at lunch and dressing up. As Chip watched the casserole being scooped onto his plate, he looked down at his game jersey. Clean and ironed, it really did look sharp. The starters had secretly agreed on wearing those the day of the game with Van Buren. Chip had told his mom that the whole team was doing it when he showed up in it at breakfast. Sometimes during the morning that big number 57 had made him pretty proud. It was a clear mark for all to see that he was one of the fourteen in school who were good enough to make the Blue and White Club. But at this moment, he wished he could bury it and put on the plainest shirt he owned.

In a few seconds, he would come face-to-face with the Blue and White decree that they would sit together at lunch. Just the starters and no one else. As he shuffled toward the milk and dessert, he saw the group at the long table next to the window in the back. They were being loud enough so that no one in the cafeteria could miss them. But someone had violated the rule.

The solid row of jerseys was broken by a red top, a white one, and a striped one. Girls. Chip could see clearly only the one on the end. It was Tammy, whom he'd met briefly at the party. There was a seat open next to her.

Chip picked up his tray and shot a glance at the left side of the room. There was Dan, already in their usual spot. P.C. wasn't there yet, though. Chip checked the ranks of blue jerseys to see if P.C. had somehow wormed his way in there. With both hands clutching the tray, he was helpless to ward off P.C.'s surprise attack. The little defensive back reached over his back and tucked a napkin under Chip's chin.

"Come on, now, slugger, we can't have you slobbering your food all over your nice clean jersey," laughed P.C. "Hey, Dan's finally come back to us from Depressionville. He can hardly wait for you to get over there so I can reveal the weekly figures on our running battle with the right side. We're getting to the end, you know. Only two weeks left." Before Chip could answer, P.C. stuck half a roll in his mouth and went back to his table.

Now what do I do? Chip thought. He looked back at the empty chair next to Tammy. She had at least talked to him at the party, and seemed the friendliest of the girls. Everyone in the place would be able to see that he was sitting with her. If that didn't impress them, what would? *What choice do I have?* Chip finally shrugged. *The starters all sit together. That's the plan.*

He walked stiffly over to the starters. He was torn between trying to avoid the looks of his friends and enjoying the feeling of importance he felt as he saw others eyeing him.

"Hi," said Tammy with a smile.

"Welcome to the bunch," said Bruce. "Pretty wild napkin."

Chip remembered the napkin as everyone at the

table laughed. He felt the blood rushing to his face to announce his embarrassment when he realized they thought it was just a gag. "Don't want crumbs on my nice clean jersey," he said, straightening the paper napkin as if it were a tie.

"Isn't this chicken stuff awful?" Tammy asked him as she gingerly chewed her casserole. Chip nodded agreement, though he didn't really think so. As he ate he thought about how the football season was turning out to be everything he had hoped it would be. Except for one thing: he wasn't a star running back yet. *Give it time,* he thought. *It's only my first year.*

The game with Van Buren erased Chip's final fear. Just before the contest, Coach Ray had announced that Eric would start—taking over for the injured Dave Atkinson at right defensive end. *Thank you, God,* thought Chip, trying to hold back a grin. After all these weeks of hassle and the bitter competition of the past week, Eric was finally out of the picture for good! Chip had the left linebacking job to himself! He celebrated by playing one of his better games in a 34-7 win over Van Buren. The highlight had come for him in the fourth quarter. He had been fending off a block, waiting to see if the ballcarrier broke through the center of the line. No runner came through, but the ball did, and it flopped right at Chip's feet. He had fallen on it and then ran off the field, holding it high in the air to show everyone who had recovered it.

Chip expected the final two weeks of the season to fly by in a blur of excitement as he enjoyed his success. But, proud as he was of his efforts, he felt his victory crumbling away. There were too many incidents like those of the Monday after the game.

Chip, Dan, and P.C. had arrived a few minutes early and had talked the new student manager, Tom, into getting a football for them. It was cool and cloudy, and it felt good to warm up by tossing passes to each other. Others apparently liked the idea, too. As more players arrived, Tom got out more footballs and games of catch sprouted up over the whole field. As Chip jogged out for a pass, Dan waved to him twice. That meant he was going to throw it as far as he could. Chip started sprinting as the ball sailed into the air. At first he thought it was too far over his head, but he kept running. Nearly tripping over a hole in the sod, he reached out and caught the ball as he tumbled to the ground. Dan was as astonished by the catch as Chip was, and ran out to congratulate him. Before Dan reached his goal, though, Chip was distracted by a sharp whistle. "Get on over here," Bruce called to him. "Let the scrubs play by themselves."

Chip gaped at him. This Blue and White stuff was getting out of hand. Dumbly, he flipped the ball back to Dan. He still liked being in with the starters, but this was getting plain mean. "Aw, I'm tired, anyway," he said to Bruce, and walked away to wait by himself for the practice to start.

Throughout the practice, Chip felt as though he had a leg on each of two ice floes that were drifting apart. Bruce and Scot were getting so obnoxious about this starter club that the reserves couldn't stand them anymore. Yet, as one who played only defense, Chip still spent most of practice time with the subs. He was getting worn out trying to get along with both sides.

Dan and P.C. had been understanding of the situation so far, and still kept him as part of their Left Side Three. Dan was back to his detective tricks, and had come up with another discovery. "Keep your eye on Scot when he's calling out signals," he whispered to the other two. "Tell me if you don't think he crouches just an inch or so lower just before the ball is hiked."

Three pairs of eyes focused on the quarterback as he called out, "Hut-one! Hut!" It wasn't much of a dip. In fact, Chip was not positive he saw it until P.C. rushed in, rubbing his hands. "By Jove, I think he's got something there!" he said.

All of Dan's tips had given the left side an overwhelming advantage in their secret contest with the right. Chip chuckled to himself when he saw Coach Ray scratching his head after a tackle by the Left Side Three. Since it was obvious that Dan and P.C. weren't the most coordinated people, Chip was getting most of the credit for the puzzling strength of the left side. But on one play, Dan anticipated the hike so well that he got by Roosevelt before the giant tackle could even move. Scot never saw what hit him as Dan tackled him before he could pitch the ball to Bruce.

Coach Ray rushed in to check on who had made the tackle. Seeing it was Dan, he stared at Roosevelt, then at Dan, then back at Roosevelt. "How in blue blazes did that player get by you so quickly?"

Good for you, Dan, Chip thought. Poor Dan deserved a break after the miserable luck he had had all year. But Chip saw Scot shove Dan off with a growl, and most of the other starters glared at him. Bruce reached up to whisper something to Roosevelt, but the tackle shook his head. Chip had seen that look on Bruce's face once before—when he had agreed to that vicious block on Eric.

This team is crazy! thought Chip. *It's like we're enemies. At least Roosevelt has some sense.*

A few plays later, Scot dropped back to pass. He sent all his backs out on pass routes, and that meant Chip was to cover Rennie. That was one situation Chip always hated. Rennie was so fast that Chip was always afraid of getting beaten on a long pass. Aided by Dan's tip-off on the play, he had backed up far enough to give Rennie plenty of room. Sure enough, Rennie was going for the long bomb. Legs churning in a full sprint, he sped downfield so fast that, even with his long lead, Chip fell behind.

Fortunately, Rennie had outrun Scot's throwing arm. Chip saw Rennie look back and suddenly stop. As the running back did so, he slipped to the ground. Chip then turned upfield just as the ball fluttered down. He had only a split second to react. He stuck out his hands, but the ball hit his thumb and bounced away.

Wincing from the pain of his jammed thumb, Chip breathed a sigh of relief. *I hope they don't run that play anymore,* he thought.

P.C. came over to congratulate him and, as usual, couldn't resist a tease. "Nice catch, Chip. You've got the hands of a surgeon."

"Oh, yeah?" snapped Rennie, getting slowly to his feet. "If you're so much better, how come you're not starting?"

"Come on, he's just kidding around," said Chip. "We always do."

Rennie said, "Whose side are you on, anyway? I wouldn't take that from a scrub."

"I'm not on anyone's side," Chip wanted to say. But he said nothing. He had the gnawing feeling he would have to make a choice soon. He felt a little hope as he saw P.C. shake his head at Rennie, more amused than angry. P.C. knew how it was, and he didn't let it bother him. If only Dan and Tom would keep playing it cool, too.

He looked over at Tom, who was scribbling something on the coach's clipboard. Ever since he had volunteered to be the manager, Tom had been exactly the problem Chip had expected. He couldn't tell a goalpost from a flagpole, and he wasn't afraid to ask the dumbest questions in his efforts to figure out the game. Compared to most boys on the field, Tom ran like a first grader. Worst of all, he still believed everything anybody told him. On Tom's first day at practice, Scot had told him that Coach Ray wanted all the tackling dummies in the front seat of his van. Tom had been struggling to get the second one in when Coach Ray had spotted him and run over to ask what he was doing. The whole team hooted for the next five minutes.

Chip always made a wide path around Tom at practice after that. *If Bruce and those guys don't like us being with subs, they'll really put up a stink about hanging around him,* he thought. Tom had bought his explanation that it was traditional on sports teams for the starters to spend most of practice time with other starters. But Chip knew that his new "buddies" were making fun of Tom. It had to hurt Tom that Chip was one of them.

For the next two weeks, Chip found himself looking over his shoulder whenever he talked to P.C. or Dan. He never called out to them, and he made sure he broke off all discussion between plays as soon as he saw the offense break the huddle. Meanwhile, the starters got worse. Some of them wouldn't speak to a player who wasn't in the Blue and White Club. Chip felt more trapped than ever. Although he loved being a starter, he welcomed the last day of practice before the final game against Madison.

As he sat on the outskirts of the Blue and White Club meeting, he started picking his name off his helmet. These meetings had become a pain. He worked off the last of the tape and started rubbing off the glue. Once he looked up and saw Bronc looking at them from a distance. Immediately, he went back to his helmet cleaning. *Why does he always make me feel guilty every time he looks at me?* Chip thought glumly. *I'm not even the one who's causing the trouble.*

The talk had turned to one of the club's favorite subjects, Eric. Actually, Chip hadn't had any problem with his old enemy for quite a while. Eric was learning a new position. It took all of his strength and stubborn determination to hold his own against the larger boys in the line. Chip had tried to give the guy a break now and then. He even told him, "Nice tackle," once, but he couldn't tell if Eric had heard it.

As much as he still disliked Eric, Chip had to admit that most of the recent scraps between Eric and teammates were started by the good old Blue and White. They had singled him out spitefully by keeping him out of the club even though he was a starter. Since Forest Grove lost its last game to McKinley, Eric could no longer be blamed for spoiling their perfect record with his penalty. But the enemies he had made had not grown kinder.

"Hey, keep it down until the bald monkey gets to his truck," Bruce told everyone. The group fell silent as Bronc walked across the parking lot. When the truck roared off, Bruce said, "OK, everyone got the plan? Tomorrow's the day we give Eric all the publicity he deserves. 'Eric Youngquist is a dork!' Write that everywhere you can get away with it. Lockers, halls, books, sheets of paper, buses, bathrooms, the whole works."

"I don't know," said Roosevelt. "We could get in trouble for that."

"It's not like vandalism," said Bruce. "We're only using chalk. Just a one-day thing to put him in his place."

"Hey! I've got a great idea!" Scot said. "We could kick the whole thing off with a grand opening. You know, Eric lives down the hill from me with his grandparents. Well, they have a big yard, and I've seen Eric raking for a couple of weeks out there. He's almost done; he must have fifty bags out there. Why don't we go and rip 'em up, and spread 'em back on the lawn!"

To Chip's horror, the starters all liked the idea. Chip sank back on the sidewalk, watching Scot take sweeping bows to the laughter and applause.

"Pretty good, huh, Chip?" said Bruce, poking Chip

in the ribs.

Chip faked a nod. "But how am I supposed to explain this to my parents?"

"Good point!" shouted Bruce. "Hey, everybody! Just tell your folks that the team wants to go over a few last-minute details before the last game. Meet at ten minutes after dark at Scot's house."

10
The New Left Linebacker

"So how dark does it have to be before it's 'dark'?" muttered Chip as he pulled back the drapes of the living room window. The sun had set, but he could still make out the autumn colors blending into the shadows. Frowning, he looked at his own front yard littered ankle deep by the fallings of a large maple. He guessed it would take nearly ten minutes for him to run over to Scot's. If he was going to go, he'd have to start soon.

He walked back and forth across the carpet, trying to figure out how he had gotten himself into the mess. He still couldn't stand Eric. There was no getting around the fact that Eric had brought his troubles on himself. The guy deserved everything they were going to do to him and more. Besides, if there was one person on earth who had a right to revenge on Eric, it was Chip. He tried to bring up those memories of when Eric had been at his cruelest, and he at his most helpless.

But those moments kept fading out of focus. Instead, he kept seeing Dan and Bronc as they talked about Eric's problems. *As if he were the victim instead of the guy who started it all,* sniffed Chip, trying to dismiss the thoughts. It didn't work. The picture that kept coming back was that of Chip in Eric's place. If Eric really was like him, if he was as desperate for approval as Chip was, then it was all just brutal. He hated that smirk of Eric's. How would it be to have twelve or fifteen of those leering faces haunting you wherever you went? How could a guy even face going to school, knowing most of the class despised you and the rest knew enough to stay away from you?

What's the use? Chip thought. *Even if I don't show up tonight, there's still all the business with the signs tomorrow.* He went to the kitchen and prowled for a snack to take with him. Jill was the only one home. She looked up from the table, where she had spread out her schoolbooks.

"Must be a really big game tomorrow," she said. "I don't think I've ever seen you so nervous."

"No bigger than usual," Chip said. "We've already lost two games, so we can't win the title anyway." He hunted in the back closet for his jacket.

Jill shrugged as she ripped out a sheet of notebook paper. "Well, you could have fooled me. You're acting just like I feel before the most nerve-racking games of the year."

Sure, Miss Perfect gets nervous before games, Chip thought as he tried to unwedge the stuck zipper in his jacket. As soon as he thought it, though, he felt small. *Why pick on her? I got myself into this mess.* Just as he was about to step out the door, he saw her back as she flipped through the pages of a book. Suddenly, he felt he had to talk to someone. He felt torn in so many ways that he couldn't stand it anymore.

"When you're on a team, do the players get along?" he asked.

"I don't know. I guess so," she said, frowning at the interruption. "Everyone can't be close friends with everyone, but we usually have a good time together."

Chip felt so tired he slumped into a chair across from Jill. "Well, we've had problems. Boy, have we had problems!" He was sure Jill wouldn't know what he was talking about. She did the right things; her teams got along. But even when he finally started to gain some success, he was a failure. For the next five minutes he told her the history of the season, and he found himself talking faster and faster, as if he no longer could keep it under control.

Jill listened silently. When Chip finished with his story and the problem of the Blue and White Club, he was as stunned by what he saw as he was with the fact that he had just spilled it out. Jill looked worried, and swallowing wasn't coming easily.

"Wow!" she started, breathing heavily. "No wonder you acted that way all night! I wish I could give you an easy answer. I suppose you've thought about doing what *you* think is right without worrying about the others?"

"That's easy for you to say!" Chip retorted, resting his chin on his knuckles. "No matter what you do, everyone knows you're great. If I was like you, I could just snap my fingers and call the whole mess off."

Jill relaxed into a warm smile. "Boy, I didn't know you had me up on such a pedestal. You think it's easy for me to block out what other people think? Why do you think I came so close to quitting the team last week?"

Chip could hardly believe it. "You did?" As he

thought about it, though, nobody in the family had even brought up the subject of volleyball lately. "You? How come?"

"Same kind of thing you're talking about. In fact, you sounded so much like me when you first started telling me you were going crazy, I thought you found out about me and were making fun." She sighed. "Pressure. People were expecting more and more from me. There I was, running my tail off, trying to live up to their expectations, like you're trying to live up to what the starters think of you. Well, let me tell you: It doesn't matter how hard you try to please them, you won't win. I had that one bad game and we lost, and everyone wanted to know what was the matter with me. And then there's Dad! You should see him when I have an important match."

"Oh, I know about that," said Chip.

"He'd get so worked up that I got upset trying to do well just so he wouldn't get upset if we lost." She sat back. "It got so hard to please everyone that pretty soon I hated the whole thing. I told Dad and Mrs. Campbell that I thought I should quit."

Chip could hardly believe anyone else felt the same pressures he did, much less Jill. "So what happened? What did you do?"

"First, Dad and I talked it out. He was good about it, too. He apologized and said he loves us and is proud of us. That he just gets carried away sometimes, wishing the best for us."

"So did that take care of it?" asked Chip. He knew just talking with Dad wasn't going to solve his problem.

"Are you kidding?" said Jill. "The big problem was at school. Everyone was talking about what I could do, and how we were a cinch to win this and that. I was always worrying about blowing it, or what people would think if we didn't win. I just couldn't take being pulled around. Well, they talked me out of quitting, but I still feel caught in the same trap."

She threw her pencil down hard as she leaned her chair against the wall. *So it's still bugging her,* Chip thought.

Jill went on. "I happened to mention it to the youth pastor at church, Pastor Wagner. He said I'm acting as though I'm not worth anything unless I do this or win that or please so-and-so. And it's so stupid; doing those things or acting that way doesn't make you different or more important. Pastor Wagner said that God accepts us the way we are, and if God accepts us, we don't have to prove anything to anyone. We're freed up to go out and play hard, have fun, help others, and do what really needs to be done. He said when you let yourself get pulled along by something you don't believe in, you're not your real self anymore."

Chip wrinkled his brow.

"I know what you're thinking," Jill said, laughing at his expression. "It's one thing to *say* you have to live up to your own standards, but it's easier to say it than to do it." She suddenly blushed. "Well, I've done it now. If I can *say* all that to a little brother, of all people, maybe I really *do* believe it!"

Chip knew he'd have to hurry if he wanted to get to Scot's on time. The fastest way was to run through the trail behind the swamp and up over the tracks to the hill. Although it was dark, there were enough lights from the houses surrounding the small swamp that he had no problem sticking to the trail.

It was better that he took that way and didn't use the streets, because he was so lost in thought he wasn't paying attention to anything around him. Once he had broken the ice with Jill, it had been easy enough to talk. But she was right. To do something about the problem was another story.

I haven't done anything I *really wanted since I stepped in that locker room door back at the start,* he thought. *Haven't even said anything I believed, either, except sometimes with Dan and P.C. Sure, Eric and Bruce and those guys started this whole mess. But I'm the one who let myself get caught in it. And it's all because I get scared. So scared that I throw away everything I really believe about God and what's right. Eric's the only one with any guts; he stands up to the whole lot of them.*

Without remembering anything about being on the swamp trail, he found himself crossing the tracks. He must have scrambled pretty hard up the hill, because he had a side ache. Automatically checking both ways for trains, he cut a shortcut onto a street.

It'd sure be easier if Eric wasn't such a creep, he thought. Then it hit him, so hard that he stopped in the middle of the street. *Who are you kidding, Demory?* he thought. *Dan and Tom and P.C. aren't creeps, and I've been treating them the same way.*

For the moment, Jill had pumped him up enough to challenge the Blue and White. He wasn't at all sure that would last, though, once he ran into Bruce and the others. In fact, he didn't have any idea of what he was going to do then. He crossed a street and went half a block further. He felt hot, but the drops of sweat on his face cooled quickly in the night breeze. Then he saw them. Everyone was there in Scot's yard. "God, help!" he whispered, and crossed the street to join them.

Eric's house was tucked into one of the few corners in the city. Although it was only minutes from downtown, a ridge on one side and the swamp on another had forced the road to twist into a dead end. There were three houses on the street, older ones by the looks of the porches and peeling paint. Eric's was the first in line.

Chip hadn't believed Scot's report of fifty bags of leaves. But he saw quickly that it was no exaggeration. It was a double lot, and there must have been twenty good-sized trees growing on it. The house was set near to the curb, with most of the yard behind it. The backyard was entirely fenced, except at the rear, where it spilled off down a hill into the swamp.

"This is the place," grinned Scot. Unlike most of the city's blocks, this one was mostly out of the range of streetlights; any light that would have hit the houses was smothered by all the trees.

"The bags must be near the garage, don't you think?" said Bruce, crouching low by the fence and signaling the others to do the same. "We'll have to be quiet about it. Why don't we circle behind the garage, get the bags, and dump them way in that dark corner by the back?"

"Yeah, less chance of getting caught," said Rennie. Scot led the way, followed by Bruce and then a string of others who looked around hesitatingly before following. Chip had meant to say something by now. But as the crouching group trickled toward the garage, he knew he just couldn't. He couldn't risk being ridiculed and snubbed just for Eric's sake. Not by himself. He wasn't a superhero; he just couldn't face them all alone. Near tears as he waited for the last person to go before him, he noticed that the other person was actually waiting for him. Roosevelt still sat on his haunches, eyes darting from the house to the group circling toward the garage.

Chip remembered the tackle's simple shake of the head during the practice when Bruce had whispered to Roosevelt about Dan. He realized, as he watched Roosevelt signal him forward, that he had been holding his breath for a long while. Letting the air out, he decided that this would be his chance. He felt as though he were plunging into an icy stream when he opened his mouth and said, "Wait a minute."

It wasn't long before the Blue and White Club

returned to the darkest corner of the yard. The long line of figures scurrying along with big loads on their backs reminded Chip of ants carting home food from a cupboard. Roosevelt had found what he was looking for, and returned from the other side of the house just before the others arrived.

Chip's heart was pounding as he took one of the rakes from Roosevelt. Although he dreaded each approaching step of his teammates, he refused to look up from his work. Even when he heard whisperings from the darkness behind him, he kept sweeping the leaves. Finally, they must have recognized him, or more likely recognized Roosevelt, since it was hard to mistake his large form even in this light.

"Have you guys lost your minds?" said Scot in a whisper.

"Probably," croaked Chip, sweeping his small pile toward Roosevelt's larger one.

"We figured this was getting out of hand," said Roosevelt.

"You picked a fine time to say that!" said Bruce, slamming his two bags to the ground. "I didn't hear anyone crying about it this afternoon."

"Better late than never," said Chip, finally looking up. It was eerie seeing all those shadows and no faces. There was no way of telling what everyone was thinking of all this.

"So maybe you don't like the idea," came a whisper that sounded like it might be Rennie. "Why come down and rake his yard?"

Chip hoped Roosevelt would answer, but the tackle silently kept on raking.

"We didn't *plan* it. Just seemed like a good idea at the moment. Look, we thought the idea of this club was fun at first," Chip said. "But look what's going on! Half the team hates the other half. About all we've done is come up with new ways to dump on everyone else."

"Come on," scoffed Bruce. "You hated Eric before the club started."

Chip's knees were shaking. As far as he could tell, he wasn't getting anywhere. Stubbornly, he went back to raking. "Maybe. That doesn't mean I have to act as mean and stupid as he did."

Chip felt a little better as Roosevelt finally spoke. "I never liked gangin' up on guys. Chip and I got talkin' about it at the last few minutes. This Blue and White stuff is gettin' too stuck up." He tied off the two bags he had finished stuffing and said, "We figured the club should do something to make up for the damage it's done before we break it up. It looks like there's about twenty bags worth of leaves left in the yard. Here's my contribution." He threw the bags at Scot's feet, hoisted himself over the fence, and walked off.

Chip felt like rushing after him. With Roosevelt gone, he didn't know what would happen. But he hadn't finished his second bag of leaves, so he kept at it. Something rushed past his ear, making him jump back. Chip saw that it was a bag of leaves, and the boy who had thrown it was coming toward him.

"Here's *my* contribution," Bruce sneered, ripping open the bag with a hard kick. After booting the bag around the yard, spreading leaves everywhere, he took his other bag and did the same. Brushing past Chip without looking at him, he, too, hopped the fence and left.

Chip shrank back toward the corner of the yard as three others followed Bruce, and then another ran after them. *Well, you've done it now, Demory,* he thought. *You just joined Eric on their hit list.* But, with his eyes growing more used to the darkness, he could make out that at least the four followers hadn't ripped open their bags. And none of the rest had moved. All were standing with their bags resting on the ground beside them, making them appear as though they were waiting at a bus stop with their suitcases.

Chip almost jumped when he heard the first whisper. It was Scot, of all people. "You've got a point, kid," he said, picking up Roosevelt's dropped rake. "If yours is a stupid idea, at least it's no stupider than anything else we've done." As if on cue, the others gathered around, helping stuff bags while they waited for a turn at a rake. Chip stared dumbly at them, and even more so at Rennie, who took his bag from him and finished twisting the top.

When Scot finished his two bags, he stepped toward Chip and pulled him out of earshot of the others. "Has Bronc been talking to you?"

"Not for a while," Chip answered.

Scot shrugged. "Just wondering. He's been after me a bit lately. He says part of being a good quarterback is being a team leader. He never really says what he's getting at, but somehow . . ."

He left the sentence hanging, but Chip nodded in agreement. *So it's not just me,* he thought. *Bronc's been working on everyone.*

They were back under the lights at the municipal park for the last game against Madison. There wasn't much grass left in the middle of the field. But somehow the bright lights and sharply marked hash marks made the field appear inviting.

Chip waited until Bronc was through giving instructions to Tom, and then approached him. "Say, coach?"

"Yeah, player?" grinned Bronc.

"I've got a suggestion for a lineup change."

"Everyone wants to be a coach. Well, you can give it to me if you can do it in forty-five seconds or less," said Bronc, checking his watch. "Just promise you won't feel bad if I tell you no."

Chip swallowed hard as he looked at the shimmering blue jerseys of the Madison team warming up. "I think you should give Dan a try at my linebacker job."

Bronc's eyebrows shot up. "That's very noble of you, but you've earned the spot."

As Bronc turned away, Chip grabbed him by the shoulder. Although it took him a bit longer than his forty-five second time limit, he told Bronc all about Dan's keen instincts and clever deductions. Bronc mulled it over awhile. "Dan figured all that out? Well, ordinarily I'd say he's too slow to be a linebacker and of course he's too thin to be a good lineman. But a guy can make up for some of that with smarts and desire. You know, he never looked too coordinated. But then nobody looks too sharp when they're up against Roosevelt." He paused for a second. "I'll let you know. Meanwhile, for heaven's sake, tell Roosevelt and Scot that they're tipping off the plays. Most likely there's no one on Madison as smart as Dan, but you never know."

Coach Ray gathered the team a few minutes later to make his usual pregame speech. He cleared his throat and looked down at his notebook. "We've got just one lineup change I want to announce. Atkinson and Demorg will alternate at left linebacker. Atkinson, take the first series."

Dan looked at Chip in disbelief and pointed a questioning finger at his chest. Chip nodded and winked. *Quit feeling so proud of yourself, Demory,* he scolded himself. *You should have given him some credit a long time ago.* But it didn't stop him from grinning.

Dan had a few problems at first. He wasn't as fast as most linebackers, and a couple of times Madison runners beat him to the outside for good gains. As the game went on, he lined up further to the outside and was able to stop those plays.

Midway through the third quarter, Forest Grove led 20-14. Standing on the sidelines between P.C. and

Tom, Chip nervously watched as the unbeaten Madison team drew close to another score. With two powerful runners and a quarterback who could throw well, they had been averaging over four touchdowns a game.

"When do you go in again?" Tom asked.

"Next defensive series." Seeing Tom's blank look, he added, "The next time our offense turns the ball over to the other team."

"How come that player is waving his hand?" Tom asked.

"That's Dan," said P.C. "Who knows what he's up to. Maybe he's trying to shoo away the only fly stupid enough to still be outdoors this time of year."

Chip held back a giggle as he saw Tom nod solemnly. It had been funny watching those two all game. Tom seemed to have a bottomless well of questions, and P.C. an equally full supply of smart answers. In all this time, P.C. hadn't noticed that Tom was taking his jokes seriously.

"Don't believe a thing that character says," he told Tom. "I think Dan's probably figured out something in the offensive setup, and he's signaling the rest."

The three watched as Madison tried a pass play into the end zone. The quarterback aimed a soft pass toward his right end, who was cutting across the middle. Chip was already slumping in defeat as he saw that the receiver was clearly beyond Rennie.

But the pass never got there. A tall frame stretched high in the air to make a fingertip grab.

"Interception!" yelled P.C. and Chip at the same time. The whole team jumped around whooping, while Dan ran off the field cradling his prize.

"Hey, I think they're going to need that thing back on the field," said Bronc, snatching the football away from the excited linebacker and firing it back to an official. "Tremendous play, Dan," he added. "Tremendous."

Dave Atkinson, dressed in street clothes, hopped over on his crutches to join the group. "How did you figure that out?" he asked his brother. "That wasn't your man. What were you doing back there?"

"I know it wasn't my man," grinned Dan. "But I found out that whenever the ball was going to go to that end, he'd always adjust his mouthpiece after taking his stance. You know, really wedge it in there tight. When I saw him do it, it seemed like a good chance to take."

Bronc stared at them, one of the rare times Chip had seen him stop in midchew. Then he turned to Chip and said, "I think Rennie could use a breather. Take over for a few plays."

"No problem," said Chip, strapping on his helmet. It wasn't until he reached the huddle that he realized the Forest Grove team was on offense! That meant that Chip was at running back! A wave of fear swept over him as Scot called out the play. But by the time he lined up, he had remembered the system. After blocking for Bruce, who hadn't spoken all night, on two plays, he leaned into the huddle to listen to the next play selection.

"Forty-two Red on four," said Scot.

Quit grinning, you idiot, he said to himself as he lined up. *Everyone in the whole park will know you're carrying this play.* He charged forward at the snap, saw a slim opening in the line and ran into it. Two linebackers closed quickly and wrapped him tightly in their arms, but he wriggled and squirmed for an extra yard. By the time he picked himself up, Rennie was waiting for him.

"Nice run," he said, slapping him on the shoulder pads.

Chip nodded and jogged to the sidelines. Seeing his dad standing alone near the 20-yard line, he veered over to him so suddenly that he bumped into a dirt-covered uniform near the end of the squad. It was Eric's.

"Sorry," Chip said. "Didn't have my turn signal on."

"Nice run," mumbled Eric, so softly Chip could barely hear it.

"Way to play tough," Chip answered. Then he jogged over to his dad, who was battling the effects of a cold with a pocketful of tissues. "That was fun!" said Chip.

"Enjoyed it myself," sniffled his dad. "You got one more yard than you should have gotten." As they watched the Forest Grove offense drive slowly downfield for another score, Dad said, "Looks like you got the game won."

"No problem," shrugged Chip. "We had it won before the game even started." As his dad's laugh was cut short by a brief coughing fit, Chip added, to himself, *In more ways than one.*

HEY! HE'S CHEATING!

Ryan stared hard at the pitcher's mound, trying to pick out the white of the pitcher's rubber from the dirt. It wasn't easy to spot. He finally detected a corner of it as the Baron went into his wind-up. The pitcher was throwing from a good foot and a half in front of the rubber.

"Hey! He's cheating!" he said, standing and pointing to the mound.

Art pulled Ryan down to the bench beside him. "Keep it down. Let's not make a scene."

This was the last straw for Ryan. How much was Art going to sit and take before something was done? . . .

Read all the Sports Stories for Boys:

At Left Linebacker, Chip Demory
A Winning Season for the Braves
Mystery Rider at Thunder Ridge
Seventh-Grade Soccer Star
Batter Up!
Full Court Press
The Great Reptile Race
A Race to the Finish

A WINNING SEASON FOR THE BRAVES

NATE AASENG

Contents

1 New Coach

"It's not like he was such a great coach," shrugged Tracy. "I mean, how many games did we win last year? Three."

Ryan squinted hard at his friend. *This whole thing must have him really upset,* he thought. *If I'd tried to say what he just said, he'd be after me with both fists flying.*

"I don't get it," said Mike from somewhere behind Ryan. "I thought everything was all set and your dad was going to coach again, Tracy."

There were twelve of them sitting on a hillside behind a banged-up backstop. From a distance they looked like construction workers on their lunch break, except that they held baseball gloves in their fists instead of sandwiches. This was the entire roster of the Braves, a summer league team in Barnes City. Not one of them had been late for this first practice of the season. Every year there was something about that first feel of a solid infield, of a real dirt pitching mound, of a home plate that was stuck firmly in the ground and wouldn't bounce away when you slid into it, that made them want to play ball.

But now no one moved toward the infield, even though it had been empty for half an hour.

"My dad *was* going to coach," said Tracy. "Now he's not. All of a sudden he doesn't have the time. But what can you do? He said he was sorry and he even found a new coach for us."

Ryan had to turn his eyes away, for he knew how Tracy really felt in spite of his casual air. In Tracy's eyes it was just a matter of which of his dad's betrayals was worse, backing out of coaching, or going ahead and recruiting this new coach. His dad hadn't really asked who they wanted for coach; he just turned the team over to someone they hadn't even heard of.

Ryan tightened some loose strings on his glove and tried to keep from muttering out loud. Obviously it didn't matter to Mr. Salesky that the Braves had been counting on everything being the same this year. They had taken their lumps last season when they were the youngest team in the league. But now they were all back, older and more skilled, and they knew their teammates well. They'd thought there weren't going to be any worries or uncertainties this year because they'd been through it all last year. And now this.

"Hey, Tracy! Isn't that your dad's car?"

"Maybe he changed his mind!"

Ryan stared hard as the blue Vega picked its way over the rutted road that led to the ball diamond. His fists were clenched with hope as Tracy's dad got out of the driver's side. But they suddenly relaxed. Tracy let out a humorless laugh when the passenger door opened and another man climbed out. One of the two men was gripping a bat in one hand and straightening the whistle around his neck with the other, and it wasn't Mr. Salesky. No, Tracy's dad had on some pressed pants and a button-down shirt, the kind that men wear under suits. Even his shoes were shined. He wasn't here to coach baseball.

"Boys," he called. "I'm sure that Tracy, uh, told you what's going on with me. I don't know if you consider it good news or bad. I know I was looking forward to the summer because you're a great bunch to work with. But I'm just going to be away too often in the next few months to do any justice to the job." He had begun by looking each of the boys in the eye as he spoke, the way he always had. But their glum expressions must have caught him by surprise, because soon he was looking only at the man next to him.

"You've never met Art Horton, I assume, since he says he hasn't met you. But I've worked out with him at the gym and I know that he'll be an excellent coach." Mr. Salesky glanced at his watch. "Well, I am no longer the coach now, just a nosy parent. So I'll get out of your way. Good luck to all of you." He scrambled Tracy's hair, waved, and climbed back into the car.

Ryan wondered why Art Horton was standing up there with such a huge grin—a silly one, really. No one else had found anything to smile about. The new coach looked like a coach, dressed in a gray sweatsuit that was too tight around the waist to be comfortable. His mustache was so thick that it covered his whole mouth whenever he stopped smiling. He squeezed the bat in one hand, sending a wave of muscles rippling through his large forearms. Ryan could guess right away that this man was a good athlete, and it scared him. There was nothing scary about Mr. Salesky when he hit a ball to you in fielding practice. But you would have to really be on your toes whenever this man pointed a bat at you.

Nobody had said a word yet. The team stared at Art as though he were a stranger grinning out of a car window and offering candy. But suddenly the man's grin vanished, so quickly that Ryan flinched.

"Gentlemen! Front and center!" shouted the new coach. "Come on, gather around. Get in here close so I don't have to scream my head off to be heard!" Ryan jumped up automatically and joined the others as they shuffled forward. Tracy took his time getting to his feet, as if to do so were a nuisance.

Art Horton stood up straight now, with arms crossed, and he was not smiling. "My name is Art Horton!" he boomed. "You will call me 'Art.' Not 'Coach' or 'Coach Horton' or 'Mr. Horton'; the name is Art! Now listen up, all of you!"

Ryan edged behind another boy to get out of Art's line of sight. He knew from Art's first words that his summer was shot. There was no way he would stick around for this kind of thing all summer. As soon as practice was over, he would quit the team and never come back. What's more, he bet that he wasn't the only one.

"Can anyone tell me how many games you won last year?" said Art, with his lip curled up almost into a sneer.

Ryan could hardly stand to stay any longer. *He knows what our record was last year,* he thought. *He's just rubbing it in.* He looked hopefully at the sun, which was sliding slowly out of sight. At least this guy had been so late in coming that there wouldn't be much time for practice tonight. The sun was nearly down, and this field didn't have any lights. He tried to picture what he was going to do with his lost summer.

"What's the matter, did you forget?" challenged Art.

"We won three," said Tracy coldly.

"Good, we got someone here who can speak. And how many games did your team lose?"

"Fifteen," said Tracy. As the best athlete on the team, he knew that none of the blame for their poor record could be put on him.

"Fifteen games? Was that fun? Did all of you have a great time losing fifteen games?" said Art. A few mumbled noes followed.

"Well, let me tell you something, gentlemen," Art went on. "As long as I am the coach here, things will be different. Because I have one job, and you have one job, and we all know what your job is. My job is to get something out of you guys, and that's what I'm going to do. I'm not here to waste my time. If I want to do that, I can watch tv reruns with the sound off. Or with the sound on, for that matter. The reason you are here can be summed up in one word. I'll give you a hint: the word has three letters. Is there anyone here who can spell that word?"

Ryan found himself cheering the sun on, pleading for darkness to end the horrid meeting. He heard a couple of halfhearted voices spelling out *w-i-n*.

Art glowered at the team. "You have a strange way of spelling, gentlemen. I always thought you spelled fun, *f-u-n*." Suddenly he broke into a laugh. "Aha! I really had you guys going for awhile, didn't I? You thought I was Old Blood-and-Guts himself. Well, I'm only tough when it comes to one thing. Anyone who isn't here to *enjoy* the game of baseball might just as well leave now."

A dozen heads turned toward each other, looking as if they had seen an animal speak. Ryan caught Joe Martinez's glance, and nodded as he saw him mouth the word, "Weird."

"All right, everyone, line up on the first base line. Would you do that?" Art called cheerily. Before the rest of the team could react, Tracy jumped to his feet and stalked directly to third base, staring at Art every step of the way. Ryan nudged Joe and they joined Tracy at third, followed by the rest of the team.

Art scratched his head. "I said 'first base.' This can mean only one of two things. Either I'm looking into a mirror or we're really going to have to go back to the basics of this game! You, sir!" he said, pointing to Tracy. "I would like your assistance for a minute."

"Oh, boy, I wonder what he's going to do to Tracy," said Mike.

"I don't know," said Ryan, who was glad at least to be out of arm's reach of the new coach. "I do know one thing. This summer isn't going to be as good as we thought."

"Look, I think he's trying to get in good with Tracy," said Mike as they saw their star player talking into Art's ear. "I'll bet he lets big shot Tracy run the whole team, just so he can get in good with someone."

"Ladies and gentlemen!" shouted Art. "I will now introduce to you the Barnes City Braves. As I call their names, they will sprint around the bases and you can give each one a huge round of applause. Leading off is the world famous batting star, the only athlete ever to get a standing ovation in 113 different countries including Upper Volta, Joe Martinez!"

Joe looked around and hestitated. Art was pointing to the basepath and making a large circling motion with his hand. Finally, Joe dashed around the bases and Art led the startled team in a round of applause.

"Second up is the man who, just this season, was voted the toughest out in the entire civilized world, Bartholomew Smith. Yahooo!

"Third, the man who has broken all of Hank Aaron's records by the age of 12, Mike Sherry!" So it went, with Troy Williams, Al Rhodes, Dave Perlock, Perry Bradovich, Randy Olson, Jimmy Amadibele (Art had trouble pronouncing that), and Justin Holmberg each tearing around the bases while the new coach shouted some wild tribute to their greatness.

Ryan was the next to the last to be called, and for some reason he felt nervous waiting for his turn. Even though he was well prepared for it, the sound of Art booming out his name made him jump. "Next up is Ryan Court! Ryan is considered too good for the Hall of Fame, so they're building a special wing in the building just for him!" The image almost brought out a grin in Ryan, but he ran smoothly around the bases, shaking his head as if the whole exercise were too childish for words. Tracy took his turn last of all, and he trotted slowly around the infield, going the wrong way. Art ignored him and began dismissing the team before Tracy had finished.

"Gentlemen, that was just to get used to having our footprints on the bases. Next time we will start beating the stitches out of that little white ball and see if we know what to do with a baseball once it has been hit. See you then." He tucked the whistle under his shirt and jogged up the hill toward Lexington Street with that bat still in his hand.

Ryan headed for the bike rack where his ten-speed was chained together with Mike's bike. "Pretty tough practice,'' laughed Mike.

''Probably my toughest one of the summer,'' said Ryan, pulling open the lock and unwrapping it from their bikes. ''I may just sit out the rest of them.''

''Not a bad idea,'' said Tracy, joining them. ''I can't tell if this guy is a baseball coach or a circus trainer.''

''Oh, I don't know. After a while I think I started to like him,'' said Mike.

''He is kind of funny,'' admitted Ryan.

''Hokey is a better word,'' scoffed Tracy.

''Don't give up on the season already,'' said Mike as they rode, standing up, over the rutted path. Even though he wasn't resting on the seat, the jarring shook him so much that his voice wobbled. He stopped to inspect his tires. ''Give it another practice or two before you quit and wreck your whole summer.''

''I have a feeling it's already wrecked,'' Ryan said, slowing down. ''Up until this we had it all planned out just perfect.''

''Aw, I may as well stick around for the practices until I get totally sick of it,'' said Mike. ''He'd have to be the world's worst coach to get me to quit baseball.''

Tracy waited with Ryan for Mike to catch up. Tracy called to Mike, ''Of course I can see why Ryan wouldn't want to play anymore. If he's too good for the Hall of Fame, how can you expect him to play with a team like ours!''

Their mission was a grim one and the faces of the three boys reflected it. Tracy's jaw snapped nervously on his gum, and Ryan and Bartholomew Smith walked with their faces scrunched in a frown. Smith told Ryan that he'd been quite willing to accept the new coach—until Art had used his full name, Bartholomew

Smith. Everyone had always called him "Smith," and if he used a first name at all, it was "Bart." But Art had said "Bartholomew," the name he hated, and now everyone was teasing him, calling him that.

The three marched in a tight group through Tracy's house to the garage and arrived in time to see the automatic door open, letting out a strong waft of gasoline. Seconds later, the blue Vega pulled in; the rumbling of even that small engine sounded loud as it echoed off the close walls of the garage. Then the motor stopped and the boys moved closer. Before Mr. Salesky could put in a word of greeting, Tracy started in. "Please, dad, I'm asking you one last time to come back and coach us."

"Please, Mr. Salesky, we're desperate!" Smith whined.

Ryan had been lagging behind the other two, and now he was glad. He'd hated the idea of putting Mr. Salesky on the spot by begging, but Tracy had insisted there was still a chance to change his mind. All that was needed was for a group of the guys to come over and show how important it was to them. But as soon as he saw Mr. Salesky's weary sigh, Ryan was sure Tracy had been dreaming. There was no way Mr. Salesky would coach.

"I know it's terrible to beg you," said Smith, "but you don't know how much it would mean to us!"

"I'm flattered that you think so much of my coaching," smiled Mr. Salesky. But when he turned to Tracy, his smile had vanished. "We've gone over this a dozen times. If I thought I could handle it, I would. But with the convention coming up, and the amount that I'm responsible for, and the time I'll have to spend out of town in the next weeks, I would miss too much."

"I know you're busy, but you promised and we were looking—"

"Tracy!" said Mr. Salesky, slamming the door. Ryan wished he could leave. As much as he wanted him for a coach, he did not want to make such a stink about it. "What more can I say?" asked Mr. Salesky. "It's not anyone's fault; it's just the way it is. Besides, Art's a better coach and a great guy, and you're better off with him."

"Art's a jerk!" said Tracy, knowing he was beaten.

"Listen to me," said Mr. Salesky in a low, even voice that had a tone of warning in it. "You don't have a right to say that about anyone. And especially not about a man you don't even know yet, who is willing to give up his time for you." He moved forward slowly, eyes only on his son. "I want you to grow up and face facts, and I won't hear another word about this. Art Horton is the coach. I am not. If you want to play baseball this summer, you'll learn to give him a chance."

Ryan did not know what effect that speech had on Tracy, but he himself could hardly keep from shaking. He felt lucky that his mom had never chewed him out in front of any of his friends. Just listening to Mr. Salesky's speech made him wonder why they wanted him so badly for a coach.

"I guess that's the end of that," said Smith after Mr. Salesky had gone.

"We really convinced him, didn't we?" said Ryan. "Now at least there's no question about it. Art Horton is the coach."

"We'll see about that," said Tracy as he stormed into the house.

2
This is Baseball?

Mrs. Court stopped and leaned backwards around the hall corner, holding onto the wall to keep her balance. Ryan thought she was going to fall over. "Ryan, it's nearly six-thirty," she said, continuing into the den. "You're going to have to be quick if you expect to get to your baseball practice on time."

Ryan looked up from his tv show and recognized that furrowed-brow look of his mom's. Pulling on his jogging shoes he said casually, "Oh, is it that late already?" But he could tell by the smile tugging at one corner of her mouth that his act wasn't fooling her. It almost never did.

"Ryan Court, we ate supper early tonight because *you* have baseball practice at six-thirty! Are you trying to convince me that you suddenly forgot all about it?"

Ryan thought about trying one more denial, but he had too much sense to go through with it. He had been putting off this decision about the team and didn't want to tell his mom about it. It had seemed like an easy way out, at least for this evening, just to let the practice time slip quietly past. He turned off the tv with a touch of his finger. "I've been thinking about whether to go or not."

"Is this the same Ryan who was out throwing a ball against the garage wall before the snow had melted this spring? The one who risked facing an angry mother when he got his pants all muddy? You must be having all kinds of problems with that new coach."

"What makes you think that?" asked Ryan.

Mrs. Court sat heavily on the couch and rubbed her feet. "You don't have to be so secretive. No one's making you play baseball." Suddenly she frowned and said, "These problems with the coach wouldn't have anything to do with Tracy, by any chance?"

Ryan tapped absently on top of the tv and smiled to himself. For once she was wrong. "No, Tracy's got nothing to do with it."

"You're sure, now?" she said with a hint of suspicion. "It's not as if that boy's temper hasn't gotten you both in trouble a few times. I hope you've learned not to follow his lead when he gets like that."

"Don't worry." Ryan thought back to some of the scrapes they'd gotten into in the neighborhood and at school. He shrugged it off, thinking, *You can't be friends with a guy since kindergarten and not get into some kind of trouble together.* Then he repeated to his mom, "Tracy's got nothing to do with it."

"Well, all right. So if you're miserable playing with your friends, just don't go out for the team. There's no sense sitting around here stewing about it."

"But I'd hate to give it up for the whole summer,"

said Ryan. "What would I do with my time?"

"You'd probably just rot and be bored to death. But at least that's better than suffering under Ivan the Terrible on the baseball field."

"Art isn't quite that bad."

"Danny!" called Mrs. Court to her younger son in the next room. "Would you please bring me the footstool from the living room?" She turned back to Ryan. "If you're trying to convince me that you don't want to play with the team, you'll have to try harder. And no, I won't drive you. My feet are killing me, and I don't want to waste gas, so you'll just have to be a few minutes late."

Often after talking with his mom, Ryan found himself doing things without really knowing why. This was another of those times. He hung his mitt over the handlebars of his bike, opened the backyard gate, and sped off. His lower gears were slipping, so he had to pedal up the final hill to the school in a higher gear. It felt as though he were lifting leg weights. Finally, with a hard push, he made it to the top and let his quivering legs dangle off the pedals as he coasted down the parking lot hill.

He was expecting to see Art hitting baseballs to his buddies, who would be scattered around the grass ball diamond. Art was swinging a bat, all right, but Ryan could see only five Braves out on the field. Tracy was not there, and neither was Mike or Joe. Since Ryan had been in plain sight of the guys while coasting down the hill, he could hardly turn around and ride away. But there was no longer any question about his decision. He would not be playing for the Braves this year. "This is absolutely the last practice," he muttered as he chained his bike to the rack and trudged toward the field.

Suddenly a flurry of action off to his left made him stop. There on the blacktop, standing in a straight line facing the school wall, was the rest of the team. At a glance he could pick out Tracy, who was taller than the rest, Mike with his shaggy brown hair, Joe with his wiry build, black hair and red baseball cap, and Troy with his afro and glasses. They were all laughing and firing baseballs at some kind of poster that was hung on the wall of the school. Ryan veered toward the blacktop away from the diamond and saw that two balls were being kept in constant motion. As he drew nearer, the picture came into focus, and he saw that it was a blowup of a snapshot of Art.

"Hey! Ryan finally showed up!"

"It's about time!"

"Come on over! We're trying to hit Art's nose!"

Ryan whirled to see what Art's reaction was, but the coach was paying no attention to them. He was busy chopping ground balls as fast as they could be fielded.

"Somebody's got a lot of guts!" said Ryan. "Whose bright idea was this? And what does the coach think about it?"

"You're supposed to call him 'Art,' not 'Coach,' " said Tracy. "And I've got news for you. This is his idea, and he brought the picture." He scooped up a ball that had rebounded off the wall, and flipped it to Ryan. "You're suppose to aim for the nose."

Ryan stepped up the baseline and threw. The ball smacked the wall by Art's shoulder. Then a whistle sounded, and Mike trotted off to join the infielders while Perry moved over to join the "firing squad."

"Art doesn't like the idea of standing around at practice," Joe explained to Ryan. "He says the more time you spend throwing and fielding and hitting, the better you'll be and the more fun you'll have. So we keep rotating, with half over there fielding and the rest working on throwing accuracy. He put up that picture for some extra incentive. It's not a bad idea. Tracy's been knocking Art silly. The picture, that is."

"And loving it!" grinned Tracy, firing with all his might. *Smack!* The ball landed near the chin of the smiling face.

Ryan joined the throwers for awhile and then took his turn in the infield. He wanted to ask Troy where he'd gotten that official referee's shirt, but Art wasn't allowing much time for chatter. The infield was lumpy and littered with rocks, so Art was taking care not to hit the balls too hard. Still, when a grounder came towards him, Joe crouched so tensely he looked like a cat stalking a bird. The ball bounced straight to him, but took a short hop off his hands and trickled over to Ryan.

"What's the matter? You scared of it?" laughed Ryan.

Phweeeeet! The piercing whistle made him jump as he was about to roll the ball back to Art. Troy had the whistle in his mouth and was pulling a yellow flag out of his pocket. He tossed it in the air and shouted, "Two-minute penalty for Ryan!"

Art signaled to Randy to take over at bat and keep hitting grounders. "Not too hard tonight," he cautioned. Then he trotted over to Ryan and pulled him out of the line of fire. "We'll wave this one off, Troy," he said. "I don't think Ryan was around when the ground rules were explained. Take a break, Ryan, and I'll tell you what we're doing."

Ryan shrugged and bounced the ball to Randy. For a second he stared at Troy as if his friend had lost his mind, and then followed Art off the infield. It was the first time he had really seen Art up close and the mustache seemed even bushier than it had at a distance. He had worked up a sweat and his sandy hair seemed almost black near the ears where the sweat ran the most.

"You see, Ryan, there is really only one mistake that you can make in this game that's serious. At least that's how I look at it. That mistake is simply not trying. You can't get anywhere in the game, you can't *play* this game unless you try. Now, backing away from ground balls is fairly common among boys your age. Why? Because you're afraid that you might field it incorrectly. So the main thing I want to do is take away that fear of making mistakes. How? By not penalizing mistakes."

He pointed to four crude stakes that he had pounded into the ground next to the eroded path that wound down into the woods from the corner of the field. "I borrowed that idea from another sport. It's called a penalty box. For the first couple of weeks that we practice, we're going to have a team referee. Troy got the job for tonight, and that's why I gave him the shirt and the flag. Whenever he hears any criticism of another guy's play, he calls a penalty. The one who did the criticizing has to spend two minutes in the penalty box throwing stones into the woods. Oh, I know some of the heckling is meant to be in fun. But I want to see what happens if we play without having to worry about getting laughed at."

Ryan nodded dumbly and returned to the infield. He had been playing baseball ever since he could remember, but on this night he felt as if he was trying out a strange game in a foreign country. What kind of practice was this?

It certainly did not help matters when Art came up

with another set of rules for a three-inning scrimmage at the end of the drills. "I'll be the pitcher for everyone," he said as the team gathered around him. "Now, I don't want anyone looking for walks. Look for pitches to hit! What kind of game is it where you stand with a bat on your shoulder hoping you draw a walk so you won't have to use it? The fun of the game is in trying to hit. So, for this game, if you swing and miss at any pitch in the strike zone, it doesn't count against you. Got that? It's not a strike.

"In the field, all you have to do is touch the ball while it's rolling or in the air and it's an out. If you make the play, then it counts as two outs. Batters still take their bases if you don't make the play on them. The only difference is that your team is charged an out if the ball is touched. Each team gets four outs when at bat. Why? Again I ask, what kind of game is it where you stand in the field and hope the ball isn't hit to you? Try! *Play* the game! I want you as hungry to get your hands on a hit ball as if it were made of solid gold."

It took a good inning and a half before everyone finally caught on to all the rules. As the team's only experienced catcher, Ryan stayed behind the plate most of the time. He wasn't thrilled to see players get four and five misses before they finally hit the ball. "This isn't baseball," he kept mumbling to himself. When it was his turn to bat he hit a hard grounder that Jimmy stopped but could not field cleanly. Ryan easily beat the throw to first, but his side was charged one out because Jimmy had touched the ball while it was still moving. "This isn't baseball," Ryan complained to Troy as he took his lead off first base.

The climax of the evening came when Troy whistled two Braves to the penalty box on the same play. Dave had popped a short fly ball into left field, and Mike, who was playing in that area, started running in the wrong direction. By the time he finally located the ball, it was too late to catch it. He was still two arm's lengths away when the ball thudded to the ground.

Tracy and Perry let out a chorus of frustrated groans at Mike's misplay. Immediately Troy blasted his whistle and threw his flag. Ryan watched the two stomp over to the penalty box. He was so busy staring at them to see if they were really going to pitch rocks that he did not notice the game was underway again. The crack of a bat jolted him, and he ducked in panic. Fortunately, Randy had hit the ball in fair territory, and catcher Ryan dropped to his knees in relief.

By the time Tracy and Perry finished their time in the penalty box, it had grown too dark to see the ball. When Smith, over at first base, squawked about not being able to see a throw, Art finally called off practice.

"Sorry about that, Smith. I don't have my watch today, and I guess I got so carried away with practice that I forgot about the time. I promise I won't keep you guys so late again. Any questions about what we're doing before we go?"

"I've got one," said Mike. "How come you have the guys in the penalty box throw rocks?"

"A little mystery of mine," chuckled Art. "The secret is buried in the Bible. If any of you happen to have one and are curious, you can snoop out John 8:7. You'll find your answer there." Ryan was startled. Was this guy a Christian? But Art said no more and briskly scooped up the bats and balls and dumped them into the trunk of his station wagon. While the boys were starting to leave, he walked over to where his picture clung to the wall in three tattered pieces. "It's frightening the way you guys took to this drill with such enthusiasm,'' he laughed as he tore it down. ''See everyone next week! Same time, same place!''

It didn't take long for the news about Randy to spread among the Braves at school the next day. It turned out that Ryan was the last to hear, and even he knew about it by noon.

Randy Olson was a big-boned guy who always seemed awkward, as if his joints needed a few turns with a screwdriver to tighten them. Yet somehow he usually managed to do well at sports. Last season he had been the only Brave to hit two home runs.

''I don't get it,'' said Ryan when Joe told him the news. ''What does he mean he can't play anymore? What did he do, break his leg?''

Joe shook his head. ''There's nothing wrong with him. All I know is that it has something to do with his parents.''

''You mean they said he can't play anymore?''

''That's what I heard.''

They were sitting at a lunchroom table next to the window, watching the rain beat down on the blacktop. Ryan had been thinking earlier that morning that they were lucky to have gotten their practice in on the night before the rain started. But the news about Randy made him wonder again whether it was any use practicing for this unlucky team. It was turning into a depressing day. The last days of school had really started to drag, and Ryan had the edgy feeling of just wanting to get the school year over with. It was hard to concentrate in class, and he felt like he did in those one-sided games when one team had to finish the rest of the game even though the other team already had it won.

Mike pulled up a chair next to them and poked around in his brown bag to get a preview of what he had for lunch. He took one look at Ryan and asked Joe, "What's wrong with him?"

"Oh, it's that bit about Randy," Ryan sighed. "That's just what we needed. With him gone, that leaves us with only eleven players. What if someone has to go on vacation or gets sick? We could end up forfeiting games right and left. How are we going to get through a year with only two reserves?"

"You're weird, Court," said Mike, biting into his sandwich. "First you tell everyone you don't think you'll stay with the team, and now you're worried sick because one guy quits."

"I want to play baseball this summer. But it seems like something keeps getting in the way," said Ryan.

"Don't complain," said Joe. "Think how Randy must feel. It's one thing if you decide you don't want to play. But when your parents tell you that you can't, wow! What kind of parents would do that to a guy?"

"I just talked to Randy and he said something about Art being the problem," said Mike. "You know, his dad was really mad about how late he got home from practice last night. But there must be something besides that. That's a dumb reason for making him quit."

"I wonder what else Art had to do with it," said Ryan.

"Who knows?" shrugged Mike. "Have you ever tried getting any information out of Randy? It's like playing twenty questions. I never met anyone who talks less than he does. Hey, Tracy! What do you know about all this?" he asked as Tracy finally emerged from the hot lunch line.

"You mean Randy? I heard Art blew it." It seemed

to Ryan that Tracy thought the whole thing was pretty funny. "The way I see it, Randy's out of baseball because Art doesn't know how to tell time," Tracy went on. "Well, I hope the great coach is proud of himself. Oh, excuse me, we're not supposed to call him 'Coach.' You know, my mom wasn't too thrilled about how late we got home last night, either."

"So Art lost track of time once," said Mike. "It happens to me all the time. I don't see why everyone's making such a big deal out of it. We're talking about twenty lousy minutes!"

"Yeah, I'd like to know what else is behind Randy's quitting," said Ryan. "I can't believe Randy's folks would come down so hard on him just for practicing late once. Maybe they know something about Art that we don't. But why would your dad pick him to coach if he was such a bad person?"

"I don't think dad knows him as well as he was pretending to," sniffed Tracy. "I think he just acted like he did so we would accept Art as the coach. Dad probably figured that was his best chance of getting out of having to coach us."

Ryan fired his paper bag into the wastebasket two tables away and got up to leave. "Great! So we're stuck with a coach that nobody wants, not even the parents. And we don't even know what it is about him that made the Olsons pull Randy off the team."

"If he had any brains at all, he would quit," said Tracy.

"You mean Art?" asked Joe. "I don't know. He seems like he goes out of his way to be friendly."

Tracy laughed as he poked at his hot dish with a fork. "You always have to watch out for people who try too hard to make friends."

3
The Last Straw

As usual, the Barnes City public pool was not opened until a couple of weeks after the warm weather arrived. Opening day was always a big event because this was no ordinary pool. It was more like a rectangular lake surrounded by a cement beach. Three lifeguard towers were spaced to patrol the entire half-block-long stretch of water. Besides being opening day, it was sunny and hot out, and as a result, even this huge pool was packed. Ryan found it impossible to swim in a straight line for long and had to weave around people like a slalom skier.

Ryan, Tracy, and Mike had each brought a younger brother to the pool. Those little guys always stayed until closing time, plus whatever extra minutes they could squeeze from the lifeguards with their pleading. But the older boys had swum their fill by midafternoon. They toweled off, put on T-shirts and shoes, and headed for the Burger House to fill the time until their brothers were done.

Mike pushed open the glass doors, which were covered with sticky fingerprints at about waist height, where small hands had touched them. But he stopped so suddenly that Ryan caught his chin on the back of Mike's head. "Don't look now," Mike started to whisper. But it was too late.

"Hey, guys!" called Art. "Come over and join me for a few minutes. There is something I want to discuss with you."

As far as Ryan was concerned, when an adult wanted to discuss something, it usually meant trouble. Tracy must have been thinking the same thing because he tried to back out the door. But Ryan and Mike had already shrugged and were walking over to Art's booth. Tracy pretended to pull a stone from his shoe and then followed them.

Art insisted that they first go ahead and order whatever it was they had come to buy, so the three of them waited in line for ice-cream cones. The coach must have long finished whatever he had been eating, if anything, because there weren't even crumbs on his table when the boys sat down next to him. A blinding glare washed over Ryan as he sat, and he wished Art could have found a spot that was out of the sun.

"How is the pool today?" asked Art. "And please don't tell me that it's wet."

The boys said nothing for a few seconds. Art had caught them by surprise, and they didn't know who should be their spokesman.

"Crowded and noisy," said Ryan, finally.

"But not bad," Mike added. "It's a good day for a swim."

"Say, I've been wanting to talk to you about a situation we have. I've been hearing some talk that Randy

Olson isn't going to play for us anymore, and I noticed he wasn't at our last practice."

"Yeah, I heard he was quitting," said Tracy. "How come?" Ryan thought he detected a nasty glint in his friend's expression. Whenever Tracy had that tight squint, it meant he was up to no good.

Art rubbed a corner of his eye as if he was trying to get out a piece of dirt. "I don't know. I hadn't gotten to know Randy at all yet. In fact, I was hoping you guys might know more about it than I do."

"His parents made him, that's about all I know," said Mike. "Randy doesn't say much about it. Or about anything else for that matter."

"Parents?" Art seemed surprised, but then quickly dismissed the subject with a wave of his hand. "Well, I didn't ask you over here to guess about Randy's reasons. But if he is serious about quitting, then that leaves us with only eleven players. That may cause problems."

"Yeah, I thought of that," said Ryan.

"Fortunately," smiled Art, "we may be able to make a bad situation work out for the best. At the church I go to, I met a family who moved into town about a month ago. They have a boy, Brad Chadwick, who happens to be your age and would very much like to play ball. Now this could be a perfect match. Our team needs a player; Brad doesn't know anyone and needs a team. I understand he lives pretty close to you fellas over on Basswood Avenue. So what do you think? Should I invite him to the next practice?"

"That depends. Is he any good?" asked Tracy.

Art laughed loudly. "Always a practical man, aren't you, Tracy? You've got a good business head on you. To be honest, I don't have the slightest idea what kind of player he is. But then we aren't asking anyone to be a superstar. We just want a good effort, and I think he can give us that. He might seem kind of awkward or out of place at first, of course. It's never easy to be an outsider breaking into a group."

That last statement struck a guilty nerve in Ryan. He wondered if Art was thinking about the cool reception the team had been giving him. But the coach gave no clues as to what he was thinking. He just kept up his good-natured smile and asked, "So what do you think?"

"Sounds OK to me," said Mike.

"Yeah, sure," Tracy said quickly. "Well, we got to run. The pool should be closing soon, and we have to pick up our little brothers."

But no sooner had they stepped outside than Tracy added, "That really burns me!"

Mike swept back his brown hair, which always fell into his eyes when it dried after swimming. "What's the big deal? We need another player. It won't hurt to give the new kid a break."

"What about Randy? Nobody gave him a break!" Tracy had deepset eyes to begin with, and when he spoke now they seemed to be dark, razor-thin slits.

"But there isn't anything we can do about Randy," said Ryan, trying to calm him.

Now that they were well out of range of the Burger House, Tracy was raising his voice. "Notice who couldn't care less that Randy had to quit! Something dirty is going on here. First, Randy has to quit because of something Art did, and Art just acts like that's fine with him. Then all of a sudden he happens to have this new guy ready to take Randy's place!"

Both Ryan and Mike stopped walking as they let this

new thought run through their minds. It was funny how Tracy could turn things around. Ryan had not been thinking that way at all. He figured the new boy would be a nuisance, one more new thing he would have to get used to this baseball season. But he had also sensed that another player was probably a good idea. And Art was looking out for some kid he didn't even know. Someone who would do that probably wasn't such a bad guy. It had only taken seconds for Tracy to wash all that away.

"He's wrecking the whole summer!" Tracy was going on. "It's like he had it all planned that way. He would probably be happy to be rid of us all so he could have everything his own way!"

"Yeah," said Mike. "He does seem to be acting kind of suspicious."

"I'm getting tired of this," Ryan moaned. "All I want to do is play baseball. All right, so this deal stinks. Art may be a crook for all I know, but what can you do about it besides quit? Nothing. And if you quit, you can't play baseball."

"I told you before, I'm figuring out a way to fix all this," said Tracy as they reached the pool.

Ryan turned away from the other two and walked down the wet concrete path to the shallow end of the pool. Suddenly irritable, he wondered why it had to be his brother who was such a brat about leaving. The swimming period had ended, but Danny was still standing in the water, driving the lifeguards crazy with his begging. One of them finally threatened never to let him back in the pool if he was still there at the count of three. Danny scrambled out as if he had just seen a shark in the water.

Ryan hardly paid attention to Danny as the two

waved good-bye to the Salesky boys and biked the final three blocks home. He was starting to feel strongly that he just wanted to play this summer, for Art or anybody. It didn't matter who. Now it seemed that it was Tracy, not Art, standing in the way of a peaceful summer. "God, don't let Tracy do something dumb. Or Art either," he whispered.

"What did you say?" hollered Danny, pumping his pedals hard in an effort to keep up with Ryan.

"Oh, nothing. I was just thinking about the Braves."

"Tracy doesn't like your new coach, does he?" puffed Danny.

"You keep quiet about that. Just don't say anything to anyone." The more Ryan thought about it, Art didn't seem like such a bad coach. Maybe he was a little pushy and a little strange. But he seemed to like coaching, and he always had time for it. That was one big difference between Art and Mr. Salesky. Art never acted as if he had something more important to get to. But Ryan did not want to take sides against Tracy, either. Tracy sometimes had a big head when it came to sports, but he wasn't really a bad friend.

Maybe they can finally patch things up, Ryan wished. *Maybe the new guy will fit in fine, and there won't be any trouble and we can get on with the season.*

Ryan could not have been more wrong. Joe Martinez's throwing arm saw to that. It all happened right in front of Ryan at the next practice. Ryan could only stand by helplessly as if he was watching a runaway car roll down a hill toward a house.

At first everything had gone fairly smoothly. School was out now, and all the guys seemed to have settled into a more relaxed mood. The players were getting used to Art, and he had most of them laughing with his chatter as he pitched batting practice. Art sent a rapid-fire stream of pitches to the plate, twenty to a batter, and each served up with some kind of comment.

"Here you go, Smith. A nice, juicy one just begging to be hit!"

"Swing easy, Ryan. That apartment building is only a quarter mile away, and we don't want to break any windows."

"That's the way to knock the shine off the ball, Perry."

"Easy on my ego, Tracy. Be a sport and miss one for a change."

Tracy had shown no signs of the bitterness he had held towards Art. All had gone surprisingly well with the new boy as well. Brad certainly was no Randy; he probably spoke more words in the first half hour than most of them had heard from Randy in a year. He was almost as tall as Tracy, which meant he was a good deal taller than the rest of the team, and he was fairly heavyset. His efforts at blending in with the team were not helped by his bright red hair and freckles. Still, no one went out of their way to be nasty to him.

Ryan knew that Mike and Smith were watching the newcomer more closely than most as he went through the batting drills. Those two were the top reserves on the team last season. Only Justin had played less. With Randy gone, that meant a starting spot would open up for one of them—unless, of course, Brad took it.

By the end of batting practice Ryan knew they were out of luck. Brad was no slugger, but he was good enough to beat them out of a starting job. It didn't seem to bother Mike that much, but Smith was far more self-conscious about his lack of skill, and he moped through several practice drills.

Although most of the Braves thought they knew what the opening game lineup would be, Art never spoke about positions or lineups. Except for Ryan, who was the only one who was interested in playing catcher, all the rest took a try at each position during fielding drills. It was not until this final practice was nearly over that Art finally got around to the most important position of all. "Who's interested in being a pitcher?"

Most of the Braves thought it was a silly question. It was only natural that their star player, Tracy, did the pitching. He had pitched every inning of every game for them the year before. No one else even moved while Tracy stepped to the mound where Art was waiting for him. Art waved the others over to their fielding and throwing drills, and asked Ryan to stay and catch Tracy's pitches.

Eager to show Art what he could do, Tracy wound up and fired hard. The ball popped into Ryan's mitt over the middle of the plate, and Tracy grinned proudly.

"Nice pitch," said Art. "But don't throw so hard until you get a few more warm-ups in."

Tracy rolled his eyes and deliberately lobbed the ball to Ryan.

"OK, I've seen high gear and low gear now," Art said. "Have you got an in-between speed you can go to for warming up?"

Ryan was glad Art was being cool about Tracy's smartalecky stuff. Tracy threw five more pitches and then Art gave him the word to "fire at will." Art encouraged Tracy on each pitch and when he told the boy to stop for the night, Ryan felt relieved. The practice had gone without problems. Maybe Tracy and Art could get along.

"Joe, let me see you over on the mound before you go!" called Art.

Like all the other Braves, Ryan had been so convinced that Tracy was the team's pitcher that he could not imagine what Art wanted with Joe. But then he heard the words that made him pound his floppy catcher's mitt in frustration. "Ryan, would you stay for a few more minutes and let Joe pitch a few?"

Ryan could not bring himself to look at Tracy. He could imagine that angry squint as Tracy tossed the ball to Joe and left the mound. *What are you doing, Art? You're blowing everything!* thought Ryan as he crouched behind the plate.

It was almost insulting for Art to have drafted Joe for this pitching tryout. Joe was a skinny boy with a dark complexion and black, curly hair who always looked as if he was ready to apologize to someone. He was almost too nice to be competitive. It had taken him all last season to cure his habit of ducking out of the batter's box as soon as the ball left the pitcher's hand. Joe was really quite coordinated when he got over his timidness, and it made it all the more frustrating to have him as a teammate. Sometimes he acted so surprised when he hit the ball that he almost forgot to run the bases.

As Ryan waited for Joe's first pitch, he felt as though he were being asked to humor his little brother. Joe had trouble believing that Art wanted him to pitch the ball, and he stood staring at Art and Tracy for the longest time. Finally he threw, and the ball smacked into Ryan's mitt.

Ryan was so surprised by the speed of the ball that he barely got his glove up in time to avoid being hit in the face. He pulled the ball out of his mitt and peered at it as if trying to figure out what was responsible for getting it to the plate so quickly. As he threw the ball back, he admitted to himself that Art really knew what he was doing. Joe must have developed his throwing arm over the past year and Art had spotted it during the throwing drills.

Art gave Joe the same lecture he had given Tracy about warming up before throwing hard. Joe nodded sheepishly and continued throwing. He had a strange motion, in that when he reared back, his glove hand swept the air in front of him as if clearing the air of gnats. When Joe finished throwing, Ryan was not quite willing to say he was as good a pitcher as Tracy. But he knew he was not too far from it.

Art patted Joe on the shoulder and called off the practice. "OK, fellas, the real fun starts at 6:30 sharp on Thursday. I want all of you to get to the diamond at least twenty minutes ahead of that. This will give us time to figure out which bench to sit on and important stuff like that." He grinned. "Remember we're playing on that field where we held our first practice."

Joe had not yet moved from the mound. Apparently he still could not believe what Art had told him about his possibilities as a pitcher. Brad finally jarred him back to reality by slapping him on the shoulder. "Quite an arm you've got. Glad you're on my side. My name is Brad. What was your name again?" Joe nodded absently until it dawned on him that Brad was waiting for something. "Oh, uh, I'm Joe."

Ryan turned away from the mound and walked over to Tracy. Although he had not actually heard Art say anything about the pitching situation, Ryan could tell Tracy knew the pitching chores were no longer his sole property. Tracy was squinting and clenching his teeth, and he stared at Art as the coach packed the balls and bats into his station wagon and drove off.

It didn't occur to Ryan to be sorry for Tracy or even happy for Joe. He was worried about the team. Tracy had been doing a lot of talking about Art before, but he hadn't done anything yet. This might have been the last straw.

Brad could not have chosen a worse time to approach Tracy and Ryan. But he had noticed all the boys riding off in twos and threes, and it reminded him of what Art had told him. "Art tells me that you guys live only a couple of blocks away from me."

Tracy squinted at him coldly. "Who cares? I'll pick my own friends. Come on Ryan, Mike."

Ryan went with him feeling terrible and worried that the summer was going down the drain again. As they walked their bikes over the blacktop, he looked back at Brad, who was standing alone on the ball diamond. Brad must have seen him because he gave a quick wave. Ryan thought about waving back. Brad had just been a convenient target for Tracy's anger, and hadn't deserved that kind of treatment, even if he was a loudmouth. But then Mike asked him what time it was, and he turned back toward his friends without lifting his hand.

4
Eavesdropping

It did not take Tracy long to come up with a plan. In fact, Ryan suspected that Tracy had been scheming all along but had never quite found the nerve to carry anything out. Art's latest blunder, however, had changed that; it was a declaration of war.

Ryan knew who was calling and why even before his mom reached the ringing phone. In cold tones, Tracy asked if Ryan could join the group that was meeting at his house. He did not need to say more.

It was a tight fit in Tracy's bedroom, with Ryan and Mike sprawled across the bed, Tracy in the chair by his desk, and Troy and Smith on the floor leaning against the wall. Ryan wasn't surprised that Joe had not been invited when he remembered the scene at the pitching mound.

Tracy outlined his case against Art while leaning over the back of his chair. Art had said that Tracy had a good business head, but Ryan thought he also had potential as a lawyer. He had prepared this plan and this speech thoroughly. First, he reported that he had talked to Randy and confirmed that Randy's parents had made him quit because of Art. As for the details, Tracy said that it was a family matter that the Olsons did not care to discuss. Then he went on about how unfeeling Art had been about Randy, lashed out at Art's "stupid" rules in practice, and hinted that the coach was trying to push new kids on the team so that it wouldn't be their team anymore.

"And now he's got it in for me." Tracy was speaking slowly and calmly. Instinct must have told him that the more reasonable he appeared, the less reasonable Art would appear. "He decided to put Joe in as pitcher instead of me. Why? What have I ever done to him? Didn't I do well last year, considering how few runs we scored? But now I can't pitch, and no one gives me a reason. All I want is a reason. Joe never asked to pitch; it was all Art's idea. Just look what that guy's been doing! He's going to mess up the whole season if he hasn't messed it up already. Don't give me any more of this 'Wait it out until we get used to each other' stuff! We've tried that, and it's only getting worse."

"What should we do?" asked Smith, glowing with excitement. Every so often Ryan couldn't stand Smith. He was the sort who loved to get in on any sort of conflict. Ryan guessed that his disappointment at seeing Brad take his starting position was making this all the more important to him.

Tracy slowly broke into a smile, as if Art were already boxed up and loaded on a truck headed out of town. "If I can count on you guys to back me up, we can have him dumped off the team in a week."

Mike and Ryan exchanged a quick, anxious glance that Tracy spotted. "Don't worry," he said. "We're not going to do anything against the law. Listen. Our first game is Thursday night, right? Well, it's simple. We don't show up. I mean, *nobody* shows up for the game!"

"Hey, decent! We're going on strike!" said Smith, clapping his hands.

"Knock it off, Smith! You want the whole world to hear us?" scolded Tracy.

Ryan shook his head. "The only ones we're hurting by quitting are us."

"Oh, no, we're not," laughed Tracy. Although he had tried to quiet Smith, he was having trouble keeping his own voice down. "When Art sees that it's just that fat creep and him waiting at the game, he'll get the message. Those two will be so embarrassed they won't show their faces around after that. We don't have to quit for the whole summer. Believe me, it's only going to take one game and then Art will be begging us to let him quit. Then the new kid won't be hanging around anymore, and the best part is, I think my dad could take over the job now. He's almost done with all that traveling, so he can't use that as an excuse. And with Art gone, we can get Randy back on the team. It's perfect!"

Ryan was sweeping his hair with a comb, wondering how he was going to say what he had to say. Somehow he couldn't seem to work up a hatred of Art. Fortunately, Mike opened his mouth first.

"You know, some of the guys think Art is kind of fun, for an adult," he said. "How are you going to get them to go along with this?"

"No problem. I keep telling you this is perfect. All we have to do is let them know what's going on, especially the way Art has been ignoring Randy.

Besides, they'll see that they don't have much choice. If the five of us don't play, they won't have a team anyway. The sooner they go along with us, the sooner we can get this whole thing straightened out."

Smith suddenly stood up and puffed out his chest. "OK, fellas, the real fun starts at 6:30 sharp on Thursday," he croaked in his lowest voice. "I want to see all of you there twenty minutes ahead of time so I can figure out how to keep my act together."

Ryan had to admit that Smith could do some great imitations. Somehow, though, he did not feel like laughing.

What he did feel like doing was riding his bike, alone. When the meeting broke up, he rushed off to his house and jumped on his bike before anyone could ask where he was going. Ryan had to get away from everyone.

He cruised the streets, distracted by his thoughts so that he wasn't riding as carefully as he should have. Something was not quite right with this business of Randy. Ryan knew Tracy too well not to notice that. It just wasn't Tracy's nature to make such a big deal on someone else's behalf. He was just using Randy's predicament for his own ends. Not that he was totally selfish; he probably would have backed Ryan in a similar situation. But for Tracy to be doing this because of Randy, whom he didn't know that well?

Ryan was nearly jolted off his bike when the wheels ran over a gaping pothole. He stopped to make sure there was no damage to his bike, and then looked around him. He was only a few blocks from Randy's house. Why not find out for himself what Randy's story was?

The Olsons' house stood on a corner lot, with

sidewalk on two sides. Ryan pedaled around the side of the house toward the front door. Subconsciously, he noticed that the car parked in front was familiar—and then he slammed his foot on the sidewalk to stop himself as he realized whose car it was. It belonged to Art, and there was the coach on the front step. *Why am I always running into him?* Ryan thought. Fortunately, he was largely shielded from Art's view by a large spruce tree, so he stayed in its shadow.

Art was talking to someone through the porch screen. As Ryan bent closer, he saw that it was an older man with gray hair and glasses that he kept polishing as he stood listening to Art. Ryan wondered why the man hadn't opened the door for the coach. It wasn't until he heard snatches of conversation that he found it was Randy's dad, not his grandfather.

Ryan knew that he should leave them alone. But there was something about the tension in the scene that froze him to where he crouched at the side of the porch. The strain of eavesdropping was made easier when the screen door finally opened and the men moved toward the end of the porch nearest Ryan.

"I want to make it clear that I'm not here to question your judgment as parents or anything like that," Art was saying cordially. "It's just that we feel bad about Randy leaving the team. Most of the boys are pretty down about it. So I wanted to come and talk, to make sure it wasn't something that I or anyone on the team might have caused."

Ryan heard a woman's voice next, and she didn't sound any friendlier than Mr. Olson had looked. "It's a long, involved story, Mr. Horton. I don't think there's much point in going into it all."

"Don't worry about my time," laughed Art. "It's

not as valuable as all that. I don't want to impose on your schedule, but as far as I'm concerned, I could stay all evening—if it would help clear things up."

"All right, fella," Mr. Olson's voice seemed to carry a challenge. "You barged in here asking for it, so I don't see any reason why I should go easy on you."

"Fair enough," said Art. It didn't sound much like Art's normal voice. Ryan figured the coach hadn't expected such a hassle when he came over to visit. He was probably squirming in his seat, if the Olsons had even offered him one. It was hard to imagine Art uncomfortable, and Ryan almost risked peeking over the hedge into the screened porch to get a look at him.

"If you really want to know the truth, then," said Mr. Olson, "it does have a great deal to do with you. The reason, one reason anyway, that we pulled him off the team was because of how late he came home that night. There's nothing so important about baseball that boys have to practice that late and risk riding their bikes home in the dark!"

"That was dumb on my part," Art answered. "Let me explain—"

"Let *me* explain," Mrs. Olson broke in. "Randall is under orders never to ride in the dark."

"In the future, we'll be sure to—" Art began.

Mrs. Olson didn't seem to have heard. "About seven years ago, when we lived on the other side of town, our daughter Julie was out riding her bike one night. It was dark and she was coming home from a friend's house. She wasn't the careless type. She had lights and reflectors on her bike. But there was a driver on the road who wasn't watching. Some people have said he'd been drinking. He claimed he never saw her until it was too late. Well, it was too late, all right! For four weeks we didn't know if she would live through it. She finally made it, but not all the way. She's off at college, crippled now. She won't be able to walk the rest of her life!"

There was a long silence. Ryan was shocked. He hadn't known much about Randy's family—certainly not this. Finally Art said, "I'm sorry."

"We've been through all the sympathy," said Mr. Olson sharply. "I mean to tell you that we won't let it happen again."

Art cleared his throat a couple of times and said, "I really am sorry for that. It's no excuse, of course, but it was my first night of coaching, and I was having such fun I just got carried away."

"Do you get carried away with your preaching, too?" Mr. Olson snapped.

Ryan's conscience had nearly talked him into leaving until he heard this. Preaching? He risked a look into the porch and caught a brief glimpse of Art's puzzled expression.

"I'm afraid I don't understand."

"Randy told us that you wanted the boys to study Bible verses," said Mrs. Olson. "No sense denying it, I wrote down the passage right here. John 8:7."

Before Art could answer, Mr. Olson continued the attack, his voice rising. "We're not about to stand still while someone sneaks his religion on our boy. We've gone the whole route on this, Mr. Horton! Used to be in church every Sunday. But not now. What's the point? There's no God in heaven if something like that happens to a person as nice as Julie. Or, if there is, I don't think much of him. So we don't talk about that nonsense in this house anymore, and no one will force it on our child. That, Mr. Horton, is why Randy will not play baseball this summer!"

Ryan heard the porch door creak open and braced himself for a quick sprint back to his bike. But Art apparently wasn't taking the hint, for Ryan saw only Mr. Olson next to the door.

"If I understand you correctly, we have two problems," said Art, more calmly than Ryan would have believed possible. "One, I was an irresponsible coach, and two, I was pushing my beliefs on the team."

"That about covers it," said Mr. Olson.

"Before you get rid of me, let me try and clear this up. First, let me apologize one more time for running practice late. If it ever gets close to being dark while we're still at practice, I'll take Randy home—I'll take all the boys home myself. May be a tight squeeze, but we'll make it.

"As for the other issue, I can't even imagine what you've been through about your daughter. You've been hit with some tough questions, and it's probably not in my power to even talk about them. I will say that I am a Christian, and that it's important to me. But you don't have to worry about me preaching. That's something the parents should take care of. May I ask you, though, if you think a person has a right to act out what he believes?"

"That depends," said Mr. Olson. The screen door clicked shut again.

"Well, listen: It's part of my belief that Randy is important, that all people are. You make him feel that at home, but I think that he—and each of us—needs to feel it from friends, too. Well, I promised not to preach, so I guess I'd better stick to that. All I want to do with the team is make a place outside the home where all the boys can feel they're worth something. I thank you for your time, and . . ."

Ryan did not wait to hear more. He knew that was his cue for a long-overdue exit. He walked his bike for a few yards back the way he had come, and then climbed on and rode off. *So much for Tracy's argument about Art not caring for Randy,* he thought. *I have to hand it to Art. He really tried. And this whole thing isn't really his fault.*

He figured that if he spread the news he'd heard, he might be able to head off the strike. But he knew before he reached home that he would not tell.

He didn't want to make Tracy mad. Besides, the whole thing would be too uncomfortable. No one among his friends talked about religion. Except for Mike, no one went to the same church that he did. The questions Ryan had heard from the Olsons about God were disturbing. Somehow he didn't feel he should be talking about doubts like that.

Worse yet, he felt he could identify with Art. Regardless of what the Olsons had said, he still felt the same way about God that Art did. What if everyone really did hate Art, after Ryan let it be known that he really admired the guy in some ways? Ryan didn't dare risk it. There was only one way Ryan could see out of this mess. That was for Randy to come back to the team.

But as the hours ticked by, no one heard from Randy. The first game of the season approached, and with it, a showdown.

5
On Strike

The same group of boys that had gathered on Tuesday met again Thursday evening in Tracy's room. Joe Martinez was also with them, squeezing between Troy and Smith on the floor. The fact that Joe would join them showed how effective their one-game strike was going to be. The entire Braves team, except for Brad, who didn't know about the boycott, and Jimmy Amadibele, who hadn't shown up, was sitting out.

The plan probably could not have been carried out by anyone but Tracy. He was the leader of the team, and not just because he could play better than anyone else. When Tracy stepped onto a ball park or a basketball court, he had a way of taking command. He knew all the rules and tricks of the game and when he wanted something done, most of his teammates figured it was a good idea to do it.

By the time Tracy finished telling everyone his opinion of the new coach, no one felt like standing up for Art. Ryan squirmed the whole time, feeling as though his insides were boiling. Tracy's pathetic tale of how Randy had to quit the team because of Art was the clincher. That even started Joe wondering. Tracy further swayed Joe by insisting that Art had brought him to the mound that night just to cause hard feelings between them.

"Ha! I would love to see Art's face about now," Tracy said. The digital clock on his bed whirred and flipped over a new number. It was now 6:20.

"I'd like to see Brad's face, too," chimed in Smith. "That guy thinks he's wormed his way onto *our* team and then, *wham*! It's just the coach and him!"

Ryan pulled out a pillow from under the covers and leaned against the wall, cushioning his head with it. He shut his eyes, doing his best to ignore Smith. He had not come over to celebrate or gloat about this strike business. It was nothing more than a chore that had to be done before things got even more out of control. It did not strike him as funny to think about what Brad or Art was going through. In fact, he was worried more than anything about what his mom would think of this whole thing. He had not told her about it nor had he even told her that there was a game scheduled tonight. Sooner or later he would have some explaining to do, and he was not sure that she would understand. She had been after him before about standing up to Tracy and his wild ideas. Actually, one reason he was over at Tracy's was so he would not have to be around to answer questions in case the phone rang.

Just then a phone did ring, and Ryan sat up quickly. The room had suddenly gone quiet, making the second ring sound as if the phone were in the room instead of downstairs. "It's probably Art," laughed Tracy nervously.

All of the boys could hear the footsteps crossing the floor to the stairway door, and they knew the call was for one of them.

"It's for you, Tracy."

"Tell him I'll call back later," Tracy called, and the others tried to stifle their giggles.

"But it's Randy Olson, and he says it's very important."

The smiles vanished instantly, as if someone had turned them all off with the flick of a switch. Tracy stepped over Troy and wedged the door open just enough so that he could get out of the room. As soon as the leader of the strike left the room, there was a different feeling in the air. No one spoke as they waited for him to get back with the news. Several were fidgeting and Ryan knew he wasn't the only one who thought, deep down, that this strike was not such a grand idea after all.

It was a different Tracy Salesky who edged his way through the door a minute later, Ryan noticed. Before, he had been so excited that, even in that cramped room, he had been unable to keep still and had been grinning with complete confidence in his plan. Now he looked like a boy who had studied all night for a test only to find he had read the wrong book.

"Randy is back on the team again," he mumbled. "He called from the corner store by the park and said we'd better get over there quick or we are going to forfeit the game."

"But what about Art?" asked Smith. "I thought Randy . . ."

Smith didn't finish the thought, and Tracy had such a glazed look in his eyes that Ryan thought he had not even heard Smith. While the others sat waiting for

Tracy to decide what to do, Ryan sprang off the bed. It had not taken him long to see that the strike was over. Randy had been one of the main arguments for the strike, and now that reason was gone. "Come on, let's go!" he said, nudging Mike off the bed. "We've only got a few minutes. Tracy, can your dad drive us? We'll never make it in time on our bikes."

"Uh, I guess so. Yeah. I mean, I'd better ask," said Tracy.

"Troy and Smith, come with us. Mike and Joe, can you round up the rest?"

"Yeah, I think I can get my dad to—"

"Then let's go!"

If Mr. Salesky had been looking forward to a quiet, relaxing evening after having returned from ten hectic days of out-of-town travel, he was going to be sorely disappointed. He had thinned out the lettuce in the garden and was doing the same to the carrots when the boys charged into the backyard.

Everyone seemed to be shouting at once. Ryan finally got the other two to be quiet and Tracy blurted out that there was a baseball game tonight and that it was due to start in a couple of minutes. "Can you take us, quick?" asked Ryan.

No sooner had Mr. Salesky started to say yes than Tracy pressed the car keys into his hand and all four boys hurled themselves into his little Vega, pleading with him to hurry. Mr. Salesky trotted over to the driver's side and backed the car out.

"Oh, no!" he said, staring at his hands as he lifted them off the steering wheel. They were caked with wet dirt from the garden, and now the steering wheel was covered with muddy handprints.

"Please! We'll have to forfeit if we don't get there

now!"

The boys kept urging him on, and Mr. Salesky had to fight the notion of speeding and cruising through stop signs. "Didn't you boys know you had a game tonight?" he kept asking over and over.

"It's a long story," Tracy said finally above the roar from the back seat. Ryan and Smith had started shouting at cars in front of them to get out of the way.

Finally, Mr. Salesky had heard all he could take. He slammed on the brakes and pulled over to the side of the road. "I'm not driving another inch until you stop acting like a bunch of fools! I don't care if it does make you late!"

Ryan wanted to scream "Come on!" and he could only keep quiet by holding his breath. It wasn't until he felt his lungs bursting that Mr. Salesky put the car back into forward gear and calmly moved back into traffic.

It's lucky we're up first tonight or we would have had to forfeit, thought Ryan as they pulled up next to the field. Randy was already at bat. Brad was there, too, of course, along with Jimmy who, it turned out, couldn't resist coming to the park to see if everyone else was really on strike.

The Giants' pitcher threw a hard pitch and Randy took it for a strike. "Three is all you get, " said the umpire when it became apparent that Randy wasn't moving from the batter's box. "Next batter!"

Randy whirled around in surprise and trotted back to the bench. "I was so worried about whether you guys were going to get here or not that I wasn't even paying attention," he said.

When Ryan finally drummed up the courage to look for Art, he saw that the coach was not smiling. Still, Art got to his feet, sent Jimmy up to bat and approached Randy. "Don't worry about it, Randy. It's hard to concentrate when you're waiting for reinforcements."

"Ryan, could you come here?" said Art after Jimmy had stepped in to hit. Ryan was expecting the worst. Without that smile, Art looked older and, well, almost dangerous. Ryan saw those biceps stretching the sleeves of Art's shirt and realized he had never made anyone that strong angry at him before. He didn't like the feeling. He was working through an apology in his mind when Art held up his clipboard full of scratched-out lineups. "Tracy is up next, and you're to follow. Start getting your muscles loose so you don't hurt yourself."

Ryan nodded and ran over to the bat pile, glad to get away from those eyes.

It was obvious that little Jimmy had been listening to Art's advice in practice. He clenched his teeth and swung at all three pitches thrown to him. The only one he made contact with, however, was the first pitch, which he fouled back behind the Giants' bench. He too was out on strikes.

"That's the way to go up there swinging!" said Art, greeting Jimmy with his old warm smile and a pat on the back. "Glad to see someone's been listening to me. You keep that up and you'll have your share of hits before the season is over."

Mike still had not shown up with the rest of the Braves, so it was crucial that the next couple of batters get on base. If they made their third out, they would have to go to the field, and without nine players to put on the field, they would have to forfeit.

Tracy did his part by lining a single past the second baseman. Ryan then made one last practice swing and took his stance at the plate. He had watched the Giants' pitcher throw to Tracy and decided he could hit against him without much trouble. The pitcher may have been a big kid with a windmill windup, but he didn't get that much speed on the ball. Ryan let a pitch go by for a ball and kept glancing from the pitcher to the rutted road that wound down the hill past the apartments. What was taking Mike so long?

The next three pitches landed well out of the strike zone and Ryan flipped his bat toward the bench as he jogged to first base. When he stepped on the base and turned back towards home plate, he saw Smith coming up to bat. Smith was such a poor hitter that Ryan was ready to concede the game. Luckily, the Giants' pitcher had not yet found the strike zone and Smith also walked to load the bases. Troy then walked to score a run.

Still there was not a car to be seen on that dirt road. Ryan sighed heavily as he stood with one foot on second base and clapped his hands, trying to spark some hope in his teammates. They were down to their last batter, Brad. It didn't matter if he made an out or hit a home run. If Mike didn't come soon, Brad was the last batter, and the Braves would lose.

Brad waited on the first two pitches, and they were both balls. Finally the pitcher floated a much slower pitch in, and it headed straight for the plate. Brad waved at it and missed by at least a foot.

Ryan couldn't figure that out at all. From what he had seen in practice, he was sure that Brad was a better hitter than he had shown by that foolish swing. An outside pitch was thrown for ball three, and then Brad grounded a pitch down the first base line. It rolled near the Braves' bench, and Art scooped it up and returned it to the pitcher. Three balls, two strikes. Ryan saw that both Tracy and Smith were staring down the road, paying no attention to Brad. Still no sign of the others.

Brad fouled off another pitch, and then the Giants' shortstop ran over to talk to the pitcher. When he left the mound a few seconds later, he was looking at the Braves' bench and grinning, and so was the pitcher. The big right-hander's next pitch made it obvious what they had been talking about. They would walk Brad on purpose, and win the game by forfeit.

By this time Ryan was convinced that the Giants' pitcher was easy to hit, and it bothered him to have to lose to such a poor team. But Brad reached out and poked at the outside pitch, barely ticking it with the end of his bat. As the Giants' catcher chased it back to the backstop, both Tracy and Smith saw a car turn into the road by the apartments. "Here they come!"

The pitcher heard their shout and quickly went into his warmup. It would take the car a couple of minutes yet to reach the ball field, and the umpire would not allow the Braves that much time between batters. Taking no chances this time, he lobbed a pitch a good five feet in back of Brad. But Brad had figured out what the pitcher was doing, and he swung his bat anyway.

"Strike three!" shouted the umpire. "That's three outs for the Braves. Giants are up."

Smith was howling over Brad's crazy swing until Ryan explained to him what Brad had done. By striking out, he had made the Braves take the field. The umpire had to allow the Braves' pitcher a dozen warm-up tosses, and that would give the car enough time to arrive. Already it was drawing near, bouncing over the ruts.

Tracy walked over to the mound, but Art called him back. "You can pitch next inning, Tracy. I can't let you throw until you've had a chance to warm up properly."

Ryan looked on in amazement as Randy went to the mound. Art must have had him warming up before the game, when no one else showed up on time. Randy looked about as awkward as any pitcher Ryan had ever seen. None of his warm-up pitches were over the plate. But on the eleventh throw, Ryan heard the car doors open and some wild cheering from inside the car. Six boys tumbled out, running as if the car were due to explode in three seconds.

"Three of you come over here, and the rest just find a position out there that hasn't been taken," Art shouted. The team arranged themselves on the ball diamond with Tracy at first base and Mike at shortstop.

As the Giants stepped up to bat, Ryan saw Mr. Salesky walk over to where Mr. Sherry was staring wearily over the top of his car. There was a lot of nodding and head-shaking among those two.

Randy found no better luck throwing strikes to the first batter than he had during his warmup. He walked the first two batters without throwing a strike. When he finally got one over on the third batter, the pitch was pounded into center field for a double. Tracy kept staring over at Art after each ball that Randy threw, but Art ignored him. After Randy walked two more batters, Art ran to the mound and Ryan joined the conference. "Don't worry about the walks; you've saved the game just by being here. But you don't have to throw so hard, Randy. Let them hit the ball and give your fielders a chance to help you."

Randy nodded and began throwing much more easily. The strikes started to come. The Giants hit two more line drives for singles, and Randy walked one more batter, but the inning finally ended when Tracy fielded a ground ball and Troy caught two flies in center field.

It did not take long for the Braves to overcome the Giants' 5-1 first-inning lead. A double by Randy brought in two runs in the second to bring them within two points. Then Tracy went in to pitch and had no trouble with the Giants' hitters. They did not even threaten to score for the rest of the game. Ryan, meanwhile, hit a home run, his first ever, and Tracy singled with the bases loaded to put the Braves ahead. By the time the seven-inning game ended, the Braves led comfortably by a score of 8 to 5.

Afterward, the Braves dutifully lined up to honor the league tradition of shaking hands with the other team. Ryan waded through the long line of dejected Giants and then noticed that Art had joined the Braves' line. It had never struck him until then that, although all coaches insisted their teams shake hands after a game, he had never seen a coach take part before.

Mr. Salesky had always had the team crowd around him after a game for a few last comments, so the Braves automatically gathered around Art at the Braves' bench. There was not any of the usual jostling and pounding that came after most victories, though. Everyone was waiting to see what Art would say about their attempted strike.

"I guess we showed them what a well-organized team can do," Art said. "After the way you guys entered the scene they must think they just played a volunteer fire department." The boys laughed nervously, still not sure what Art was thinking. Ryan thought Art seemed more business-like than usual, staring at his clipboard as he spoke.

"Look, I'm not sure I know what this was all about

tonight,'' Art started to say.

''It was just a mistake,'' Ryan blurted.

''Really, it's all been cleared up now,'' added Mike eagerly.

''That's nice to hear,'' said Art, sounding as though he did not believe it. ''I would appreciate it, though, that if there are some problems in the future you would talk to me about them. We don't always have to agree, but . . . Well, good game,'' he said suddenly. ''I'll see you next week. Will someone help lug the bats and balls to my car?''

Mr. Salesky was beaming over his son's pitching performance. ''You boys played well,'' he said. ''Maybe later on someone can tell me why I had to set a land speed record to get over here. But for now, if you still have any energy left, why don't all of you scoot over to McGraw's corner store and I'll get you a treat?''

''Decent!'' shouted Smith. Those who had bikes rode them while the latecomers trotted across the field toward the store. It would take less time for them to run there than it would for a car to wind through that rutted road.

Mr. Salesky walked alone toward his car, flipping the keys in his hands. As he started the car, he noticed one of the Braves still standing near the bench. He recognized him as the new kid, and shouted, ''Hey, son! Go on and join them. I'm treating all of you!''

Brad started to shake his head, but Ryan had seen what was going on. ''Come on, Brad!'' he shouted with a wave. He called to the group of boys who were leaping and howling their way across the sparse grass of the outfield. ''Hey, we can't leave out the guy who saved the game for us!''

Brad was not the fastest runner, and by the time he

reached the others, who had slowed to a walk while waiting for him, Ryan and Troy had finished explaining just how Brad had saved the game.

Tracy, who was always impressed by a good piece of strategy, said, "That was quick thinking. Not many people would have thought to swing at an impossible pitch. You know, when we figure up batting averages at the end of the year, we'll let you count that as a hit instead of a strikeout. Come on, let's beat dad!"

But as Brad huffed to keep up with his teammates who were congratulating him, his smile showed that, at the present time, he couldn't care less about his batting average.

The Braves were hoping to hear how Randy happened to rejoin the team. But no sooner had they flopped down on the sidewalk outside the store with their bottles of pop feeling cool in their hands than Randy gulped his down and headed for his bike. "Gotta get home before dark," he explained.

It took most of the week and a lot of stubborn questioning before the Braves managed to badger Randy into telling most of the story of Art Horton's visit to the Olson house. Ryan felt a little guilty about eavesdropping that night, so he acted as if the whole thing were news to him too.

Randy even managed to tell his sister Julie's story, and Art's reaction to it. When he finally finished, Smith asked, "So why did your folks change their minds?"

Randy shrugged. "They didn't say much to me about the Braves after that, but late last night they told me I could play in the first game. No, I don't know what changed their minds. Art did, I guess."

"It's not necessary. That's all in the past," said Art as Ryan tried to make a formal apology for the team at practice. "Maybe we know each other a little better now. I will tell you one thing, though," he said sternly to the group gathered around him. "I'm tired of being the target of all this abuse. From now on, you aren't going to have me to pick on!" Without another word, Art stomped over to his car and climbed in.

"What's he doing! Is he quitting?" whispered Mike.

But seconds later he was back, carrying a large, rolled-up sheet of paper. He worked the rubber band off and held up the picture. His huge grin was answered by the Braves when they saw that it was a shot of baby Ryan blowing out his birthday candles. His cheeks were puffed up as though he were going to pop, and his eyes bugged out of his face as he strained to douse all the flames. "Here is your throwing target for tonight, gentlemen. Aim for the cheeks!"

"How did you get that?" gasped Ryan.

"Mothers are wonderful people," he said with a wink. "Let's go, now. Troy, Ryan, Joe, Brad, and Jimmy, take this fine portrait to the wall and start throwing. The rest of you take fielding practice. Except for Tracy and Ryan." Ten heads turned toward the boys he had named. "I'd like you two to do the hitting for me for a bit."

Art stood behind the boys as they sent high, bouncing hits at the infielders. Tracy hit balls to the first base side and Ryan to the third base side. After a couple of hits Art said, "Keep hitting while I talk to you. Actually, I asked you to hit so we could talk without the others hearing us." Ryan glanced suspiciously back at him, then sent a hard grounder to Smith.

"I've felt a little friction between us since the first

time we met, and I admit it's partly my fault. I've got to remember to explain things more thoroughly. Keep on hitting. I'll be honest, I'm guessing that you guys are the team leaders, and that you had a big part in last Thursday's little drama." Tracy started to protest, but Art made a swinging motion with his hands while nodding at the bat. Tracy went back to hitting, but he said, "It was my idea, not Ryan's."

"But it's partly my fault, too, I guess," said Ryan. He was having trouble concentrating on his hitting, and missed the ball completely on his next swing. "I was the one who started talking about quitting on you in the first place."

Art stopped the conversation until Ryan had a chance to hit a couple of solid grounders. "Like I said, I'm not concerned about what's past, except that I would like to know how we got to that point."

"I guess it started when you dumped Tracy as pitcher," said Ryan. He figured he might as well be honest and get to the bottom of this. "He was the pitcher all last year, and he did a good job for a lousy team."

"Ask anyone; I'm the best player on the team," said Tracy.

"I don't have to ask," laughed Art. "I've got eyes. So you thought I brought Joe in to pitch just to get at you? Better hit one to Mike, Tracy, he's starting to look bored. I should have told you my two reasons. First, Joe isn't nearly the athlete you are, Tracy, but he does have a good arm. I've watched him throw against that wall, and it almost hurts to see my picture taking some of those hits. He might even be a touch faster than you. You know that Joe can't contribute as much with his bat or his fielding as you can, so it makes sense to let him use his arm. That gives him a better chance to enjoy a little success. The other reason is that I need both of you to pitch."

"We only needed one pitcher last year," said Ryan. Since Tracy had cleared him of any blame for the strike, he felt like backing him up.

"Do you ever wonder why you never see me throw very hard?" asked Art. "I used to be a pitcher, but now I have trouble even bending that arm. That's what comes from throwing too hard and too often at an early age. Eighteen games is too much strain on a young arm, I'm afraid. It would be better for both you and Joe if you pitch every other game."

"Well, if I'm such a great athlete, why did you put me on second base for the next game? Third base and shortstop are where the action is," said Tracy.

"That may be true on the pro level," said Art, "but I don't think that this league is quite that caliber. My guess is that there aren't many boys who will get a bat around when they hit against Joe. Since most boys hit right-handed, that means most of the balls will be hit to the second base side."

Ryan knew how Tracy appreciated good sports strategy.

Tracy stopped hitting for a moment. "I guess maybe I didn't understand what you were doing."

"Glad we could talk," said Art. He took the bat from Tracy and held his hand out for Ryan's. "Your turn to field. Now that we have that straightened out, we can go to the next problem. When practice is over, I'll tell you why Tracy will be benched in game four, and why Ryan will always bat ninth."

Both Ryan and Tracy spun around, their mouths hanging open.

"Don't worry," said Art. "You'll love my strategy!"

6
Heckling Points

It took the Braves only two more games to match their entire win total of the year before. Following their opening victory was a 9-5 win over the Dragons and a surprising 5-2 win over the Rangers. The Rangers had finished first the year before, but apparently some of their best players had moved on to the league for older boys.

Ryan had clipped out the most recent standings in the newspaper, as had most of the Braves. It didn't matter that the paper printed only the records and scores of the games without mentioning names or details. That one listing, "Braves 3-0," was proof to the world of what they had accomplished.

There had been some wide-eyed gawks before the second game when Smith, Mike, and Justin were put into the starting lineup and Troy, Brad, and Perry went to the bench. It wasn't until the middle of the third game that Ryan saw Art was serious about having no starters, reserves or pinch hitters. Everyone took turns starting, and everyone got a chance to play several innings of every game. The pitchers were taking turns on the mound, Joe surviving a shaky start against the Dragons and Tracy throwing well against the Rangers. Ryan wasn't sure if it was the system or the winning that was responsible, but he could not remember ever having so much fun in league baseball.

He had not been on the field more than two minutes during the game against the Barons when he sensed this game would be different. Jerry Gordon and Chuck Brock were wearing black and red Baron T-shirts, and the sight of them brought scowls to most of the Braves. Those were the kind of guys who kicked books out of your hand onto the sidewalk and then laughed about it.

The Braves were supposed to be in the field to start the game, but the Barons did not allow them any practice time. They stayed on the infield, throwing the ball around, snapping their gum, and spitting on the base paths. Ryan did not even want to go near them.

Art was no help at all. He sat scribbling on his clipboard on the end of the low bench with its green paint almost completely peeled off. After a quick glance at his watch, he whistled the team to gather around him. He took a deep breath of air, as if savoring it, and then rubbed his hands together. "What a night! Great night to be outdoors and playing a little baseball. I envy you guys! Wish I could be out there myself."

"I wish you could, too," said Smith. "Then we could really knock the ball down their throats!"

"It's too good an evening for losing tempers." Art smiled. "Pay no attention to our worthy opponents. We're here to play baseball, not to get into a spitting contest."

Ryan laughed along with the rest. He could feel his

stomach settling a bit now that he knew Art was aware of their opponents and was not bothered by them.

Art then read off the lineup and grinned as he said each name, as if this player were a secret weapon about to be sprung on the opponent. Tonight's lineup card was full of erasures and scratched-out names, so it was obvious that Art had been having trouble getting it right. But the list he finally settled on was:

1. Troy	second base
2. Brad	left field
3. Dave	right field
4. Justin	first base
5. Smith	center field
6. Mike	third base
7. Randy	shortstop
8. Joe	pitcher
9. Ryan	catcher

All eyes immediately turned to Tracy. Never in his sports career had he been put on the bench to start the game, and most expected to see some show of temper from him. Ryan wasn't worried, though. Art had already explained his system of rotation to everyone. Although Tracy was not thrilled with the idea, at least he knew it was nothing personal. He merely shrugged, plopped himself down on the bench, and said, "Go get 'em, guys."

Ryan bent down to start fastening his catcher's gear. He had been catching for a couple of years now, but he still had trouble getting his shin guards strapped on so they felt comfortable. As he worked at them, he tried to fight off feelings of embarrassment for batting last in the lineup. Art had explained to him that, since no one else wanted to catch, Ryan would be the only one to play all the time. He felt it was only fair, then, to have Ryan let everyone else hit first. Ryan had to agree, but it did not make it any easier to bat in the position usually reserved for the worst hitter.

Ryan was not the only one feeling embarrassed. Tracy had never been shy about letting people know how good he was at sports. Now some of the Barons, seeing him on the bench, could not pass up the chance to hoot at him. "Hey! Big star's sitting on the bench now!" "How're you doing, scrub?" "Hey, scrub, you're an all-star at collecting bench splinters!" As the inning went on, the remarks from the Baron bench grew worse.

Ryan thought the inning would never end. Jerry Gordon even had the nerve to laugh at Tracy while waiting for one of Joe's pitches. Ryan wanted to take a swing at him, and he could imagine how Tracy felt. He wondered how Art was able to keep their star on the bench with all that going on. *Come on, Art,* Ryan said to himself after Joe walked Jerry. *Let Tracy come in. Give him a chance to shut them up.*

Joe escaped the inning without allowing a run, and the Braves trotted silently to the bench. Art was stroking his mustache and frowning as Troy picked up a bat and started swinging on his way to the plate. "Are these guys unusual or are there other teams in the league that act like that?" he asked.

"They're the worst," said Ryan, angrily bouncing his catcher's mask off the dirt.

"They're even worse than last year," complained Mike. "They must have a real zero for a coach. Look at him! He just lets them say whatever they want."

Ryan followed Art's gaze over to the Barons' bench. Their coach didn't seem to be a threatening man. He was small and heavy with wavy brown hair edged in gray. He sat on the end of the bench, leaning forward with his hands gripping his knees, and he didn't seem to hear what his team was shouting.

Art shook his head and said, "No sense in saying anything back to them. A big reaction is just what they want. Just pretend we're playing a team of chattering zoo monkeys." He patted Tracy on the knee as he said it, but Ryan could tell it wasn't easing Tracy's nerves. His friend stared over at the ground around first base, and his arms were crossed tightly over his chest. The Salesky squint was back.

As soon as Troy stepped in to bat, the heckling got worse. They shouted, "Look out!" as the pitch came in and laughed when Troy missed the ball. The pattern was repeated for every Brave batter, getting louder with each swing and miss.

When the Braves took the field after failing to get a hit, the Barons started in on Joe. They made fun of his arm, his nose, his windup, and his occasional wildness. They also kept after Tracy, who was still steaming on the bench. After allowing the first two batters to get hits, Joe got himself under control. He reared back and fired as hard as he could, causing a loud pop in Ryan's mitt. As the Baron batters were called out on strikes, one after another, Smith and a few other Braves started talking back to the Barons' bench.

"Come on, let's not get into that," said Art firmly as his team came in to bat. "Let's go. Justin, let's see you take some good whacks at the ball."

Justin had been afraid to swing the bat the year before, and a few of the Barons remembered it. Jerry and Chuck roared so loudly when he walked up as the cleanup hitter in the lineup that even their own coach slapped them on the arms and told them to keep it down. Justin bought himself a few seconds of silence with a long foul down the first base line before finally striking out. As he trudged back to the bench, he muttered, "That pitcher seems like he's so close."

The Barons' pitcher was a large kid, and Art nodded sympathetically. "Yeah, he's a big one, all right. Don't worry about it, though. You really gave that foul ball a ride. Next time you might straighten it out, and then he won't look so big. Remember, the better the pitcher, the more fun it is to get a hit."

Smith followed with a ground ball that the first baseman scooped up easily. Smith was out at first base and he kicked the dirt as if disgusted with his poor hit. But Ryan guessed that he was putting on an act. *Smith's probably thrilled he was the first person not to strike out,* he thought. *Oh, great! Mike's up now. Justin, Smith, and Mike. How's that for a powerful lineup?*

Mike gamely battled the husky, red-haired pitcher to a three and two count. He was one of the smaller players, and when he went into a crouch at the plate he offered a small strike zone. With two strikes on him he always choked up on the bat, almost as though he were going to bunt. While Mike waited for the pitch, Smith was still griping at the end of the bench. "That pitcher's so big he looks like he's throwing from only ten feet away."

Ryan did not like to hear about how fast or big a pitcher was. It just made batters worry before they went up to hit. But it struck him as strange that both Smith and Justin thought the pitcher seemed so close. Ryan stared hard at the pitcher's mound, trying to pick out the white of the pitcher's rubber from the dirt. It wasn't easy to spot, since it was nearly covered with loose dirt, but Ryan finally detected a corner of it as the Baron went into his windup. "Hey! He's cheating!" he said, standing and pointing to the mound.

Everyone was busy watching Mike foul off the pitch, and no one but Art seemed to have heard him. Art pulled Ryan down to the bench beside him. "Keep it down. Let's not make a scene."

This was the last straw for Ryan. How much was Art going to sit and take before something was done? That pitcher was throwing from a good foot and a half in front of the pitching rubber! "Come on!" he shouted at Art. "Look at his—"

"I know, I know," Art interrupted. "He's not staying on the rubber. Look, Ryan, I don't like this whole scene. That team is out of control, and if we don't keep our cool, then no one will." They both watched as the pitcher, clearly ignoring the pitching rubber, fired a pitch past Mike's flailing bat. "Here's what I want you to do. We'll let the umpire handle it. When you're alone with him between batters this inning, ask him if he would watch that pitcher's foot. Ask him only once. Tell him I suggested that you ask, and then don't worry about it. It's his job to enforce rules, not ours."

Joe was still firing strikes in the third inning and it was only three pitches before the first batter was out and Ryan had his chance. It was all he could do keep from yelling, but he turned to the umpire and said, "Coach wants me to ask you to watch their pitcher. See if his foot is on the rubber."

"Don't worry about it, son," said the umpire, marking down the out on his card. "Let's go! Next batter."

Ryan pounded his mitt in frustration. He wasn't too sure about this umpire. In his opinion, the man wasn't doing too well at calling balls and strikes, and now he didn't seem to care that the Barons were cheating. He bent down wearily and held up his glove for Joe. The Braves' pitcher threw, and Ryan reached out to grab the ball over the outside corner of the plate. But he flinched as a bat swung and smacked the pitch solidly to centerfield.

Had there been a fence on the field, the Braves might have held the hitter to a triple. But the ball bounced high off the hard outfield surface and rolled on as if bouncing down an asphalt runway. The batter was already crossing the plate by the time Smith finally caught up with the ball near the infield of the ballfield on the other end of the park.

Trailing 1-0, the Braves finally got a base runner in the third inning when Randy walked. Joe struck out on a pitch thrown from in front on the rubber. Ryan glared at the umpire as he strolled to the plate. Why wasn't he doing anything? One ball and two strikes were both thrown so hard that Ryan could not get his bat around in time, and he watched them go by. Then came another hard pitch, headed straight for the plate. Ryan swung but hit nothing, and he dropped his bat and walked back to the dugout.

"Balk!" shouted the umpire. "I've warned you already about staying on the rubber, son! Runner moves to second base and that's a ball, not a strike, on the batter. Come back, son, you're still up."

Ryan spun around in time to see the Baron coach charge off the bench at the umpire. "What are you doing?" he screamed. "That batter is out! Get him out of here!"

Ryan backpedaled toward his bench. He didn't know if he was out or safe, but he knew he didn't want to be anywhere near an angry coach.

"The pitcher's foot was two feet in front of the rubber, and it wasn't the first time," said the umpire sternly. "You tell him to pitch from the rubber or take the consequences."

"You're crazy," said the coach. "Their pitcher's been cheating the whole game and you never called it on him. Anyone who wasn't blind could see Darrin's foot was right on the rubber! You're ruining the game for my boys!"

Ryan instinctively dodged as a shadow flashed by him, but it turned out to be Art. "If you're concerned about ruining the game," he said calmly, "cut out some of the talk from your bench."

The Baron coach refused to back down. "You can't take it, huh?" he sneered. "Your little feelings get hurt?"

"That's enough!" said the umpire. "You play baseball by the rules, and you start playing it now! Any more of this and I'm calling the game off and reporting you to the league. That goes for both sides. Now, batter up. Let's see, what have we got? Uh, three balls and two strikes."

The Baron coach had started back to his bench, but he whirled as if hit from behind with an egg. "*Three* balls? Is that what you said?" He scanned the hill behind his bench and picked out a man in a suit who was sitting alone. "You, sir! What was the count before that last pitch?"

"One ball and two strikes."

"Mmmm, that's right," nodded the umpire. "Sorry, it should be two balls and two strikes."

"No, you said 'three balls.' You had the count wrong and we're going to protest this game. I'm reporting *you* to the league."

Art stretched his arms wide. "Think of the kids," he pleaded.

"No," said the coach, turning his back. "You heard him give the wrong count, and we're protesting." It probably didn't help his temper any when Ryan singled to score Randy. By the end of the inning the hoots from the Barons were so bad that some spectators were getting angry. Art called his team together before they went to the field for the fourth inning. Tracy finally had his turn to get into the game and Ryan bet he was so angry he would wear a hole in the catcher's glove if he were pitching. But he would be taking Troy's spot at second base.

It seemed to Ryan that, for some reason, the tenseness was gone from Art and that familiar grin and twinkle of the eye was back. "Don't worry about that protest they're talking about. That coach doesn't have a leg to stand on, and he'll realize it once he cools down. Look, I know how tempting it is to want to beat this team 100 to zip," he said. "They probably deserve to have it happen. But we're not going to turn this into a war or a grudge match."

"You mean we have to keep taking it from them?" asked Tracy.

"Oh, no," Art laughed. "We came here to play a game, and that's just what we're going to do. I think I've got a game that will turn their tactics upside down. Here's the deal, gentlemen. Every time you get heckled or insulted, it's worth one point. Troy is through for this game, and did a mighty fine job, I might add, and so he will keep score. Just raise your hand whenever it happens to you. Now, if you can pile up 200 points in the four innings we have left, you win the prize."

Ryan was not impressed. "What's the prize?"

"There's a certain big league ballplayer coming to town to speak at a high school banquet. It so happens that we played together in college, and I know him pretty well. If you get your 200 points, I'll arrange for him to come to our next practice."

"Which player is it?" asked nine Braves at once.

Art let the suspense linger for a few seconds. "Tony Dalton," he said finally. No one needed to ask who Tony Dalton was. The Chicago right fielder had almost led the league in home runs the year before.

Joe had barely reached the mound when Ryan saw him shoot his right hand in the air. *I wonder how Art comes up with all these ideas,* Ryan thought. Already he felt as if some pressure had been lifted. It was great to see Joe laugh and raise his hand after each pitch and to hear the cheers from the fielders as the "insult" total rose. He looked over to the Baron bench and saw that, although the heckling was as strong as ever, the Barons did not seem to be enjoying it as much.

At the end of the fourth inning, Troy announced that he had counted 97 points, and Art led a loud cheer to celebrate. "You're halfway there, fellas. Keep up the good work."

By the time Ryan batted in the fifth, the Braves held a two-run lead and the Barons had quieted considerably. The Baron's catcher spat to the side as Ryan dug his back foot into the batter's box. "What are you morons up to?" said the catcher. "You must be cracked."

Ryan whistled to the Braves' bench and held up two fingers.

"Got 'em," answered Troy. "We're up to 134."

"Awright!" shouted Smith, who was leaning on

Troy's shoulder, helping him count. "We're going to break it easy!"

Ryan felt such relief at the turn of events that he felt certain he would smack at least a double. But he swung too low on a high pitch and fouled out to the catcher. Ryan pounded his bat until he heard the laughter from the Barons. The anger disappeared and he jogged over to Troy after carefully looking over the Barons' bench. "I think I got five at once," he announced.

He gave Tracy a pat on the shoulder as his friend moved up for his first time at bat in the game. The sight of the big second baseman seemed to recharge the Baron bench. Ryan wasn't sure how much of it Tracy would stand for. He'd seen him get into fights for less cause than he had tonight.

"Hey, chump, swing!" shouted the Barons as the first pitch came in to him. Tracy stepped back and glared at the catcher, who had shouted the loudest. Then suddenly, he shot his fist in the air and nodded at Troy.

Ryan couldn't contain himself any longer. He jumped high in the air as he cheered along with the rest of the Braves. *Art's plan is working!* he thought. *Even Tracy's having fun with it.*

Tracy clouted the next pitch to left field and raced to second base well ahead of the throw from the outfield. "You run like a chimp," said the second baseman. "That should have been an easy triple."

"Two!" shouted Tracy to the Braves' bench.

"We're up to 148," answered Troy.

But the total stayed at 148 as the Braves prepared to bat in the sixth. Their lead had stretched to 6-1 and the Barons suddenly were not saying anything.

"No way we're going to reach 200 now," Tracy said

to Ryan. "They haven't said a thing for the last five minutes."

"Maybe they figured out what we're up to and are trying to wreck our chances," Ryan answered. "I wouldn't put it past them."

"I can see these guys aren't cooperating anymore," Art broke in. "But I'll tell you what. I'm so proud of you guys that I'll get Tony to practice with us if you reach 150."

"Awright!" howled Smith.

"Now don't get so carried away that you're begging for insults," warned Art.

It didn't look as though the Braves would reach even 150. No one on the Barons' bench was paying much attention to the game any longer. Tracy came to bat with two out in the sixth. With Joe protecting a 7-1 lead, this was probably the Braves' last inning to bat. Fortunately for the Braves, there were a couple of Barons who couldn't resist some final barbs about Tracy's starting the game on the bench.

"Hey, scrub!" "Hey, benchwarmer!"

The Braves broke into cheers even before Tracy got his hand in the air. They were still celebrating when Tracy hit a home run. Ryan was there to meet him at home plate as Tracy sprinted in. "Way to go, slugger! How many guys can be a hero twice in one time at bat?" he said as he slapped hands with him.

As the mob of Braves stumbled over each other on their way back to the bench, Ryan saw a familiar-looking older man come over and shake Art's hand. The man had been sitting on the hillside along with the other Braves' parents since about the third inning. Ryan knew all of the parents who regularly attended and often took his own "roll call" of them between innings. But he couldn't quite place this man. It was not until after Joe had notched the final strikeout in the seventh inning and Ryan saw the man surrounding Randy with a hug that he realized it was Mr. Olson.

"Boy, that Art never runs out of tricks, does he?" said Mike, after they had shaken the hands of some quiet and confused Barons.

"He's smart. You gotta give him that," said Tracy. "I guess we could have done a lot worse for a coach. Look at who the Barons got!"

"Yeah, I'll take Art," said Ryan. He'd defend his coach against anyone now.

"You're not kidding," grinned Mike. "We're unbeaten, after all!"

There are more important things than a winning record, Ryan thought, though he didn't say anything to Mike. *That's the way Art feels, I know, and that's why I like him.*

7
First Place

The second they heard the front door open, Tracy and Ryan dashed across the living room. The newspaper carrier who had so routinely pulled on the handle jumped back in surprise as the two boys charged at him. Before he had a chance to drop the paper in the doorway, Tracy snatched it away with a quick "Thanks" and dove to the floor. He tossed away the outside section as if it were only a wrapper, and found the sports section. Within seconds, Ryan and Joe were flanking him on the rug, each with elbows on the floor and chin resting in his hands as they found the standings.

The Braves were listed on top, with a record of 12 wins and 2 losses. Directly beneath them were two other teams with the same mark, the Rangers and the Hawks. The Braves had been beaten by each of them in the past two weeks. The Hawks had first pulled them from the unbeaten ranks with a 3-2 win in eight innings. Then the Rangers had won their return match with the Braves 6-3. Tracy had pitched that night and had not had a very good game.

"Hey, look!" said Ryan. "They put in a bit about our last game. 'Tracy Salesky collected three hits to pace the Braves to a 7-3 win over the Cubs.' How about that? You're famous."

"Had to do something to make up for the way I pitched against the Rangers," Tracy muttered.

Ryan and Joe had seen what they were after, and they slowly rose to their knees. But Tracy was still studying the standings. "There's a list here of all the games left on the schedule," he said. "The Rangers and the Hawks play each other next week. One of them has to lose, and I hope it's the Rangers. That way, they'll be out of the running and we'll get to play the Hawks in our last game. Hey, can you believe it? If we beat the Hawks then, we win the title."

"You make it sound like such a cinch," said Joe. "We have to win our other games first."

Tracy ran his finger down the schedule. "Ha! We play the Jaguars next, and they're 8 and 6. After that, all we have left are the Pirates and the Rockets. We could beat them in our sleep."

"The Jaguars won't be easy," Joe warned. "We only beat them by one run last time."

"Well, don't worry about them," said Tracy. "It's my turn to pitch again, and I'm going to make up for the way I stunk up the game last time I pitched."

Ryan glanced down at the schedule and did some quick figuring of his own. "That means you're going to pitch the last game against the Hawks," he said, whacking Joe on the arm.

Joe frowned. "I think I'd rather see Tracy pitch that one."

"No chance," said Tracy, folding up the paper.

"Art isn't going to change anything around. In his system, it doesn't matter who we're playing. He just plays you when your turn is up."

"You can't argue with the way things have turned out," said Ryan.

"I just hope he realizes we have a good shot at the championship," said Tracy. "Chances like this don't come around too often."

"What are you getting at?" asked Ryan suspiciously.

"All right, I know Art's doing a good thing by giving everyone a chance to play and all that. And he's just crawling with ideas, and he has a good point about making the game fun. And I admit he was right about letting both you and I pitch, Joe, because it turned out that you're better than we ever dreamed. But say it comes down to that last game with the Hawks. How would you like to get that close to a championship and then have to sit on the bench for a couple of innings—and end up losing?"

"I don't know," sighed Ryan. "But I do know that Art's run things pretty well so far with his team effort idea."

Tracy ignored him. "I don't know about you, but I'd never get over it. Do you know what it means to win the championship? We would go on to the regional tournament, and then we'd be just two games away from going to state!"

"Is that state tournament a pretty big deal?" asked Joe.

"Is it?" laughed Tracy. "Just think of it. A trip down to Charlesburg. We'd stay in a motel with a pool, and eat at fancy restaurants. Probably get to see the capitol building. They'd let us play on one of their best fields with fences and a grandstand. Who knows, we'd probably get our pictures in the paper along with some big articles, and we'd be famous around town. My dad says it's been twelve years since a team from Barnes City ever made it to state."

The whole description made Joe so nervous he couldn't sit still. He excused himself and ran home. Ryan had not known about all that went with winning a championship, and he had to admit it sounded better than anything he had ever hoped for. He pictured himself hitting a ball over a real fence, and seeing a crowd stand up and cheer as he rounded the bases, hearing someone boom his name over the loudspeaker. *Batting ninth for the Braves is Ryan Court. . . .*

"Think of it," he said aloud. "First Art brought Tony Dalton to one of our practices, showing us how to hit, and then we get a chance to go down to Charlesburg and play in the big time, all in the same year. How do you know all this stuff about the tournament, anyway?"

"If you read the sports section, you find out lots of things," Tracy said. "Last year a team from Red Prairie won the tournament, and they got to ride through their town on a fire engine with a police escort."

"Yeah, it sure would be nice," said Ryan. All this talk was starting to get him excited and the Hawk game was still two weeks away.

"I just hope Art realizes how important it is to go all out for that Hawk game," Tracy said.

"It's not like he hasn't given everyone lots of chances to play all year long," reasoned Ryan. "Maybe for a game that important he might change his system a bit." Suddenly he got up and went to the door. "Aw, who are we trying to kid? Art isn't going to change. You know how he always plays down the winning angle. By the way, what time is practice tonight?"

"Seven. He said it would only take forty-five minutes."

No sooner had everyone arrived at the ball field than a small cluster of boys walked up to Art. Mike led the way and Ryan could tell he had something important to say. It made him a little nervous, because Mike was one guy who would say whatever came into his mind. Justin and Smith walked behind slowly, as if Mike was dragging them by a rope. The closer they got to Art, the more Smith tried to lag behind as if he were not part of the group.

"Art, some of us have been talking about the season and the standings, and it seems we're in pretty good shape for a championship," said Mike loudly. Obviously, this little speech was meant for all the Braves to hear.

"Yes, well, those things sometimes happen in life. I guess we just have to learn to live with it," Art answered in a mock serious tone. "Seriously, though, the whole team has done well, and I'm proud of you. Every single person on this team is playing the game and looking like he's having fun doing it. When that happens, you're bound to have a little success as well. And a little success is like sugar: it helps make things a bit sweeter."

"We know," said Mike. "I think all of us appreciate your system and the good job of coaching you've done. We've learned a lot, and I think most of us would have liked playing this way this season even if we weren't leading the league."

"Tied for the lead," corrected Tracy.

"All right, Mike. What's on your mind?" laughed

Art. "When people start telling me how wonderful I am, I get suspicious."

"The three of us have talked it over, and we realize that the Braves are very close to winning the title. And we've kind of decided that it wouldn't bother us if you switched the system some. You could put the best players in for the tougher games."

Art stared at Mike as if he were trying to crack a code. "Is this your idea, or has someone else been putting ideas into your head?"

Ryan was wondering the same thing, and he nudged Tracy. But Tracy shook his head and shrugged his shoulders.

"No one said anything," Mike said. "The three of us have been talking. You made this into a good team, and we feel we're a big part of it. We want to do whatever we can to help the team. If that means sitting out a game or two, well, we've gotten more playing time this year than last year."

"Who decided that you three aren't as good as the rest?" challenged Art. Despite his coach's seriousness, Ryan had to choke back a laugh. For Smith was glaring at Mike as if to say, "Yeah, who put me in with you scrubs, anyway?" No wonder Smith had been trying to hang back in the shadows. He still really thought he was better than many of the players on the team. *I wonder how Mike talked Smith into going along with this,* Ryan thought.

"I think everyone on the team knows who the better players are," said Mike stubbornly.

Art pulled off his baseball cap and smoothed the hair on the back of his head. "OK, I'm not going to mislead you and say that the three of you are all-league candidates. At least not this year. But you've all improved tremendously since the first time I saw you play. You guys have added a lot to this team. You've played the game as hard as anyone here, and that's the only thing that counts, remember? That effort has paid off for you. Come on, each one of you has gotten some good hits this year and I'm not ashamed to have any of you out in the field playing your positions.

"As for this championship talk, that isn't the main thing we're here for. I'm not going to sacrifice any of you, or anything I believe in, to win. You start doing that and pretty soon baseball isn't a game anymore. The pressure gets greater and you start being afraid to go out and have any fun. I keep telling you, success is like sugar. A little tastes great, but too much can make you sick."

Art looked over at Randy standing close by and poked him in the stomach. "I promised I wouldn't preach at you, and now listen to me. Let's just keep doing what we've been doing, and enjoy ourselves, and we may even win a championship. And *you* might get the winning hit," he said, pointing a finger two inches from Mike's nose.

Ryan figured that was the end of it, but Mike wasn't taking no for an answer. "There are others with a better chance of that. You know we have two tough teams and two easy ones left on our schedule. We can still keep the system of equal time for all. Just put us in against the Pirates and Rockets and make sure Tracy and Randy get in against the Jaguars and Hawks."

Mike glanced around for support and Justin finally backed him up. "It would probably be more fun that way, anyhow. I'd rather play the Pirates and Rockets. At least I have a better chance of getting a hit off them."

Ryan thought back to the evening when Justin hit a double. *He's right, that was against the Pirates the first time,* he thought. Mike's argument was making more and more sense to him.

Art smiled but shook his head. "I don't know. You're getting away from the fun of challenges. If you start shying away, then you're spoiling everything we've tried to do so far."

"But we're not backing away," said Mike. "Give us a chance to help win our two games and give them a chance to win their two. We get equal playing time, we're both helping the team, and we both get our own challenge."

"We'll see," Art said, shaking his head. "I'll give the three of you credit for a very noble offer but, you see, I'm an old guy and I'm kind of set in my ways."

He hobbled as if arthritic over to his station wagon and struggled to get the hatchback open. "I'll admit your request caught me by surprise. Well, I don't like to be outsurprised by you young whippersnappers, so I brought one of my own. According to some of your parents, it's about time we had a dress code on this team. From now on I'm going to get tough on you and insist that you all wear one of these to our games."

With that he pulled open his shirt like Clark Kent changing into Superman, and there on his chest was a white T-shirt with "Braves" written on it in red. He then passed out shirts and Ryan examined more closely the red stripes down the sleeves and the piping around the lettering. "Look at these!" he shouted to Tracy, who needed no urging to do just that. "Wow! And pants and caps, too!" Art had pulled open a box of caps, each with a *B* stamped on the front.

"Thank your parents for the funds," said Art. "And

make sure that when you wear it at our games, the word *Braves* is on the front. Like I said, it's a very strict dress code."

No more was said about Mike's idea.

The Jaguars were the best hitting team the Braves had faced all year. They probably would have run away with the league title if they had found someone who could pitch as well as they hit. As Ryan caught Tracy's warm-ups, he was wishing that Joe could be pitching this game. Joe had gotten better with each outing, while Tracy was starting to have trouble getting batters out. Ryan had heard Art tell Tracy several times to quit trying so hard and relax. He wondered if Tracy was trying too hard to top Joe's performances.

Art had stuck to his system. Tracy was on the mound, and both Mike and Smith were starting in the outfield. Smith had already just missed being hit by two practice balls while admiring his new shirt. Ryan hoped he could pay more attention to the game once it started.

The Jaguars were eager to hit against Tracy. Although they had lost to the Braves earlier in the year, they had scored six runs off him, and were confident they could get even more this game. Ryan could tell that by the look in their eyes as they watched Tracy warm up. There wasn't much chatter among the Jaguars; they stepped to the plate quickly and never took their eyes off the pitcher.

It didn't take long before Ryan realized Tracy was in trouble. The first pitch bounced three feet in front of the plate and skipped past Ryan all the way to the backstop. When Tracy did get the ball over the plate, the Jaguar hitters pounded it. After the first batter walked, there was a single, a single, and a triple in rapid succession, and each crack of the bat sent new pains through Ryan's stomach. Then Mike misplayed a fly ball and threw it wildly over Brad's head at second base.

At the end of the inning, the Braves sprinted toward their bench like people caught in a rainstorm dashing for shelter. Ryan saw grim faces everywhere and knew that everyone was feeling what he was feeling. *What if we blow it?*

"That's OK, we'll get them back," he said to Tracy. "We can score off their pitcher."

Tracy turned away without answering. He stalked off to the far end of the bench, where Art finally cornered him. "Your pitching form is fine, Tracy, and you've got plenty of speed on it. But, you know, your next meal doesn't depend on your striking out everyone. Relax, throw your best stuff, and if they can hit that, they deserve to win."

But at the bottom of the inning, Ryan was beginning to think the Jaguars did deserve to win. He buried his head in his hands as Brad watched a third strike go by. Something was wrong. Brad had never let a strike go by without swinging at it, especially not with two strikes on him. What was happening to the Braves? He looked down the row of faces to his left and could have sworn he was with a family that was watching their house burn down.

Art tried his best to shake the team out of their panic. "Hey, we're not playing the New York Yankees tonight! These are the Jaguars. You know, lovable little cats? We're here to play baseball, and you act like you're on deck for a Russian roulette match. The best effort I've seen tonight is when Mike chased that triple out into the weeds in left field."

If the Braves' batters were not getting the message, at

least Tracy appeared to have settled down. Although fighting another wild streak that caused him to walk four batters in the next two innings, he kept the Jaguars from scoring both times.

In the bottom of the third, Ryan finally got his first chance to bat. Suddenly he understood why all his teammates had been standing as if frozen in the batter's box. He was so desperate for his team to win that his arms were shaking and his spine was buzzing like a tuning fork. The first pitch came in waist-high and overly fast, but when he swung, he missed and nearly tripped over his own feet.

He gulped and glanced back at the bench. *May as well forget about a championship,* he thought. Then he caught sight of Art. The coach was smiling and holding his bat tightly under his chin.

"Ryan, if you squeeze that bat any harder you're going to leave fingerprints!"

Ryan backed out of the batter's box and looked at his hands. The knuckles were white as he clutched the bat. He grinned sheepishly at Art, dropped the bat, and shook both hands down at his sides.

"Just relax, Ryan, and I'll guarantee you an all-expenses-paid tour of the basepaths."

Ryan nodded and stepped back into the batter's box. Suddenly the bat didn't feel so heavy in his hands. It seemed to jump out at the next pitch, and sent the ball soaring into center field. Ryan had nearly reached first base when he saw that the ball would not be caught. He sprinted as hard as he could around the bases and did not even have to slide as he crossed home plate well ahead of the throw from the outfield.

"That's the spark we needed!" he heard Art saying as the team escorted their puffing catcher back to the bench. "Now listen to me, guys. Losing is no problem as long as you get beat despite your best effort. Don't beat yourself by worrying. Get loose out there."

Although the Jaguars scored another run in the fourth, Ryan could feel that things were turning in favor of the Braves. His teammates were talking, and diving for ground balls, and swinging at anything that came near the strike zone. Brad, Randy, and Tracy each hit doubles in the fifth inning as the Braves closed the gap to 7-5. Both the Braves and their parents were so caught up in the action that all were standing as the team came up for its final chance at bat. There was still tension in the air, but for Ryan it had changed from a stifling pressure to excitement.

Tracy led off with a hard-hit single to center field. Ryan and Mike jumped on top of the empty Braves' bench and cheered. Al then grounded out to first, moving Tracy to second base. But the lull in the Braves' celebration was quickly broken when first Dave and then Perry walked to load the bases. Ryan and Mike slapped hands atop the bench.

It was then that Ryan noticed Troy standing near Art and practically falling over him trying to get noticed, and it occurred to him that Troy hadn't gotten in the game yet. Every Brave had played in at least a few innings of every game before, and Ryan stopped in midyell as he tried to figure it out. This was a key game, and Troy was a good hitter. Did Art just get caught up in the excitement of the rally or did he know that Troy hadn't played yet?

Jimmy then swung at a pitch with two balls and no strikes on him and popped it up to third base. The Jaguars' third baseman grabbed it and reached over to tag Tracy, but Tracy had already scrambled back to the base. The Braves' cheers stopped quickly as they realized they were down to one out and that Smith was due to bat.

Just then, Ryan figured out what had happened with Troy! Art had been saving him just in case he needed a good hitter in a tight spot at the end of the game.

"Hey, Troy can pinch-hit!" he said to Mike.

Both of them looked at Art, but the coach made no move to call Smith back from the on-deck circle. Mike jumped down and grabbed Art by the arm. "It's OK to pinch-hit this once," he pleaded. "Think about poor Smith. If he strikes out now, he'll feel worse than anyone. Do him a favor and let Troy pinch-hit for him."

Troy joined the small circle, and his wide eyes were doing a better job of begging than Mike was. Still Art seemed to be debating. Ryan knew what must be going on in Art's mind. He had never had anyone pinch-hit for someone else before. He had saved Troy for just such a moment, but now wasn't sure he could go through with it. He really didn't believe in it.

Ryan was torn. He hated to see Art default on his system of playing everyone equally, regardless of ability. But he wanted so badly to win.

Smith had almost reached the batter's box when Art finally tapped Troy's shoulder and nodded toward home plate. Smith wouldn't believe it at first when Troy grabbed his bat from him. He clung tightly to the bat and looked back at Art.

"Troy's up," said Art. "He hasn't been in all game."

Smith let go of the bat and stomped angrily back to the bench. *Cut out the act,* thought Ryan. *You're glad Troy is getting you out of a tough spot.*

Troy was so eager to hit that he chased an outside pitch and missed badly for strike one. But he caught the next pitch squarely and lined it just past the third baseman.

"Fair ball!" shouted the umpire. Tracy scored, then Perry, and finally, with a leap of joy, Dave soared high in the air and landed on home plate with both feet. He was quickly buried under a mob of Braves.

"What a game!" shouted Ryan from the bottom of the pile. "What a game!"

8
Blisters

The meal was never officially over at the Courts' house until the dishes were done. Danny was not much help; he usually created more of a mess than he cleaned up. So it was left to Ryan and his mom to wash whatever wouldn't go in the dishwasher.

Without even changing out of his Sunday clothes, Ryan ran the water into the sink and collected the dishes. As she always did when it was Ryan's turn to wash, Mrs. Court dipped a finger into the dishwater. Ryan had given up trying to make the water hot enough to suit her. In fact, he knew better than to let the water get too hot because his mom would automatically make it still hotter.

"Wasn't that Randy you were talking to in church today?" she asked as the steaming water streamed into the sink. "I don't think I've ever seen him in church before."

"He's been coming the last couple of weeks. His parents are thinking about joining the church."

"That's nice. You'll have to introduce me to them sometime. Are they switching over from another church?"

Ryan risked touching the water with his finger. Pulling it back quickly, he wondered how he was going to find the dishcloth under the suds without scalding himself. "No, they weren't going to any church. Randy's folks wouldn't go to one ever since his big sister had an accident riding her bike. She got hit by a car and can't use her legs at all."

"Oh, that's awful! I wonder what it was that changed their minds about coming to church, then."

"Randy thinks it had something to do with Art," Ryan said. "He was over to see them when Randy almost quit the team. I don't know, maybe they liked how friendly he was and how much he likes giving his time to other people and things like that. He's very active in a church across town, you know."

"Maybe they saw that it hadn't done them much good to be off to themselves for so long. Sometimes it takes a long time for the bitterness to go away," sighed Mrs. Court. "I remember how I felt when your father and I split up." She rubbed her cloth on a plate until long after it was dry. "But I do hope it turns out for the Olsons and they find what they need at our church. We should include them in our prayers tonight. You know, this coach of yours sounds like he's really something.'

"He is," agreed Ryan. "Best coach in the league. I've always liked playing baseball, but this has been the best year ever! Did you see that long article on him in the paper?"

"I'm afraid I missed it. Well, I can hardly wait to meet him. I am sorry, Ryan, that I haven't been to one of your games yet. I'll have to be sure and make it to this next one. When did you say it was? Monday?"

"Yeah. It's a big game, too!" said Ryan. The thought of the championship game got him so excited he no longer noticed the heat of the water as he scrubbed a frying pan. "You couldn't pick a better game to go to. We're playing the Hawks, and they're tied with us at 15 and 2. The winner gets first place and goes on to the regionals."

"Oh, dear," frowned Mrs. Court. "I wish it wasn't one of those crucial games. You know how worked up I get watching these things even when they aren't for championships. It seems the game always gets close at the very end, and I get all caught up in it. I get so nervous I can't even watch and my stomach gets to be such a wreck I can't eat for days!"

Ryan grinned to think of his mom at the game. Her once-a-year appearance at his game was about the only time he ever saw her lose her cool. "We'll try to make it easier on you this year. Maybe we can get a big lead on them in the first inning. Then with Joe pitching you won't have to worry about the score, and you can sit back and enjoy the game."

"I thought Tracy was your pitcher," she said, inspecting the frying pan in the sunlight and finding it clean.

"I told you about Joe and Tracy taking turns. Joe seems to get better every time he pitches. Did you know that he hasn't given up a run in his last two games? Even Tracy knows that Joe is the best pitcher on the team."

"And how is Tracy living with that fact?"

"Oh, you know Tracy," shrugged Ryan. "He likes to be the best. I think it's bugging him so much that he's pitching worse instead of better. He talks mostly about his hitting these days. Of course, he keeps track of everyone's average and he's way at the top, hitting over .400."

Mrs. Court didn't seem to be listening to Tracy's batting statistics. Instead she had pulled open a cupboard door and was peering at a calendar taped to the inside of it. "Monday the 28th. No, I don't have a thing on for that evening. But what's this you've got on the 27th? I can't read your writing."

Ryan shook the suds off his fingers and studied the calendar. "That's the 'Walk for the Hungry.' Don't tell me you forgot about that, too!"

"As a matter of fact, I hadn't," she smiled. "I was just wondering if you still planned to go on that."

"Of course," Ryan said. "Mike wants to go on it, too. Hey! You still haven't sponsored me yet. Can I put you down for ten cents a mile?"

"You mean I donate a dime for every mile you walk? How far is this? Thirty-one miles, I thought you said. Sure, I'll sponsor you, but what kind of shape are you going to be in for your game on Monday?"

Ryan unplugged the drain and thought a minute. "I never realized the walk was the day before the game. Oh, it won't matter," he said, finally. "I suppose my legs will get a little stiff but I'm not fast enough to steal bases anyway. And how much ground does a catcher have to cover?"

"I hope you know what you're getting into," said his mom. "That thirty-one miles is nothing to sneeze at."

"Can I go with Ryan on that walk?" begged Danny, who had stopped running laps around the house long enough to see if there was any action he happened to be missing out on.

"No, you can't," said Mrs. Court. But as he charged

out the back door, she chuckled. "He would probably have less trouble than anyone. The way he goes around here, thirty miles would be a snap!"

Art Horton was the last person Ryan would have expected to throw his immediate future into confusion. And yet there he was, peeking out from beneath his car, with oil streaked on his forehead and dripping from his hand, and he was saying. "You're going to walk thirty-one miles the day before the Hawks game? Are you serious?"

Ryan tried to laugh off Art's reaction, even though he had biked over to the coach's house to make sure going on the walk was OK. "Come on, it's not a race. I can go as slow as I want."

"Have you ever walked that far before?" came Art's voice, echoing from under the station wagon.

"Well, no. Not that I ever kept track."

"I'm going to be honest with you, Ryan," said Art. "If you do go on that walk, you'd better plan to forget about playing on Monday."

Ryan couldn't believe his ears. What had happened to all Art's talk about not letting winning get in the way of life? Where was Art, the caring Christian? Ryan bent down to get a look at Art's face to see if he was really serious. As soon as he did so he nearly bumped into Art, who had finished changing the oil.

"You would bench me for that?" asked Ryan. "I thought you weren't big on a lot of training rules. Besides, some of the kids at our church have been planning on doing this walk for a long time. It's all set up. I thought you said we shouldn't be taking these games so seriously."

Art smiled and tried to rub an itch on his forehead

without getting more oil on his face. A fresh black streak over his left eye showed he wasn't successful. "Oh, I don't mean that I'm going to punish you for not saving your strength for the game. But I don't think you'll be physically able to play a hard-fought game the day after such a walk. You might, but I'm not at all sure. Could you hand me some of that paper toweling?"

Ryan tossed the roll of paper to him and leaned against the car. He hadn't thought going on the walk would be such a big deal. He tried to find out what Art really wanted. "So you don't think I should go?"

"Oh, no, I'm not making that decision for you," laughed Art. "That's up to you. What do you think you should do?"

"I wouldn't want to miss that Hawks game for anything."

"I wouldn't want you to, either. You're my only catcher."

"But still, I'd feel kind of funny about skipping out on the walk."

"Let's try to figure a way out of this, then," said Art. "How about if you sponsored someone else this year instead of walking?"

"I could," agreed Ryan. "But I'm kind of short on cash. I *do* have a decent pair of legs."

For the first time that Ryan could remember, Art seemed tired. He didn't bother to pick up the empty oil cans; instead he scraped them toward the garage wall with his foot. "I'm glad to see you're so concerned about this hunger thing. It's a Christ-like attitude, and I'm all in favor of that. I just wish the timing were better. You know *I* can sympathize with what you're doing, but the others are going to be much tougher on you if you can't answer the bell on Monday."

"You mean Tracy and the guys."

Art nodded. "They'll probably think that you're letting them down. Really, though, the one I'm worried about the most is you. You've worked as hard as anyone this season. I wish you could work something out so that you can do what you feel is your duty to this cause and still play against the Hawks. It's an experience I wouldn't want you to miss. Whether we win or lose, just to have played in a title game is an important moment."

A half hour before the Sunday starting time for the walk, Ryan was still mulling over his decision. Every time he thought his mind was made up, all the arguments against his decision rushed into his mind to tip the balance the other way. It was like leaning first one way and then another to keep a canoe from capsizing. It only rocked the boat even more. As usual, Ryan put off his final choice, hoping it would somehow take care of itself. He got home early from church and ate lunch by himself under the shade of a maple tree in the back yard. Already it felt so warm and humid that there seemed to be steam rising from the grass.

As much as Ryan admired Art as a coach, his warnings about going on the walk should have been enough to talk him out of it. Ryan felt surprised that Art hadn't been able to convince him. But there was something a little different about the way Art was acting. He was still pleasant and acted like he had all the time in the world to spend with each boy. But Art had said "my team" once when talking about the Braves in the past week. Maybe it was just a slip of the tongue, but it didn't sound like the same Art who had always played down his own importance to the team.

Ryan had almost talked himself into pulling out of the walk and sponsoring Mike, who didn't seem concerned about spoiling his chances in the Hawks game. After all, no one was counting on Mike to do much. But the thought kept coming back that the walk was important. Those Bible verses about feeding the hungry kept creeping into his mind, almost as irritating as a commercial that you can't stop humming. He remembered his mother encouraging him to stand up for what he felt was right.

"Ryan! Are you coming? We don't have much time!" It was Mike, his shoulders already shiny with sweat even though he was only dressed in shorts and a tank top. He sat on his bike, fanning himself with a fishing hat and holding sunglasses in his other hand.

Ryan found himself going the easiest way with his decision. Mike was urging him on, and Ryan was not set against the idea firmly enough to offer resistance. If he had really thought the walk would be that tough, he would probably have stayed away. But he had never been too tired for baseball in his life. He felt he could probably walk the thirty-one miles and still have the energy for a few innings before nightfall. *How tough can it be if you're only walking?* he thought.

Ryan had found out how tough the walk could be, and the ugly white bubbles swelling under the skin of his feet were lingering evidence. The late July sun had grilled the streets of Barnes City, and Ryan's feet had not been up to it. The lone pair of socks in his shoes had not been enough protection against blisters.

When he arrived for the Hawks game, Ryan was determined not to let on about his feet. As if the game weren't special enough, his mom had come and was sitting next to Troy's parents on the hillside. But not even the wads of cotton taped over his toes and feet could make the pain bearable when he walked. It felt like a dozen separate fires were burning on his shoes.

Gritting his teeth, Ryan tried to jog over to the first base sideline to help Joe warm up. He thought he detected Art studying him as he ran, and he gave an extra springy hop to show the coach that he had never felt better. He was glad his face was turned so Art could not see him wince when he landed. When he dropped into his catcher's crouch, he nearly fell over from the pain. Not only were his feet throbbing, but his legs were stiff and tender. Ryan saw Joe take deep breaths between pitches and thought, *I'll bet I'm the only one on the team who isn't thinking about the Hawks. Why did I ever go on that walk?*

Ryan knew that it was all over for him when he saw Brad approaching.

"I guess Art wants me to try catching for awhile," said Brad. "It sure wasn't my idea! You must be feeling pretty bad!"

Ryan handed him the mitt and tried to jog back to the bench. The sharp jabs of pain, however, made him struggle to keep up a good limp.

"How was the walk?" asked Art. "Look, I talked Brad into taking over the catching for today. You're in no condition for it. Come on and take your shoes off. There's no sense in making your feet worse than they already are."

Tracy and Smith were swinging bats, preparing to hit first, when they saw Ryan grimly unlacing his shoes. "What is this?" asked Tracy. "I thought you said you were feeling great!"

"Look at those feet!" Smith pointed. "You really must have ripped them up on that walk yesterday."

"You mean you went on that thirty-one mile thing the day before the championship?" asked Tracy. "I though you had more brains than that, Court. This is for the league title, you dope! You're just going to go give it to the Hawks!"

"Leave me alone," said Ryan bitterly.

Ryan was hoping Art would defend him, but only Mike hobbled over. "Hey, don't just pick on him. I went on that walk, too, and the same thing happened to me." From the way he walked it seemed his feet were just as bad as Ryan's, but Mike had not made any effort to hide the fact. In fact, he was so amazed at the size of his blisters that he could hardly keep quiet about them.

"*You* don't happen to be our only catcher," snapped Tracy, stepping back and swinging his bat. "You had to do something stupid! Way to go, Ryan!"

Despite Ryan's optimistic predictions to his mom, the Braves did not look like they were going to run away with the game. Even Tracy struck out in the first inning as the Braves failed to score. Fortunately, Joe was in top form and he fired the ball past most of the Hawks before they even swung.

Ryan did not feel like leading the cheers from his spot on the bench like Mike was. Instead he studied his replacement as catcher. Brad seemed to do fine—as long as the batters did not swing. But whenever the bat flashed across the plate, Brad shut his eyes, and the ball usually bounced all the way to the wire backstop. Brad must have been under orders not to even try to throw out baserunners. When the Hawks finally got a single, their player stole second and third base while Brad held the ball in his hand and stared at them.

One batter hit the bottom of the ball and lifted an easy pop-up right over home plate. Ryan jumped to his feet from force of habit. That ball would have been his to catch. But Brad had not seen where the ball went. He whipped his head from side to side searching for it, while it landed only two feet away from him, barely in foul territory.

"If it had been any closer it would have hit him," Mike muttered.

Ryan looked out to second base and saw Tracy squinting at him with his hands on his knees. Then Ryan turned away and scanned the hill for his mom. She caught sight of him and mouthed, "What's wrong?" Ryan pointed to his bandaged feet and his mom winced. Then she quickly looked away as Joe's next pitch came to the plate. The batter swung and missed, ending the inning and leaving the runner on third base. Ryan saw his mom's shoulders collapse in relief. *She really does get into the game,* he thought, *even when I'm not in it.*

Somehow Ryan wished it could be someone other than Tracy to get the Braves' first big hit. When the star player lashed a long double to score two runs in the fourth inning, Ryan was the only Brave who did not let out a whoop of triumph. He saved his applause for when Randy drove Tracy home with a single.

The 3 to 0 lead held up until the sixth inning. Suddenly Joe, who had been breezing through the Hawk lineup, ran into some problems. He walked the first batter, who then stole second. Then he followed with a pitch that seemed to float toward the plate at only half speed. The batter lined it past third base and sprinted around first and second bases. A run scored as the batter dove into third base, knocking down Perry, who was waiting for the throw from Smith.

"Come on, Joe!" shouted Ryan. The crowd behind the Hawks' bench suddenly came alive after several innings of frustrated silence. They shouted their encouragement to the next batter, a well-built, left-handed hitter whom Ryan recognized as the league leader in home runs.

Just as the batter stepped to the plate, Art called time-out and bolted to the mound. Ryan could hardly stand not knowing what they were saying; as catcher he was always a part of the conversations on the mound. He craned his neck, trying to see around Art's back to get Joe's reactions. Joe seemed to be pointing to a spot low on his back. Art nodded and rubbed the area for a few seconds, then patted him on the back and left.

Art's strategy was obvious from the first pitch. Brad stood up and moved far to the left of the plate while Joe went into his windup. Joe lobbed the pitch to Brad so far from the plate that the batter had no chance to swing.

"Intentional walk," nodded Mike, as Joe threw three more similar pitches. "With that good a hitter up, it was a good idea." The Hawk fans did not think so, and they booed loudly.

"I sure hope Joe can get us out of this mess," whispered Ryan. The pitcher seemed to be bearing down harder than ever, chewing furiously on his gum. With three balls and two strikes, Joe reared back and fired. Strike three!

"That's one out. Hang in there, Joe!" said Ryan. He glanced back on the hill and saw his poor mother clenching her fists so tightly he could almost see her knuckles turning white from where he sat.

Joe threw to the next batter, who swung and missed.

But Brad also missed the pitch, and the entire Hawk bench screamed, "Go! You can score!" Fortunately for the Braves, the runner on third hesitated. He started to sprint home, then stopped and finally scrambled back to third as Brad chased down the ball and threw to Joe covering home plate. The other Hawk runner had no trouble moving up to second base.

The players on both teams had barely settled back on their benches when the Hawks' batter hit a soft liner to Perry at third base. Perry jerked his glove up in front of his face and caught the ball. He then saw the Hawk runner scrambling to get back to the base and he touched the bag with his toe just ahead of the runner.

"Double play!" shouted Mike, and he ran to join the crowd of Braves who were hugging Perry and Joe.

"Hey! Come on, we've got one more inning to play, guys," warned Art. But he must not have been too worried about losing the lead, because he let Ryan bat in the seventh. Mike was offered a turn, too, but he claimed he could hardly stand up. Ryan was able to hit a ground ball to the shortstop, but was thrown out easily as he limped toward first base. It was the third out of the inning and Ryan returned to the bench while most of his teammates rushed out into the field. As Ryan sat, he was shocked to see Joe sitting next to him. A quick glance at the mound showed him there was no mistake; Tracy was getting ready to pitch the final inning.

"How come Art took you out and put *him* in to pitch?" said Ryan, barely masking his disgust for Tracy. He remembered each of Tracy's cutting remarks, word for word.

Joe didn't seem overly thrilled for a boy who had held the Hawks to one run through six innings. He stiffened his spine with a grimace. "Something's wrong with my back. I don't know; what does a pulled muscle feel like? Anyway, I started getting these pains in my back at the start of the last inning. Sometimes it really hurts to throw, like the time that guy hit a triple."

"What did Art say about it?" asked Ryan softly, eyeing his coach. Art was chattering constantly, trying to keep Tracy loose and build his confidence. It seemed as though the entire crowd sitting behind the Braves' bench was doing the same.

"He wanted to know if I could hang on and finish the inning. I told him I could try, and he said that if I could pitch out of trouble he would get Tracy to finish up, and we'd win the title."

"Well, you did your job. Great game!" Ryan told him, slapping him on the knee. "Thanks for getting me off the hook. If we'd lost because I couldn't catch, I don't know what I would have done."

"Thanks," shrugged Joe. "It wasn't your fault you got those blisters. Just one of those things."

"Come on, Tracy, fire at will!" shouted Art. "Don't worry about the hitters; they can't hit what they can't see! That's the way to dent your catcher's glove!"

Tracy seemed to be enjoying the role of relief pitcher. He was so confident on the mound, for a change, that he almost grinned while he pitched. A walk and a base hit made him a good deal more serious but the Hawks could not get another run across the plate. Tracy fielded the final ground ball and rushed over to first base to make the play himself.

It spoiled a moment that Ryan had been dreaming about for weeks. They were the champs, and were going on to the regionals. But Ryan shook Joe's hand and limped up the hill to talk to his mom. "Tracy, you hot dog!" he muttered to himself.

9 Tournament Game

Once the car left the Barnes City limits, Ryan hardly said a word. He sat in the back seat with Jimmy and Joe, each of them staring silently out of the windows. The front seat, meanwhile, was alive with chatter. Mike and his dad joined Brad in commenting on everything from the Hawks' game to the height of the cornstalks along the highway.

Ryan could not decide if he wanted the two-hour drive to Silver Heights to pass quickly or not. In a way, he could hardly wait to get his chance to represent Barnes City in the Region Six Tournament. It was an honor he had long dreamed of. But his dreams had always left out a few things. In them he had always been a hero, playing to the roar of the crowd and the crackle of a loudspeaker. Now he realized he had as good a chance for failure as success. *This really is the big time,* he thought. *What if it's too much and I play a bad game in front of everyone?*

One glance at Joe told him that his teammate was thinking the same thing. Joe's normally tanned skin seemed almost pale as he stared, unseeing, at the rows of corn rippling past his window. At one point Mr. Sherry caught sight of him in his rearview mirror and asked if he wanted him to stop the car for a minute. Joe shook his head.

They always say that it's the waiting that gets to you the most, Ryan thought as he turned back to his own window. *It's Tracy's turn to pitch this afternoon. Poor Joe is going to be a basket case by the time it's his turn tomorrow.*

The plain, black and white sign that announced "Silver Heights, population 19,200" sent a fresh current of tension through Ryan. Mike's dad slowed down and followed the two cars ahead of him as they snaked through the side streets on the west end of Silver Heights. There was another sign hanging on a wire mesh fence: "Silver Heights Municipal Field." Ryan fumbled with the door handle, got out of the car, and gawked. He had heard that Silver Heights had a great playing field for a town its size, and now he saw that it was true. There was a covered wooden grandstand, painted green, rising up from behind the backstop. About halfway along the basepaths, these stands gave way to bleachers. There were loudspeakers tucked into the corners of the roof over the center stands, and a large scoreboard loomed over the centerfield fence. A fence! Ryan grinned eagerly at the wooden boards, plastered with advertisements, that ringed the entire outfield. Never before had he played in an enclosed field.

As Ryan walked closer to the field, he marveled at the

basepaths, so smooth the dirt seemed to have been sifted and pressed down. The grass was thick and green, almost like a living room carpet with a well-groomed pitcher's mound in the middle of it. Then there were the foul lines marked off in white chalk. "This sure is the big time," whistled Ryan.

"I don't feel very good," he heard Joe say. "I hope Tracy can pitch both games."

"Come on, do you want to lose?" Ryan asked him. "We aren't going to the state tournament with Tracy pitching." He thought back to that morning, when the Braves had piled into the three cars for the trip. Tracy's dad had held his car door open for Ryan, but Ryan had refused the offer. He lied about having already promised Mike he would ride with him, and then had been relieved to find there was actually room for him in the Sherrys' car.

"But what if I blow it?" asked Joe. "What if—"

"Hey, none of that now," said Art, approaching and grabbing Joe around the shoulder. "You'll feel better once the game starts. Just relax. After all, you're probably the best pitcher in this tournament. Your opponents are the ones who should be worried about blowing it!"

After running his team through some fielding drills to get them used to the field, Art gathered his players in the dugout on the third base side. It was a real cement dugout with steps and a floor. Art sat on the top step, looking down at his players.

"Don't be psyched out by the field," he said. "It's a nice place, so I want you to enjoy it. But remember, it's still a ball field. Same shape, same size as what you usually play on."

"If you think this field is good, wait until we get to

state!" said Tracy.

"I like your confidence, Tracy, but remember it won't be easy. I was talking to the sports editor of our newspaper, and he said that no team from Barnes City has gone to State for eleven years."

"Twelve," corrected Tracy.

That little fact did not help Ryan's peace of mind.

"I've done some scouting over the past couple of weeks," Art continued. "From what I've been able to snoop out, the team from Crawford is far and away the best of the three other teams in the tournament. Don't start snickering at Crawford just because they're a small town. They play a pretty solid game of baseball. The other teams are from Silver Heights and from Stormview. Now I've just been given the draw," he said, waving a small slip of paper, "and guess who we get in the first game?"

"Crawford," groaned a small chorus.

"Smile when you say that," Art grinned. "That's right, we get Crawford. What's the difference if we play them today or tomorrow? We're going to have to beat them to get to the state tournament. Now, since they seem to be the toughest opponent, we'll meet them with our toughest lineup. Over the last half of the season we did best with Joe as pitcher. This is no insult to you, Tracy, because you're a fine pitcher, but I think we should let Joe pitch against Crawford. You have to admit that Joe may be one of the top pitchers in this part of the state. We'll go with Tracy then in tomorrow's game."

Tracy looked as though someone had just run off with his wallet. Ryan smiled to himself, because he knew that Tracy had told everyone he knew that he was going to pitch today. He had even talked some girls into coming to Silver Heights to watch the game.

Joe, meanwhile, was stunned. Sweat broke out over his eyebrows, and he began fidgeting with his glove.

"Here's our lineup," Art said, unfolding another slip of paper from his hip pocket:

1. Troy	first base
2. Tracy	second base
3. Ryan	catcher
4. Randy	shortstop
5. Brad	right field
6. Perry	third base
7. Al	center field
8. Dave	left field
9. Joe	pitcher

Ryan was mildly surprised that Art had again broken from his "no-favorites" system of lineups. Of course, it was a tournament. That made a difference. He was definitely glad Tracy wasn't pitching.

As Ryan walked along the fence to find a spot to help Joe warm up, he saw a long line of cars entering the parking lot. Fans were starting to fill the bleacher seats, and the public address system crackled as an unseen announcer began welcoming people to the game.

Ryan bent down about forty feet from Joe and held out his glove. He felt more confident about the game now that Art had put him at the heart of the batting order instead of in his usual ninth position. "Warm up slowly," he said. "Art says that when you've got so much nervous energy it's easy to start throwing too hard. Lob it in here, and save your fast stuff for the Crawford Colts."

After a few tosses Joe complained, "I don't know.

Something doesn't feel quite right."

"Don't start in on that," said Ryan. With his own nerves racing full speed he had little patience left for Joe. "Relax, will you? Just throw it like you usually do, and let the batters fall over themselves trying to hit it."

The Crawford Colts were to bat first, and Ryan took his position behind home plate. Nothing was second-rate at this field; the plate was shiny and the lines marking the batter's box were so white and clean that Ryan did not want to step on them. As the first Crawford batter was announced, the crowd began shouting, and Ryan's whole body felt numb with tension. He was glad he was facing the field and did not have to look at the crowd behind him.

"Stay loose, Joe!" Art shouted from the dugout steps. "I want you so loose that the flesh is just hanging from your bones. Don't clench that arm and get those muscles all tight. Ease up, leave your muscles free to work, and airmail that ball to home plate!"

The first Crawford batter was a small boy, and somehow that helped bolster Ryan's confidence. He crouched low, eagerly awaiting the pitch as Joe rocked back on his right leg and brought his arm forward. The ball rushed toward the plate and Ryan threw out his arm as the pitch sailed outside.

He returned the ball to Joe, who was shaking his head over something. Joe wound up and threw again. This time Ryan saw the bat nearly sweep over the plate and then pull back. "Steeeerike!" boomed the umpire.

The umpire was a large man with bushy eyebrows and a no-nonsense expression. He looked like he knew his business. Ryan flipped the ball back to Joe, who was still frowning despite the strike call.

The third pitch did not seem to be thrown very hard,

and the batter hit a sharp line drive to second base. Tracy took two quick steps and grabbed the ball across his left shoulder. He grinned, pulled the ball out of his glove and held it high for everyone to see. "See that, Joe, you got fielders today. Don't worry about those Colts."

The fielders had no chance on the next pitch as it seemed to jump off the bat into left field. *He pulled the ball to the left,* thought Ryan, staring at the Crawford player as he pulled up at first base. *What's wrong with Joe's fastball?*

The next batter fouled a pitch down the third base line and then doubled to left field.

"Come on, throw the ball! Don't lob it!" howled Tracy.

A terrible feeling was starting to come over Ryan as he watched Joe wind up. The pitcher was not rearing back all the way, and he held his arm close to his body, more like a shot-putter than a pitcher. The ball floated to the plate so easily that Ryan wanted to jump out and knock it away before the batter had a chance to swing. But the Crawford hitter waited for it and blasted it over the left field fence. He was still running the bases with the crowd cheering and the loudspeaker blaring out his name when Ryan went out to the mound. He felt his cheeks burning as he watched the batter touch home plate for the third run of the inning. Here they were, Barnes City champs, and they were being pushed around as if they had never won a game all year. All because Joe was scared out of his mind. Inside Ryan, all the tension about winning the tournament burst out in a flood.

"Look what you're doing, you chicken!" he snapped. "Would you just throw the ball? Just throw your normal speed and we might have a chance. And stop moping and wishing you didn't have to pitch to-day!''

Tracy had not bothered to join them on the mound, but he made his disgust known. ''You choker! You *would* fall apart in the big game!'' he shouted loudly enough for everyone to hear. Ryan heard Art shout at Tracy, telling him to knock it off.

It was as slow and painful a torture as Ryan had ever known. Joe walked the next batter and then gave up a long double, scoring a run. Finally Art ran out to the mound and Ryan jogged over to join him. He pulled a wet hand out of his catcher's mitt and dried it on his shirt.

''Chicken!'' spat Tracy, kicking the dirt by second base.

''Hey, what's wrong, pal?'' said Art. ''You're not throwing the way you have all year.''

Joe was trembling as he pounded the ball in his mitt, and Ryan saw his bottom lip quiver. ''It's my arm. I can't throw.''

''Excuses, excuses,'' muttered Ryan. ''Get Tracy in the game before they laugh us out of the ballpark.''

''Lay off, will you?'' snapped Art. ''What is it, Joe? You can't get loose? Sometimes it takes twice as long to get loose when you're nervous for a big game.''

''I don't know,'' Joe said. ''It hurts.''

Art frowned and sighed heavily. ''All right, take it easy on this batter. Throw four pitches way outside and throw them easy to see if we can't work the kinks out of your arm. Then pitch to the next batter and we'll see what happens.''

Joe followed instructions, but it did not seem to help. After giving up a walk, he had to dodge a line drive that sailed past his shoulder and into center field for a hit.

Tracy was stomping around second base like an enraged rooster. "You're throwing like a girl! What is this? Big star chokes when the chips are down!" Art finally trudged out to the mound, flipped the ball to Tracy and escorted Joe back to the dugout.

Ryan watched in anger as many of the fans offered Joe polite applause for his effort. *As if he deserves that!* he thought.

By this time, Tracy felt angry enough to throw the ball through a wall. Although he was unusually wild and walked two batters, he escaped the inning with only one more Colt run crossing the plate.

No one coming off the field even approached Joe, who was slumped in the far corner of the dugout, his face buried in his hands. Art walked over to say a few words to him, but he did not respond, and Art finally went back to his position on the steps.

Ryan glared at Joe and threw off his chest protector. "What a baby!" he muttered. The game he had looked forward to for so long had turned into a nightmare before the first inning had been half over. Things did not get better as the afternoon wore on. Ryan struck out his first two times at bat. The Crawford pitcher was tall and thin and had an arm like a whip. It was bad enough that he could throw the ball so fast but he also had a sidearm motion that made the ball seem as if it were heading straight for the batter. Ryan had not even gotten a good swing during either of his strikeouts.

Even Tracy was called out on strikes, though he refused to accept the call. He stood on home plate, arguing that the pitch was low, until even the Braves were telling him to sit down and forget it. If Art had not finally come out and pulled Tracy away from the plate, the Braves' star would have been kicked out of the game.

Tracy may have been behaving poorly but even Ryan had to admit he was pitching one of his best games. Except for allowing two runs in the third inning, he kept the orange-capped Crawford team under control through six innings.

Ryan refused to talk to him or offer any encouragement, however. Ever since Tracy's remarks about the Walk for the Hungry, Ryan had decided he did not need a conceited show-off for a friend. He never visited the mound, and merely tossed the ball back to Tracy and waited for the next pitch. In a way, he was not sorry to see Tracy completely lose his cool. He knew how much Tracy had played this game up to his friends and how it must be tearing him apart to have his great Braves team look foolish in front of such a big crowd. *It's your own fault. You should keep your mouth shut once in a while,* thought Ryan.

The final straw for Tracy came in the seventh inning. He had been burning the ball in as hard as he could, walking two and striking out two. A Crawford player finally got a bat on the ball and hit a weak grounder to shortstop for what appeared to be the final out of the inning. But Randy kicked the ball, crawled after it, and then threw wildly trying to trap a runner off second base. By the time the ball was retrieved, two more runs were in. Tracy threw down his glove, walked over to Randy, and chewed him out. He paid no attention to Art's order to get back and pitch.

After all that, it was a relief to Ryan when Brad hit a high pop-up toward first base in the bottom of the seventh. The Crawford first baseman cruised under it, caught it, and jumped high in the air. The game was over with the score 9 to 2 in favor of the Crawford Colts. As he watched the celebration, Ryan decided that he had never spent a worse two hours in his life. From the first slow pitch to the last inning—in which the Colts had put in all their reserves—it had been embarrassing.

Many of the team's parents, as well as a group of the Colts themselves, were starting to mill around the dugout, trying to console the losing team. But after listening to a series of "Too bad it turned out that way" and "It was just one of those games," Ryan felt like screaming. He pulled off his Braves' shirt and replaced it with his blue windbreaker. He didn't want to be with the Braves or even be known as one of them at that moment. Everyone had seen what kind of a team the Braves were. The Braves were the team with the spoiled brat, Tracy, who had acted like a hotshot idiot in front of everyone. They were the team with the pitcher who panicked and could not have struck out anyone even if all the batters had been swinging pencils instead of bats. And they were the team that had managed only five hits and two runs off the Colts. One of those runs had been in the seventh inning when the Colts' top pitcher had left the game.

Ryan charged out of the dugout, but found an orange-trimmed uniform blocking his way. "Nice game," said the blond kid who had hit the home run in the first inning. "Too bad about your pitcher getting hurt. I think you guys could really have given us a close game."

Ryan allowed the boys to shake his limp hand, and then turned away. He pushed past some parents standing by the gate and went into the parking lot. "The pitcher was hurt, huh?" he scoffed. "Yeah, sure."

10 The Phone Call

Never had a baseball game seemed so boring to Ryan. Art had insisted that, out of politeness, they should stay to watch the contest between Silver Heights and Stormview. They stayed and sat in a clump at the far end of the right field bleachers, but few of them actually watched the game. With their hopes of a championship dashed, they didn't care which team won. Ryan noticed that neither Art nor Joe was sitting with the team, and it bothered him that they'd gotten out of staying.

It seemed typical of the team's luck that day that the game went into extra innings. The Braves grew so eager to leave that they began cheering for whichever team was at bat to score the winning run. In the ninth inning, Stormview finally broke the tie and sent most of the hometown fans away disappointed in Silver Heights' 2-1 loss. As the Braves filed out of the stands, Art reappeared and asked to meet with the team in a corner of the parking lot.

Art told the glum group that they had nothing to be ashamed of. Most boys their age would have given much to have even made it to the regional championships. They had enjoyed a rare chance to play in a championship game and they had played hard.

"None of you backed away from the challenge," Art continued. Ryan was one of several boys who snorted and looked around to see where Joe was. Apparently he was still hiding somewhere.

"It was your coach who ruined your chances in this game." Ryan didn't believe he was serious till he saw that Art was looking into the eyes of each player. "I just got back from a clinic a few blocks away from here. They took a look at Joe, and it seems that he hurt his arm. It doesn't appear to be serious, but it was bad enough so that he shouldn't have pitched for at least four or five weeks. Now that was more than a bad break; it was bad coaching. The doctor thinks that he probably hurt it in the Hawks game. Remember when his back was bothering him and I left him in to finish the inning? It's very likely that Joe put some extra strain on his arm trying to compensate for his back pain.

"Of course, I was too blind to see this. To begin with, I should have recognized what had happened and gotten him out of that game as soon as he complained of the pain. I didn't, and the end result was that this turned out to be a rough game for all of us, especially Joe. I never thought I'd pull that kind of dumb stunt as coach. I tried to talk Joe into coming back with us to the motel, but he went back to Barnes City with his parents. He's taken this pretty hard, and the comments some of you guys made were pretty vicious. I don't know who was worse today, you or me!"

Ryan was stunned. He had not thought he could feel any worse than he had right after the game. But as Art's words sank in, and he thought back on the stinging accusations and taunts he had thrown at Joe, he felt even more like running away and screaming. He had thought that he was a Christian, that he was better than Tracy. Now he wished more than ever that they had never left Barnes City that morning.

It was to have been a special night. Some community groups in Barnes City had put up the money for them to stay overnight at the motel between the two days for championship play. It was a nice motel, and Ryan kept thinking about how fun it could have been to stay there. But after the disaster against the Colts, it only seemed like a place where the guys had to hang around together and kill time. No one looked forward to the meaningless third place game they were to play the next day against the Jets of Silver Heights.

Some of the players, led by Mike and Troy, tried to shake off their disappointment, and they jumped into the motel's heated swimming pool. Before long they had a rough game of keepaway going with a plastic football that Brad had brought.

But Ryan didn't feel like joining in. He walked out the front door and across the parking lot down to the end of the sidewalk. The sun had just set, the shadows were growing long, and the air was quickly turning cool. Ryan sat down where the concrete ended and a long row of evergreen shrubs began, and found the sidewalk still warm from when the sun had been out.

Ever since the team had left the park, he had been haunted by a picture in his mind of Joe sitting in the corner of the dugout. Those red eyes were looking toward the field, yet not focused on any of the action.

I really stuck it to Joe when he was down, thought Ryan. *I hate this whole day and this whole team.* He thought, bitterly, how easy it was to blame it all on one person. When he'd found out that Joe was not to blame, he had tried to work up a hatred of Art. After all, he was the one who had caused the trouble with Joe's arm. But it was not Art who said those things to Joe. No, Ryan Court had played a big role in the horrible things that had happened that afternoon.

"Mind if I join you for a few minutes?"

Ryan saw his coach standing in the shadows, stroking his mustache. *You picked a bad time for this. Leave me alone,* Ryan thought. But he said nothing, and Art's knees cracked as he bent down to sit beside Ryan.

"It's a good night for reflection," said Art. "No moon or stars to distract you." Ryan merely stared at his thumbnails, so Art went on. "It's been quite a year, wouldn't you say?"

"Yeah," Ryan answered wearily. "But something went wrong somewhere. We had it going so good, and then it all blew up on us."

"Well, that's what comes from inferior coaching. Here I spent all this time spouting off about playing the game the way it's meant to be played, and seeing that everyone gets something out of it. I said we weren't going to let winning control us. Then look what happened! I started letting all my principles slide. I guess I had forgotten how strong that urge is to grab first place. You start tasting a little success, and pretty soon all you can think about is more success."

There was a light shining on Art's mustache and it made the bristly hairs seem wilder than ever. Ryan shrugged and said, "It could happen to anyone."

"Well, I'm leading up to an apology, I guess." Art

smiled. "I started sacrificing players, looking for an edge, and now I wish I could step outside myself long enough to give me a good pounding. We really paid the price to win, but we didn't get anything for our money. Let me ask you: how much did you really enjoy that past couple of games?"

"I've had more fun at the dentist's office," Ryan said.

"I thought so. There was no sense of fun or joy. We lost our perspective on the game, and you can pin that on the coach."

"No, we're to blame for that, too," said Ryan. "We were talking all the time about going for the championship. You know, benching Smith and Mike and Justin against the Hawks. And all that stuff about going to State started with us. I never heard you talk about it."

"Well, we all got caught up in it. The point is, what can we learn from all this?"

"I know what I've learned," snorted Ryan. "I thought we were hot stuff, and now I know better."

"Don't be so hard on yourself, Ryan. You made a better effort to keep things in perspective than most of us did. I'm still kicking myself when I think of how little support I gave you when you went on the Walk for the Hungry. There you were, trying to do what you felt was right, and I gave out the impression that I thought a baseball game was more important."

A swarm of gnats suddently hovered around Ryan's face, and he stood up to swat them away. "Well, whatever you did was nothing compared to what I said to Joe. I just can't believe I did that to a friend of mine."

Art did not reply for a moment. Then he said, "Do you think God knows anything about baseball?"

Startled, Ryan stared suspiciously down at Art. "What?"

"Just give me a few more minutes of your time and I'll be grateful," said Art, patting the sidewalk next to him. "When I was in college I also thought I was pretty hot stuff, as you called it. You know why I thought so? Because of this, right here." He held his right arm up for Ryan to inspect. "Can you believe it? I thought I was an important person because this arm could throw a ball faster than other arms could. I guess I thought that way until the day this arm broke down and couldn't throw hard anymore. There I was at age 19, washed up as a major league prospect. Yep, the scouts never looked at me after that.

"I had been counting on that arm to prove I was somebody, and when it failed me, I no longer had any proof. Ryan, I spent three years fooling around and getting myself in trouble because I thought I was a failure. I thought that until the day I walked into a church. There I talked with someone and found out that, even though I had given up on myself, God hadn't. He still cared."

Art seemed like a different person to Ryan. Maybe it was the weird combination of night lights and shadows, but as he watched Art, it seemed as though he had been introduced to him for the first time. He wasn't a flawless grownup. He was just another person, a friend with both strengths and problems. "Glad to hear it helped you, I guess," he said. "But what does that have to do with—"

Art held up a hand. "Just give me another minute. It takes a long time for thoughts to find their way out of this dense head of mine. I was going to say that, when I realized what I had done to the team today, and especially to Joe, I had that same low feeling. I felt like giving up. I had a perfect excuse, having just wrecked a season for thirteen great fellas. Fortunately, it didn't take me as long this time to figure out that God hasn't given up on me now, either. I spent some time talking to him about it. I still don't feel good about what I've done, and I may have some scars for awhile, but I think I'm ready to learn from what happened. I'll apologize to all the guys, and go on from there."

Ryan felt himself wishing he could forgive himself the way Art had. "Art, for you that's OK. You're a good person. But in my case you're not talking about a little slip-up or a wrong choice. I really came down hard on Joe—and I'm talking about mean, cruel stuff—when he was already down. The way I've been taught, that's the kind of stuff God really hates. I can say I'm sorry, but it doesn't change anything. You know what it would be like if I wanted to pray about it now? It would be like—like wrecking a guy's car and then asking him if you could borrow it again the next week."

Art chuckled softly. "I don't know. It seems like the best time to ask for help is when you're at your lowest."

Ryan felt strange talking to Art about God. He did not really know him that well, and the only times he had ever spoken about religion were at church or at home with his mom. But somehow he did not quite want to let go of the subject yet.

"Don't you ever wonder what's the use?" he said, looking Art in the eye for the first time. "I really care about doing the right things, you know. Treating people right and all that. But it doesn't matter how hard I try. It often ends up like this. I either keep my mouth shut when I should speak up, or else I say something when I shouldn't."

Art had a funny look in his eye, as though something had just occurred to him. "Ryan, do you remember back in our early practices when we had that system? When you weren't penalized if you swung at a ball in the strike zone, and when you got an out in the field if you so much as got your glove on the ball?"

Ryan nodded. He had almost forgotten about that time in the season.

"I really think God is the same way toward us," Art went on. "He doesn't expect perfection all the time. He wants us to try. Jesus wouldn't have had to save us if we could be perfect on our own. So I don't think God's Word is just a blueprint to show us where we've goofed. It's also like our practice drills, to get us thinking the right way about getting involved and trying."

Ryan thought hard for a moment, trying to connect everything Art was saying. "You mean what I did to Joe was like an error, a bad one? And God can forgive a Christian's errors—he just wants us to keep trying?"

Art shook his head in amusement. "Why is it that you can say better in two sentences what I've been rambling on about for five minutes? Well, I've imposed myself on you long enough. Brrrr! What's autumn doing here so soon? It's only the beginning of August." He rose to leave, but Ryan followed him in.

"The deal is, we're supposed to forgive other people's sins like God forgives ours, right?" Ryan continued as they entered the lobby. The shimmering light from the overhead chandelier nearly blinded him after the darkness outside.

"That the way I understand it."

"Well, I guess that's a start. Thanks, Art. By the way, have you seen Tracy lately?"

"He was in his room last I checked. See you later."

It was a good thing that the motel desk clerk had been willing to part with a fistful of change in exchange for their dollar bills. Neither Tracy nor Ryan had any idea how much a long-distance call to Barnes City would cost, and they were not taking any chances on coming up short. Between the two of them, Ryan figured, they now had enough change to play video games all night, but he wasn't interested in games now.

Tracy sat in the booth while Ryan stood in the doorway. The light over their heads was the only one turned on in the entire hall, except for the red exit signs on either end. Ryan had been surprised and relieved when Tracy volunteered to make the call. He did not like to talk on the phone, and thought he would blow the whole thing by forgetting exactly what to say.

While Tracy spoke with the operator, Ryan thought back to his resolution a half hour earlier after his talk with Art. Tracy had been on the bed in his room, watching tv when Ryan found him. It had not taken much to break the flimsy barrier between the two friends. All Ryan had said was, "You pitched a good game today. Best I've seen you throw all year. Too bad we didn't give you much support—especially me."

Tracy had responded more warmly than Ryan had expected. They both apologized for their behavior of the past weeks, and then Tracy explained the events behind his change in attitude.

"When I walked out of the dugout after the game, my dad was trying to cheer me up by telling me what a great game I'd pitched and how he'd never seen one team have so much bad luck in a game," Tracy had said. "But I was so mad I wasn't listening much to what he said. I was really teed off at Joe for his pitching, and at Randy for his error, and at that umpire and myself, too, for striking out.

"It was pretty crowded outside by then, and everyone was talking at once, so you couldn't hear much of what was said. But I heard some girls mention that number 12 on the Barnes City team. So I stopped to listen, and I heard them laughing about what a poor sport I was, and how everyone in the stands from Barnes City must have been embarrassed.

"I knew dad must have heard, but he didn't let on, and I realized that if everyone was talking about me now, it must have been worse during the game. Then none of my teammates were talking to me, especially not you, and suddenly I just wanted to dig a deep hole and jump in."

Ryan and Tracy had then talked about what they could do to make up for their remarks. Both had agreed that this phone call would be a good start.

Ryan could tell from the silence that Tracy was waiting for someone to pick up the ringing phone. His quick, deep breath gave Ryan warning that someone was home.

"Joe? Hi, this is Tracy. I called to, uh, apologize for that happened in the game today. Yeah. Ryan's sorry too. How's the arm? Well, keep soaking it, if that's what they said to do.

"Say, Joe, we really acted like creeps this afternoon, and we're sorry. We should have known something was wrong. I mean, when do ordinary humans pull the ball against a healthy Joe Martinez? Listen, the season isn't over. I know it's only for third place, but come on, a game's a game. We want you here. It's our last chance to get back on track as a team. Yeah, I know about your arm but we've got that figured out. Why don't you play first base tomorrow? That way you won't have to throw, and you can still get in the game. Ryan says he doesn't think Art will mind at all.

"What? So, maybe you'll make some errors. Who doesn't? You know Art doesn't ask for anything but a good effort and we know you always give that. Boy, do we know! Come on, get your dad to drive you back here tomorrow. The game is at noon."

A good effort is what God wants too, Ryan thought as Tracy hung up the receiver. He felt a little better already.

The Silver Heights stands were quite empty compared to the day before, and those fans who were there were lazily stretching out on the bleachers to enjoy the sunshine and the cool breeze. On one side of the field, the Silver Heights Jets, in their black and silver jerseys and caps, lifelessly tossed baseballs back and forth.

The Braves, meanwhile, huddled tightly in their dugout, and many of the Jets stopped to see what they were up to. Suddenly the team burst onto the field, carrying Joe above them. The mass of players cheered and escorted him to the infield, where the three boys who had been carrying him on their shoulders planted him on first base. As they clapped and whooped, a small segment of the Barnes City fans joined in with their applause.

Ryan trotted down the first base line toward home plate. Even if it was only a third place game, the field had been prepared flawlessly. He felt the smooth dirt of the base paths under his feet and it made him feel so light that he sprinted the rest of the way to the plate.

As he settled back in his crouch, the crisp lines of the batter's box brought back a few painful memories from the day before. But he looked out over at his teammates spreading out in the field. There was Joe, gritting his teeth as he concentrated on catching the practice throws from his teammates to first base. Smith was back in center field, pounding his glove and howling and watching his shoes settle into the lush outfield grass. Mike was on third base, gamely trying to get the best of a ground ball Joe had thrown to him. He knocked it down with his glove and crawled after it, then fired a high throw that Joe was barely able to flag down.

Tracy grinned at Ryan from the mound and asked if he was ready. After a few warm-ups, the rest of the Braves tossed their baseballs out of the field and started yelling encouragement to their pitcher.

"Go, Tracy!"

"Don't let us get bored out here. Give us something to catch!"

Ryan tossed the last warm-up pitch back to Tracy and nodded to the umpire. As the Jets' batter shuffled up to the plate, Ryan took a last look toward the dugout. Art was no longer on the step. In fact, he was sitting on the grass next to the fence with his hat off and a huge grin on his face.

"Hey! What a day!" he shouted. "Wish I was out there myself. Hey, Ryan, do you think I could pass for age twelve?"

"You'll have to shave off your mustache first!" Ryan shouted.

The Jets' batter stepped back and stared disbelievingly at the chattering infield surrounding him. He turned to Ryan and scoffed, "Don't you guys know this is only for third place? The game doesn't mean a thing."

Ryan grinned back at him. "Oh, yes it does!"

Again the guard ducked in and slapped at the ball. It bounced off the side of Ben's leg and rolled out-of-bounds. Without thinking, Ben shoved the pesky opponent hard with the heel of his hand. "Get out of my face, shrimp!" he said.

A blast from a whistle pierced the gymnasium. The official ran towards Ben. "Technical foul! If I see that again, son, you're out of the game."

No one needed to tell Ben that he had just made a fool of himself. By the time he reached his chair he was so frustrated and angry at everyone, including himself, that he wanted to cry.

Read all the Sports Stories for Boys:

At Left Linebacker, Chip Demory
A Winning Season for the Braves
Mystery Rider at Thunder Ridge
Seventh-Grade Soccer Star
Batter Up!
Full Court Press
The Great Reptile Race
A Race to the Finish

Full Court Press

NATE AASENG

Contents

1
The Toe

"Do you suppose I could find an incredibly strong kid somewhere to help me haul these things?"

Benjamin Oakland continued to dribble with his left hand as he turned to look at his father who was holding a square slab of concrete. Ben could see a stack of similar slabs weighing down the trunk of their car.

"Sure, Dad." The boy flicked one more shot at the basket. When it clanged off the rim, he retrieved it and shot once more from in close. Ben's hands were growing cold. A November breeze chased away any warmth that the sun might have given, so he had little control of the ball. Again the shot missed its mark. Frowning, he attempted one more lay-up. This one was successful.

Despite the brisk weather, Ben's short brown hair was matted with sweat. Except for slightly hollow cheeks and eyebrows that tufted at the peaks, he was a very average-looking boy.

After tossing his basketball in a cardboard box in

the garage, he peered into the open trunk.

"Be careful with those—they're heavy," said Dad, his hands grimy from preparing the ground for the blocks. "Just bring a couple of them out back."

Ben hoisted one and grunted at how heavy it was. "Where's Ken?" he asked. Whenever there was work to be done and Ben was doing it, his first thoughts turned to his older brother. In the Oakland family, the older you were, the more slave labor was expected of you. Ben wanted to make sure the oldest slave was not getting away with anything.

"He's coming," said Dad as he hauled his load through the back door of the garage.

Reinforcements quickly arrived, but not the kind Ben was looking for. "Can we help?" asked little sister April, bouncing across the garage floor. Apparently she included Nick, the youngest of the Oaklands, in the offer.

"Look out. This is too heavy for you," Ben said. "Stay out of my way." The rough corners of the concrete were biting into his already stiff fingers, and Ben was glad when he reached the backyard and set down his load.

"I've got some gloves you can use," Dad said, seeing Ben wring his hands. "Just bring a couple more of those. Ken can handle the rest."

"Nah, I'll be all right once I get these gloves on." Although not particularly fond of work, Ben was not about to back down from the chance to show he was at least as tough as Ken.

"Get out of the way, please," he said, irritated, as Nick and April tried to help him carry the next load. "It's too heavy for you. Why don't you go find that lazy Ken and tell him to get down here." April scampered away, eager to deliver the message, with Nick trailing.

By the time Ken arrived, Ben was on his fourth slab. Although his arms were beginning to shake from the exertion, Ben pretended to be okay.

"Why don't you take a break—this isn't a fire drill," Dad said.

"I can get another one unloaded first," Ben said. This time, though, he could feel the strain all the way through to the sockets of his shoulders. He took shorter, more hurried steps toward the door. But there was Nick, blocking the exit with his wagon. "Come on, you guys are making it twice the work! Get of of here!" Ben grunted.

By the time he squeezed past Nick, Ben felt his grip beginning to slip. He lurched out the door but before he could set the block down, he caught his foot on a roll of sod that Dad had pulled up to make room for the blocks. Ben stumbled, and the concrete ripped off one of his gloves as it slid out of his grasp. The edge of the concrete block landed with crushing force squarely on Ben's big toe.

Ben's screams were enough to summon Mom from the basement. Bare arms crossed to ward off the outdoor climate, she pushed her way past the curious brothers and sister. Dad was doing his best to calm Ben who was still hopping around on one foot and yelling.

"Tom, what was he doing carrying those heavy blocks?" scolded Mom.

"He thought it was a basketball and he dribbled it off his foot," said Ken.

"This is not a time for cute remarks," Mom said, angrily.

"They weren't heavy!" Ben answered through clenched teeth and tears that were beginning to spill from his blue eyes. "I tripped on that sod. Oh, ow!"

"I'm sorry. I shouldn't have left that sod there. I thought there was enough room to get through," said Dad. "Can you settle down enough so we can have a look at it?"

When Ben finally submitted to an examination, the Oaklands peeled off a blood-stained sock to find an ugly, swollen mess.

"Whew!" whistled Ken. "Looks like you really nailed it."

"Does it hurt?" asked April.

"No, it tickles!"

"We'd better have a doctor look at it," Dad said. He searched the pockets of his baggy garden clothes, then got up and hurried inside the house.

Nick kept complaining that he couldn't see, so Ken picked him up and held him over the wound. "If you were a horse we'd probably have to shoot you," Ken said to Ben. "Isn't that the pits, though? The only three things you've talked about for the last five months are basketball, basketball, and basketball. Now here it is, less than two weeks before the season starts, and you get yourself so mashed up that you'll have to sit out a couple of months."

Until that moment the searing pain had blocked out all other thoughts and feelings. But it was as if Ken's words struck a nerve even more sensitive than those in his feet. All of a sudden Ben shrieked and slammed his fist into the lawn.

"What did you do now?" Dad asked, coming out of the house.

"I didn't touch him," Ken said, putting Nick down. "I just said it was too bad he was going to be laid up for the start of basketball practice."

"Why couldn't you just carry your own stupid blocks?! Idiotic sod! You can just take your whole patio and . . ."

Mom's eyes flashed alarm as Ben continued to beat the earth. "Benjamin, calm down. That's just going to make it worse. Try to relax, would you?"

"I can't figure out what I did with the car keys," Dad said, his jaw clenched in frustration.

"I know! They're still in the trunk. I saw them there!" said April, proudly.

When Dad and Ben finally got in the car, and those begging to come along had been shooed away, Dad tried reassuring Ben that it might not be as bad as he thought. "Sometimes these things look worse than they really are. And even if you have to sit on the sidelines awhile, it might not be all bad. You'll be raring to go just about the time everyone else is getting a little tired of the game—you'll give the whole team a lift."

Ben didn't answer. For one thing, the toe still throbbed so badly he thought it might explode. For another, he could not imagine anyone getting tired of playing basketball. But the most important reason was that November 8 had been circled in purple marker on his calendar since early last spring. It had been tough counting down the days until that first practice.

If there was one thing Ben was no good at, it was waiting. As soon as he became aware of some future event, it was as if someone planted a noisy clock in the center of his brain. No matter how he tried, he could not stop thinking about it until it nearly drove him crazy. Now, just as he was nearing the end of the wait—this!

Slumped back in the rear seat, resting his leg on the seat, Ben brooded about the injustice of it all. There he was being a good kid, helping his parents, working hard and not even complaining. And what was his reward?

A half hour later, Dr. Weber filled him in on the details of his "reward." It was more like a prison term. Ben had been sentenced to at least two weeks of no activity, and then at least two more of light activity, which meant something other than basketball. After that, Dr. Weber would check to see how he was doing. Then, just *maybe*, he would give the okay.

As they were leaving the doctor's office, Dad tried to cheer Ben up. "It turned out better than I thought," he said. "You just clipped the fat part of your toe. When I first pulled off your sock, I thought you might have broken the thing in a dozen places."

But Ben wasn't listening. "Dr. Weber didn't say that I couldn't shoot baskets, did he?" he asked, hobbling through the parking lot on crutches. "That isn't really any kind of activity. I mean, I can shoot baskets standing still."

2
Homework

Whether or not Dr. Weber approved of Ben shooting baskets, Mom made it clear what she thought of the idea. "No activity means *no activity*, young man." He could not even bounce a basketball sitting in a basement chair without the little kids complaining about the noise.

"Come on! They can hear the TV. They're just being twerps, as usual," he grumbled. He expected his sore foot to win him some sympathy but Mom seemed to be going out of her way to make him miserable. Ben could have sworn she was glad he smashed his toe, just to keep him away from the thing he loved most in life. She insisted there would be no bouncing basketballs in the house, even in the basement. Ben couldn't even win that one.

Resenting his family's lack of understanding and frustrated by the slow healing of his toe, Ben could hardly stand to be around the house. For the first time in his life he was actually glad for the end of the long Thanksgiving weekend so he could get back to school and be with normal people. By that time he could have done without the crutches, but he liked to use them anyway. As long as he had to have an injury, he might as well look like a real injured basketball player!

After supper on the Tuesday after Thanksgiving, Ben went out into the darkness, clomping his way down the street to their church. The River Metro basketball league included both school and church teams. This fact had caused Ben a great deal of anguish during the early days of November. Everyone knew how good Ben Oakland was and they had all been begging him to join their team. Ben took it for granted that Pine Knoll School would have a better team than Faith Church. In fact, if he joined the Pine Knoll team they would easily be the best in the league. Pine Knoll also had a better coach—one of the school gym teachers. Faith had John Buckwell's dad for a coach. You could never tell how much dads knew about a sport—sometimes they just coached as a favor to their own kids.

But when Paul Schmidt and Dave Yamagita joined the church team, Ben decided to go along with them. When it came right down to it, he could not walk out on his closest friends. *Pablo and Rags owe me one for this,* he thought, using their pet names for each other. Ben's nickname was "Oak."

Ben maneuvered his way inside the door of the church gymnasium. Already there were echoing volleys of basketballs bouncing off the floor. This was the Faith Falcons' third practice. Despite the fact that it was sheer torture watching everyone else shoot, Ben could not stay away. At least here he could hold and bounce a basketball without getting chewed out. Every once in a while, when Coach Buckwell's back was turned, he even put up a shot.

"Hi, legless," greeted Pablo.

"Hi, brainless," Ben answered with a smile. They got no further into conversation before Coach Buckwell blew the whistle and gathered the troops under one basket. Ben scooped up a basketball, rubbed his hand over the worn, pebbled surface, and sat down next to the door.

The coach started them off with a lay-up drill. A few lay-ups told you all you needed to know about a person's basketball skill, Ben decided. You could tell that Rags had played before. He took his two steps and gently one-handed the ball up to the backboard. Although he didn't always make the shot, he knew what he was doing. Too bad he was so short. Pablo was an in-betweener. Big boned and solidly built, he relied much more on strength than grace. He sometimes took too many steps and often bounced the ball too hard off the backboard. But at least he had the general idea.

Then there were the Austin Lunds of the world. Austin could not run and dribble at the same time. His imitation of a lay-up was to clumsily bounce the ball two dozen times as he made his way toward the basket, then stop and shoot with two hands from underneath. Austin was not the only one who played like that, but he stood out from the others for a very good reason: Austin Lund was the tallest kid that Ben had ever seen. At six feet, one and a half inches, he even looked down on Coach Buckwell.

Austin did not go to Pine Knoll School, and Ben had never been in the same Sunday school class with him at Faith. The few times he had seen him around the church, he assumed that Austin was three or four years older. So when he saw Austin at the Falcons' first practice, Ben got excited. What an advantage to have someone that big playing under the basket!

That excitement, however, had lasted only as long as it took for Austin to "jump" for a rebound in the Falcons' first practice. Ben was not sure Austin's feet ever left the ground. It didn't matter much though, because the ball went through Austin's hands and hit him in the face. Ben had never before considered basketball a dangerous game. But as Austin sat on the sidelines holding a tissue to his rather large nose, Ben got the feeling that any time there was a ball in flight, the poor guy was not safe.

On this evening, Austin managed to avoid any embarrassing collisions with the ball. But that was the best that could be said for him. Coach Buckwell was trying to practice a full court press on defense. It seemed a good idea to have four players taking chances and swarming all over the dribbler while the giant waited under the basket as the last line of defense. Unfortunately, the last line of defense might as well have been made of air for all the good Austin was doing. The poor guy never met a fake that he didn't fall for. Pablo gave him the same fake three different times, and Austin went for it every time. As for shooting free throws, Austin was doing well if he hit the rim. One of his shots went *over* the backboard.

"At least he must be stronger than he looks," Ben commented later. "He's so skinny I didn't think he could throw a ball that far."

"Austin may be a giant, but I don't think he's going to do us any good," Pablo said afterwards. As the next largest player on the team, Pablo would probably end up playing center. He did not look forward to trying to shoot over kids who were four inches taller.

"This stuff's all new to him," Rags said.

"Yeah," Ben agreed. "I wonder what planet he's been living on. I can't imagine how someone that tall managed to avoid basketball for so long. Maybe if we work with him, he'll start to catch on. It would be a shame to let all that height go to waste."

"You know what will happen?" Rags sniffed. "He'll be the one who ends up making a million dollars playing pro basketball just because he's 7 feet tall."

"Well right now it doesn't matter how short you are," Ben comforted him. "If you played one-on-one with him, you could beat him blindfolded."

That night, Ben leaned back in his chair and wadded up a small piece of paper. "Lakers lead by four, with three minutes to go," he imagined. "The pass goes in to Ben Oakland. Magic Johnson is all over him. Here comes James Worthy on the trap. Oakland fakes a pass and cuts right through the double-team. He goes up." Ben fired the paper ball toward the wastebasket next to his bed. The wad bounced off the bedspread and into the basket. "He's hacked on the arm by Johnson but the shot goes in anyway. Oakland steps to the foul line with a chance for a three-point play."

Just then the door opened. Dad poked his head in and immediately saw the pile of spitballs lying beside the wastebasket. His dark eyebrows raised in suspicion. "Got your homework done?"

Ben straightened his chair and glanced at the open pages of his math book. "Just about."

Dad walked in and bent over Ben, one calloused hand leaning on the desk. "Suppose you show me what 'just about' means."

"Oh, I just have a few problems left on this page." Ben took up his pencil and began studying the next problem.

"How many?"

"Just five or six," Ben sighed, sounding exasperated. "It won't take me that long."

"Uh-huh. You've been sitting up here for more than an hour. And how many problems have you done in that time? Don't answer, I can see only two on your paper. Two down, six to go and you call this 'almost done'?"

"I don't get it, though," whined Ben. "This stuff's too hard."

"How would you know?" asked Dad. "I see you've spent the whole time taking target practice. Do you know what time it is?"

Ben glanced at his digital clock. "About 10 o'clock."

"Nearly quarter *past* 10 o'clock!" Dad said sternly. "You've got 20 minutes to work on your math. After that it's lights out. Whatever isn't done, isn't done and you can either get up early and do it or explain to your teacher why it isn't done. Understand?"

Ben did not answer. He hated math and he hated getting chewed out. It was all Dad's fault anyway. If he hadn't made him carry those blocks and left the sod right in the middle of the doorway, Ben wouldn't be missing so much basketball. If he could just play a little basketball every day, maybe he wouldn't be so bored. Then he would be able to get his math done. But no, he just had to sit and watch without even bouncing a basketball, thanks to Mom. They didn't even try to understand. They just liked bossing people around.

"How come I'm the only one who ever has homework?" Ben grumbled, poking the lead of his pencil through a hole in his sweatpants. "Ken's just sitting downstairs watching TV."

"That's because he sat down and did his homework instead of filling up wastebaskets with tiny packages. Now I mean it, 20 minutes!"

Twenty minutes later, the door burst open. Ben slammed shut the basketball magazine that he had been reading and spread his math paper over the top of it. Desperately, he hoped it was Ken coming to bed. But he could sense immediately by the size of the shadow that it was Dad again.

Without a word, Dad crossed the floor and snatched Ben's paper. It was virtually unchanged from the last time he had seen it. A second later he unearthed the *Pro Basketball* magazine. Dad did not get *really* angry often but Ben knew this would be one of those times. Ben was caught totally defenseless—he could not think of a single excuse—and he sat there almost in shock at his own stupidity.

"That does it!" Dad said, biting off each word. "I gave you 20 minutes to work on your assignment and you thought it would be cute to ignore me and read a basketball magazine. You're grounded for the week, and that includes basketball practice."

"No!" Ben said defiantly. His embarrassment had turned to anger on hearing the punishment. Why did they always pick on basketball? It was the one thing in the whole world that he really cared about. He'd already been cut off from it, and they still could not leave it alone. "You can make me go to bed earlier or fine me or make me do dishes for a week but you can't keep me out of basketball!"

"Don't tell me what I can and can't do! You're not setting the rules here! Furthermore you are not going to any basketball practices, healthy or not, unless you have every assignment finished by 9 o'clock in the evening every single school night of the year. Do you understand me?"

There it was again! Always out to get basketball! First Mom and now Dad. A pair of tag team wrestlers. They find the spot where they can hurt you the most and then take turns stomping on it until you give up. It was just mean and spiteful. "I'm not missing any basketball," he insisted, coldly.

"That's up to you," said Dad. "But what I said stands. If basketball is getting in the way of the important things you have to do, then you'll have to learn to do without it. Now can I trust you to get to bed or do I have to stand here and watch you do it?"

When Ken came to bed a few minutes later, Ben pretended to be asleep. He was finished with trying to be reasonable with people in this family.

3
The Mystery Note

The Oakland family penitentiary was at least bearable during December. Ben had to respect the threat of losing out on basketball, so he always finished his assignments by the appointed time. He also knew better than to bring on more arguments by being openly rude or by being too silent. Since he wanted as little to do with his family as possible, he decided it was best to meet the minimum standards of behavior. He would not be unpleasant but he would not be pleasant, either. He would answer questions but he would not volunteer any information. Even April and Nick got the cool treatment. Maybe they were just little kids, but they were part of the whole situation.

The day finally came, a week later than promised, when Ben was given permission to play some basketball. The toe still had to be heavily wrapped, and Ben was forbidden to take part in competition until after New Year's Day. That meant that he would miss the first two games, which were scheduled for the week after Christmas. But at least he could practice.

Even though a dusting of snow was swirling in the driveway under thick clouds, Ben ran outside with his basketball. Never mind that the ball lost some of its bounce in the cold weather, and that the thick gloves hampered his shooting. This was basketball, and there could be no Christmas present that would equal the thrill of watching that first shot swish through the net.

At Tuesday night practice, Ben felt as though he could soar higher and run faster than anyone else. There was no place on earth he would rather be than on a basketball floor, and it was not costing him a cent to be there!

Coach Buckwell dampened some of the fun by enforcing the doctor's ban on all competitive drills. "The more careful you are in this sport, the more you get stepped on, it seems," Coach told him. "For now, just join in the shooting and passing drills and hold off on the scrimmages. Listen up, everybody!" he called, in his gravelly voice. "Listen up. I want you all to pair off and just practice passing and catching. Mix in some bounce passes."

Pablo whistled at Ben to join him, but Ben shook his head. He had been fascinated by something he had read in a sports article about how the true measure of a great player is that he can make everyone around him play better. Ben decided that if he wanted to be great, he would have to work on doing that. What better person to practice on than Austin Lund? As tall as he was, if someone could teach him to play ball, he could make the Falcons one tough team.

"Go ahead with Rags," Ben said to Pablo. "I want to get to know our giant a little better. Hey, Austin! Over here."

Austin seemed surprised to have been singled out. As he jogged over, Ben noticed that his small head made him look even taller. Austin was so timid on the court that Ben was surprised at how friendly he was. "So you're Ben. I hear you're pretty good."

Ben grinned. "And you're Austin. I hear you're pretty tall."

Austin shook his head. "Just a vicious rumor. I only look tall because I'm so skinny, and because my head is so high off the ground."

"Have you ever played basketball before?" Ben asked as he tossed him a chest high pass.

Austin's hands gave away the answer before the fellow could open his mouth. He stiffened up as the ball came toward him, as if this were a difficult trick he was being asked to perform. "I've never played any sport before," smiled Austin, after making a bobbling catch.

"How come?" Ben asked, casually latching onto Austin's pass with one hand.

"I never thought I was any good. I know, I know," he laughed. "You can't imagine what ever gave me that idea!"

"So what made you try now?" Ben purposely threw soft passes. This was almost like playing catch with Nick.

"I keep growing and everyone says I should play basketball. You know, if you have webbed feet you're supposed to swim. If you have feathers, you're supposed to fly. If you're tall, you're supposed to play basketball."

"How do you like it so far?" Ben risked a bounce pass to Austin and to his surprise, the guy caught it.

"It isn't so much a matter of liking it as it is just surviving," admitted Austin. "When I come out here I feel like I'm in a foreign country where everyone knows the language but me."

"Well, how smart are you? You know this game is just as much mental as it is being coordinated."

"I'm the most brilliant C student in the whole metro area," smiled Austin. "It's funny. People see how clumsy I am at sports and they automatically think I'm a superbrain."

"Well, it works both ways," Ben said. "People see I can play basketball and they think I'm stupid. Shoot, my parents think I'm stupid *because* I play basketball. But, hey, don't worry about it. Being tall really will make it easier for you. You'll like the game once you get used to it," Ben said. "Here, throw the ball straight out from your chest, not from the side. Keep doing it as hard as you can; don't worry about hurting me."

Austin did as he was told, and Ben actually

thought he could detect some improvement. "Thanks for the help," Austin said when a whistle blast ended the drill. "Most of the others act like I'm some kind of freak."

"Hey, you work hard, you can help this team," shrugged Ben. "Tell you what. I know the janitor at this church pretty well. If you want, we can come over here every afternoon during winter break and I can work with you."

The suggestion seemed to stump Austin. "Well, that's really a nice offer. Maybe I could. You got any tips on playing defense?" Austin changed the subject. "I think it's even more embarrassing having people score against me than it is not being able to score against them."

"Didn't the coach tell you anything?" Ben asked, in a voice low enough so that Coach Buckwell couldn't hear. "The best tip on defense is don't look at the other guy's head or you'll get faked out. Keep your eye on his belly button. There aren't too many guys who can fake with their belly button."

"All right. Except that most kids' belly buttons are quite a ways down there."

Ben romped through the lay-up drills without a miss in six attempts. At the free throw line he sank 6 of 10 shots. That was a little below average for him, but he still tied Rags for the best mark on the team. Austin kept his streak alive by missing all 10 of his. After that, Coach Buckwell put the team through scrimmages. Ben begged one more time to join in, but was waved away. He moved off by himself to the far end of the court to practice dribbling with either hand.

Coach Buckwell was determined to use the full court press on defense. That meant they were to guard the other team closely all over the court and never give them a chance to rest. The only defender who was to fall back on defense was the center. Unfortunately during this evening's practice, the press only worked when Rags was playing defense. Whenever Rags was on offense he just dribbled past the defense as if they were flags on a ski racing course. In the mass of confusion, one of the forwards would always get open under the basket. Rags would simply throw a long pass to Pablo, who would fake out Austin for an easy basket. There was one hopeful moment when Austin actually blocked a shot, but Pablo retrieved the loose ball and laid it in for the score.

"When you get in the lineup we can probably work the press pretty well, Oak," Pablo said to Ben as he and Rags waited for their ride after practice.

"Coach will have to put Pablo in at center, though," Rags said, after checking first to make sure that Austin wasn't around. "Austin just isn't ready for prime time."

"I don't think he ever will be," Pablo said. "He could be the most improved player on the team at the end of the year and still be the worst player in the league."

"Give him time," Ben said. "He's never played before. I predict he'll do some serious damage before the season's over."

"He's already done more damage to his nose than any player I ever saw," said Rags.

"Don't be so hard on him," Ben said. "Have you ever talked to him? He's really kind of funny."

"You mean he talks just like he plays?" chuckled Pablo.

Ben shrugged them off and sat down to put on his boots. Three inches of snow had fallen since school was out, and his mom always had a fit about him getting his "expensive" basketball shoes wet. That was typical, the way she cared more about his shoes than about him.

As Ben slid a foot inside one boot, though, it brushed against a lump. Thinking the liner in the boot had gotten bunched up, Ben stuck his hand in to straighten it. But instead of finding soft fabric, his fingers touched something colder and smoother. It was a bright blue envelope.

"Do you always have mail inside your boots?" laughed Rags.

"What's it say, Oak?" asked Pablo. "Who's it from?"

Ben tore open the unaddressed envelope. Inside was a small sheet of paper with a note. The printing was so childish that Ben could hardly read it. Rags, peering over Ben's shoulder, figured it out before Ben could hide it.

" 'Hope you had a nice practice. We're pulling for you all the way. Signed, Order of the Broken Arrow.' Whoa, pretty heavy stuff!" said Rags. "Oak's got some secret admirers!"

"Did one of you guys stick this in here?" demanded Ben. Both his friends denied any knowledge of it. "So who put it in? Did you see anyone messing with my boots?"

"You had your boots out here in the hall, Oak," said Rags. "It could have been anyone. We never would have seen them."

"This is weird," frowned Ben.

"Aw, enjoy it!" said Rags. "How many guys have their own fan club? I don't know how you do it, you sly fox! Girls are so hot on you they start sending notes. Boy, that's rough."

"What makes you think this is from girls?" Ben asked.

"I'll bet it was the crutches," Pablo said. "I read that girls really go crazy for guys on crutches. I could use some attention like that. Could one of you guys step on my foot, just hard enough so I have an excuse to use them?"

"How about if I step on your face?" Ben shot back. "Maybe the girls will think that's an improvement."

"Here's our ride," said Rags opening the door and letting a cool rush of air inside. "You'll just have to suffer with being popular."

"Can I have your autograph?" Pablo called back

as he followed Rags to the idling car.

"For a dollar," Ben answered. Now that the others were gone, he unfolded the crumpled paper and reread it. This was really strange! In a way it felt good to have someone claiming to be a fan of his. Even though he was too suspicious to trust it completely, just reading the words and pretending gave him a small ego lift.

But Ben had no more patience for mysteries than he had for anything else. The clues kept nagging at him. The babyish writing really had him puzzled. And who or what was the Order of the Broken Arrow? As he walked home he tried to figure out who would do such a thing. But even after running a long list of acquaintances through his mind, Ben could not even come up with one suspect.

4
The Shot

Ben sat glumly on the edge of the stage, wondering why he had bothered to put on his red Falcons uniform. After all, Coach Buckwell had made it clear that Ben would not be playing in this game against the Patterson Panthers.

As he watched the two squads miss shots, kick the ball around, and throw passes out-of-bounds, Ben could hardly believe they had spent a month practicing basketball skills.

"I could score 50 points against these guys," he thought. Having to sit there on the bench watching a game was much harder than watching practice. It was all he could do to keep from running out and grabbing the basketball.

Although this was the first game Ben had seen, it was not the Falcons' first game. They had been manhandled by the Lincoln Bay Lakers 46-10 just two nights earlier. Ben's absence had been the result of more troubles on the home front, on Christmas Day, of all times.

It all started when Nick asked Ben to read the books on dinosaurs he had gotten for Christmas. In the spirit of the season, Ben had turned up his personality a notch on the pleasantness scale, and had already read two books to his younger brother that morning. By the time Nick came begging for a third reading, Ben was busy working on his Boston Celtics team picture jigsaw puzzle, a surprise gift from Mom.

"I'm sorry, Nick, I already read to you twice," he had said. "Now I'm in the middle of something I want to do. Get Ken to read it."

"Ken's helping April with that stupid Magic Dungeon game."

"How about Dad or Grandpa?"

Nick clambored up the stairs only to return to the basement with an irritating news bulletin. "Grandpa's playing with April and Mom says they're busy making dinner and you're not doing anything so you have to read it to me. So there!"

Had he remained calm and taken some time to think about it, Ben might have had realized that Nick was not the most accurate reporter. As a matter of fact, the kid had twisted Ben's statement to Mom as well as Mom's message to Ben. Ben's blue eyes flashed anger, however, and rather than checking out Nick's story, he called off the Christmas truce.

"Sure, I'll read it to you," he said, as Nick climbed on his lap. Flipping quickly through the pages, he read, "Dinosaurs were big creatures. They ate elephants and bananas and slept in abandoned garbage trucks and now they're all dead. The end." With that he slammed the book shut and booted Nick off his lap.

"That's not what it said!" Nick screamed. Seconds later most of Ben's jigsaw puzzle pieces were dashed to the floor and Nick's bottom was swatted as tears and angry shouts drowned out the Christmas music on the stereo. Mom, who had been frantically trying to get a perfect meal together while everything was still hot, blew her top.

Tired of being pushed around, Ben refused to apologize. Despite Dad's and Grandpa's best efforts at peacemaking, the argument grew more heated until Ben stomped off up to his room.

"You're not missing Christmas dinner!" Mom yelled up to him. "If you don't come down right now, you can forget about going to your basketball game tomorrow."

Ben had not come down, and it had been a thoroughly miserable Christmas for everyone, especially with all of it happening in front of Grandpa. Dad backed up the punishment of missing the first game, and so Ben had been spared the agony of watching his team get creamed.

Mom gave up speaking to him after that, and for a time the little kids stared at him as if he were some dangerous criminal. Ken kept telling him he was "immature," and Dad had been surprisingly quiet on the whole subject. The only relief Ben found during the week had been those afternoon practice sessions at the church gym with Austin. The big guy seemed eager to learn and Ben was eager to teach him. They fired passes at the wall from close range and tried to catch them; fortunately the finger Austin sprained was on his left hand. Then they worked on shooting free throws, and shuffling the feet on defense. Ben even taught Austin the hook shot and had him repeat the maneuver again and again.

The second session didn't last as long as the first, and Austin kept glancing at his watch. The big guy didn't always seem to be paying attention to what Ben was saying, especially after the first half hour. But Ben was seeing improvement. If they kept at it every day of vacation, there might be some hope for the new center.

In this game against Patterson, though, Austin Lund was hardly a beacon of hope. After entering the game in the second period, Austin only touched the ball once—when a rebound bounced off his shoulder and into the hands of a Panther. On offense, Rags looked at Austin several times, but always thought better about risking a pass to him. Fortunately, the Patterson guards were having such trouble handling the ball that they never got any fast break chances against Austin.

Just before halftime, though, Austin produced a blunder of such magnificence that even his opponents were wincing in embarrassment for him. The gangly center was knocked over in a scramble after a rebound. A Panther was called for the foul, and that put Austin on the free throw line, all by himself, in front of everybody. As the referee handed him the ball, Austin blinked and gulped and trembled as though he were facing a firing squad.

After bouncing the ball for what seemed like five minutes, he summoned the courage to risk a shot. He bent his knees the way Ben had shown him. But as he let the ball go, he lost his balance and teetered over the foul line. Swinging his arms to regain control, he struggled to keep his feet behind the line as the ball sailed in a high arc toward the hoop. All of his efforts were in vain. He crashed to the floor in the lane without anyone touching him.

Miraculously, the ball went through the net, but that only made matters worse. The referee took away the point because Austin crossed over the foul line. Ben thought it was an act of mercy when Coach Buckwell promptly removed Austin from the game. It was especially thoughtful of Coach to put in three substitutes at once so that Austin would not feel like he was yanked out for sheer clumsiness.

"Doesn't look good for us," said John Buckwell, the coach's son, as he sat down next to Ben. His round face was flushed. John was the heaviest of the Falcon players, and after several minutes of chasing the Panthers around the court, he seemed glad to have a replacement.

"We're only down by four points," shrugged Ben. "The game isn't even half over."

"Yeah, but this is supposed to be the worst team in the league," huffed John as he wiped his forehead with the bottom of his shirt.

The statement jolted Ben out of his slouch. "Where did you hear that?" he asked. Even though Ben had not been involved in the loss to the Lakers, he was ashamed of the score. The thought of adding to that humiliation by losing to the worst team in the league was almost more than he could take.

"They lost by 20 points to the Redeemer Rockets in their first game," John said. "A lot of those Rockets go to my school, and they aren't very good."

Nobody scored in the final two minutes of the period, so the halftime score stood at 13-9 in favor of the Panthers. Rags had scored seven of the Falcons' points and Chris Moret, one of the reserve forwards, had scored the other basket on a rebound. Pablo had tried two shots early in the first quarter and both had been blocked. After that he seemed only too eager to pass the ball.

As the group gathered around Coach Buckwell in one corner of the gym, several of the players were complaining to others about their poor passes. For some reason, it took the Coach a long time to get his thoughts together. Twice he asked for quiet, but each time he got it, he just ran a large hand through his wavy, grayish hair and stared at the floor until the chattering started up again.

"My toe feels great," Ben said. "I got it all taped up just in case. Can't I play, please?"

"You guys want to play?" Coach said. "Then let's have it quiet." Several more seconds went by before he said, "All right. You're doing fine. I see lots of hustle. There's a lot of mistakes but they're hustle mistakes and those will go away once you get some experience. You need to think about what you're doing, now. David, don't start dribbling as soon as you get the ball. When you catch the ball you have two options: you can either pass or dribble. If you start dribbling right away and then have to stop, then your only choice is to pass the ball. That makes it too easy for the defense. Look for the pass first, then dribble."

"Can I play? Just a few minutes," begged Ben. "The toe's perfect and I promise I'll stay out of traffic. I'll just play around the outside."

Coach turned on him slowly, his gray eyes peeking out of his thick eyelids. "Do you understand English? Your doctor said to avoid contact 'til after New Year's. That's final. Now, second half," he started. Obviously Ben had distracted him because he stared at his sheet of paper for several seconds before continuing. "Remember I'm going to give everyone some playing time. We'll keep getting fresh troops in there so we can always play tough, full court defense. Chuck and Nathan at guards to start out with. Chris and John at forward. How's the elbow, Austin? You ready to play?" Austin nodded nervously and Coach finished, "Austin at center."

Ben trudged back to the stage, flanked by Rags and Pablo. "You guys can't let these jokers beat you," Ben said. "We'll never be able to show our faces at school again."

"What do you want from me?" Rags said wearily. "I'm doing everything I can."

Pablo glanced up sheepishly. "I didn't have a very good half. I don't think I was warmed up enough. Maybe it's because I had to sit in the cold car for five minutes before Dad finally got ready." He glanced up at the rows of chairs on the stage to see if his dad was close enough to hear.

Ben thought again about how nice it would have been to have played on the Pine Knoll team. They had some good, tall players like Rudy and Rich. If he were on the Pine Knoll Knicks he wouldn't have to worry about the teasing at school, or about being embarrassed by his own teammates. Except for Rags, the Falcons were too slow. Except for Austin, who hardly counted, they were too short.

Ben was tempted to take a dig at his friends for insisting they play on the church team. But they were discouraged, and you had to give it to poor Rags—he was playing his heart out. Ben refused to lose hope. Things would be different once he got back into action. If only Austin could learn a few of the basics, then Pablo could play forward where he could do a better job, and then they'd do all right.

The Falcon unit that Coach Buckwell sent out did nothing to change the team's fortunes. In five minutes they went scoreless, and gave up two baskets to the Panthers.

"Come on, now. It's 17-9. Don't let them get away from you!" Ben shouted as Rags, Pablo, and John ran out onto the court. He could not sit still and began fidgeting on the stairs leading up to the stage. School vacation would soon be over and he knew just what he would hear even before he got his coat off in the classroom. Rudy would be laughing his head off at how the Falcons lost to the crummy Panthers.

Rags was all over the court, his straight black hair whipping from side to side with each screeching halt and change of direction. By the end of the quarter, the team had cut the margin to 18-15, thanks to two steals by Rags in the Panthers' backcourt, and foul shots by Pablo and Nathan.

"You're getting them, now!" Ben said, as the Falcons huddled up before starting the final period. "Keep on them!" He was so pumped up he didn't know what to do with his hands. He kept clenching and unclenching his fists and trying to keep his stomach muscles from tying themselves into knots.

The final quarter was pure agony for Ben. Rags would steal a pass only to slip and lose the ball to the Panthers. Pablo would block a shot only to have the nearsighted referee blow the whistle on him for a foul. Austin would catch a ball under the basket only to have it knocked out of his hands before he could try a shot.

The clock wound down to two minutes, one minute, 30 seconds. Trailing 22-19, Rags charged down the court toward the Falcons' basket on the far end of the court. He sent a long pass to John who tossed up a desperate, two-handed shot.

"There are 25 seconds left, John," Coach Buckwell called calmly to his son. "Get a better shot than that." Ben, still pacing the stairs, threw his head back in despair and pounded the tiled wall with his fist. The shot missed the rim, the backboard, everything, but landed squarely in the chest of a very surprised Austin. After staring at the ball for a second, he was spurred into action by a dozen cries from the parents' section far down the court.

Austin eyed the basket, hesitated, and then shuffled the ball to Pablo, who was standing just a foot away. Pablo, who had been getting in position for a possible rebound, nearly dropped the unexpected pass. But he managed to bank the ball off the backboard and into the net.

"All right, Pablo!" shouted Ben. After anxiously checking the scoreboard clock, he joined the screams of "Defense! Defense!"

Rags was scurrying from player to player like a waterbug, swiping and slapping at the ball. He tipped one pass but a Panther got to it first. More Falcons swarmed around the kid who picked up the ball.

"Don't foul him!" said Coach Buckwell.

The Panther twisted and turned but was surrounded by red jerseys, each of which seemed to have three hands. Instead of trying to pass the ball, he clutched it tight against his chest and bent over it with his body. After a few seconds, the referee signaled a jump ball.

"Who's going to jump it, ref?" shouted one parent. It was a good question. There were at least three Falcons who had tied up the Panthers.

"I hope it's not Rags," whispered Ben. As the shortest player on the floor, Rags could not hope to win a jump ball. The referee selected John for the jump-off. As the ball hung in the air, neither boy could gain control of the tap. The ball fell to the floor where Rags pounced on it.

"Time out!" called Coach Buckwell. There were nine seconds left. The Falcons huddled anxiously around their coach. "All right, all right. Here's what we're going to do," said the coach. There was no bickering or chatter as the players waited for the formula that would give them the win.

As the team waited, hardly daring to breath, the coach mulled over his options. The silence was hardest on Ben, who blurted out, "Put me in, Coach! I can make the shot. I don't have to drive into the middle or anything. All I have to do is stand out there and shoot it."

Coach's black eyebrows took on a menacing appearance as he turned to Ben. But then his look softened, as though Ben's suggestion had suddenly walked over and slugged him in the face.

Sensing the coach's hesitation for the first time, Ben stepped up the pressure. "I only have to stand and shoot, just like I've been doing in practice all week. There isn't a *chance* of getting hurt. I promise! Just pass me the ball and, boom! I shoot before anyone knows I have it."

As the referee blew the whistle summoning them back onto the court, Coach Buckwell finally spoke. "Okay, we'll try it. John, pass the ball in to Dave. Dave, get down the court fast and drop it off for Ben. Ben, you shoot and then back out of the way. The rest of you be ready for a rebound. You understand that, Ben? You're just shooting, nothing else!"

Ben nodded eagerly. He could hardly believe it! He was getting in the game, and with everything on the line. All he had to do was make his shot and the Falcons would win. He could show his face at school and not have to take any of Rudy's smart talk.

As Ben trotted off to center court, it never occurred to him that he might miss the shot. Number 14 in the black Panther uniform trotted toward him. "I'll have to lull this guy to sleep," Ben thought. Most of the parents were yelling encouragement to both sides as John tossed the ball in to Rags. The little guard zoomed down the court with a Panther right by his side.

Ben stood with his hands on his hips, as if he was just going to watch Rags take the ball to the hoop.

His defender turned to watch, too. Just then Ben took two quick steps toward the middle. The defender, caught by surprise, dashed after him. As he did, Ben stopped, took two steps the other way and held his arms out for the ball. The defender was still several steps away when Ben lofted his shot.

The ball ripped through the net cleanly with two seconds to spare. Ben ran and jumped across the court toward his coach as if powerful electrodes were wired to his shorts. Some of his teammates leaped off the stage and ran toward him with their fists pumping the air. But Coach Buckwell grabbed the leaders by the backs of their jerseys and jerked them back.

"His foot, his foot! Come on, don't go jumping on him! Hey, get off the court! There's still two seconds left."

Ben, grinning broadly, accepted hand slaps from all the Falcons on the bench. The team was so excited that no one remembered to take Ben's place on defense for the last two seconds. Fortunately, the Panthers were unable to get the ball across midcourt. The Falcons hopped up and down like a batch of red-coated popcorn bursting with the excitement of the win.

They savored the win for nearly ten minutes, exchanging their personal stories of what happened in those final seconds. The Falcons finally broke off and attached themselves to their parents. Ben was riding with Rags's parents tonight. When it seemed they were ready to go, he searched for his coat in a corner of the stage.

Stuffed in the pocket was a familiar blue envelope. Ben stepped back behind a stage curtain and ripped open the envelope. Reading hastily, before Rags or Pablo could see him, he found that same childish scrawl that he had seen before.

"Congratulations on waiting it out! Now you'll be free to play. May your season bring you all the joy you have hoped for. The Order of the Broken Arrow."

Following Pablo's hint that the letters were from a girl, Ben had meant to keep these notes a secret. But this one did not sound like anything a girl would write. It sounded more like an adult. He stuffed the letter in his pocket. As he came out from behind the curtain, he scanned the gym for clues as to who might be writing him notes. Nobody seemed to be giving any secret, sly glances or pretending that they did not notice him.

This is really weird, he thought.

5
A Suspect

It was a toss-up as to which was gloomier—the cold gymnasium lit up only by a row of small windows near the ceiling, or Austin Lund's face. This private practice session with Ben, two days before the end of winter break, was the worst yet.

It was not Austin's play that was so depressing. In fact, his free throw shooting had improved, he was catching the ball better, and he was starting to learn some things about playing defense. But Austin had arrived a few minutes late without a trace of spring in his step. It took him forever to peel off his coat. When Ben tossed him the basketball, Austin's expression reminded him of the way April looked at a pile of broccoli on her plate.

Every movement seemed to be an effort for Austin. But the worst part was that he didn't remember anything. He would nod while Ben spoke about using his body to shield the ball from defenders. But just 30 seconds later he would hold the ball right out where Ben could slap it away.

"Is something bugging you?" Ben asked. "You've been out to lunch ever since you showed up here."

Austin gulped and said, "Well, you see, I've been thinking about this quite a bit, and I don't really know if I'm into basketball all that much. I mean, let's face it, the whole thing has been pretty much of a disaster."

"I keep telling you that's just because you're new at it. Look how much better you're getting. You just have to keep working. It'll come."

"So will the glaciers, if you give them enough time," said Austin. "I just don't know if it's worth all the time I'm putting into it."

"You can't get anything really worthwhile in life without paying the price," Ben said. He felt a little odd giving someone else one of the very lines that he hated getting from his parents. Well, if that's what it took to keep from losing the tallest player in the league, that's what Ben would do.

"On the other hand," sighed Austin, "there's no sense in beating a dead horse. I don't exactly get the feeling that the one reason God put me on this earth was to play basketball."

"He made you tall, didn't He?" challenged Ben.

"I'm not sure that has anything to do with it," Austin said. For the first time since Ben had known him, Austin shook off his timid posture and started to get angry. "Look, God gave me a big nose, too. Does that mean I'm supposed to be a comedian? I get pretty tired of people telling me what I'm supposed to do just because of how I look."

"No one's forcing you to do anything," Ben said, innocently. "I just thought you might like some extra help so you could make use of your size and really help the team. If you don't care about that, fine."

"I appreciate all the help you're giving me, Ben. But it's just too much. I can't be spending so much time at it. I've been so busy with this I haven't had any time to even do my art lessons, and my parents are paying a lot of money for those."

Art lessons? Ben almost laughed at the idea. *How could someone as awkward as Austin ever learn how to handle a paintbrush? He'd probably miss the paper half the time.* "You mean you're quitting the team?" hc asked.

"I didn't say that," Austin replied. "I know I'm not much good, but it is kind of fun being on a team. You know, a bunch of guys all pulling for each other; it's really a different feeling. After you made that last shot to win the other night and we were all going wild, that was great! I don't mind the regular practices and I like getting a chance to play every game. It's just that—" Austin started fidgeting and his gaze dropped to the floor.

"You don't want any more of these extra practices," sighed Ben. So much for the big center they needed to win the championship.

"Yeah, I guess that's it," Austin said sheepishly. "You never seem to get tired of basketball but I just can't take so much of it."

"Fine," Ben shrugged, trying to hide his disappointment. "Just trying to help."

Austin straightened up as though a heavy weight had been lifted from his shoulders. "Want to finish with a free throw contest? Best out of 20 shots?"

Ben accepted the challenge and easily won, making 14 shots to Austin's 7. As they scooped up their jackets, Austin found a blue envelope lying next to their boots. "What's this? It's got your name on it."

Ben stared at the envelope. No one else had entered the gym the whole time they were practicing. "Did you see anyone come in here when you showed up?" Austin shook his head. "Somebody keeps slipping me secret notes. Whoever's doing it would make a great spy." He opened the note and read it.

"No matter where you go, no matter what you do, we are always thinking of you. The Order of the Secret Arrow." The whole goofy thing was starting to get on his nerves. He showed the note to Austin.

Austin's eyes grew wide with horror. "Sounds like a death threat! You think the Panthers are mad at you for that last shot?"

"No," laughed Ben. "I thought they were love notes at first. Maybe they still are, but they're so strange. I can't figure it out. I guess I'm just stuck with a secret admirer. Sure wish I knew who it was, though. Seems like a younger kid, especially with handwriting like that. But the words sound too grown up."

"Wow! It must really be something to be such a star," said Austin, shaking his head.

The notes kept coming. Ben had come to expect finding them at practice, but the matter really got serious when he opened his school locker and a blue envelope fluttered to the ground. Rags happened to be with him and he shook his head in bewilderment.

"They're everywhere," Rags chuckled. "Somebody really has it for you bad, Oak. It's almost scary."

Ben read the message, which was very similar to all the others. Then he ripped it into tiny pieces and dropped them in a wastebasket.

"This has gone a little bit too far," Ben said. "I don't mind having a fan club, but I don't like the idea of somebody on my tail everywhere I go."

"So what are you going to do?" Rags asked.

"I need some help," Ben said. "Whoever it is always waits until I'm not looking before making a move. They're sneaky enough so that I can't catch them. What I need is for you and Pablo to keep an eye out for me. You might be able to spot them doing something while my back is turned."

"I can't spend the whole day out in the hall watching your locker," Rags said.

"Neither can the note sender," said Ben. "I just want you to keep an eye on my locker whenever you happen to be out in the hall. Let me know if you see anything strange going on."

"If I told you everything strange I saw going on in this school, we'd never have time for anything else."

"Just do it, would you?"

Rags saluted. "Yessir. I won't let you down, sir."

"And tell Pablo."

It was Pablo who came bursting into the lunchroom with the report two days later. "Oak! Rub my head, would you? Maybe some of what you got will rub off on me!"

Ben let the bite of peanut butter sandwich rest in his mouth for a moment. "What is your problem?"

"My problem is that Ms. Marinetti isn't in love with me."

Just then Rags trotted through the doors, scanned the room for a moment, and rushed over to them. A stern glance from the principal slowed him to a fast walk, but he was nearly breathless when he reached Ben. Rubbing his friend's shoulders like a trainer soothing a prizefighter he said, "Oak, you sly fox! How do you do it?!"

Staring up at his two grinning friends, Ben swallowed the sandwich and said, "Is your disease contagious?"

"I sure hope yours is," said Pablo, grabbing his hand. "Here, touch me!"

"I'm sorry to hear about the loss of your brain," said Ben, turning away from them. "But then I heard you weren't really very close to it anyway. Let me know when you get back to reality."

Pablo and Rags pulled out chairs, one on each side of Ben. "We did it, Oak," said Pablo. "Superspies at your service. We found out who your secret lover is."

"She really messed up this time," added Rags. "Pablo and I were at opposite ends of the hall and we both saw her slip a *blue envelope* under the door of your locker. Caught her red-handed, both of us."

"Really?" Ben didn't know which of his friends to turn to. "So come on, already. Who is it?"

"You sly dog," said Rags.

"We should make him pay," said Pablo to Rags. "This info's worth a fortune. We'd never have to work for the rest of our lives."

"If you don't tell me now, there won't be any rest of your lives to worry about."

Rags and Pablo grinned at each other. "Are you ready?" asked Pablo. "It's Ms. Marinetti!"

"Very funny," said Ben, sarcastically. It was ridiculous enough that they chose someone from the school staff as the supposed letter writer. But Ms. Marinetti, the new librarian, was the most gorgeous woman any of them had ever seen. "Big joke."

"We're not playing with you, man!" said Rags.

"Get this!" said Pablo, sitting on the end of his seat. "I'm coming up the stairs and the first thing I see is Ms. Marinetti kneeling on the floor shoving a blue envelope in the bottom of your locker."

"I swear it's the truth!" said Rags. "I saw it, too."

"You guys, this isn't even funny," sneered Ben.

"Okay, you don't believe us?" said Pablo. "You know that powerful perfume she's always wearing? Run by the library and get a whiff of it and see if it ain't the same stuff that rubbed off on the letter."

Ben still didn't really believe it, but if these two were acting, they were doing a better job than usual. When he got to his locker, there was a corner of a blue envelope hanging out. Ben pulled it out and read, "These notes are just to let you know how special you are. Enjoy the day. Order of the Broken Arrow." Ben ran the envelope by his nose and, sure enough, there was an unmistakable scent to it.

"You sly fox," Rags said, chucking him under the chin.

6
Miscalculation

Ben finished the school day in a daze. Ms. Marinetti in love with him? There were movie stars who would have given anything to have her looks. He knew he was in way over his head on this one. "Come on, I'm just a kid," he kept saying to himself. The whole notion had him so dumbfounded that he was glad he had a basketball game that night. If there was one thing that could get his mind off Ms. Marinetti for a while, it was basketball.

Unfortunately, while Ben was running through a pregame lay-up drill, he spotted her coming through the double doors of the gym. Rags saw it, too, and as he flipped a rebound to Ben he said, "Sly dog!"

Ben could not believe it. Here was the moment he had been waiting for. After all these months of waiting and six weeks of nursing an injured foot, he was finally going to do what he loved best in life—play a game of basketball. And now something had come up that totally distracted him. *She* was here to watch him play.

His walk took on a slightly cocky swagger as he tried to live up to the role that had been thrust on him. He decided that he would put on a show for her that she would never forget.

The Richland Raiders were a well-coached team. Unlike many players who would pass only when it was certain they could not get a shot off, the Raiders passed the ball around, looking for a good shot. Even with Ben joining Rags at the guard position, the Falcons' full court press was unable to force many turnovers. If not for the fact that the Raiders missed a large number of open shots, the Falcons would have been in deep trouble.

As it was, Ben was able to match points with them. Drawing extra strength as he felt the eyes of Ms. Marinetti on him, he kept driving into the lane for lay-ups, or faking a drive and firing up a longer shot. By the end of the first quarter, he had already scored 12 points, more than the Falcons' entire team had scored in their first game.

Sitting on the bench in the second quarter, Ben risked several sidelong glances towards Ms. Marinetti. She was playing it as cagey as ever. In fact, she was going out of her way to make it look as though she were really cheering for the Raiders. When they tied the score just before halftime, she even jumped to her feet and clapped her hands.

Nice act, he smiled to himself. *But you're wasting your breath. I'm wise to you now.*

Having served his time on the bench, Ben

expected to play the entire second half. This time they would be going for the basket right in front of Ms. Marinetti. *Yessir, Ms. Marinetti,* he thought. *Sit back and enjoy the show. There's no way these clowns are going to stay with us.*

The Falcons wasted no time in regaining the lead. Rags forced a bad pass in the Raiders' backcourt. Ben intercepted and laid it in for the score. It was all he could do to resist looking to see her reaction.

Ben felt so strong and sure of himself that he almost toyed with the defenders. Even when he was double-teamed, he could sometimes get both opponents off balance with a clever fake. He missed a couple of shots, though, and after a third straight miss, he was angry enough at himself that he bulled over a couple of Raiders to get the rebound.

The referee blew his whistle and called out "Red, number 22, over the back on the rebound. Blue team's ball." Ben stared at the referee for a moment with a sarcastic smile. Then he shook his head as he retreated downcourt for defense.

Coach Buckwell finally took him out of the game with two minutes to go. But as he slumped into the chair feeling pleasantly fatigued, he knew the game was over. The Falcons were ahead 37 to 30. He glanced back up at Ms. Marinetti and saw her smiling and talking to a woman sitting next to her. He knew he must have made her proud. By his own unofficial count, he had scored 28 points, nearly enough to beat the Raiders all by himself.

"This is the life," he thought. "Man, I love basketball!" Having someone like Ms. Marinetti backing him was frosting on an already delicious cake. "It's nice someone cares about what I do," Ben thought. His own parents had not even bothered to show up.

The game ended at 38 to 34. Ben hardly noticed the congratulations from his teammates, and his mind was too busy with other things to offer many himself. He was more curious to see what Ms. Marinetti had put in the note that he knew he would find in his boots.

"Pretty soon maybe we'll be able to talk. Hope you enjoyed your game. Thinking of you, Order of the Broken Arrow."

"Wow!" said Ben.

"If I were you, I'd ask her to marry me quick, before she changes her mind about you," said Pablo.

"Would you stop being such a dork?" said Ben. But he could not help feeling proud. Of all the guys in the whole school, or in the whole world, who thought Ms. Marinetti was a knockout, it was he, Ben Oakland, who had the rights to her.

The three of them were squeezing their way through the front hall traffic toward the waiting buses. "The note said she wanted to talk to you, man," Rags said. "So what are you waiting for? She's probably all alone in the library."

"Chicken!" said Pablo.

Somehow having Ms. Marinetti in the palm of his

hand brought out the daring in Ben. Without a word of explanation, he left his two grinning friends standing in the bus line and threaded his way through the crowd toward the stairway.

Ms. Marinetti was not exactly alone in the library. But the five or six students sharing the wide open spaces of the room with her were spread out far enough away that it would be possible to hold a private conversation. She was sitting underneath a buzzing fluorescent ceiling panel, logging in some data on a computer terminal. Her blonde hair was curled back from the sides of her face and her long eyelashes blinked frequently as she studied the data.

Ben walked toward her. His heart suddenly jumped as he picked up the scent of that perfume. She gave no hint of noticing him. He felt foolish just standing there, so he picked up a reference book that happened to be nearby.

Several times he glanced up at her, and finally she happened to look up as well. Ben's mouth instantly dried into a desert. "Hi," he croaked.

"Hi, Ben," she smiled. "Anything I can help you with?"

Ben reminded himself that she was the one who was crazy about him. "Maybe," he said innocently. "Is there anything I can help you with?"

She raised a curious eyebrow as she typed in some more numbers. "Ach, dummy!" she said, erasing some numbers off the screen. "Well, are you any good at databases?"

"I don't know, I'm pretty good with computers," he said, coming around the side of the desk.

Ms. Marinetti stared at him as he crossed into her forbidden work space. Then she laughed and jabbed at a few more keys. "That's all right. I'd better do it myself. That's what they pay me for. Are you sure there isn't something you need?"

"Well, we could talk," he said smugly, taking his cue.

Ms. Marinetti swept a lock of hair back and stared blankly into space. "I get a lot of requests during a day, but this is a new one on me."

"It seems to me it was someone else's idea."

The librarian looked past his shoulder to see if someone were lurking around the doorway. Seeing no one, she sat in silence for a few seconds and then said, "Do you really have something to do in here or are you just playing games?"

Enough of this playing around, thought Ben. "Well, I just wanted to let you know that I really appreciated the notes," he said.

"I'm flattered," she said, studying the sheaf of papers again. "I hope that means you'll return those books before the end of the year."

Ben cleared his throat. "I have two witnesses who saw you put a blue envelope in my locker."

Ms. Marinetti broke into such a high-pitched laugh that the kids in the far end of the library turned to look at them. "So, that's what you're talking about. Don't mention it. Glad to do it."

"It is confusing, though," said Ben, coyly, closing in on the subject. "I mean, why was it written in children's handwriting?"

"I give up," said the librarian, as if she were the model of patience. "Why was it written in children's handwriting?"

"Are you going to pretend you don't remember what the note said?"

Ms. Marinetti's tolerant smile vanished. As she stared squarely into Ben's eyes, he suddenly felt as shaky as if the library rug had turned to quicksand. "I don't care for what you're implying. I don't read other people's notes. I saw the note sticking way out of your locker. Someone brushed against it, knocked it out, and I picked it up and put it back."

"Just kidding," Ben said, with a hollow laugh. He felt the shame rising into his face and it felt hot as molten lava. Now he was confused, unsure. But what about the basketball game last night? Trying to wiggle out of the idiotic spot he had blundered into, he cleared his throat and said, "Actually, I just came to say I saw you at the basketball game last night."

Ms. Marinetti's anger had gone but the smile that reappeared on her face had left behind a good deal of its warmth. "That's right, you were playing for that red team, weren't you?"

"I, uh, just wanted to ask what you were doing there."

Leaning on one elbow the librarian said, wearily, "My boyfriend coaches the Raiders. Now is there anything else about my personal life that I haven't covered?"

Ben felt like his head was so full of blood that it sloshed when he shook it. He shrugged and said, "Bye" and walked out of the room, lashed by pangs of shame. If the earth was not kind enough to swallow him up, he planned to take the next flight out of the country to some remote place where no one knew what kind of a total idiot he was. By the time he walked all the way home in the cold shadows of a waning sun, he had calmed down a little. But he was certain he would never enter another library for as long as he lived.

7
Good Shots

"Coach Peters, there's a spy in here!" Rudy Trabor announced over the echoing thunder of a dozen bouncing basketballs.

"What are you talking about?" asked the physical education teacher. Mr. Peters was a walking advertisement for either shampoo or hair spray. His styled black hair always looked freshly clipped and it seemed locked into combed position.

Rudy pointed toward a figure in the doorway. "That's one of the players on the team we're going to beat tomorrow," he said, loudly enough that Ben could hear him.

Mr. Peters looked at Ben and smiled. "Doesn't bother me. We don't have any gimmicks or secret plays." Turning to his team, he said, "It's all you fellows can do to just learn the basics. And if we don't have a better practice today than we did last time, Ben should find it very entertaining. Maybe it's a good thing he's here. After watching you clowns, he'll go back and tell his team about what a bunch of bozos the Pine Knoll Knicks are, and they'll get so overconfident that maybe we'll have a chance."

Ben smiled to himself. Mr. Peters was his idea of a coach. The man knew what he was talking about, took no nonsense from anyone, and his practice sessions were all business. Compared to him, Mr. Buckwell was just a motorist studying his road map, trying to figure out how to get back to the main road.

Contrary to what Mr. Peters had suggested, Ben saw nothing in the practice session that made him overconfident. Greg Murphy was a deadly shot and he got rid of the ball so quickly that it would be tough to stop him. "I'm guarding him," Ben thought, his nerves starting to jump as he considered the challenge. Rudy and Rich Silas both had talent to go with their height. Rudy was especially strong and he played hard. Ben could see that Pablo and Austin were going to get worked over.

The Falcons' only chance was to stop the Knick guards before they could feed their big men under the basket. At least Coach Buckwell had been aware of his team's shortcomings and insisted that they practice that full court press. If a team could outshoot and outrebound you, your only hope was to try to force them to make mistakes. "Rags and I will pick them clean," Ben vowed, grimly.

He knew he should have left before the practice ended. But he could not resist hearing Mr. Peters's little pep talk at the end. Coach Buckwell never gave pep talks. "Just remember, the people who start the game aren't necessarily the ones who will finish it," Mr. Peters was saying, his chin jutting out, daring anyone to challenge him. "I'll be watching to see who really wants to play ball. The people who want to work hard and do what they're supposed to are the ones who play on my team. Remember, eat a light meal at about five and be at this gym by 6 p.m. If you come later than that, don't expect to play."

Ben zipped up his jacket and began to walk out the double doors thinking about what might have been if he had joined the Knicks. It was hard to believe that both the Falcons and the Knicks were 4-1. Ben felt like a volunteer fire fighter who had just watched the professionals in action.

"Hey, Oakland!" called Rudy, before Ben could escape. Ben pretended to ignore him and kept walking slowly down the hall. Once upon a time he had gotten along reasonably well with Rudy, but lately the kid had been pretty obnoxious. Pablo said it was because Rudy had expected Ben to join the Pine Knoll team and had bragged that they were going to go undefeated.

Rudy followed him into the hall just far enough to yell, "We're going to wipe the court with you guys!"

Ben turned and smiled. "Your coach doesn't seem to think so. See you around, Bozo."

"He's just bluffing," said Rudy with half a sneer

curled across his freckled lips. "Too bad you joined the losers when you could have been on a winner."

Ben laughed. "Our record's the same as yours. Better put some pants on. It's cold out here in the hall. Wouldn't want you to get sick and miss the big game."

Rudy's deep brown eyes overflowed with spite. "I hear you tried to make a basketball player out of that big ox. Didn't work, did it?"

This guy's really a moron, thought Ben, angrily. "I'd rather have Austin on my team than you any day," he snapped.

"You won't be saying that after I get through with him tomorrow," leered Rudy.

"He can outplay you any day," Ben shot back. Immediately, he knew it was a stupid thing to say. Austin couldn't outplay a fence post half the time, much less Rudy. But Ben was not going to stand there and listen to someone make fun of his teammates.

"Ho, ho!" scoffed Rudy, twirling his sweatshirt around his index finger. "Care to put some money on that? Twenty dollars says I outscore and outrebound him at least three to one. Make it four to one."

Ben's eyes narrowed in hatred. Mr. Hotshot had him boxed in now. Ben would never live it down if he backed off his support of Austin. On the other hand, betting on Austin was like betting on an ice cube to freeze a blast furnace.

The lean, muscular form of Mr. Peters appeared around the corner to save the day. "You want to bet on games, you'll do it from the sidelines," he said to Rudy. "I don't need ball players who mouth off. If there's any talking to be done, the coach does it. Understand?"

Ben wished he could see Rudy's face, but the boy was facing the coach and pulling a sweatshirt over his head. *Serves him right,* he thought, biting his cheeks to keep from laughing out loud. *We'll see who picked a bunch of losers!*

That night Ben went out after supper and shot baskets in the shadowy light of an outdoor lamppost. For more than an hour he pumped shot after shot at the hoop. *I'll beat those Knicks by myself if I have to,* he thought.

Only the sight of Ken's desk lit up in their bedroom window saved him from disaster. Tossing the ball back into the garage, he raced upstairs and finished his math assignment at two minutes before nine. There was no doubt in his mind that his parents would have banned him from the big game if he had been so much as a minute late.

It felt funny being the visiting team on his own school court. It made the place look different. Ben was not sure if it was because he had never been in there at night, or whether it came from being surrounded by teammates he had only seen in a church setting. The floor seemed shinier and the gymnasium smaller than usual. It even seemed as though he had to make adjustments in his shot to keep the ball from bouncing too hard off the backboard. Strange, he had never had any trouble with that backboard before.

While retrieving a ball that had been struck in midflight by another ball, Ben watched Austin warm up. For a moment he studied him with Rudy's critical eye. No grace or quickness. Rudy would eat him up. If only Austin could somehow block a shot, then Rudy might be intimidated by those long arms hovering above him. It was not impossible. Austin was so tall that he had managed to block a couple in the Falcons' last game without leaving his feet. Actually, that was the only way he could block a shot, because he never did leave his feet.

Austin took a couple of dribbles and then swung his arm in an arc over his head. The ball swished through the net. He broke into a wide smile, which he shared with Ben. "Finally nailed one of those buggers," he said.

"You ready to try one in a game?" he asked hopefully.

Austin's brow furrowed in a deep, soul-searching meditation. His smile resurfaced a few seconds later accompanied by a weak nod. Ben did not take that as a promising sign. *Sure, he'll take the shot, but he doesn't expect to make it,* he thought. *That isn't going to help us much tonight.*

After shooting just enough to get loose, Ben returned to the folding chairs that had been set up for the Falcons. He did not want to waste any of his strength. As he sat there, loosening his laces to straighten out the tongue of his shoe, Coach Buckwell crossed the floor and sat next to him.

For a few moments the coach stared silently as if his thoughts had been left behind on the other side of the court. Then he focused on Ben and said, "You know, you took quite a few shots last game."

"Made quite a few, too," Ben said, defensively.

"Yeah, well, they weren't all good shots. And the rest of the team was standing around waiting for you to score." Ben had never really talked to Coach Buckwell at this close range before. Now he could see the jowls shaking as Coach chewed his gum. "It gets them into bad habits. Did you see how lost they looked on offense whenever you left the game?"

"I don't have to leave the game," Ben said. "I never get tired."

The coach raised one of his droopy eyelids higher than Ben had seen them before. "This team isn't called 'Ben Oakland and His Faith Falcons,' " he went on, in his patient, halting voice. "We've got to find playing time for everyone, and we've got to find shots for other players."

"I don't think the others mind," Ben said, trying to copy the coach's patience. "After all, they want to win."

Coach started to speak, then cleared his throat.

"Yes, they want to win. And I think our chances are better if you don't play one against five on offense."

Ben, who had expected to win this argument easily, grew irritated at the coach's insistence that he change his style of play. Well, it was a poor time to ask for this. He had already calculated that he would have to play the game of his life and score at least 30 points in order for the Falcons to beat the Pine Knoll Knicks. If he started giving up shots to other players, it was as good as handing the ball over to the Knicks.

Ben's silence had given Coach a chance to collect some more thoughts. "Instead of trying to shoot with two guys hanging all over you, take advantage of it," the coach said as blandly as if he were asking Ben to pass him a container of water. "If there are two guys on you, that means one of your teammates is wide open. Do what you've been doing and get the defense to come after you. Then dump to the open man."

"Sure," said Ben, looking away. "I'm not a ball hog. I don't care who gets the points, just so we get them. As long as our guys can make their shots, I'll feed them all night long. But if they don't, then it's up to me." *There, that ought to settle him,* he thought. *What could be more reasonable?*

"The goal is to get good shots," insisted Coach. "The team that gets the most good shots usually wins. If we miss the good shots, we miss. There's nothing you can do about it. But that doesn't mean we ever stop playing for the good shots."

What's the point of arguing? thought Ben. He nodded to the coach and trotted back onto the court to warm up. *I'll try it for a while,* he thought, watching Rudy jump for a rebound and then snap a pass to another Knick. *But this is one game we* have *to win.*

Coach Buckwell collected the team around him a few minutes later. As usual, he asked for quiet several times before he found something to say. "Okay, boys. Starters will be Dave and Ben at the guards, Chris and John at forward, Paul at center. Remember to play full court press all the time; we'll need it. Don't worry about getting tired, we'll get a fresh player in for you."

Like the rest of the team, Ben was waiting for something more. But the coach had apparently said all that he planned to. He sat back in his chair and scribbled some notes down on his pad.

"Play ball!" said the referee, after a sharp blast on his whistle. The referee was a big guy with a crew cut and a forehead that looked like it was carved out of rock. *No one's going to pull anything past this drill sergeant,* Ben thought as he trotted out to the jump circle. Immediately he sought out Greg Murphy.

"Hi, Ben. Are you guarding me?" Greg asked, tucking in his blue shirt and smoothing some of the crinkles out of his gold shorts.

"Only when I don't have the ball," said Ben.

"Want to give up now so I don't have to wear myself out?"

"Nah, go ahead. Wear yourself out."

"How come Rudy's so quiet?" Ben whispered to Greg. Rudy was waiting inside the center circle, hands on his hips. When Pablo arrived for the jump, Rudy simply shook his hand and then crouched into position.

"He won't be if we win," Greg whispered back.

Pablo jumped high for the opening tip, but Rudy was four inches taller and won it easily. No sooner did Casey Pendleton grab the ball for the Knicks, however, than Rags was all over him.

"A little help! A little help!" Coach Peters was yelling to his Knicks. Greg immediately ran back toward his teammate. Ben jogged behind him, giving Greg plenty of room, inviting the pass. Before the ball even left Casey's hands, Ben made his move. He cut in front of Greg, tapped the ball with his fingers and sprinted after it. Catching up to it just before it rolled out of bounds, he stopped and layed it in for two points.

Was that a good enough shot, Coach? Or should I have passed it? he chuckled to himself as he looked back down the court toward both benches.

"Press!" shouted Rags, jumping in to harass the Knicks as they tried to pass the ball in bounds.

Almost forgot, Ben thought, turning around to find Greg. This time the Knicks were able to break through, although John nearly deflected a pass into

Chris's hands. The Knick guards were already so flustered by the Falcons' attacking defense that they were not even thinking about getting a shot. It was all they could do to keep the Falcons from getting the ball. One of the Knicks finally kicked the ball away before they were even able to take a shot.

"Time out!" shouted Coach Peters. Ben was so fascinated by the tongue-lashing that the Knicks were getting during the time-out that he didn't even hear what his own coach was saying. It didn't matter much; Coach Buckwell didn't really have anything to say except "Good work" and "Keep it up." Coach Peters, meanwhile, was loudly demanding to know who wanted to play tonight and who didn't care, adding his opinion that there were many more in the second category than the first. The coach seemed so genuinely upset that Ben began to wonder if it really was so much fun playing for him after all.

After the time-out, the Falcons brought the ball downcourt. The Knicks tried to answer the Falcons' full court press with one of their own. That lasted only as long as it took Rags to speed past two defenders and race downcourt. Leaving blue-shirted bodies lying in his wake, Rags steamed toward the basket and flipped the ball to an unguarded Pablo. Pablo easily sank the shot. Ben rightly guessed that it was the last time the Falcons would see the press that game.

Pine Knoll finally worked the ball in close to the

hoop to Rich Silas. His shot from close range bounced off the rim, but Rudy grabbed the rebound. His quick flip from the left-hand side of the basket also bounced out, but he again came away with the rebound. His second follow-up shot rolled around the rim and in. The Knicks were on the scoreboard.

Under newly shouted orders from their coach, the Knicks hurried back to guard their basket and let Rags walk the ball upcourt. As Ben had expected, Greg guarded him closely. No problem; he could get rid of Greg. But no sooner had he caught the ball and dribbled around Greg than Rudy stepped in to block his path.

Rather than trying to shoot over his tall opponent, Ben dribbled away from the basket. Again he drove around Greg only to run straight into Rudy, who had stepped out to meet him. *That means that someone's open*, he thought. It wasn't Pablo, who was working under the shadow of the much taller Rich. That meant Chris was unguarded.

After faking a pass to Rags, Ben zipped a pass to Chris. Ben's fake had fooled more than just the defense, though. Chris was staring straight at Rags when the ball hit him in the chest and bounced out-of-bounds. "How about that?" Ben muttered, resuming his argument with the coach. "Was that what you call a good shot?"

The Knicks missed an outside shot, but again four long arms branched out over Pablo's outstretched hands. Two of them belonged to Rich, who wrestled the ball away from his teammate Rudy and banked an easy shot off the backboard to tie the game at 4-4. "They're doin' a lot of shoving under the basket," Ben complained to the referee, who ignored him.

Again, Ben charged into the lane. This time he knew what to expect. *Here comes those freckly legs*, he thought as Rudy moved toward him. Ben shoved a pass to the unguarded Chris near the sideline. Although he stood less than eight feet from the basket, Chris hesitated and looked for Ben.

"Shoot it!" screamed Ben.

As if the ball had suddenly grown hot, Chris instantly flung the ball well over the basket. Not only did the miss give the ball back to the Knicks, it seemed to ungag Rudy's mouth. "Air ball!" he said, mockingly as he collected the miss and handed it to Casey.

Before he could complete the handoff, Rags zipped in from nowhere. He slapped the ball away and went up for the shot. He missed, but the embarrassed Rudy fouled him, and Rags was awarded two shots.

While Rudy was being yanked from the game by an irate coach, Rags Yamagita made one of his two foul shots to put the Falcons back on top. It remained a close contest throughout much of the first half, until Rags, and then Ben were taken out. The Falcon substitutes were not as effective with their press, and the Knicks were able to move the ball inside to take advantage of their height.

After Rudy and Rich played volleyball rebounding each other's misses, Coach Buckwell turned to Austin. "They're killing us under the basket. We need some height."

Never before had Rags, Pablo, and Ben all been on the bench at the same time. Never before had Chris, Nathan, John, Donny, and Austin all been out on the court at one time. The three friends stared at each other glumly as the Knicks moved out to a 16-11 lead. "We don't have anyone in there who can score," muttered Pablo.

"At least they're getting good shots," Ben snorted sarcastically.

By the time Rags returned to the game, the Knicks' lead had grown to 20-11. Austin had not played badly on defense. In fact, he had pulled in one rebound and had stunned Rudy by blocking one of his shots. It was funny watching Austin lope down the court after making the block. "He's so excited you can almost detect some spring in his step," said Rags.

Ben did not return to action in the first half. While he watched, grinding his teeth at the sorry spectacle, the Pine Knoll Knicks pulled away to a 23-11 lead at halftime. The worst part of it was that Rudy was starting to play with that sick, cocky "I told you so" grin of his.

8
The Lay-up

That did it! The Knicks were going to die! So much for these good shots that his teammates were so scared to take! Those guys had not scored any more points with Ben passing off than they had in the last game when he had been shooting the ball. Meanwhile, Ben had totaled only four points. The Knicks were sure to be having a good laugh about that. *A good shot is a shot that has a chance of going in,* he decided. *It doesn't matter where Chris or Rags shoot from. They can't make it so it's automatically a bad shot. Anything I shoot has a good chance of going in. Therefore any shot I take is a good shot.*

Ben began firing from the opening moments of the second half. More than that, he had decided to take charge on defense. When the Knicks were on offense, he would guard Greg only until the ball went into the middle. Then he would charge in and try to strip the ball away from the Knicks' two tall players. The tactic worked well. Along with several steals they gained off their press, the Falcons were able to slice the lead to 26-24 by the end of the third quarter.

To his surprise, Ben found himself on the sidelines for the start of the last period. As he sat there, burning the coach with an accusing stare, Coach Buckwell said, "You're playing hard. You need a rest. For crying out loud, you don't have to do everything yourself."

"Wanna' bet?" Ben felt like saying.

One person who was playing more than usual was Austin. Although he still appeared to be thinking out each move, the big guy was actually posing some problems for Rich and Rudy. They were so used to being the tallest players on the court that neither knew much about how to get a shot off against a taller player.

Austin looked so much more comfortable on the court than he ever had before that Ben almost risked a pass to him. The big fingers were outstretched, almost as if he *wanted* the ball, and he was shielding his opponent with his body. Ben started throwing the ball to him, then thought better of it. The memory of too many bumbled passes in practice was still too fresh. Instead he dribbled left, dribbled right, dribbled left, and finally worked his way between three Knicks defenders. He flung up an off-balance shot that bounced high off the rim and went in. That closed the margin to 33-30.

Neither team was able to score for the next few

minutes. Finally, with two minutes to go, the full court press again claimed a victim. Lurching as if he were ready to drop from exhaustion, Rags hounded Casey into using up his dribble. As the Knicks' guard sought out someone to throw to, Rags punched the ball out of his hand. Both players dived for the ball. His face twisted with strain, Rags batted the ball away from Casey toward the free throw line.

Chris got there first and picked it up. He started to dribble, then saw Ben coming up behind him. As if caught red-handed stealing something that belonged to Ben, Chris shoved the ball at Ben, who made the lay-up.

Coach Buckwell immediately called time-out. He escorted the dazed Rags to a seat and sent in Nathan to take his place. "One point! One point!" said Ben as he rushed up to each of his teammates to encourage them. "Two minutes left, we're only down by one. Let's win this just the way we beat the Panthers."

First they had to stop the Knicks, and they had to do it without Rags. The little guy gamely offered to go back in but Coach Buckwell congratulated him on playing hard and sat him in the seat next to him. That was the seat reserved for someone who was not going to be playing.

For the next minute and a half, Ben played his own version of defense. Instead of playing man-to-man defense, it was more like man-to-ball defense. Ben simply went after whoever had the ball. He nearly stole the ball from Casey, and nearly forced a jump ball against Rich. But in the end, all he succeeded in doing was getting in the way of his teammates and tiring himself out.

Casey fired a quick pass to Rudy, who tossed it back to Greg near the free throw line. Because Ben had chased the pass toward Rudy, he was too far behind to recover. Greg was wide open for the shot. The Knicks' ace shooter, who had been shut down by Ben most of the night, dribbled one step closer and fired. With a tremendous effort, Austin ran in from the side and launched himself several inches off the floor. His long arm rose high in the air and struck the ball with a THWACK!

He blocked the shot so completely that the ball nearly stuck to his hand like flypaper. No one looked more surprised than Austin to see the ball wind up in his hands. As the Knicks retreated on defense, Austin held the ball proudly. It obviously had not occurred to him what to do next.

Ben shot an anxious glance at the scoreboard clock. Some of the numbers were not working on it, and it took two seconds before he figured out there were 19 seconds left. "Throw it here quick!" he shouted.

Austin did as he was told and Ben dribbled toward the waiting Knicks. His own teammates might as well have been invisible. Ben was looking only at blue and gold uniforms, trying to figure out how to get a shot off. After a couple of seconds, he decided to win the game just like he had before—a long shot would be better than trying to beat three or four Knicks up the middle. He charged forward, getting the Knicks defenders back on their heels. Suddenly he stopped and raised the ball just above his forehead.

It felt bad as soon as he let it go. Desperately he charged in for the rebound. But he stepped on Austin's foot and both of them fell heavily. Rudy was holding the ball high over his head as if it were a trophy fish.

Scrambling to his feet, Ben lunged at the ball. Just in time Rudy fired it downcourt to Rich. Ben could hear the seconds ticking down in his head. He raced downcourt to where Pablo was badgering Rich, arms waving like a willow in a storm. Rich tried to pass it to Greg but he floated a soft pass that John was able to intercept.

Ben saw the clock flash six seconds. "Throw it here quick!"

John did, but two Knicks stepped in to block Ben's path. There was no way he could get close enough for a good shot. He would be lucky to reach mid-court before the final whistle blew.

Suddenly he saw Austin limping near the free throw line far down the court. The collision with Ben had stunned him and he had been slow in getting up. In the mad scramble of the final seconds he had been left behind near the basket. Ben quickly fired a one-handed pass down the court.

It was coming hard and Austin put his hands in front of his ducking head to protect himself in case he missed. He did not catch it cleanly, but knocked it down and picked it upon the bounce. Three seconds left. All he needed to do was dribble in about five steps and lay the ball in to win.

Austin brought the ball up to his chest and crouched. Too late, Ben saw what was happening. "No!" he screamed in horror. Instead of driving in for the easy lay-up, Austin launched a shot from the spot at which he had caught the ball. The shot clanged high off the backboard and bounced to the left side. Austin chugged after it but by the time he retrieved it, the game was over.

Ben swung a fist wildly in the air and stamped a foot. Frustrated as he was, he would not say anything to Austin, of course. But how dumb could you get? *A simple lay-up*, he thought to himself. *That's all you had to do. We had this game won! Shoot, if you knew how to jump you could have dunked the ball!*

Not even a pat on the shoulder from the Knicks' coach could calm the rage that was boiling in his guts. "Nice game, Ben," said Mr. Peters. "Your guys played a great game. I don't think we deserved to beat you."

The gym teacher went on to congratulate the rest of the Falcons for their effort. Ben watched him with resentment. *Yeah, it's easy to be nice when you win. Unless, of course, your name is Rudy Trabor,* he thought, catching sight of the freckly face. Rudy was strutting off the court with that sick grin. He aimed a finger at Ben as if it were a gun, pulled the trigger, then blew the smoke away from the barrel.

Sure, you weasel, Ben thought, turning away from him. *Lucky stiff!* Rudy was playing it smart. If he had dared come close to Ben with that stupid grin of his, Ben would have slugged him—he wouldn't have cared how many people saw him do it.

"Tough loss," said Ben's dad, offering him his sweat jacket. "You guys have nothing to be ashamed of."

Austin does, thought Ben. *Why couldn't it have been anyone else? Even Donny had at least a 50-50 chance of making a lay-up.* April and Nick were chasing each other around Dad's legs, yelping and giggling. Ben wished they'd have stayed home. All he needed now was some noisy kids getting on his nerves.

"Did you win?" asked April, sucking on some strands of her long hair.

"Yeah, we beat them 100 to nothing."

April's eyes grew wild and she immediately repeated the news to Nick before the two enjoyed a sprint across the wide-open spaces of the gym.

"Man, you sure put a scare into those guys," Ken said, walking over with Mom. Ben had not even seen Ken during the game; he wondered if he had come in late. "They thought it was going to be easy. Guess you showed them."

"They won, didn't they?" muttered Ben.

"Only as far as the final score," smiled Mom. "Why don't we celebrate with a trip to the Dairy Queen?"

"Celebrate what?" Ben grumped to himself. "Can't anyone around here read a scoreboard? We lost! I'll be hearing about it at school for the rest of the season." Memories of the game and especially those final 20 seconds so filled his brain that he failed to notice anything unusual as he slipped on his jacket. For once there was no secret message waiting for him at the end of a game.

9
Technical Foul

The radio station had given up trying to keep pace with the flood of cancellations being phoned in. "I think it's safe to assume that all events scheduled for today anywhere in the city and outlying areas have been cancelled," chuckled the announcer. The blizzard had dumped such an avalanche of snow on the city that only the extremely foolish, and those with four-wheel drive vehicles and a good reason for being out, tried to plow through the snow-clogged streets.

Many hearty souls who tried to get an early jump on their shoveling were quickly beaten back to the shelter of their homes by the bitter cold and the driving blasts of wind. Over the roar of the arctic fury, Ben could only occasionally make out the drone of a faraway snowblower.

Throughout the entire block there were only two ribbons of concrete that had been shoveled out from under the snow. One was a portion of driveway near the end of the block. It had been cleared by an overeager man who had promptly gotten his car stuck in the street after traveling all of four yards. Some helpful neighbors pushed the car back to the garage, and the driveway was fast filling up with a fresh dump of snow.

The other cleared area was the basketball court on the driveway at 2134 West Sheridan Avenue, dug out moments ago by Ben Oakland. Ben was sweating heavily even as he tucked his chin further into his collar to keep it from freezing. Wearing a stocking cap underneath his hood, with only his eyes and part of his nose poking out from under a scarf, Ben leaned the shovel against the side of the house and began shooting at the basket.

After a gust of wind carried one of his shots nearly to the roof, Ben confined his practice to short- and medium-range attempts. He kept wiggling his fingers in his gloves in an effort to ward off frostbite. Occasionally he had to pull his fingers out of their slots and clench them together to bring some warmth back to them.

The ball hardly bounced and it felt as hard as a brick when he rebounded a missed shot. But he was too busy replaying the last loss to take much notice of either the weather or the frozen ball. His mind had set up a two-man obstacle course between himself and the basket. There was Greg; there was Rudy.

For nearly half an hour, he spun and twirled, trying to keep control of the low-bouncing ball with his gloved hand. The loss to the Pine Knoll Knicks hurt every time he thought about it, which was at least several times a minute.

Of course it was worst whenever Rudy was around, smirking. At least there had been enough highlights during the game to provide ammunition for Ben to fight back. If Rudy talked about Austin's last shot, Ben reminded him that Austin had blocked one of Rudy's shots. But nothing could really erase the sting of defeat.

Every time the ball bounced off the side of the hoop or fell off the backboard, it sent a surge of anger through him. Each miss was a reminder of the shot he had missed near the end of the game. He was all through blaming Austin. "If I had made my last shot like I was supposed to, there wouldn't have been any lay-up for Austin to flub," he thought.

Mom opened the front door a crack and winced at the fury of the storm. "Benjamin, I'm worried about you!" she shouted. Ben could barely hear her, and the swirling snow made it just as difficult to see her. But it was not difficult to tell what was on her mind. Ken had already called him a certified looney for going out to play in a blizzard.

"I'll be coming in pretty soon," he shouted through his scarf. He doubted that she could hear that but it did not really matter. The door shut. Ben moved out toward the street, hunting for the free throw line. Already there was only a corner of blacktop near the garage that was still black. Ben had to scrape a line in the newly arrived snow where he thought the free throw line lay buried.

Even though the wind kept blowing his shots way off course, Ben refused to make any allowances for it. *There's no wind on a basketball court*, he thought. *I'll just practice shooting it up the way I'm supposed to and who cares if it goes in*.

Thanks to the wind, few of his shots did hit the basket. But Ben continued his practice until his eyes stung and his forehead throbbed from the force of the cold. *I hate those Knicks!* he thought as he brought the ball into the house and peeled the gloves off fingers that felt twice as thick as usual.

Coach Buckwell tried again to explain to Ben that basketball was not meant to be a one-man show. In fact, he used very close to the same words he had used the other night. But if those words had not been enough to convince Ben before the loss to the Knicks, they certainly carried no weight after it.

"I liked what you did the first few times down the court," Coach Buckwell said. Warm-ups had been delayed by the fact that 24 rows of chairs were sitting in the middle of Faith gymnasium. Several boys started removing the chairs while Ben's dad got a key to the storeroom. "When they double-teamed you, you immediately found Chris open."

"Yeah, and he just stood there with it," said Ben. As far as he was concerned, that was the end of the argument.

"He's not used to shooting," Coach said, rubbing one of his sleepy eyes. "You're in such control out there that some of those guys think they can't shoot without your permission. I guarantee you that if you keep finding the open man, pretty soon they'll know what to do with it. It may not pay off right away, but in the long run we'll be better off for it."

In the long run? thought Ben. *Who's he kidding? We only have five games left.*

The Faith gym was the smallest court in the league. Even though spectators pushed their folding chairs up against the wall, they still had to be careful that their toes did not touch or cross over the sideline.

Tonight's opponent was the Holy Family Flames. *We're the ones who should be called the Flames,* Ben thought, comparing the Falcons' bright red uniforms to the navy blue and gray of the Holy Family team.

Ben had been expecting a tough game. After all, the Flames had just beaten Pine Knoll to hand the Knicks their second loss. Greg Murphy had told him about one Flame player with thin, almost white hair who had muscles like a weight lifter. The guy was a tough, rough player who led the Flames to a four-point win.

Unable to see anyone on the court he would be afraid to arm wrestle. Ben asked one of the Flames about him.

"That's Jesse. He's got the flu," the boy said.

Ben smiled for the first time since the loss to the Knicks as he repeated the news to Rags and Pablo. "That makes our job easier," he said.

"You know what they say," Pablo nodded. "It's better to be lucky than good. If we beat them, we'll be 6-2, and in a four-way tie for first place."

"Who would have believed it?" marveled Rags.

"What do you mean 'who would have believed it'?" scolded Ben. "I expect to win every time we play."

"Yes, and I admire that," said Pablo, backing away from him. "No wonder Ms. Marinetti likes you so much!"

"Shut up!"

Coach Buckwell assembled his troops and read out the starting assignments in his usual monotone voice. "David and Ben at guards, John and Chris at forwards, Austin at center. Let's go!"

Ben was several steps onto the court before the last name sank in. "Did he say Austin?" he asked Rags. Sure enough, Pablo was shrugging at them from the bench while Austin was adjusting his socks and walking out with the rest of them.

Even with his size advantage, Austin barely won the opening tap. Ben scooped up the ball and cruised down the left side of the court. Only one player came out to challenge him; the rest had all paired up against the other Falcons. "That makes me the open man," he grinned to himself. He faked a pass, which got his opponent lunging for air.

"Shoot it, Ben!" said Donny, who was sitting with the other Falcons on the sidelines just a few feet away.

As Ben went up for the shot he heard Pablo answer, "You don't have to tell that to Ben. He'll pass up a shot about once every solar eclipse."

Although the shot went in, Ben did not get his usual stroke of pleasure from watching the net ripple. His own friend was talking about him as if he were a ball hog or something. *Coach wanted good shots, well, there it was,* he thought. *Couldn't have been easier if they had given me an escort to the basket.*

As he backpedaled down the court, he was so furious with Pablo that he forgot about the full court press. "Hey, Oak, get your buns back here!" yelled Rags, who had dogged one of the Flames only to see him bounce a pass to a completely unguarded teammate.

The close walls were awful. Ben could clearly hear some tittering among the parents at Rags's impolite comment. *Really funny,* he thought, angrily. *OK, everyone thinks I'm just a hotdog scorer? All right you guys, let's see who thinks they can shoot the ball!*

Holy Family missed their shot and Austin rebounded. Rags loped down court and automatically passed it to Ben. "Start cutting to the basket," Ben snapped at him. "Don't just stand there."

Rags did as he was told but the defenders had

heard the same message and knew what was coming. They closed in on Rags, cutting off the passing lane. "Don't just stand there," Ben waved at the others. "If someone wants the ball, you'd better move around."

He dribbled slowly as he stood about 20 feet from the basket, waiting for a teammate to break clear. He was not even paying any attention to the little Flame who had moved in to guard him more tightly. Once the guy even tipped the ball, but Ben recovered it. Of the four choices of targets, Austin seemed the best bet, so Ben whipped the ball to him, perhaps a little harder than he should have. Austin juggled the ball but came up with it. Then, taking a deep breath as if about to dive under water, the big center swung into a hook shot. The ball bounced off the front of the rim and the Flames rebounded it.

Ben gave him an almost fatherly smile before going back to work on defense. This time the Flames scored to even the game at 2-2. *Okay, who wants the ball this time?* Ben said to himself, again dribbling slowly, watching his teammates. The little Flames defender was growing more and more bold. Ben tried to ignore him but the guy would not quit. He kept sneaking in and getting a hand on the ball.

Growing irritated, Ben nearly shoved him with his forearm but checked himself in time. Again the guard ducked in and slapped at the ball. This time he ticked it enough so that it bounced off the side of Ben's leg and rolled out-of-bounds. Without thinking, Ben shoved the pesky opponent hard with the heel of his hand. "Get out of my face, shrimp!" he said.

A blast from a whistle pierced the gymnasium and a small man in a striped shirt ran towards Ben as if he were going to place him under arrest. "Technical foul!" he said. "Blue team shoots a free throw and then gets the ball out-of-bounds. If I see that again, son, you're out of the game."

Coach Buckwell beat the referee to it. He held a short conference with Pablo who ran in to take Ben's place. No one needed to tell Ben that he had just made a fool of himself. By the time he reached the row of folding chairs by the exits he was so frustrated and angry at everyone, including himself, that he wanted to cry. He headed for the last chair in the row but Coach Buckwell patted the empty chair next to him. Ben debated ignoring him, but something inside told him that he had already stirred up enough trouble for one day.

He slumped into the chair and stared at the floor. At the moment he did not have the slightest interest in the basketball game that was going on.

While keeping his eyes on the game, Coach Buckwell asked, "Do you know why you hit him?"

"No," said Ben, and at least for the moment, it was the truth.

"He made a good play on you," said the coach, still watching the game. "You weren't expecting that, were you?"

"No," Ben admitted.

"You didn't take him seriously enough. Then he embarrassed you by beating you, and you hit him. Maybe you should sit and think about that for a little while." The coach spoke without a trace of anger or any other kind of emotion. It suddenly flashed through Ben's mind what the Knicks' coach, Mr. Peters, would have done if he had been Ben's coach.

Ben sat silently, still feeling as though tears might come at any moment. *Fine, I'll think about it,* he thought. *That'll do a lot of good!* The "little while" that Coach Buckwell had spoken of turned out to be the entire game. As he realized he was not going to get back into the game, Ben felt more anger flowing into his already confused swirl of emotions. This was a game that they could have won easily if he had played.

But as it turned out, they won anyway. By playing forward instead of center, Pablo found it much easier to get off his shot, and he made the most of it. Austin figured out what to do with that extra length of bone that he had been blessed with. He blocked several shots, sank two out of five free throws, scored his first basket on a rebound shot, and even made one of those hook shots he had been practicing. This, along with the usual thievery from Rags and a few scattered points from the other players propelled the Falcons to a 27-22 win.

Rags and Pablo tried to console Ben, but there was not much they could say. Ben's dad surprised him by putting a hand on his shoulder. *I'm surprised he'll admit that this little hothead is his son,* Ben thought. But Dad could not think of much to say, either. Ben's teammates were too thrilled over their own efforts to get bogged down in his gloom for more than a few seconds. Ben overhead more than one Falcon remarking, as if they still could not believe it, that they "had done it all without Ben."

Yeah, well, what if that Jesse character had shown up? Ben thought, as his giddy teammates congratulated each other. *Where would you be then?* The place suddenly felt hot and stuffy, and Ben wanted to get out as quickly as possible. Dad quietly nodded when Ben told him not to wait, that he needed to walk home alone.

It isn't fair, Ben thought as he sat in the hall to put on his boots. *I've always treated them well when I had a good game and everyone else messed up.* He could not begin to understand how he had gone from star of the team to a dirty player and a ball hog who hardly felt like part of the team at all. This was basketball; he was supposed to be having the best time of his life.

Something in the left boot was pinching his toe, and Ben absently pulled off the boot. Digging around for the problem, he discovered a familiar, crumpled object. It was square and very blue.

Not wanting anyone else to see it, he quickly slipped his foot back into the boot, put on his coat and hat, tucked his gloves in his armpits and stepped outside. He waited until he was under the first streetlight before taking out the envelope from his pocket. The paper was already cold and he hurriedly warmed his hands in his gloves before reading the note. This time the message was different and totally took him by surprise:

> The Lord bless you and keep you,
> The Lord make his face shine upon you.
> The Lord lift up his countenance upon you and give you peace.
> Order of the Broken Arrow

Ben had heard the words 100 times at least, in church. He had daydreamed through them, talked through them, and absently recited them. Now for the first time, these were words addressed only to him. They seemed to jump out at him from the page. The words were talking to him now—maybe they always had, but he had never heard them. At the moment it was hard to imagine that they had been written with anyone but him in mind. Ben was not sure exactly what they meant, but it was impossible to read them and still feel completely alone.

"Thanks, whoever you are," he said out loud to the mysterious sender of the note.

10
Night of Terror

Camp Drury was a 1,600-acre woodland playground filled with snow, deer, birds, and other creatures. There were two snow-covered lakes tucked back in the middle of the pine forest, one steep, open hillside on which a toboggan run had been built, and almost complete privacy for the scout troops who used it. These advantages more than made up for the crude indoor facilities. The concrete bunkhouse was equipped with a refrigerator, stove, sink, and a showerless bathroom. They did not make up for the fact that, for the first time in many months, Ben Oakland would not be within 20 miles of a basketball hoop.

It was a poor time for such a situation. The Falcons were now 8-2, still tied for first place, with only two games to go. The last thing Ben wanted to do was spend a weekend without any kind of practice.

Not that things were going particularly well for him on the court. Basketball was no longer the simple game it had been at the start of the year. Now it seemed as though a panel of judges sat ready to rule on every shot he took. Ben had made a conscious effort to pass off whenever double-teamed. But now he sometimes felt guilty shooting even when he was wide open. Was it a "good" shot or a selfish one? Was someone going to gripe because their best shooter was still taking more shots than some of the others? Ben could hardly tell anymore.

Half of the group of 16 boys was perched atop the bunk beds that were scattered around the room. The rest had been nabbed for cleanup duty following a supper of barbecued beef sandwiches, carrots, and potato chips.

"Can we go exploring after we get these done, Mr. Barton?" asked Pablo, as he sloshed water in the large, battered pot that had held the barbecue.

The leader, a short, thick-bearded man with swatches of blond hair surrounding a bald spot, looked at his watch. "You've got free time until 9:30. Then we're going to roast some marshmallows outside and tell stories. I don't want you going too far off at night by yourselves, though. Where are you going?"

"We thought we'd try to find a toxic waste dump so we can get rid of the rest of the barbecue," Pablo said. Mr. Barton glared at him.

"Pablo and Ben and I just want to do down to the lake for a little while," Rags offered.

Although the weather was exceptionally mild this

evening, it had been bitterly cold for most of January. Ben knew that the ice would be solid well into spring. A trail led straight from the cabin to the lake a half mile away. Since they could not get lost or fall through the ice, there was no reason not to let them go.

Mr. Barton arrived at the same conclusion. "All right. Just stay together and don't do anything dumb. You got flashlights? And bring along a compass just in case."

Ben rolled his eyes at Rags on hearing the last comment. He wondered if Mr. Barton ever so much as went to the grocery store without a compass. Their departure was delayed when Mr. Barton inspected the pot and told Pablo to come back and do a better job of washing. But it was not long before Ben and his two friends stepped out into the night. They flicked on their flashlights but found that they really did not need them. A three-quarters moon was just about directly overhead and lighted up all but the densest portions of the woods. The air was so still that nothing could be heard but the crunching of their boots over the snow.

"I love the smell of pine," said Rags.

"Wooo, aren't we romantic?" teased Pablo.

"Hey, if you lived downwind from the paper mill like I do, you would appreciate what clean air was," said Rags.

"Do you realize that our last game against Brook Manor could be for the championship?" asked Ben.

"If we beat Meadow Hills and then Brook Manor beats Pine Knoll, we'll be the only two teams with a 9-2 record."

Rags and Pablo looked at each other. "The kid's talking basketball again," said Pablo. "Should we dump him in a snowbank?"

"Give him one more chance," said Rags.

Ben managed to stay off the subject as they wound down the trail to Crescent Lake. The moonlight that reflected off the white snow spread an amazing amount of light over the lake. Ben could clearly see the expressions on his two friends' faces.

"Look! Deer tracks!" shouted Rags, pointing to a cluster of prints that crossed the lake. "I wonder if they're still around."

"If they were, you just scared them off with that noise," scolded Ben. They followed the deer trail as it cut across the narrow section of the lake to where it led into the forest, but saw no sign of the animals.

"Whew! I'm hot!" Pablo said, unzipping his coat. "That was dumb of me to wear this sweatshirt underneath."

"I wonder if it's warm enough for snowballs," Ben said, dipping his gloves into the snow. Surprisingly, the snow held together.

"I suppose you're going to roll some basketball-sized snowballs and run us through a little passing drill," said Pablo.

"No, I'm going to make a baseball-sized one and rub it in your face," laughed Ben, charging. That set off a brief, three-sided snowball fight that was brought to an end by a chunk of snow that hit Pablo's neck and slid down his shirt. After that they began rolling snowballs.

"We're Troop 101," said Rags. "Why don't we make our sign right out in the middle of the lake? Pile up three snow balls for the ones and roll one gigantic ball in the middle for the zero."

The three worked hard at their project. By the time they shoved and strained at the last and largest of the snowballs, their necks were soaked with sweat. Just as they wheeled the five-foot diameter "zero" into place, Rags said, "Hey, we're not alone. See those lights over there? Over there," he pointed, "by the summer overnight camp."

Sure enough, at least four flashlight beams could be detected. Faint peals of laughter carried across the lake.

"I wonder who it is," said Ben. "Mr. Barton said there wasn't going to be anyone else up at Camp Drury this weekend."

"Must be our troop then," Pablo said. "I guess we weren't the only ones who wanted to go out for a walk."

"It's got to be the whole troop," said Rags. "They're building a fire. Looks like we're having the marshmallow roast down here."

"Come on," said Ben. "Why would they come all the way down here to build a fire? Especially without telling us?"

"They knew we were down here at the lake," Rags said. "It must be them! Who else could it be?" Their line of sight was blocked by pines and shrubs and the newly kindled fire was still too small to cast much light on any of the figures.

"Let's ambush them," Pablo whispered excitedly.

"How?" asked Rags. "We're standing out here in the middle of lake with the moon shining all over us. How can they miss us?"

"Just get off the lake and come around from the back side. We can spray them with smallbore snowball fire before they know we're there."

Rags and Ben agreed. They walked back towards the eastern shore, in no apparent hurry. As soon as they were off the lake, they plunged into the shadows. Pockets of deep snow, past their knees in spots, slowed their progress and it was not until fifteen minutes later that they began to approach the campfire from the wooded hill.

Ben found to his disgust that the snow was not as sticky in the more shadowed woods as it was out on the lake. He had to press hard with his soggy gloves to get it to hold together. "We'll have to carry one in each hand," he whispered. "We won't have time to make any once we start firing."

They slid and crawled down the hill, trying to keep from disturbing too many branches. Something did not seem quite right to Ben. He was not able to recognize for certain any of the laughs he was hearing. At last they reached the outhouse and found the snow more packed and easier to walk on. With Pablo in the lead, they crept forward to the last stand of scrub pine ringing the circle.

Peeking through white-dusted boughs, Ben saw a sight that froze his heart. His inner suspicions had been correct—it was not Troop 101!

Instead he saw five boys, probably high school aged. Their faces glowed in the yellow of the campfire and Ben did not like what he saw. Some of their eyes were glazed over, others looked as wild as those of a pony in a snake pit, and still others had that narrowed squint of plain meanness. There were beer cans lying around the edges of the circle and liquor bottles propped up next to the logs. One of the trespassers, dressed in baggy army fatigues and sporting a shaved head was swigging from his own bottle. A greasy-haired member of the gang was passing around a roach clip while another was snorting something out of his hand.

"Let's get out of here," mouthed Pablo, eyes shining white in the semidarkness. As they crept back along the outhouse path, it seemed as though they were making ten times the noise they had made on their way to the campfire. Ben wanted to break into a run. He nearly tripped as he walked up Pablo's back.

They had nearly reached the outhouse and were about to head back into the deep snow when a crash right in front of them made them all jump right off the ground! The outhouse door opened and out staggered a boy in an open hunting jacket, flannel shirt, and blue jeans. As he saw them standing, frozen by fear, his nearly shut eyelids snapped open.

"Hey, looka we got here!" he roared drunkenly. In the distant, flickering light of the campfire, he looked like a maniac, leering at them with his mouth wide open and that crazed glint in his eye, with uncombed hair shooting out at all angles from his head. Just as Ben was about to make a dash for the deep woods, the guy seemed to guess his thoughts. "Uh-uh," he said, shaking his head. He withdrew his hand from his coat pocket and slowly aimed a gun right at Ben's eyes.

Ben could not even summon the strength to close his eyes, but stared straight ahead. His head was swimming. He tried to find some proof that this was a dream. Slowly the barrel of the gun moved and pointed at Rags, then at Pablo.

By then some of the others had arrived to see what the fuss was about. Laughter and a torrent of filthy language spilled out of their mouths.

"Hey, lookathat," spluttered the one with the shaved head. "One of em's godda shnowball. They were gonnatack ush."

Ben saw that his friends had had the good sense to drop their snowballs some time before. He opened his hand to let his drop but the evidence clung to his glove so stubbornly that he had to shake it off.

"Yeah, they were gonna ambush us," said another.

The long-haired one roared with laughter and said, "Big tough guys, huh? Look at the weapons these big guys carry. Snowballs!" He moved closer, his breath stinking. "Want to see a weapon, boy?" His tongue flopping out of his mouth, he held up a large hunting knife to the light. "Show 'em yours, Brodie."

"I already did," said the outhouse visitor, taking turns pointing his revolver at the three of them.

Ben was too scared to even think. His eyes were cemented to the small black cylinder that he realized might be the last thing he ever saw. These guys were out of their minds—so wasted they didn't know what they were doing. They could squeeze a trigger and wake up the next morning without a clue as to what they had done.

"What are you doin' here?" asked the one called Brodie, weaving toward them, sweeping the air with his gun. Neither Ben nor his friends said anything, nor did they dare look at each other. "You know what I ought to do?" Brodie said, his face twisted from the effort of his speech. "I ought to blow your brains out."

"Yeah, blow their brains out!" roared a voice from back at the campfire. All the others laughed.

"No, I godda a bedder idea,"said Brodie, spinning the chamber of his weapon. "Let's make 'em play roulette."

More roars of approval. "Just how lucky do you feel?" cackled the one with the shaved head.

Another belched after taking a long drink from his bottle. "Aw, let 'em go."

"Thad woun't be 'spitable," said Brodie, who was having trouble spinning the chamber. "Come on, be palsh!" he said, leaning close to Ben's cheek and lowering his voice to a whisper. "Wan get high, man? We're gonna. Ain't we, guys? Ain't we gonna?"

"No, thanks, we have to go," Pablo finally said in a shaky voice.

"Aw, come on!" He called them a long string of unprintable names, which the rest repeated. Pablo kept shaking his head. Ben could not keep his eyes off the gun. He winced every time Brodie's finger started tapping on the trigger.

The boy who had stayed at the campfire staggered through the screen of small pines and collapsed in the dirt near their feet. "Blow their brains out, blow their brains out," he muttered over and over before passing out.

The others thought his behavior extremely funny. "Bulldog's really gone, man!" laughed the long-haired one. "Out cold! Let's take him down to the water."

"Yeah, throw him in the water!" roared the shaved one.

As Ben gaped in disbelief, Brodie tucked his gun inside the waist of his pants and grabbed the unconscious boy by the foot. "Down to water!" he howled. The rest all tugged at various limbs. Some of them were pulling in different directions, so hard that the boy momentarily woke from his stupor to swear at them.

Ben perked up as he saw an escape route opening up in this nightmare. If only he could be sure if they were faking or not. Could anyone really be so stupid as to stand out in the snow and not remember the lake was frozen? If the drunken teenagers were that far gone, maybe there was a chance of escape.

Rags was thinking the same thing. He touched Ben's arm and nodded in the direction of the woods. Ben shook his head. He could still see the handle of the gun as Brodie and his laughing bunch of buddies dragged their load toward the lake.

"Back up slow," Ben whispered. Whatever they did, they did not want to attract attention and remind anyone of their presence. *Just keep quiet, and don't panic,* he thought. *And don't faint,* he added to himself, feeling his stomach walls cave in from the terror.

The first section of the short drop from the camp to the lake was steep. As soon as the first of the trespassers struck that, they toppled over each other. Brodie had to let go of one leg, and he fell backward, laughing all the while.

"Go!" whispered Rags and Ben at the same time. Not wanting to get bogged down in the deep snow and steep hills in back of the outhouse, they tore off down the main trail back towards the lodge. Rags was much faster than the others, and he was soon flying out in front. All three of them stumbled at one time or other on a hidden root or rock or dip in the road, but they were too frightened to allow themselves to fall.

Fighting for his balance after one such stumble, Ben kept seeing a vision of drug-soaked monsters chasing him. He kept listening for the sounds of gunfire, ready to flinch at the first shot. But whether their tormentors had forgotten about them or been too wasted to chase them, there were no shots, no pursuing footsteps, no voices except for several different octaves of faraway laughter.

Rags was far out in front now and not looking to see who was behind. Feeling quite sure that they were not being followed, Ben eased up and waited for Pablo. But the memory of that gun and those crazed eyes spurred him back to a full sprint before he could draw a full breath.

By the time Pablo and Ben reached the bunkhouse, Rags had already been there long enough to arouse some action. Mr. Barton was charging down the trail to help them, while two of the boys ran down the main road toward the caretaker's cabin.

Fourteen pairs of eyes were staring out the window of the locked lodge when the flashing lights arrived about 15 minutes later. Two squad cars pulled up next to the building. After speaking to Mr. Barton, one of them radioed for more help. It seemed like a long time later that five muttering, cursing boys marched clumsily up to the parking lot, surrounded by four uniformed guides. Several minutes after these five had been packed away in the squad cars, two other officers arrived, each with the arm of a very limp and unspeaking person draped over his shoulder.

The officers seemed to be in no urgent hurry, and so Ben assumed that no one had gotten hurt. As the piercing red and blue lights disappeared around the bend, Mr. Barton looked at his watch.

"Nearly 11 o'clock. Anyone still want to roast marshmallows and tell stories?"

They passed out marshmallows to the boys who ate them cold, straight from the bag, and curled up in their sleeping bags. But it was a long time before Ben fell asleep. It was not unusual for him to lie awake at night, but for the first time in many months, he was not thinking about basketball.

11
Grandpa

By the time Ben returned home, his memories of that night's events were diluted by many hours of snow soccer and tobogganing. As a result, he was able to tell the story to his parents and older brother calmly, as if describing a story he had heard from somewhere else.

Deep down, though, the events had upset his sense of security, and he didn't even squirm when Mom hugged him close. "It'll be a long time before you go on one of those trips again!" she declared, firmly. Even though he did not agree, Ben decided to save that argument, if it ever really came up, for a later time.

At dinner the next evening, Mom seemed unusually quiet. She didn't even get up to serve dessert. Kids always set the table, Dad put on the meal, Mom served the dessert—that was how life had gone for as long as he remembered. But this time she sat as if she simply did not have the energy to lift a piece of apple crisp onto a plate. Dad went over to the counter to do the honors.

"Who wants ice cream with theirs?" he asked. The question was scarcely out before it was answered with a chorus of "me."

"Me, too," Dad said. "Too bad we don't have any. Who wants a big piece?" Ben and Ken stared at him suspiciously this time. Only April and Nick piped up, echoing each other with their usual enthusiasm. "Okay, big pieces for April and Nick. Small ones for the rest," said Dad.

Ken and Ben started to complain but Dad ignored them and gave both a normal-sized piece. "If by some miracle you can't finish, will you give the rest to the boys?" he asked the younger ones. Both agreed, and Dad winked at the older boys. It was a pretty safe bet there would be leftovers from those two plates. Mom still said nothing, except a quiet "thank you" when Dad set her dessert in front of her.

"You look tired, Mom," Ken said. "You gettin' sick?"

Mom shook her head. She and Dad exchanged a look and then she said, "We got some bad news today." Ben put the spoonful of apple crisp back on his plate. Bad news had a way of ruining a good taste, so he would wait a bit for his dessert. "The nursing home called this morning," Dad continued. "Grampa's not doing so well. Mom has been there most of the day."

Not so well could mean a lot of things, Ben

thought. *Some of them pretty bad. What does she mean?*

April immediately had her thumb in her mouth and was climbing on Mom's lap. "Is he going to die?"

"No, no," comforted Mom. "But he's going to need quite a bit more care from now on. He's had another stroke and . . ." Her eyes grew misty.

"He'll have to be in a wheelchair from now on," Dad finished. "And he will need some help doing very ordinary things, like eating and getting dressed. I don't think he'll be able to visit us anymore."

Ben did not like the silence that followed. He waited for someone to break it. Ken finally did. It was one thing older brothers were good for. "We can still visit him, can't we?"

"Yes," Dad said. "In fact it would be a good idea. Mom said he's not complaining about anything, but she can tell it's not easy for him."

"He's always been able to take care of himself," Mom said. "He even mowed his own lawn up until two years ago."

"How old is Grandpa?" Nick asked.

"He's only 74," Dad said.

"When were you planning on going?" Ken asked. "I could go tomorrow or the next day, but I've got to study for that big biology test tomorrow. I suppose I could go tonight anyway," he shrugged.

"No, you take care of your schoolwork," said Mom. "You can go another time."

"I want to go visit our Grampa," said April, bouncing insistently on Mom's lap.

"Me, too," chimed in Nick.

"Nick, you were up *very* early this morning. You can't be out that late. And, April, you have school tomorrow morning."

"I hate school!" frowned April.

"Were you planning on going tonight?" Ben asked.

"I was going to go after I finish some papers I need to get in the mail," Dad said. "Is your homework done?"

"Don't have any," Ben said. As soon as the others were all excused from the table, Ben finally began digging into his apple crisp. Mom was still at the table, sipping on a cup of coffee. He saw more wrinkles and creases on her face than he had noticed before and he felt bad that they had not been getting along. Not that it was all his fault, of course.

"What was Grandpa like when he was young, Mom?" Ben asked.

"Don't talk with your mouth full," she said. "When he was young? Oh, he was always playing around, teasing like your dad. He used to love sports just like you do," she added, taking off her glasses and rubbing her eyes. "Mostly it was softball and tennis, and later on golf." She snorted a little laugh. "He used to play your sport, too, but that was before I came along. You should see some of his old high school yearbooks. I guess he was quite the player. I seem to remember he won some honors. Most valuable something or other—I don't remember."

She looked at him over her cup of coffee. For a moment Ben saw that sparkle or something in her eyes that always made him feel good. "So maybe you come by your love for basketball honestly," she smiled.

Although he did not say anything, Ben was grateful for the remark. For a while he had come to believe that everyone else in the family considered basketball to be some sort of disease.

Ben had learned his lesson last time he was at the Silver Haven Home. Old people like it hot. Ben could be baking to death and still Grandpa would complain of a draft in the room. This time he came prepared, wearing only a T-shirt under his winter coat.

This evening they took the elevator to a part of the home Ben had never seen before. The employees at the Silver Haven Home seemed friendly as they bustled around, yet as soon as the elevator doors opened, Ben detected that unpleasant odor. Half a dozen or so people sat around in the lounge, shriveled into their wheelchairs. Some of them greeted Ben and his dad as they stepped out. Ben answered them more pleasantly than he would have answered most people. One woman sat muttering to herself. The only thing Ben could understand was that she constantly repeated the word "piano."

They crossed the lounge and began hunting for Room 334. Dad found the sign that indicated that rooms 318-338 were down the hallway to the right. The door was open. But through the doorway all they could see was the shape of some feet under blankets at the bottom of a bed.

Dad knocked on the open door. "Grandpa?"

After a few seconds a weak voice asked them to come in. Ben hoped that his face did not give away the dismay that he felt upon seeing Grandpa. He was even thinner than Ben remembered. One side of his face drooped as if the flesh were sliding off the bone, a silvery stubble of whiskers showed on his chin.

"Good to see you, Grandpa," Ben said, trying hard to be cheerful.

"Eh, who's that?" Grandpa's face looked like that of a small child suddenly realizing he was lost in the middle of a large fair.

"Ben!" Ben knew he had to speak loudly to Grandpa.

"Elmer, it's Tom Oakland," said Dad. "Audrey's husband. And this is our son, Ben."

"Oh, yeah," said Grandpa with a pained smile. "Thank you for coming. It's good to have visitors. What day is today?"

"It's Tuesday, Elmer," said Dad, loudly. "Tuesday, January 31st."

"What am I supposed to be doing?" Half his mouth did not move when he spoke, and this made him very difficult to understand.

"Nothing, Grandpa," Ben offered, as he moved to the opposite side of the bed from his dad. Dad indicated that he should pull up the chair near the wall. "You can just talk to us."

Ben sat there nervously for a minute. There didn't seem to be much to talk about. All he could think of was to ask how Grandpa was feeling, and that did not seem to be a subject worth exploring.

"How's the Chevy working?" Grandpa finally asked.

"It got us over here tonight," said Dad. "Starts even on the coldest mornings. I have to admit, you sure know how to pick cars! We haven't had a bit of trouble with it in six years."

More silence. Grandpa seemed to have great difficulty getting his breath. It was even harder for him to turn his head, so he only looked at Dad.

"You never told me you were such a good basketball player," Ben thought to say at last.

"Huh? What did I forget?" Grandpa asked, his face contorted as he tried to shape it into a questioning look.

"You didn't forget anything!" Ben said, even louder than before. "Mom told me tonight that you were a star basketball player in high school. You never told me about that." It was amazing to think that this aching, worn-out old body had once been able to dribble and jump on a basketball court.

"Oh, that was a long time ago. Long time."

"What position did you play?"

"Oh, a little guard, a little forward. I could play both, you know."

Ben hoped it was not just his imagination that Grandpa seemed to be perking up a little. Grandpa's breath still rasped, and many of his facial muscles were still frozen. But that anguished look seemed to have faded, and his mind seemed sharper.

"Were you a scorer or a rebounder or a playmaker, Grandpa?"

"Oh, I was a shooter," Grandpa smiled, and his chest rattled with kind of a cough, as if he were trying to laugh. "I admit I wasn't much else. All I really knew how to do was shoot."

"What was your best game?"

Grandpa sat silent for a long time. Ben was ready to give up on that question and ask another one. "24 points against Heartland, 1928. We won the game by two points in overtime," Grandpa said. With a great effort, aided by Dad, Grandpa turned his head toward Ben. The eyes that had looked bewildered and vacant now focused clearly on him. "Didn't you win a game in overtime a little while back?"

Ben sat closer to the bed and leaned one elbow on it. "Well, almost. It wasn't quite overtime but I made a shot with time running out that won the game. I didn't know you knew about that." Grandpa just looked at him for a while. "Got any advice for me, Grandpa?" Ben asked. "Our team might be playing for the championship in a couple nights. I could really use some good pointers."

"Yes, I have one," he said, struggling to get his lips to form the sounds. "Two hands. You're always more accurate with two hands."

Dad grinned at Ben from across the bed and shook his head. Grandpa had always insisted that the prehistoric two-handed set shot was the best way to score from long range.

The old man's eyelids suddenly grew droopy and Ben cast a worried look at his dad. Dad stood up and bent over the bed. "He's just tired," he said. "I think our visit probably wore him out. Especially being so late in the evening."

The eyelids pulled open and stared at Ben. In a couple of seconds Ben saw a hint of recognigion. "I'm sorry, but I am tired," Grandpa said. "Could you read for me out of my Bible? It's the last thing I do before bed."

Dad found the book, a large-print version, open on the bedstand. Ben thought that Dad was going to read it, but Dad handed the open book across the bed to him.

"What do you want me to read?" Ben asked.

"The next chapter."

"The whole thing?"

"Yes."

It was the twelfth chapter of Luke. Ben glanced ahead to see how far he had to go and his heart sank when he saw that this chapter went on for 59 verses. He read about hypocrisy and sparrows and then came across a story that was at least partially familiar. "The land of a rich man brought forth plentifully," he started. Ben read how the rich man kept tearing down barns and building bigger ones to hold all the grain he was harvesting. Just when he was feeling wonderful and secure, wham! "This night your soul is required of you; and the things you have prepared, whose will they be?"

It gave him the creeps to read that verse: it brought back so vividly the memory of the campfire and the crazed teenagers and the dark barrel of the gun pointed at his head. Ben kept reading to the end of the chapter, but even as he did, he kept seeing the gun.

During the drive home Ben leaned against the cold vinyl of the car door. He tried to imagine Grandpa pumped back up with blood and muscle and energy, running around a basketball floor. But the image of Grandpa kept dissolving into a picture of Ben Oakland on the court. Pretty soon the picture reversed itself and he imagined himself, 65 years from now, lying in a bed, trapped in a body that no longer worked. Trapped in a body that couldn't play basketball. Shoot, it wouldn't take 65 years—Grandpa had not been able to play real basketball for years, decades. Here was a man who had been a star player, and what did it mean now?

Boy, it all goes away so quickly, he thought. *It was a good thing basketball wasn't Grandpa's whole life.*

"This night your soul is required of you and the things you have prepared, whose will they be now?"

What would happen if I went tonight? Ben thought. It was a scary thought, but one that he couldn't help thinking. In fact, he had been forced to think it dozens of times since that night with the gun. How could he help but think of it?

Well, what would I have to show for myself besides basketball? he thought. *Nothing. Basketball's my life.* He had said those last three words many times before, only before he had been rather proud of himself. It did not sound very smart right now. *I can never get enough of basketball.*

"This night your soul is required of you; and the things you have prepared, whose will they be?" The phrase would not go away.

I never could get enough basketball, he admitted. *I can't help myself. I can't get enough points, enough wins. Tear down old barns, get new ones. More, more. Then it goes and what are you left with? Parents you can't get along with. Refs who think you're a crybaby. Teammates who think you're a ball hog. Opponents who think you're a poor sport.*

What else do I have?

12
Brook Manor Mavericks

The eleventh round of games on the schedule went exactly as Ben hoped it would. The Falcons boosted their record to 9-2, thanks to a 36-20 win over Sun Creek. Brook Manor then knocked Pine Knoll out of a first place tie with a 50-45 victory over the Knicks. That left the Brook Manor Mavericks tied for the top spot with Faith going into their final game showdown. One of them would be the champion.

"Could you stop drumming your knees?" Mom said to Ben as Dad pulled into the parking lot. "You're shaking the whole seat."

"I can't help it, I'm nervous," Ben said. He had found that after such a long period of not really speaking to his parents, it was not such a cinch to reopen communication. But at least he did not feel like he had to avoid his family anymore.

Brook Manor was the oldest elementary school still in use in the metro area, and the largest. The bricks had turned nearly black with age, and there weren't many growing things on the property even when the winter snows left. It was close to the business section, bounded on one side by an auto repair shop, and by a railroad track cordoned off by a chain link fence on the other. Behind the school stood a row of houses, and in front of it ran a main street carrying traffic into downtown.

"Are you going to win?" April asked as they piled out of the car.

"If I knew the answer to that we could have stayed home tonight," Ben said, speaking more loudly to be heard over the traffic. He took a deep breath. "Gotta keep control," he kept reminding himself. "It's just a game. All right, it's the most important game you've ever played in, but it's still a game."

There was a surprise waiting for Ben when he walked into the gym. Hanging across the entire length of one of the purple walls was a giant banner that read: "FIRE UP, FAITH FALCONS!" At the end of the fancy lettering was a lifelike picture of a red falcon soaring across a mountainside.

"Wow!" said Ken. "I thought you guys were the visiting team tonight! Looks like you own the whole gym. I've never even seen a sign like that at any of the *high school* games. I suppose next you'll be telling me you have cheerleaders."

"Yep. And television time-outs, too," nodded Ben. "But really, who do you think did that?"

"Almost looks professional," said Mom.

"Did you hear that?" Pablo said to Rags as they trotted over to greet the Oaklands. "Mrs. Oakland says it was done by a professional. That means Austin can't play on our team. We're not supposed to use professionals."

"Austin did that?" exclaimed Ben. "That's right, he told me he was an artist."

"He didn't lie," said Dad.

Ben tossed his jacket into a corner and ran out to where Austin had just begun to take some practice shots. "You mean to tell me this is what you were doing when you could have been practicing basketball?" Ben scoffed, surveying the mural. Austin stopped in his tracks. His shoulders slumped in a look of guilt and disappointment.

"Sure wish I could draw like that!" Ben added with a grin.

Austin broke into a relieved smile. "I wish I could play basketball like you."

"Well, if we ever find a genie and a magic lamp, I guess we'll know what to wish for."

Players from both teams trickled into the gym until at last two full teams were shooting at baskets on opposite ends of the court. Many of the players spent as much time sizing up the opposition as they did warming up. Each practice shot was examined as an omen of what was to come. Whenever a purple-shirted Brook Manor player missed a shot, the Falcons' hopes would rise. With each shot their opponents made, the Falcons' confidence would drop.

Pablo had seen enough to draw his own conclusions. "Looks like we're in trouble, Oak."

"That's a great attitude, Pablo," said Ben, who was practicing free throws and ignoring the Mavericks. "What makes you say that?"

"Are you blind? Look at them shoot!"

"Yeah? What about it?" Ben swished his third shot in a row.

Pablo was so concerned about the situation that he had not taken a shot for several minutes.

"Look," said Ben, putting a hand on Pablo's shoulder. "I know they've got a guy named Tyrone who's as good as anyone we've played. I remember him from a summer basketball clinic. But I don't know anything about the rest." He leaned close to Pablo's ear and cast some secretive glances left and right. "You know what Brook Manor is saying right now? They're looking over here and saying, 'Oh, no! They got a little guy who's going to run the pants off us. And look at that giant they've got playing center! We'll never get a shot off! And there's Ben Oakland, the guy who smacks you if you play him too close. Shoot, we might as well go home and mail in the score!"

Ben turned and sank another free throw. "And they're probably worried sick about that number eight who is so good he doesn't even have to warm up," he added. It took a couple seconds for that to sink in before Pablo called him a turkey and started shooting baskets.

Ben could hardly wait for Coach Buckwell's words of wisdom before the start of the game. This was for the championship, after all. The coach had to at least *try* to say something inspirational.

"Okay, listen up, guys," said the coach to nine players who had been waiting for him in silence for at least half a minute. "We're going to have to use the press. Play as hard as you can, and I'll keep substituting to keep you all fresh. David and Ben start at guard, Paul at center, Chris and Donny at forward." With that he rubbed his pocked cheeks and sat back in his chair.

Somehow it seemed comforting to hear Coach say the expected words. He might not know as much about the game as some other coaches, and he might not be much for pep talks. But he was always there for you, and he was fair. You had to give him that.

"Nice to know some things never change," Ben said to Rags as the two trotted onto the court. "Same speech for the 12th straight time."

"Except for the lineup," said Rags. "Why is he starting Donny?"

Coach's speech had started out so familiar that Ben had not listened to the end. "Really? Donny's starting?" He looked around and saw Pablo standing in the purple circle at center court. "And Austin's on the bench? He's been playing pretty well lately. Maybe Coach plans to substitute often and doesn't want all the best players on the court at once."

Tyrone walked over to Ben. Neither of them

offered their hands but Tyrone said, "How you doin'?" as they positioned themselves for the jump.

"I'd probably be doing better if you weren't guarding me," answered Ben.

"Just don't even be thinking about driving on me and we'll get along all right," smiled Tyrone.

"I like to live dangerously," said Ben. That brought a chuckle from Tyrone.

The Brook Manor Mavericks easily won the tap and raced downcourt before the Falcon defense could get organized. A couple of quick passes later, Tyrone banked in a short shot. Ben could have kicked himself. He had been unable to fight through the traffic, so Tyrone had been left all alone.

Rags ran the ball upcourt. Immediately after crossing the center line, he tossed the ball to Ben on the left side. Ben turned and found Tyrone crouched in front of him, one hand outstretched. Relaxing his muscles, Ben started to toss it back to Rags. Just before the ball left his hands, though, he pulled it back and burst past Tyrone. The Mavericks were prepared. One of the forwards stepped in to block his path. It was all quite familiar by now. Immediately Ben slid a pass to Chris who was standing unguarded at the side of the basket.

By the time Ben had opened his mouth to yell "Shoot!" Chris had already arched the ball into the air. It dropped through cleanly to tie the score. "Nice shot!" grinned Ben, slapping Chris's open palm.

"Nice pass," Chris beamed.

"Anyone feel like playing defense?" shouted Rags. Three purple-clad Mavericks were having no trouble playing keepaway from the lone Falcon defender in the backcourt.

"Sorry," said Ben, rushing up to reinforce him. But it was already too late. The Mavericks were rushing the ball towards the basket. Again they were able to get a shot from close range and, although it missed, they put in the rebound. "Get in the game, Oakland!" Ben said to himself angrily.

On offense, Ben repeated the same move he had tried last time, but Tyrone was already wise to him. Ben had to back out and give up the ball to Rags. Rags passed to Donny, who seemed happy just to have a chance to handle the ball. Donny passed to Pablo who backed in and looked for a shot. He tried to force it through the taller Mavericks and missed badly. But he was fouled on the play. He made the first foul shot and missed the second, leaving the Falcons one point behind.

This time the Falcons unleashed their full court press. The Mavericks had obviously prepared for it. Both of their forwards hovered near midcourt to help out in case the guards got trapped. But there was no way to prepare for Rags's quick, windmilling hands. He picked the guard clean and coasted in for a lay-up to put the Falcons into the lead.

After that, Tyrone took over most of the ball handling for the Mavericks. Ben was happy to see it.

Although the Falcons might not be able to get as many steals as usual, Rags's hounding defense and the double-team traps set by the other Falcons would take a lot out of the Mavericks' star. As a result, he might not have as much energy left for scoring and defensive work.

Unfortunately, there were other Mavericks who could score, even if Tyrone ever did show signs of tiring. They scored three straight baskets, two from in close and one from long range, while the Falcons could do nothing.

Into the game came Austin and John, out went Pablo and Donny. Austin's height had an immediate effect on the Mavericks' inside game. After Austin blocked the first shot taken against him, Brook Manor started thinking twice before shooting from in close. It did not seem to matter, though, because the smaller of the Mavericks' guards got hot from the outside. After the guard popped in two long-range shots, a weary Rags was taken out for a rest in favor of Nathan.

With the score now 14-5 in favor of Brook Manor, Ben began to tighten up. This was the title match. All that buildup, all those days and nights of thinking about it and preparing, and here the game was getting away from them even before the first quarter was over. With his jaw clenched he took the ball into the lane. As usual, Tyrone stayed right with him. This time Ben made his move toward the basket and fired. Swish! The score stood 14-7 as the whistle sounded ending the first quarter.

With Rags out of the game, the Falcon press was not nearly as effective in the next period. Tyrone galloped across the center line and sped for the hoop where Austin stood ready to challenge him. As Austin stretched out to challenge the shot, Tyrone slipped the ball to a teammate coming in from the other side. The Maverick cut in behind Austin for an easy basket to make it 16-7.

Ben took the ball as it fell through the net and slammed it on the floor before putting it back in play. Again he tried to work around his defender, and could not do it. He was forced to toss up an awkward shot that somehow went in. Sixteen to nine.

Tyrone answered with an almost identical shot, forced by Ben's tough defense. Ben ground his teeth. He was playing his heart out and somehow could not cut the gap.

Tyrone played him even closer this time down the court. *That means I should be able to drive around him*, Ben thought. He tried once, twice, and finally slid around his opponent's shoulder. Immediately two Mavericks stepped in to plug the middle. Ben kept going and launched a shot just as he crashed into one of them. The ball bounced off the glass into the hoop.

A shrill whistle echoed off throughout the gym. The referee put one hand behind his head, signaling a charging foul on Ben. "No basket!" he said, as he pointed toward the basket that the Falcons were defending. "Purple ball."

Ben bounced to his feet, so angry the veins ere bulging in his neck. With his arms clenched at his side, he ran at the referee, "He didn't have position!" he shrieked.

The referee stared at him coldly. His hands seemed to be twitching slightly. As Ben stared in anguish, he saw those hands begin to form a "t" signaling a technical foul on Ben.

13
The Last Shot

Before the referee could complete his sign, Ben beat him to it with a "t" of his own. "Time out!" he said, clapping the flat of one hand against the upraised fingers of the other.

The referee hesitated a second, then blew his whistle. "Time out, red team," he said.

"Whew!" thought Ben as he walked back toward the Falcon chairs with his head down. He exhaled deeply a few times to try and let out some of the frustration, then dropped heavily into the chair next to Coach Buckwell.

"You got to take me out," he said, resting his eyes in the palms of his hands.

Coach Buckwell had nothing to say during the time-out other than "good job" and "Paul, go in for Ben." It was not until the referee had resumed play that he spoke to Ben. "What's the problem? You hurt yourself?"

Ben pulled his hands away from his eyes and waited for his vision to clear itself of those swirling colors. "I'm not hurt. I just lost control," he said bitterly. "I was trying, I was really trying, but I can't do it. I just can't stand losing! I started acting like an idiot again. I don't know why I do that!"

Coach Buckwell slowly scratched an itch on his leg. "That was my fault, Ben. It's a coach's job to get a player off the floor when he starts to get that way. You showed a lot of class taking yourself out."

Ben accepted the praise silently. He wanted to believe what his coach was saying but there were too many facts in the way. He had come into the game with what he had thought was a new attitude, only to find that he had not changed much at all. The only new thing was that now he was able to recognize when he was acting like a fool.

"We'll get you back in there in the second half," said the coach. "For now, just sit back and close your eyes. Oh, and someone asked me to give you this."

His thick, hairy hands were holding out a blue envelope. "Who gave you this?" Ben said, sitting upright.

"Someone," said the coach, turning his attention back to the game.

Ben turned the envelope over in his hand for a few seconds. Should he be reading this in the middle of a game or should he wait? Curiosity won out and he tore open the top. This time the letter was not written in that juvenile script but in flowing, adult handwriting:

"Ben,

However the game turns out, you have a right to be proud. It's a blessing to see the effort you put out. You and all the Falcons have been a joy to watch.

Order of the Broken Arrow

P.S. The ref blew the charging call!"

Ben whirled around. The letter writer had to be in the gym at this moment! Frantically he searched the spectators' faces for some give-away clues. But all he saw were parents earnestly watching the game, some younger children paying far less attention, and a custodian who passed through the gym, looking at his watch. No one was giving away anything.

"What are you looking for, Ben?" asked April, sitting in a row of chairs directly behind him.

"Nothing," he said, and he began to turn around. Suddenly an idea struck him. "April, come here." She bounded off her chair eagerly, pigtails flopping. "April," he whispered, "did you see anyone give my coach a blue envelope?"

April's lips snapped shut as tightly as if someone were trying to force a spoonful of spinach down her. Her shoulders stiffened as she shook her head quickly and scurried back to her chair. "That little squirt knows and she's not telling," he thought. But there was someone else there who could not keep a secret for anything. "Nick, come here," Ben beckoned.

Nick hopped down from his chair in a perfect imitation of April. "Nick, old buddy, this is really important. Did you see anyone give a blue envelope to this man sitting next to me?"

You would have thought he had threatened Nick's life. The kid stood almost paralyzed, looked pleadingly at Mom and Dad, and then shook his head. The answer to the mystery was just beginning to dawn on Ben when he saw the buttons. Both Mom and Dad were wearing small black buttons on which was drawn a white arrow with the shaft broken. Order of the Broken Arrow. That's who had been sending those notes all along! How could he have been so dumb?

Ben pushed through the Falcons' row of seats and kneeled between his parents. "I should have known it was you," he said.

"We didn't tell," insisted April.

"Why should you have known?" asked Dad.

"I don't know, I just should have," said Ben. "Thanks. There were some times when the notes really came in handy." This was getting to be a humbling night in many ways.

"Our pleasure," said Dad.

Then, whispering so she wouldn't disturb those around watching the game, Mom said, "You know we weren't communicating very well for a time. It just seemed like things had gotten so bad between us that we couldn't talk to each other. So if we can't talk, how do we let you know we really care about you? We hoped this might help break the ice."

"Maybe we won't be needing to use notes

anymore?" Dad suggested hopefully.

"Maybe not," Ben said. "So tell me, was it April who printed all those notes for you?"

"Excellent deduction, Sherlock," said Dad. "It was good penmanship practice for her."

"And what is the Order of the Broken Arrow?"

"Broken arrow—no more war?" said Mom.

Ben nodded. "Well, I'm sorry to have to say this, but you're both dead wrong about one thing."

"What's that?" said both parents suspiciously.

"The ref was right. I charged."

By the time he got back to his seat next to Coach Buckwell, the half was nearly over. Ben could not believe he had totally ignored nearly a quarter of play in a championship game. Fearful of what he would see, he checked the portable score board perched on the scorer's table. Incredibly, the Faith Falcons had closed the gap to 24-22.

"How did that happen?" Ben asked Rags as the Falcons walked off the court at halftime.

"Who knows?" smiled Rags.

"No, I mean how?" Ben said. "I didn't see what happened after I left. Who scored for us and what happened to Tyrone?"

Rags couldn't help laughing. "Are you serious? You didn't watch any of it? What's the matter, did the game get too boring for you?"

"Would you just tell me?"

"Sure," Rags shrugged. "As soon as you left the game, Tyrone sat down, too. He was pretty tired and they must have figured that with you out they could afford to give him a rest. After that they started to have trouble against our press. Austin blocked another shot and scored a basket on that miserable excuse for a hook shot you taught him. The rest was just like the last couple of games. With Austin drawing attention near the basket, Pablo had room to shoot and he hit a few of them. John got a basket after a rebound and I made a couple of free throws and here we are!"

"Listen up, boys," Coach Buckwell called. Ben could not help but think it was probably the last time he would ever hear that familiar call. He would miss it. It wasn't just the game of basketball he would miss; it was all these guys playing together. Maybe that was the mark of a good coach. "They've been getting a number of baskets from that guard, number 16," he said, consulting his notes. "Don't worry about that. If he can keep making those from out there, then they deserve to win. I'd be surprised if he does. Keep the press going hard. We'll keep substituting to keep fresh. And, Austin, when you're in the game, give Ben some help with that number 5. He's dangerous."

"He crossed us up," grinned Rags as they took their positions on the court. "Added a new wrinkle to the standard speech."

Ben had been sitting so long that the drafty gymnasium air had chilled his once sweaty body. He wished he could have shot a few baskets before getting back into action. As he performed a few hops and short sprints to loosen up, he saw Tyrone coming toward him.

"You okay, man?" Tyrone asked.

"Never better," Ben answered. "And you? How's the wife and kids?"

Tyrone laughed and then broke some welcome news to him. "Coach wants me to concentrate on bringing up the ball and scoring. He doesn't want me wearing myself out trying to chase your hide all around the court. So you're safe; someone else will be guarding you from now on."

"Wish I could say the same for you," Ben answered. "I still got you. Just don't be trying to drive on me and you'll be all right."

"I like to live dangerously," said Tyrone.

In getting rid of Tyrone, Ben felt as though he had been released from a straitjacket. He repeatedly drove into the lane for lay-ups or else passed off to an open Falcon for an easy shot.

Tyrone was equal to the challenge, however. Now that he had gotten used to the Falcons' full court press, he cut through it easily. Although Ben made him work for everything he got and forced him to take some off-balance shots, the Maverick star kept scoring. Austin's shot-blocking had intimidated a couple of the other Mavericks, but he could not seem to get a hand on anything Tyrone tossed up. Worse yet, Austin was constantly being pushed out of position for rebounds. One of the

Brook Manor forwards scored an easy rebound basket to push his team ahead 38-37 at the end of the third quarter.

Austin trudged wearily to the last chair in the row, where he would be sitting at the start of the final period. Ben followed him to give him some encouragement. "You know, Austin, you're doing a lot of things right. You just need to be more aggressive. You're being too gentle out there. Do you realize you haven't been called for one foul all year long?"

Austin rubbed a bead of sweat off the end of his large nose. "You're right!" he marveled. "I haven't committed a single foul, have I?"

In the final quarter, Ben scored two more baskets before sitting down for a rest. He expected to see Rags hop off his seat to take his place but instead the coach sent Donny.

"Why didn't you sent Rags in, Coach?" Ben asked.

Coach Buckwell waited so long to answer that Ben was not sure he had been heard. "We'll turn Rags loose with fresh legs the last two minutes. He should be able to make something happen."

Meanwhile Tyrone was still making things happen for Brook Manor. Just as Coach Buckwell had predicted, the Mavericks' other guard started missing his shots. But Tyrone had twice muscled his way into the middle to pull down rebounds. Now that Austin was out of the game, the Brook Manor center also started to take the ball to the hoop. He scored twice against Pablo to put his team ahead by four, 45-41.

"Ben, Austin in. Donny, Paul out," Coach Buckwell said. Although many in the crowd were beginning to squirm from the mounting pressure, the coach showed no emotion, as usual.

Ben scored on a drive to the basket. Tyrone answered with a high-arching shot from beyond the free throw line. The Falcons were still four points behind. The clock showed 3:42 to play.

As Ben dribbled downcourt, debating his next move, a familiar face came up to challenge him. Tyrone winked and inched closer, ready to pounce the instant Ben made a move. The move caught Ben by surprise. He checked his teammates and his gaze lingered on Austin, who had his arms stretched out, begging for the ball. Austin's powers of persuasion worked, because Ben found himself lobbing a pass to him. The tall center bobbled the ball, then took a long awkward step and swung his arm around. The hook shot rolled around the rim twice before dropping through.

"Two points behind," thought Ben, "We've got to stop them here."

Ben clung to Tyrone like a tight-fitting jacket and the Brook Manor star was finally forced to give up the ball to a teammate. A shot went up and bounded high off the rim. As he outfought a Maverick forward for the ball, Ben caught a glimpse of disaster out of the corner of his eye. There was Austin pushing the Maverick center, as plain as if they were two kids fighting over a toy. A whistle blew; the foul was called. Instead of it being the Falcons' ball, Brook Manor had a chance to add to their lead at the free throw line. Yet there stood Austin looking quite satisfied with himself.

"What do you think you're doing?" challenged Ben, feeling his frustrations slipping out of control again.

"I fouled him," Austin said, innocently. "You said I was supposed to be more aggressive, didn't you?"

Ben stared stupidly at Austin for several moments. "Look," he said, trying hard not to laugh at Austin's ignorance. "Never mind what I told you. No more fouling, okay?"

As the Maverick center stepped to the line, Rags dashed into the game for John. "Two-minute warning," Rags said, grimly. Ben looked over at Tyrone, who had his hands on his knees and was breathing heavily. He could not help thinking that Coach Buckwell was right. A fresh Rags romping among tired bodies with two minutes left in a championship game could create some problems for the Mavericks.

The center made his first shot and missed the second. Brook Manor now led, 48-45. Again Tyrone was all over Ben. Ben passed to Austin who was called for traveling. Before Ben had time to be disappointed, there was Rags bouncing along the end line, ready to deny the inbounds pass. The other

Falcons joined the attack. Tyrone could not get open for the pass. Instead the throw went to another Maverick who dribbled the ball off his knee.

Ben and two Mavericks chased the ball from different directions. Ben got there first, just before an on-rushing Maverick who knocked him to the ground. Foul.

"You okay?" Rags asked him.

Ben nodded and accepted his friend's offer of an outstretched arm. After shaking his head to clear the fuzziness, he sank both free throws to pull Faith within one point.

Brook Manor tried a dangerous inbounds pass to Tyrone, who had to outleap Chris and Ben for the ball. He fought his way past Rags and into the front court. Gulping air, Ben moved over to challenge Tyrone. Less than a minute remained. This was a defensive play he just *had* to make.

"David!" shouted Coach Buckwell. "Switch with Ben!"

Quickly Rags cut in front of Ben and started waving his hands all over Tyrone. Ben felt hurt at first that he had been taken off the Maverick star, but it took him only a couple seconds to appreciate the move. Rags was fresh. Short, but fresh and as pesky a defender as there was. Tyrone tried to move in, thought better of it, and passed in to the center. Feeling Austin's shadow over him, the center immediately fired it back to Tyrone.

This time the Brook Manor star backed Rags in

toward the basket. Closer and closer he got, while Rags fought him tenaciously for every inch. Finally Tyrone turned around and jumped. Rags was far too short to challenge the shot but Austin had somehow guessed what was coming. As the ball left Tyrone's hand, Austin's bony fingers rose just high enough to tip it off course. John grabbed the rebound and flipped it to Rags who sped down the court at top speed.

Unable to set up their defense, Brook Manor had lost track of Ben. Rags was the first to spot him cutting under the basket. His pass was so hard it stung Ben's hands and he nearly lost it out-of-bounds. But he recovered, and stepped back to put in the lay-up. The Falcons were ahead!

This time Ben's mind was totally on the game. "Press!" he shouted. He stood by the end line to deny the pass while Rags became Tyrone's second layer of clothing. Suddenly the passer's eyes grew huge. He reared back like a football quarterback and threw as hard as he could. Ben whirled around to see what was happening.

Apparently the pace had been too much for Austin who stood gasping for air in the Mavericks' backcourt. His absence had left the Maverick center all alone under the other basket! Rags had seen the danger, too. He had left Tyrone and started streaking down the court a second or two before the pass was made.

The ball was traveling so high and fast that the

Maverick had to first knock it down with his hand, then catch up with it. This delay was just enough for Rags to arrive on the scene. The Maverick took two dribbles towards the basket. As the ball hit the ground for the last time before he jumped into his lay-up, Rags slapped the ball backwards towards center court.

Bodies were spread all over the court by this time. Chris reached the ball first near the half court line and threw it to Ben who had hardly moved from under the basket.

"This will clinch it!" he thought as he turned toward the basket. There was no Maverick within 20 feet of him. Such a surge of energy flowed through him that he could almost imagine dunking the ball. But before he laid the ball up, he saw Austin trotting in.

Without quite thinking why, Ben stopped and flipped the ball to Austin. "It's all yours," he said. Austin cradled the ball in one huge hand and took two choppy steps. As Ben gaped in horror, Austin missed! Tyrone roared in to take the rebound. Dribbling madly back the other way, the Maverick looked feverishly at the scoreboard and saw "01." Gathering all his strength, he unleashed a shot from near center court.

The ball seemed to hang in the air for several seconds, aiming straight for the Mavericks' basket. But it just missed, banging the front rim so hard that the entire backboard shook.

The Falcons dashed around the court trying to find each other so they could share their celebration. Amid the madness, Ben saw his parents hoist April and Nick high in the air and twirl them around. The only sane Falcon backer seemed to be Coach Buckwell, who was calmly walking over to shake hands with the Maverick coach. The last thought that occurred to Ben was that he was glad it was Coach Buckwell taking that little walk instead of, well, instead of anyone else.

When the chaos finally settled, Austin sheepishly stuck out a hand to Ben. "I don't know if I have the nerves for this sport," he said. "Art is much more peaceful. You know, I appreciated the thought. But you should have taken that last shot yourself."

Ben grabbed his hand and slapped him as high up his shoulder as he could reach. "Maybe," he grinned, as April and Nick charged full speed into him from across the floor. "But somehow I don't think Coach minded. Hey, it's like any gift—it's the thought that counts."